PRAISE FOR *THIS GIRL'S A KILLER*

"Completely riveting. When I wasn't reading about Cordelia Black, I was thinking about her. Utterly obsessed and ready to support all of Cordelia's wrongs!"

—Jesse Q. Sutanto, bestselling author of *Vera Wong's Unsolicited Advice for Murderers*

"Blood-splattered, witty, and sharp, *This Girl's a Killer* is the BFF serial killer thriller you need in your life."

—Dea Poirier, bestselling author of *Next Girl to Die* and *The Marriage Counselor*

"In her fierce and feminist debut, Emma C. Wells combines taut thriller plotting with sharp, sassy humor and introduces an indelible antiheroine I'd follow anywhere. Cordelia Black is the ultimate girl's girl, and as far as I'm concerned, she's done nothing wrong ever in her life. All hail the new queen of the 'good for her' genre!"

—Layne Fargo, author of *They Never Learn*

"Emma C. Wells has a hit on her hands with this debut! *This Girl's a Killer* is a darkly delicious ride. Expertly dancing on the thin line between villain and antihero, Cordelia Black (what a perfect name!) is a woman with a killer style. She's on a mission that will have you questioning your ethics as you root for her ruthless brand of justice. With a sweet, found family, heart-pounding moments of suspense, and an ending you'll never see coming, *This Girl's a Killer* will stick with you for a long, long time."

—Xio Axelrod, *USA Today* bestselling author of *Girls with Bad Reputations*

THIS GIRL'S A KILLER

A NOVEL

EMMA C. WELLS

For those who could've used a killer in their corner.

Cover design by Tim Green/Faceout Studio
Cover images © CSA-Printstock/Getty Images, Tissen/Shutterstock
Internal design by Diane Cunningham/Sourcebooks

Published by Poisoned Pen Press, an imprint of Sourcebooks
P.O. Box 4410, Naperville, Illinois 60567-4410
(630) 961-3900
sourcebooks.com

Cataloging-in-Publication Data is on file with the Library of Congress.

Printed and bound in the United States of America.
PAH 10 9 8 7 6 5 4 3 2

A QUICK NOTE ABOUT CONTENT WARNINGS FOR THIS BOOK.

Dear Reader,

This Girl's a Killer is about friendship and found family. It's also about trauma and, well, a serial killer. Cordelia Black commits murder. It is violent and she enjoys it. Specifically, she kills predators—very bad men who've committed crimes against vulnerable people. While Cordelia's violence happens on page, the actions of the men she kills does not. Their crimes are mentioned, but not discussed in detail, and are absolutely not glorified in any way.

It's important to me that readers who need content warnings always feel safe and respected when choosing (or not choosing) one of my books. I also realize that the thriller genre relies heavily on twists and turns, and for some readers, content warnings are viewed as spoilers. I don't want to spoil anyone's fun.

If you are concerned about the content/triggers found between the pages of this book and would like more information than what is provided above, you can find a detailed list of content warnings on my website, emmacwells.com under the Menu tab labeled Content Warnings.

Stay stabby (and safe),

Emma

NOTHING STAINS LIKE RED FROSTING—NOT EVEN BLOOD. The last thing I needed was the sugary red concoction smeared across the tan leather of my car's interior. But love makes us crazy, which was the only explanation for why I zoomed toward Oak Road Middle, making up for lost time by going double the posted twenty-miles-per-hour speed limit with thirty rainbow cupcakes balanced precariously in the passenger seat.

I hit a pothole, and the plastic clamshell lid of the bakery box popped open for the fourth time. I reached over with one hand and clamped it closed. Again. It was a risky game I was playing, but if anyone understood that middle school was its own circle of hell, it was me. If having rainbow cupcakes to share with her class the week of her birthday made my goddaughter's sixth-grade experience even a bit better, well, she would have the damn cupcakes.

My phone rang through my car's speakers, right as I wheeled into the school's long driveway. I was tempted to ignore it, but Diane's name appeared across the screen on my dash. While I was good at many things, I'd never been good at ignoring my best friend. Besides. She'd text if I didn't answer—and keep texting until I responded.

I pressed the button on my steering wheel. "Hey, you."

"Hey yourself. Did you remember the cupcakes?"

Like I'd forget. Being Sugar's godmother was the most important role in my life.

Well. One of the most important roles. There was the other thing—that additional role I filled—necessary as it was violent. But these two parts of myself were so tangled together that trying to separate them was absurd. Besides, Sugar and Diane were at the center of both. There was nothing I wouldn't do for my best friend and her daughter. Nothing I hadn't done.

I rolled my eyes. "Are you serious?"

"I know, I know," Diane said. "You'd never forget Samantha. I also know you hate last-minute changes to your schedule. I wouldn't have asked, but there's an audit here because the hospital overspent on a stupid waste incinerator and—"

"Diane." Best to interrupt her before she got started on work drama. She could talk about Mercy Hospital's audit for an hour.

She plunged ahead as if she hadn't heard me. "And my boss is being a real pain so I can't leave. And—"

I spoke louder. "Diane. It's fine. Really."

"You're sure?" She paused, and the background sounds of the Mercy Hospital accounting department filled the car. "Thanks again, Cor. Truly."

"No worries. Happy to do it." My voice was airy—the opposite of how I felt. "I'm delivering them now."

"Oh." Diane's answer was a single syllable, but the smirk, clear in her tone, spoke volumes.

"Oh, what?" I asked.

"Nothing. I'm surprised is all."

"Surprised about?"

"Is Cordelia Black—Queen of the Clock, Punctual Princess—running late? Because Samantha's afternoon break started fifteen minutes ago and—"

"Nine minutes," I interrupted, flipping on my blinker and pulling into the school's parking lot. "Sugar-Bug's break started nine minutes ago, not fifteen, thank you very much. And it's not my fault, okay? My last meeting ran long, then there was this jerk cop who crashed into me at the bakery. He knocked me off my heels and—you know what? Why am I explaining this? I need to find a parking spot."

"Wait, don't freak out." Diane laughed. "I'm teasing."

"Who's freaking out? I'm not freaking out." I wasn't. Not on Diane—I could never. True, getting her cupcake 9-1-1 text while tethering a monster to a table wasn't ideal, but if my ride-or-die needed me, I was happy to help. Especially with Sugar-Bug. *If* I seemed a tiny bit stressed, it was because the jerk at the bakery had thrown me behind schedule and now every passing minute felt like a personal insult.

"If you say so," Diane said, and there it was again. The smirk. "I was thinking...why don't you come over after work? Your date with the Fumble hunk is tonight, right? Bring some wine and get ready at my house. I'll do your hair—just like our college days." Diane and I had been thrown together by chance over a decade ago—roommates in the freshman art-major dorms at LSU. Though we'd both changed our paths by graduation, we'd remained inseparable.

"You don't know he's a hunk," I reminded her. "No photos on Fumble, remember? It's their whole stupid schtick."

"Yeah, yeah. But you don't know he's *not* a hunk," she countered. "Would it kill you to hope for the best? To be a little excited?"

"What makes you think I'm not excited?" I wasn't excited. At all. I'd only signed up for Fumble Online Dating because Diane had been way too eager to create my profile. Honestly, I'd expected her to forget about it and move on to the next shiny new dating trend and I'd be off the hook. No such luck; my dating profile had become her latest hyperfixation.

She snorted. "Please. I can read you like a book, even through the phone. You're a terrible liar. Come over, okay?"

"Yeah. Fine." I spied an open parking space a few rows over. Another vehicle was circling the lot. "Now I really have to go." I stomped my Louboutin to the gas. This spot was mine.

"Wait! I have something else to tell you, but...I guess you can find out tonight."

"Sounds goo—fuck!" An orange tabby darted in front of my car. I slammed on the brakes, causing the pastry box to pop open. It slid forward in the passenger seat. My arm shot out and smashed the lid down, smearing rainbow icing against the clear plastic. "Fuck," I repeated, this time softly. At least I'd kept them from flying onto the floorboard.

"You okay?"

"Yeah. Peachy." I frowned. Our original agreement was I'd place the cupcake order, and Diane would handle pickup and delivery. The last-minute change of plans shouldn't have been a big deal. Considering everything else I'd accomplished that morning, delivering an order of cupcakes wasn't difficult. So what if I'd had to rush things along in my workshop? I built buffers into my schedule for just such an occasion. Diane liked to joke that schedules were my entire personality, and she wasn't exactly wrong.

Yet here I was—running late with a carton of trashed cupcakes that were more smeared finger paint than gourmet rainbows.

"Okay. If you say so." Diane sounded unbothered as ever. "See you tonight. And thanks again,"

"Sure." I ended the call. Three feet in front of my car, the orange cat sat on its haunches, staring at me as he dragged his tongue over his patchy fur.

I tooted the horn. "Move it, roadkill!"

The cat never blinked as he shot his hind leg into the air, and went to work on his nether regions. Yards away, a tan SUV slid into my parking space.

Because of course it did.

I clenched and unclenched my grip on the steering wheel. There was no point in getting worked up over being a few minutes late; everything was fine.

It was fine that Sugar's birthday cupcakes, special ordered from the best bakery in town three months ago, were garbage. *No big deal.*

And so what if, thanks to an orange fleabag, my only parking option was the overflow lot near the athletic fields. Did it really matter that, in these heels, that parking lot might as well have been miles away? Or that I was now a full—I glanced at my phone; *oh god*—twenty minutes behind schedule. I hoofed it toward the main building.

It. Was. Fine.

The heel of my Louboutin snagged a crack in the sidewalk, pitching me forward. I steadied myself, somehow hanging on to the cupcakes—not that it mattered. They couldn't have looked worse.

How did Diane—who was never on time—live this way? Because I was lying to myself—it was not fine. It was horrible.

Sweat had collected in my armpits and between my breasts by the time I pushed through the school's entrance, signed in at the office, and hurried to Sugar-Bug's classroom. Mr. Lopez saw me coming through the window in the classroom door and pushed it open before I could knock. He wore his signature expression: lips pursed, eyes twinkling (yes, twinkling; seriously, I'd seen diamonds with less sparkle).

With his mop of black waves framing his chiseled face, Sugar's teacher would've been more at home on a soap opera than leading a sixth-grade class. *Jesus.* No wonder most of the moms and some of the dads had crushes on him.

"Sorry I'm late." I thrust the oversized box into Mr. Lopez's waiting arms.

He shrugged. "No worries. The closer to final bell I can wait before giving them sweets, the better." Mr. Lopez paused and looked down at the clear box. "Uh...did something happen? I mean, they're kind of..."

"What? Are they not good enough?" I snapped, immediately regretting it, because Mr. Lopez was being nice. What he clearly wanted to ask was, *What the hell did you do to these things?*

It would've been a fair question.

"Sorry." I glanced down and shook my head. "Let me start again." My fingertips rested on the teacher's arm as I forced a friendlier tone. "What I mean is, there was this whole thing with this orange cat and slamming on brakes and—you know what? Let's just say, it's been an adventure." I smiled. "Hopefully these are still okay to give to the kids?"

"Are you kidding? I could pass around a tub of frosting, and they'd love it. Don't even worry about it." Mr. Lopez chuckled. "Oh, before I forget: Samantha could use a little extra time with prealgebra. Perhaps a tutor?"

I nodded. "I'll make sure it happens."

"Good, good." With that, he took the cupcakes into the classroom. I checked my phone. There was no time to stick around and gauge Sugar's reaction to her ruined birthday treat. Poor thing. I'd make it up to her later. Another video game should do the trick. After all, it was Sugar's world; we were just living in it.

I flew down the stairs and out the door, mentally calculating the best route for making up lost time, as I artfully avoided sidewalk cracks. Even with the buffers built into my schedule, thanks to both the asshole at the bakery and the marmalade menace in the parking lot, I was cutting it too close for comfort. Showing up late was not a good look—and this doctor had the potential to be a profitable business partner.

The Jimmy Choos I planned to buy with the commission check from this pharmaceutical sale were poetic—navy silk wrapped in beaded silver accents that, in certain lighting, twinkled like stars in the sky. I wasn't religious, but they spoke to me on a spiritual level.

I flung open the car door and sank into the driver's seat, pressing the start button. The engine roared to life, blasting delicious air-conditioning, just as my phone rang through the car's Bluetooth. This time, however, it wasn't Diane on the other end. It was my boss.

I reversed out of the parking spot, clearing my throat before I answered the call. *In control. Perfect as always.* "This is Cordelia."

My boss's tone was stilted. "Good. You answered."

"Margery." I worked to sound upbeat—not an easy task at the moment, but the last thing I needed was Margery on my case. "You know I always answer. What's up?"

"Your afternoon meetings are cancelled," she said.

"What?" I punched the brakes, my car sliding to an abrupt stop in the middle of the school driveway. This day kept getting better. "You know how I feel about changing my schedule. I'm the senior salesperson with a trusted track record, and if you think—"

"Cordelia, save it. This isn't about trust." Her annoyance was clear, and I could see her in my mind. Margery Huang, pharma sales shark and all around badass, seated at the mahogany desk that filled her office, her posture rod-straight, and her silver-streaked black hair tugged into its usual no-nonsense ponytail. I'd once overheard an intern whisper that Margery's flawless ivory complexion glowed because she moisturized with the tears of her subordinates. It was believable, which was one of the reasons I admired her. Unfortunately, the sentiment wasn't mutual.

My voice remained cool, despite the alarm bells clanging in my mind. "What's going on?"

"We have a problem. Bosephan is being pulled from the market. Pronto."

"I'm sorry?" I pressed the button on my steering wheel to turn the volume up on our conversation, as if that would help Margery's words make sense. "My connection must be bad. It sounded like you said we're pulling Bosephan?"

"Yes. A few hours ago we got wind of a class action lawsuit. Rumor is the higher-ups have known about it for a while and have been trying to make it go away...but it isn't. Trust me when I tell you I waited as long as I could to make sure this was real."

"And is it?"

"It's serious," she said.

All visions of Jimmy Choo and his poetic, soul-speaking footwear vanished. If Margery said it was serious, it was serious.

"Why? What are they saying is happening? I mean, the side effects list is long and thorough..."

"Blood clots. Stroke. They're saying Meyer Pharm knowingly downplayed the risks."

"Did they? I mean, did we?"

She sighed. "I don't know. I'm in sales not science. That's not important. What *is* important is covering our asses."

"It's important to me." I'd touted the safety and efficacy of Bosephan to every doctor I visited, and because of my pitch, they prescribed the sleeping pill to their patients. Bosephan was *my* account. Sure, there were other salespeople assigned the drug, but I was top tri-state earner for the past two years. I knew Bosephan's listed side effects like the back of my perfectly manicured hand.

The pill was a modern rebrand of an erectile dysfunction medication that Meyer Pharmaceutical shelved in the nineties. Its original reason for being pulled—a side effect of intense drowsiness and painful morning wood if whoever took it didn't find "release" before falling asleep—was what made it a miracle drug for many women with insomnia. It wasn't often prescribed to cis men, but no peen, no pain, no problem. At least that's what I'd been led to believe and what I'd assured my clients was the truth.

The idea that I'd played a part in harming innocent people made me ill.

"All I know," Margery continued, "is it's a PR nightmare, and Meyer doesn't want to deal with the repercussions. There's an audit, and I have to turn over all of our sales and samples info, so I'll need your notes and logs ASAP. Cordelia, they want it gone. Like yesterday."

"Yesterday?" This was bad.

"Yesterday," Margery repeated firmly.

I leaned into my headrest, eyes closed as I massaged my temples with my index fingers, doing my best to stave off the dull ache humming at the base of my skull. It was quiet hum for now, but was capable of growing into a stress-induced, debilitating roar. Ask me how I know.

I focused on inhaling slowly—in through my nose, out through my mouth—while envisioning my happy place. *Silver table, rows of shelves, plastic spread over the floor, all perfectly tidy. Everything in its place.* Another deep breath.

"Cordelia? Are you still there?" Margery's voice pulled me back into the moment. "This is a very big deal."

No shit, Margery.

An audit of my Bosephan sales account could mean trouble. Not like smushed cupcake trouble—but the kind of trouble that could land a woman in an orange jumpsuit—possibly for a very long time. Possibly for murder. I hated orange—it washed me out. So yeah. I'd say it was a big fucking deal.

"Cordelia?" My boss's voice grew impatient.

I opened my eyes to see the orange tabby trot past my window. *Smug bastard.* I thought it was black cats who were unlucky.

"Are you there? Cor—"

"Sorry," I interrupted. "I—my cell signal isn't great." I cleared my throat. "And yes. Of course. I'll get my logs to you as soon as I can."

"See that you do."

We disconnected, and I hit the gas, gunning it off the school grounds.

This whole lawsuit was probably nothing to worry about.

Probably. Taking chances was a luxury I couldn't afford. This would be bad for anyone, but it would be next-level for someone with my unique situation. The sharp tips of my manicure dug into the leather of the steering wheel until my nail beds ached.

At the red light, instead of continuing in the direction of my office, I turned left, heading toward the highway that would take me to the other side of town, toward Practical Family Medicine.

In my five years working with Bosephan, I'd given out tons of samples. Which was no big deal—that's what they're for. Salespeople like myself gave samples to the doctors who grew to love the medication, so they prescribed it often, and my commission checks kept me in designer labels.

Which was great, because looking well-off and put-together made my *other* job easier. Or maybe it was more of a hobby? Depended on how you looked at it, I guess. Personally, I considered it a calling.

Either way, appearances mattered. And commission from Bosephan sales allowed me to *appear* like the type of person who was above getting her hands dirty.

But a pay cut—even a deep one—wasn't enough to send me into panic mode. However, skimming off the top of my stash of samples was unfortunately a fireable offense—with possible legal consequences. An audit from my company could (and likely would) lead to a criminal investigation that could lead police to a particular workshop. One housed in a storage unit outside of town. That would not do.

I glanced in my rearview mirror. My company-issued tablet sat on the backseat, but old-fashioned paper forms worked better for this arrangement. With one hand on the wheel, I reached behind me and pulled my leather work bag to the front passenger seat and unsnapped it. *Good.*

The folder with the required paperwork was tucked inside, exactly where it belonged. Everything was going to be fine.

I'd sacrificed too much to get here. I'd done things I couldn't undo. Scary things. Things that hurt. Things like lying to people I loved, because regardless of what Diane thought, I was a great liar...when I had to be. And then there was Joanie...I could never forget Joanie.

Getting rid of her had taken everything I had. That itself proved Cordelia Black wasn't afraid to do the difficult thing. I'd be damned if, after everything I'd poured into creating this life, undocumented sleeping pills led to my unraveling.

I merged onto the highway. There was no reason to panic—I'd assessed the risk before the first time I'd ever slipped one of the perfect little pills into a predator's drink. All I had to do was stick to my plan.

Which was easy—because it was a great plan. A solid plan. Meticulous.

The plan's name was Dr. Robin Ezelle, and she'd be happy to see me—or at least happy for the money I gave her. Same as she'd done many times before, she'd sign the logs saying she'd received my missing samples, and I'd slip her cash for her trouble.

It had been months since I'd paid her a visit, which okay, I could now see was not so meticulous after all—leaving so many samples unaccounted for. But in my defense, this whole fiasco sprang up out of nowhere. Bosephan, in its current form, had been around for years with zero issues. I'd grown complacent—and a person with my particular interests (*Hobby? Calling? Proclivities?*) could never be complacent. Lesson learned.

Deep breath. *Yes.* I was in control. Of the situation. Of everything.

This was the major difference between who I was and who I'd become.

Once upon a time, I'd been a scared throwaway girl who would've given in to anxiety. Who would've squirmed and flailed.

Now, I simply adjusted my course.

Now, Cordelia came out on top. Always.

BY THE TIME I MADE IT TO DIANE'S THAT EVENING, IT FELT like days, not hours, had passed since my panicked phone call with my boss.

Which made the fact that there was a pickup truck parked on the street in front of Diane's house *just perfect*. Diane was enough for me, but occasionally she tried to usher me into her small group of work friends, inviting me to bachelorette parties and girls' nights. Thanks, but no thanks.

I eased on my brakes as I pulled past the truck, slowing almost to a stop. A turquoise Mercy Hospital parking tag, same as the one in Diane's Jeep, hung from its rearview mirror.

After the emotional suck-fest of my day, adding a party crasher to the mix was the last thing I needed or wanted.

Because you want to know what had happened to my plan? My perfect plan—my *meticulous*, foolproof paperwork-fixing plan?

It was not so foolproof, it turned out.

After the phone call with my boss, I'd driven straight to

Practical Family Medicine, ready to get a handle on things and get back to my perfectly orchestrated life. You know. The life where I *didn't* worry about my company getting the police involved because of unaccounted sleeping pills, and those cops snooping around until they found out things about me they most definitely did *not* need to know.

But it was going to be fine—because of my plan.

Except.

When I stomped into the doctor's office, the receptionist sounded almost gleeful when she told me Dr. Ezelle—my one-woman key to safety—had suffered a stroke.

Okay, fine. No big deal. Cordelia Black could handle it. Determined to put this problem behind me, I'd driven straight to the hospital, where I'd lied to the nurse's desk. *I'm here to see my cousin. Poor thing had a stroke.* Easy. With the forms tucked beneath my arm, I'd marched into Dr. Ezelle's room, convinced this was nothing but a small snafu.

I wasn't prepared for what I saw.

Dr. Robin Ezelle lay curled into herself, tiny and fragile in the hospital bed. Her gray hair frazzled around her sallow white face, while tubes ran into her nose and burrowed beneath the delicate skin of her arms. Machines beeped, and on the overhead television, a woman guessed the price of a crate of toothpaste with an audience cheering her on. I stared at the doctor's limp body until a nurse bustled into the room.

"Sweetie, don't give up hope," she'd said, patting my arm, mistaking my bewilderment for grief.

I gripped the forms to my chest. My whole stash of samples were now unaccounted for, the papers left unsigned. And me, unprotected.

"Will she wake up today?" I asked, the perfect amount of concern in my voice.

"Anything's possible," the nurse said, but the way she hadn't looked at me felt intentional.

I'd made an excuse and bolted.

Now, I shifted into park and cut the ignition. Slumping in my seat, I stared through the windshield at the modest two-story bungalow that was practically my second home. Diane and Sugar were the only family I had. The only real family *I'd ever* had.

But if this Bosephan fiasco spiraled into something bigger—if there was a legal investigation—they, nor anyone else, would ever look at me the same.

It wasn't fair. The work I did—the necessary *good* work—would be laid bare, distorted. Picked apart by the press like vultures tearing meat from bone. No one would care that the men I killed were monsters. I'd be painted as psychotic. *A psychotic, man-hating bitch.*

Because yes, that is what I was doing in my workshop. I was getting rid of bad men.

Bile crept up my esophagus. I swallowed, but its taste remained, sour and acidic like a bite of rotten fruit.

A curtain moved in Diane's front window, and Sugar appeared. She smiled her big brace-faced smile and waved. If I wasn't inside in five minutes, she'd be at my car, talking nonstop without taking a breath.

God, I loved that kid.

It had always been the three of us—Cor, Di, and Sugar-Bug—and there was nothing I wouldn't do to protect that. Losing Diane and Sugar because of *fucking medication samples* could not happen. I wouldn't let it.

The folder holding the forms sat right there, on the passenger seat—what was I waiting for? I dug a pen from my glove box. Damn it, I'd handle this now and put it behind me.

I thumbed through the stack, backdating each form and scrawling Dr. Ezelle's chicken-scratch signature. If push came to shove, once the doctor recovered, she could be convinced to say the signatures were hers. I was a fair person; I'd even send her the usual payment. It was fine.

There. I signed the last page with flourish. *Done.*

I rolled my shoulders and relaxed my jaw, and the bile that had risen like mercury in an old-school thermometer dissipated. Everything would work out because I would make it work out. I always did.

I grabbed the bottle of white I'd bought on the way over and jogged up the brick pathway, pausing outside the front door. Following dangerous men for hours—*drugging them, trapping them, making them pay*—didn't faze me, but the idea of losing my family sent my anxiety into a tailspin.

Luckily, coming out on top of crappy situations was peak Cordelia. I was an expert at managing *all* circumstances. My entire life was proof, wasn't it?

Shoulders straight, chin high, *easy breezy beautiful fairy godmother*—I twisted the doorknob and let myself inside.

Sugar was in the living room parked in front of her game console, playing the Zelda game I'd given her for her birthday. That explained why she hadn't rushed out to my car—the girl was obsessed with Zelda. She tossed her controller onto the couch and bounded toward me with open arms, giggling. "CiCi! What were you doing out there for so long?" She didn't pause for me to answer. "Thanks for the cupcakes! They were hilarious!"

I squeezed her tight. "Sorry about that, kiddo."

"Don't be sorry, everybody loved them. Devon Castello smeared the icing over his face. It was *so* funny." She stepped back and smiled at me slyly, the way she did whenever she said the name *Devon Castello*. "They were so much better than those weird cookies you brought last year."

"The macarons?"

"Yeah." She scrunched her nose. "Those."

"Oh, come on. They weren't *that* bad." Last year, for Sugar-Bug's birthday, I'd driven to New Orleans and bought pink and green macarons from my favorite high-end confectionary. The fancy desserts weren't cheap, but as a kid, I'd never had so much as a birthday cake. Sugar deserved the best.

The macarons, however, were a complete fail. Apparently standing out was not the goal in fifth grade.

"They were pretty." She shrugged. "But cupcakes are better."

"Even smushed?"

"Especially smushed."

"You're a mess, you know that?" I shook my head and started up the stairs. "Your mom working on a project?"

"You know it." Sugar rolled her eyes. "Get ready. She's going to introduce you to her new boyfriend." She stuck her finger in her mouth and made a gagging sound.

I gripped the banister, freezing in place. "Boyfriend?"

I'd expected someone because of the truck parked out front. But boyfriend? We spoke every day and Diane hadn't mentioned a boyfriend. She hadn't mentioned a guy at all.

"Yeah—*Simon*. Mama's nervous because she doesn't want you to be *mean*." She wrinkled her nose, and lowered her voice to a conspiratorial whisper. "He's *such* a nerd, CiCi. His hair is so oily. It's like those old timey movies. He just slicks it back. Complete weirdo." She giggled as she dramatically pushed her strawberry curls away from her face with both hands. "We'll have to do what we always do."

Was I really that predictable?

I shrugged. "Your mama is perfectly capable of choosing who she wants to date without our input."

"Sure." Sugar-Bug grinned, eyes shining. She skipped back into the living room and grabbed her controller. "Whatever you say."

Okay, *maybe* I was a little hard on Diane's dates. And *maybe* I'd helped her come to her senses regarding one or two. Three, *maybe*. But only because, let's face it, she had horrible taste in men. The women she dated were questionable, but the guys? Ugh. My best friend deserved someone worthy of her. If such a person existed.

I wasn't mean. I was fair.

In college, Diane had blushed and rolled her eyes as her mother, visiting for parents' weekend, told stories of how little-girl Diane always brought home strays—mangy cats and dogs, baby birds fallen from their nests. Even now, she'd rescue busted pieces of furniture from the roadside to, as she called it, *give them a second chance*. My bestie had a big heart and wanted to save things. That included men, it seemed.

But I knew something Diane had never been forced to learn. Not all things deserved saving. My bestie needed me to be the voice of reason whenever she brought home a sad sack with mommy issues.

Simon. He was probably a real piece of work.

"Go ahead," Sugar called in a singsong voice, and I paused on the top stair. "You'll see—he's a big angry dork."

Angry? Why would Sugar call him angry? I filed away the thought to examine later. It was time to meet this secret Simon for myself. I couldn't help but smile. After the day I'd had—it would be nice to blow off some steam.

Diane was in her spare bedroom clutching a paintbrush and squatting next to a half-painted aubergine dresser. A few copper ringlets escaped her topknot and framed her round freckled face.

A man stood next to her.

Simon. My gaze traveled over his lean frame—black button-down with the sleeves rolled up, tucked into belted jeans. His blond hair slicked away from his angular face, exactly as Sugar had described. Bad hair was unfortunate, but it wasn't a deal-breaker.

He leaned close to Diane, the muscles in his forearms dancing as he used his own brush to create messy strokes on the sad piece of furniture.

He was definitely her type. Slightly dorky. A little preppy. And he was tall.

Petite Diane had a thing for tall men, and Simon was at least six two.

I leaned against the doorframe, but they were too caught up in their own world to notice. Fine—it gave me a chance to observe this *Simon.*

He wasn't ugly. But he wasn't exactly handsome, either. His complexion was smooth enough to suggest at least a basic skin care routine—not a bad thing—but not *too* smooth, with the first signs of a five o'clock shadow along his cheek and jaw. His eyes were a cool gray, and his hair was blond enough to make me wonder if it was professionally lightened. Probably not, considering the dated cut and style.

Overall, everything about him was average. Perfectly ordinary.

Too ordinary? I frowned.

Simon made messy streaks with the purple paint, the corners of his lips twitching as if he were forcing the smile he wore. "Babe." His voice carried more bass than I expected. "If you need a dresser, I can buy you one."

Diane laughed and swatted at him. "Stop. I could buy my own if that's what I wanted—this is better. Trust the process. Besides, isn't it fun?"

"If you say so." He shrugged and repeated, "Trust the process."

It would've been fine—a flirty, bantery moment—except Simon didn't sound flirty. Besides his twitchy smile, he sounded annoyed. Sugar's words came to mind—*an angry dork.* Ugh. What did he possibly have to be annoyed about?

At best, Simon was *bland*, while Diane was *everything*, and he should feel lucky to be here, in her home, working on one of her projects. He should feel lucky she even looked his way. He should *not* be annoyed—not with Diane. And he definitely shouldn't be angry.

I'd only been here, casually spying, for a few minutes, and already something about this man made me uneasy. His slicked hair, his tucked shirt, even the smile on his face...it all felt fake. And as someone who wore disguises on the regular, I prided myself on spotting authenticity.

Simon, though? He was too...too *curated*. The kind of man you saw all day long, but could never quite recall. Handsome enough, but wholly uninspired, like a xeroxed copy of Harmless-Nice-Guy.

Which I hated, because in my *professional* opinion, forgettable men were the most dangerous. Pretty privilege was real and handsome men got away with a lot—but it's those forgettable faces you had to watch out for. *Don't look behind the curtain—no one here but Harmless-Nice-Guy.*

Is that you, Simon? I'd find out.

His eyes met Diane's, and his smile grew until a dimple cratered his cheek. He seemed so sure of himself. I was embarrassed for him, really. Diane would see right through this act.

Except...Diane smiled demurely up at him, and he tenderly

wiped a fleck of paint from her cheek. He leaned forward. *Shit.* They were going to kiss.

I cleared my throat and the couple froze.

"You're here." Diane turned toward me, awkwardly stepping from Simon's arms. She wiped a hand down the front of her overalls, leaving behind a smear of paint. "Good."

I held out the bottle of wine, my gaze still crawling over Simon, as my best smile slid into place like the mask it was. "Who's this?"

Diane narrowed her eyes, a warning for me to behave—because while I did have my secrets, on the phone earlier, she hadn't been completely wrong. She knew me better than anyone. "Cordelia, meet Simon White. We...work together." She beamed. "Cordelia is my best friend—the one I told you all about."

"Work together, huh? Is that what the kids are calling it nowadays?" I gave an exaggerated wink.

"My very *sarcastic* best friend," Diane added, the edges of her words tight. Her message was loud and clear—*Play nice, Cor.*

No worries there. I always played nice, until I had a reason not to.

"I'm only teasing," I said. "Sugar told me your boyfriend was upstairs."

"Boyfriend? He's not... We're not..." She stuttered, flushing beneath her tawny freckles.

Good. If she was embarrassed—maybe they hadn't discussed being exclusive yet.

Simon stepped forward and thrust out his hand. "Boyfriend, huh? I like the sound of that. Nice to meet you, Cor."

Of course he does. My eyes narrowed, and I gave his hand a firm shake. "It's Cordelia. Only Cordelia."

"My bad," he said with irritating Nice-Guy enthusiasm. Like a camp counselor or sitcom dad. The act—because of course it was an act; no one actually sounded like that—set my teeth on edge. And his twitchy smile—*so nice*—never reached his gray eyes.

I glanced at my best friend. *This guy, Diane?* But her smile never faltered.

Maybe she was right. Maybe I needed to chill.

But that was one thing I'd never been good at: chilling.

It wasn't the craziest idea that Sugar's description (*such a big angry dork...*) and Diane's failure to mention his existence (*How long had they even been together?*) set me up to for instant dislike.

And because of my nocturnal pastime, I've been known to see a predator crouching behind every bush, even when there wasn't one.

Fine. I'd play nice. I'd smile. I'd joke. I'd *nicely* give him the boot. Because this guy? He would have to find another bush to crouch behind. Diane's was off-limits.

Diane shook her head. "Cordelia's all snark, no bite. I promise. Now, why don't we get this bottle open, hm?"

I gave my bestie a salute. "Yes, ma'am."

Diane dropped her paintbrush into a mason jar of cloudy water. I followed her downstairs to grab glasses and a corkscrew from the kitchen, Simon directly on our heels.

"I hate to sound rude," I whispered furiously. "But this was supposed to be a girls' night? I mean, I *am* getting ready for a date."

I tossed a look over my shoulder as we entered the kitchen. "Not that it isn't lovely to meet you, Samson."

"It's Simon. And I'm not staying—Diane asked me to stop in to meet her amazing friend." He snaked a long arm around Diane's waist and tugged her close. His fingers dug into her hips as he raised his eyebrows, and was it my imagination or did he seem smug?

Diane leaned into the embrace, her petite frame tucking against his broad chest, before smiling apologetically my way.

Okay. Sure, maybe I was overreacting. Maybe Simon was perfectly fine. Maybe he was a genuine Nice-Guy.

And maybe the Manolos Diane ordered from Wish were the real deal.

"Hmph." The sound escaped before I could stop it. Diane shot me another warning glance.

If Simon noticed the silent conversation happening in front of him, he ignored it. "I'm sure we'll be seeing a lot of each other, Cor... uh, Cordelia."

"Sure." I shrugged. "Maybe."

He dropped another peck on Diane's head. His eyes widened. Something on the kitchen island caught his attention. Reaching across the stacks of bills and scattered junk mail, Simon picked up a mailbox flyer that featured a conga line of grinning animals dancing across the top. *Everyone goes wild for Zippity Zoo Fest*, it read.

"Hey! You want to check out the zoo festival on Sunday? It's supposed to be a lot of fun," he asked Diane.

"Of course not," I said, at the exact moment Diane chimed, "Heck yeah."

I propped against the countertop and held out my hand. Simon slid me the mailer. "I thought we decided to skip this year."

Diane dragged me to the festival-slash-zoo fundraiser every year since Sugar was a toddler. When she'd brought it up yesterday, Sugar had proclaimed herself too old—zoo festivals were for kids, and she was a tween. This was more than fine with me. I hated zoos; the locked-up animals were depressing. The festival, with its stroller-crowded sidewalks and shrieking toddlers, only added to the misery.

Diane shrugged. "Next year, Samantha will be a teenager. Let's go one more time. As a kind of farewell to a childhood tradition. What do you say? It'll be fun."

Ever since Sugar started her period last month, Diane had grown sentimental over anything and everything concerning her daughter's childhood. A few days ago, I'd caught her slumped over an envelope of baby teeth, bleary-eyed and weepy. Motherhood did strange things to people.

Sugar groaned loudly from the living room. If eavesdropping were a recognized sport, she'd be an Olympic athlete. Deep lines appeared between Diane's furrowed brows.

"I know the festival has a lot of memories attached to it, Di, but we can make a new tradition," I said, meaning it. "Something fun that doesn't involve caged animals and crying babies."

"Sounds good to me!" Sugar yelled.

Diane shook her head, opening her mouth to reply, but Simon stopped her.

"I was actually asking if you and Sugar wanted to go." He trailed a hand to her shoulder, cutting his gaze quickly my way, then back to Diane.

"Oh?" I said, and should've won an Oscar because somehow, I managed to sound neutral instead of murderous. Chipper, even. Did this asshole think he could intercept *our* weekend and push me out?

"But no worries," Simon continued. "I have an idea."

Unless Simon's idea was to leave and never come back—I didn't care what he had to say. But I pasted on my friendliest grin and leaned against the counter.

He tucked a ringlet behind Diane's ear as he spoke. "Why don't I take you and Samantha to Zippity Zoo Festival; then you and Cordelia can meet up some other time and start that new tradition she mentioned?"

The zoo flyer fluttered from my hand, joining my stomach on the floor—because what the fuck did Simon think he was doing? The muscle in my jaw twitched.

His smile widened. "Everybody wins."

Everybody wins? Diane and I did not need him telling us we could *meet up some other time*. Sure, the festival was as much fun as licking batteries. Had I hoped this would be the year I *finally* talked Diane out of going? Yes. But at the end of the day, if Diane wanted to wade through a crowd of screaming kids while the hot Louisiana sun warmed piles of animal shit, then of course I'd do the damned thing. Because she was Diane and I would do anything for her. Just like she'd do anything for me.

Simon could fuck all the way off with his *ideas*.

The corners of my smile strained, and I waited for Diane to tell him thanks but no thanks.

"Oh." Diane bit her bottom lip. "Um. Yeah. Okay. That could be fun."

"What?" My gaze ping-ponged from bright-eyed Diane to Simon and his fake Nice-Guy face.

"I'll stay home with CiCi," Sugar whined from the living room. "You and *Samson* can go without me."

I smirked. *Atta girl.*

"You're coming with me—we're spending the day together. That's the end of it," Diane called in a singsong voice, ignoring the dig at Simon's name. Annoyance played over his face—rapid blinks, ticking jaw—but disappeared in an instant. *Interesting.*

"Aw, man," Sugar groaned.

I crossed my arms. How did I handle this situation? It would feel so good to tell him off, but bitchy wasn't the move; Nice-Guys loved playing the victim. *No.* There was only one way to handle a man like Simon White. I had to out-nice him.

"Don't worry," I called loud enough for Sugar to clearly hear. "I'm going."

"Yes!" Sugar squealed.

Diane's brows shot upward. "You are?"

Half a second delayed, Simon echoed, "You are?"

"Of course I am." I turned to Simon, cocking my head to the side and oozing sympathy. That's me. Kind. Sweet. *Right.* "That was such a nice offer, Sam—I mean Simon. But totally not necessary. The zoo festival's important to Diane, so no way I'd miss it."

"You wouldn't?" Diane smirked.

"Don't I go every year?"

"But I thought—"

"I said I wouldn't miss it," I snapped.

Simon's jaw clenched, his shoulders stiffening, and for the briefest moment, I saw something in his eyes—a passing flicker of coldness that made the secret place inside of me stand and take notice.

A person can disguise everything about themselves, but the eyes are the window to the soul. I could always spot a monster by his gaze—but Simon wasn't a monster. He was only a jerk. *An angry dork* as Sugar-Bug noted.

But why was he angry?

Did Diane having friends bother him? Or was it being challenged that pissed him off?

He hadn't liked it when I'd corrected him about my name. Was that it? Was it being corrected? Or being corrected *by me*?

It didn't matter—*because news flash, Simon*—Diane and I were family. Ride or die. Vintage. When Diane came to her senses and realized she was too good for this forgettable waste of time, I'd still be here.

"What about the crying babies and caged animals?" Simon asked, his voice warm and friendly, the cold flicker nowhere to be seen.

"What about them?" I deadpanned. "Who doesn't love crying babies and caged animals? Sounds like a party."

A peel of high-pitched laughter rolled in from the living room.

"Great. The more the merrier."

How kind of him to approve. The discipline required not to roll my eyes—it was impressive, if I did say so myself.

"I should be saying that to you." My voice bordered on saccharine. "After all, it is something *we* do every year."

Simon blinked again, and for a moment, it almost seemed like a faint, wispy movement swirled behind his irises. *Smoke?* My predator brain perked up.

The thought caught me off guard. He was hiding something—I suspected a temper or all-around crappy attitude—but smoke? The idea prickled my insides. Sugar was only a room away, and his arms were draped over Diane. I stared into his face, leaning slightly over the counter.

No. His eyes were gray. Cold. But clear.

"Cor? Are you okay?" Diane reached across the bar and touched my arm.

"Huh? Sorry. I thought... Never mind." I shook my head. "What was I saying?"

"How you adore the zoo now, apparently?" Diane was loving this.

"Right. It's a *tradition*." I used her word. "A tradition for *the three of us*."

"And now it'll be four." Simon grinned broadly, his eyes flashing to mine in a way that said, *Your move*.

Diane smiled between us, catching my eye with the same silent plea. *Be nice, Cor. Please.*

Damn it. Simon had to go. But I had to be smart about it; I couldn't hurt Diane. I wouldn't.

"Right. This time it'll be four," I agreed.

"Damn it," Sugar grumbled from the living room. The corners of Diane's lips twitched, but she pretended not to hear the swear word as she circled the island and threw her arms around my neck. "This will be so much fun—I know you two are going to love each other. And—bonus!—there's a new giraffe baby."

"Can't wait." Simon beamed. He liked that he'd won.

"Me neither." I made a show of looking at the clock blinking on the stovetop. "Now, I need to hurry or I'm going to be late for my date."

"Oh. Right, sorry." Diane nodded. "Bye, Simon. See you Sunday."

"Yes. Goodbye," I chimed. Take that, you smug asshole.

"Good to meet you, Cor"—Simon paused with an *oh shucks* smile—"I mean *Cordelia*." He crossed in front of Sugar in the living room. "By Sammy."

"It's Samantha. Only Samantha. I already told you. Not Sam. *Never* Sammy." My goddaughter spoke without looking away from her game on the television screen. "Only CiCi gets to call me by a nickname."

Simon glanced at Diane as if he expected her to say something—maybe order Sugar to be polite or chastise her for speaking her truth—but my bestie only shrugged.

Simon left, closing the door behind him, and the electricity that charged through my nerve endings vanished.

Diane said, "You're such a bitch."

Was I? Possibly.

I grinned. "You love me."

"And my daughter is turning into you."

"You're welcome."

She sighed. "I guess there are worse people she could imitate. Now let's drink this wine. You always bring the good stuff."

As Diane retrieved the wineglasses, my eyes settled on the place where Simon had stood moments before. Maybe that lingering feeling that something was off—maybe it was nothing. Or possibly his attitude could be explained away by nerves. Diane was out of his league. I, her adoring best friend, obviously didn't like him. Neither did Sugar. It was enough to throw anyone off their game.

But.

Maybe...

Maybe it was more.

Whatever was up with Simon White, I didn't like it one bit.

The moss-green vanity chair cut into my lower back as Diane ran a brush through my tresses. This ritual was left over from our college dorm days, back when we got ready for each date together. I'd done our makeup. Di had done our hair. We'd abandoned the tradition, except when nostalgia hit. And when it did, it always made me remember how special our friendship was.

When Diane had been *very* pregnant our junior year of college, and her blood pressure spiked, I'd rushed her to the hospital. On the way, she'd passed out in the car, her head lolling listlessly to the side as spit caked in the corners of her mouth. It was the most afraid I'd been in my entire life. Growing up in a den of junkies, always hungry, always a little sick in the way that poor kids are—I could handle a lot. I could handle doing the hard things. I could handle getting rid of Joanie. I could handle bad men—monsters.

But I couldn't lose Diane. That I couldn't handle.

With ugly, snotty tears streaming down my face, I'd promised her I would always look out for her. If she'd stay alive, I'd protect her and the baby at all costs. It was a promise I took seriously, one that became a mantra in my life, shaping every direction of every decision. She was my family.

Across Diane's bedroom, a small television sat atop a chest of drawers, tuned to a local channel Diane had been watching earlier that day. We'd left it on to cover our conversation in case Sugar got it in her head to snoop and listen outside the door. It was mostly ignored, until it played a commercial for the evening news.

Photos of Baton Rouge men—all different, except for a single common thread—lined up across the bottom of the screen. My ears perked, and I focused on the television through the vanity mirror as the reporter spoke somberly into a microphone. *"Still no leads on the area's missing men. Could there be a serial killer in the Red Stick? News at ten."*

Serial killer.

I loathed those words. They weren't fair—not when used against me. Had I made those men disappear? Okay, yes—but I dealt in karma—not murder. It wasn't like I skulked around, killing randos. My work was decent and good—but I wasn't an idiot. Rapists and murderers and abusers might go free, but the one who brought them justice would not.

It was why I'd freaked out about the Bosephan paperwork. When you lead a life like mine, there's no room for error.

But—I inhaled a deep breath—*it's fine.* The reporter said so himself—*no leads*. Besides, he hadn't said victims. He'd dubbed my monsters as *missing*. *Missing* meant no bodies. No bodies meant no murder—and certainly no *serial killer*. The whole thing was irresponsible reporting—someone should complain.

"Earth to Cordelia?" Diane tapped my head lightly with the comb.

"Hm?"

"Everything okay?"

"Yeah." I caught her gaze in the mirror. "Just...indigestion from the wine, I guess."

"I told you not to drink so fast." Diane frowned. "You aren't twenty-one, you know."

"Yes, mother. Is that why you smacked me with the comb? To remind me to drink responsibly?"

"You're a real riot, you know that?" She rolled her eyes. "Were you listening to anything I said? I asked why you were so rude to Simon. You were only teasing him, right? With the whole *Samson* bit?"

"You want to know how I feel about Simon?" I served Diane my snarkiest smile. "You sure?"

"Yeah." Diane adjusted the part in my hair, then lifted a piece and sprayed coconut-scented dry shampoo. "Sometimes I can't tell when you're teasing and when you're serious."

"Okay. You asked," I said. "Simon. Well. Something's off with that guy."

"Here we go again." Diane worked the hair product into the roots of my hair with her fingertips. "How could you possibly know that? You talked to him for like ten minutes."

Diane hadn't detected Simon's *offness*—and I couldn't blame her. She'd had the kind of childhood where teachers taught, coaches coached, clergy preached, and uncles gave appropriate hugs and twenty-dollar bills on holidays. Even when she'd ended up pregnant from a creep, she'd pretended everything was fine. It was easier to believe excuses than to believe someone you trusted would purposely deceive you.

If there was anything wrong with Simon, no doubt Diane and her kind, optimistic heart would miss it.

Good thing she had me.

"Diane." I turned in the chair and looked her in the eye. "Why did you ask, if you think I haven't been around him long enough to have an opinion?"

"I don't know." She shrugged. "I guess I wanted your first impression, you know? I thought you'd say something about his hair."

"At least you aren't delusional about that." I turned back around and Diane picked up the curling iron and began working it through my ends. "What was he going for—nineteen-eighties stockbroker?"

"You're such a snob."

"I know."

"Hair can be fixed," she said, picking up another section of mine. "And *delusional*? Really?"

I looked at her in the mirror and shrugged. "You asked me, remember?"

"I know he's a little nerdy, but I like it," Diane said. "Especially after CrossFit Chad."

I scrunched my face and, in a husky voice, said, "'I'm sorry, I can't eat that. I have to hit my macros.'"

Diane cackled and set the curling iron on the vanity table. "He was pretty, though, wasn't he?"

"Only if you like six foot three, deep-bronze skin, with piercing dark eyes and a six pack," I said.

"Ew. Gross." Diane scrunched her nose in mock disgust. "Who likes those things?"

Truth was, I'd liked Chad for Diane. He was safe—what you saw was what you got: tall, handsome, and not too bright, but sweet as cherry pie. She'd gotten bored with him quickly (there are only so many times a woman can listen to a man talk about Turkish get-ups and dead lifts), and he wasn't able to deal with Diane's diet soda and Doritos addiction.

"You're right about one thing," I said. "Simon is Chad's polar opposite."

Diane shook her head. "I don't know if you mean that as an insult or—"

"At least he's better than Bethany," I interrupted. It was a dirty move—but mentioning Bethany was a guaranteed subject change.

Diane stiffened. "Do you always have to bring up Bethany?"

"Diane. She stole your clothes."

"She did not 'steal my clothes.'" Diane wiggled her fingers in air quotes. "She borrowed them."

"Yeah, and then you broke up, and she moved away and took all your things with her," I said. "That's stealing."

Scarlett bloomed over Diane's cheeks. It was one of the things I loved most about her—how she wore every single emotion on her face, bright and honest as a blinking neon sign.

"You aren't funny." She picked up the comb and yanked it through my ends a little rougher than necessary.

"Oh, I think I'm a little funny." I laughed.

"I really liked her." Diane words were as breathy as a teenager sighing over a crush.

"Yeah, you did." I snickered. "Right up until she packed a suitcase full of your clothes and skipped town."

"It's not funny." Diane huffed. "Cordelia, it's not." The more she insisted, the harder it was to hold back. Belly laughter is contagious, and soon Diane's shoulders were shaking, neither of us able to speak.

When she finally caught her breath, her eyes went dreamy. "At the time, I thought what Bethany and I had was special." She shrugged. "I'm hoping this time it's for real, ya know? With Simon."

So much for a subject change. "Seems a bit soon for that kind of talk, don't you think?" I asked.

Diane ignored me. "Simon isn't obsessed with his looks like

Chad, and unlike Bethany, he has a stable, good job. And oh my God, he's sweet, and so funny."

"Bullshit." I pictured the twitchy-lipped guy I'd met. "He is not."

"Cordelia, he is—he has to be comfortable around you for that side of him to come out. He writes me these funny little poems. They're sweet and hysterical, and dorky. But—"

I interrupted. "At least you don't have to worry about him stealing your clothes, I guess."

"I'm serious," she said. "I like him, and it's important to me that y'all like each other."

My heart ached because Diane was so desperate to be loved. It wasn't something I understood. She was enough for me. Diane and Sugar and I? We were a family. If she needed someone else to feel complete, then I wanted her to have that. But Simon? Ten minutes with the guy, and I knew he wasn't it.

"He likes kids," she continued. "Do you know how hard it is to find someone in their thirties with no crazy-ex baggage, who likes kids? He's a fucking unicorn, is what he is."

I leaned toward the mirror and wiped away a smudge of lip liner. "What about Mr. Lopez? He's right there—single, the right age, devastatingly handsome, likes kids."

"Yeah. I'm not sure he's into women."

"So ask him," I said.

Diane shook her head. "I couldn't date my daughter's teacher."

"If you say so."

"I do. Say so, I mean." Diane pumped shine serum into her hands. "Can you give Simon a chance? A real one? Please? For me?"

"Diane." I inhaled a contemplating breath as she put the finishing touches on my hair. "I know I've been a little judgey in the past—"

"A *little* judgey? Ha!"

"Yes, a *little*. It's only because you deserve the best. That's what I want for you. I don't think it's Simon." Understatement of the decade. "But if you do, then okay. I'll give him a fair shot." What could it hurt to humor her for now?

Diane's eyes were puddled sunshine. She draped an arm over my shoulders and gave me a squeeze. "That's all I want."

"Good. Me too. Now." I ran my fingers through Diane's glossy, smooth handiwork. "I'm going to shimmy into my dress and go on this pointless date to listen to some idiot talk about bitcoin or fantasy football or god knows what else, while I stuff my face with surprisingly decent seafood. You, on the other hand, are going to have an amazing night polishing off the rest of the Pinot and bingeing Netflix. Or maybe you'll finish painting that dresser."

Diane snorted, because we both knew she wasn't finishing the dresser any time soon. She had a knack of turning day projects into month projects, but she adored the process, which I understood in my own way.

Diane and I were like two sides of the same artistic coin. We each took dirty, broken subjects through a metamorphosis. Her preferred canvas was old furniture. Mine? Well...

My fingers twitched with anticipation. My canvas was waiting for me—my prize for getting through this date.

I sighed, quelling the excitement that knotted in my middle, then pulled my little black dress from its hanger on the back of the bedroom door and wiggled into the fitted frock. Diane tugged up the zipper.

I adjusted the waist and hemline, then smoothed the material with my palms, frowning at my reflection. I looked great. The dress was perfection and the stilettos I planned to wear gave me ballerina calves. But all this effort for some guy who probably wouldn't look up from my tits all evening? Ugh.

Diane clocked my frown and threw herself onto her bed, tucking her arms behind her head. "You don't have to seem so miserable."

"Don't worry about me." I pulled my black Valentino from the top of Diane's vanity and dug around for my perfume, dabbing it behind my ears, my wrists, and between my breasts, then set my handbag aside. "I'm fine."

"Are you?" She sat up and hugged her knees to her chest. "Because you could've fooled me. You look about as happy as if you were going to a funeral or something."

"Not true." I clapped my hands and bounced on my toes. "*Golly, gee.* Is this better?"

"Seriously," Diane said, ignoring me. "You've found something wrong with every single man you've gone out with. How can you tell anything after one date?"

"Okay. That's not fair. I'm not"—aggressive air quotes—"*finding something wrong*. I refuse to ignore red flags."

"What about Lewis? He was nice."

"Seriously?" I'd gone out with Lewis two months ago. "He was missing all his top teeth, Diane."

"That's not necessarily a red flag." She sighed. "Dental is expensive."

I narrowed my gaze, and she held up her hands in surrender.

"Okay, fair enough. I know you've always had thing for nice teeth. Fine. Andre, then—what was wrong with him? He was handsome and could cook—yes, please." She raised her brows.

"Andre the chef?" I crossed my arms. That date was several weeks ago, and my cheeks burned with the fresh memory. "Yeah, I thought he was cute too. Until I let him go down on me, and he said my pussy has good mouthfeel."

"Oof. I forgot about that." Sure she did. "Yeah. You're right. There's no coming back from something so..." Diane winced and squeezed her knees together. "*Mouthfeel.* What does that even mean?"

"It means..." I paused, then shook my head. "He should stick to his kitchen because he didn't know what the hell he was doing in the bedroom."

"You know who did?"

"Don't say it," I ordered with mock authority.

Diane smiled demurely. "Bethany."

I grabbed a throw pillow from the foot of the bed and tossed it at her as she dissolved into contagious laughter. This—laughing myself stupid with my best friend—was exactly what I needed after my crazy day.

"Sweetie," Diane said. She inhaled a deep breath, smothering the remaining giggles. "I know I can sound pushy, but I only want you to be happy."

"I *am* happy," I said. "If I don't seem excited about yet another blind date, well, I'm thirty-three years old—this whole process… it's exhausting." I tugged my best friend to her feet and laced my arms around her waist. "But I'm lucky to have you in my corner. I love you."

"Same." She squeezed me back. "And I love you too. Forever?"

"And ever." It was our affirmation to each other—a promise that began when Diane found herself single and pregnant and too afraid to tell her parents. The man who'd knocked her up had overdosed shortly after, and Diane and I only had each other.

Her hand trailed my arm to my wrist. She ran her fingers over the grubby braid of neon pink yarn I wore as a bracelet. "You know, you don't have to wear this if you don't want to." Sugar had made one for each of us—Diane and me—on Mother's Day when she was in fourth grade. "Samantha won't notice."

"You know I'd never do that." The bracelet never came off. It was tucked carefully into my disguises when hunting and underneath gloves when delivering justice in my workshop. It was a constant reminder that someone cared about me—two someones—and was the most valuable thing I owned. "It's vintage, you know."

Diane held up her arm, showing her matching orange bracelet. "Oh, I know."

I stepped into my date-night Louboutins. Unlike my work pair, these were silver with a higher heel. "How do I look?"

I did a little turn.

"Killer," Diane said.

"Perfect—that's exactly what I was going for."

THE RESTAURANT WAS A TRENDY SEAFOOD PLACE WITH A ridiculous name. *Joe Fish.* With its industrial speakeasy décor and dim lighting, it fit the bill for blind dates perfectly: Always crowded, so my dates never felt too intimate. Always noisy, which was great because I loathed pointless small talk. The food was always good, because if I had to be here, why not at least enjoy dinner?

A couple of the guys I'd met from the dating app turned out to be real gems who I hoped would find happiness with someone else. Others made my skin crawl. One was even on my watch list—when enough time passed so as not to draw attention—we would meet again. The thought of taking him to my workshop awoke a wonderful tickle inside.

That tickle had bothered me once upon a time. Back then, I'd thought, *Am I any better than the predators I put down, if I enjoy the process?*

The answer? Yes. I am (and was and always would be) better.

Because what I did was important. It was messy and dangerous—the fact that I enjoyed it was a bonus.

A wonderful, delicious bonus.

Maybe it had to be that way. Like sex. Sex is messy with an element of danger, but it's necessary. *Absolutely* necessary if humanity wants to continue. But as necessary as it is, would people do it if it didn't give them pleasure? If it didn't fill a longing?

No. Of course not.

If we didn't enjoy sex, we'd say, *Let someone else do it*, and keep saying it right up until mass extinction.

Instead, many people crave it, and our species continues. Maybe that thrill that climbed my spine, with each kill rooting itself in my very being, maybe that was my evolutionary reward.

Or maybe not. Maybe giving bad men what they deserved was simply...satisfying.

I bypassed the hostess stand and headed for the bar, sliding onto my favorite stool. As always, I was early.

"Back again?" Jeremy the bartender was a nice guy. He had a thick mustache and wore suspenders with everything.

"You know it." Of the many times I'd been on dates at *Joe Fish*, Jeremy had worked the bar during six of them. After my fourth visit, he'd stopped asking what I wanted and expertly mixed my Tito's and soda.

He wedged a slice of lime onto the rim of the glass and pushed it toward me.

The best thing about Jeremy was that he didn't have comments. No *You must be picky*, or *You'll find someone one day*. He did his job. Accepted his tip. And moved on. Basically, he was the perfect bartender.

I sipped my cocktail and watched the table in the corner. Still empty. My Fumble match had ten minutes before he was officially late. If this were a real date, I'd finish my drink, pay, and leave without waiting around to introduce myself.

But I was here because I'd promised Diane I would be. And because this was what single millennial women did. So I did it too. Blending in was exhausting.

Thirty minutes later I was finishing a soda and lime when a man was shown to my table.

There was something vaguely familiar about the way he raked his fingers through his curly dark hair. He placed a pastry box on the table, then seemed to think better of it and picked it up. Then set it down. Then opened it and adjusted it slightly. He glanced around the restaurant floor and smiled a perfect gleaming smile. The kind of smile that would've been right at home in a toothpaste ad.

The kind of smile a person remembered, and damn it...*it was him.* The cop from the bakery. The man who'd made me late to Sugar's school.

Earlier, he'd only looked up from his phone because when we'd collided, he'd dropped his own order—a single cupcake. The whole thing would've been kind of funny, except the man had rolled his eyes, as if it were my fault—even though *he* ran into *me*—and acted annoyed when I hadn't stopped to help him pick up his precious lonely cupcake. Who does that?

Apparently someone four inches taller than me, with olive skin, curly brown hair, and great teeth.

Because Diane was right. It might be strange—but I noticed teeth.

It wasn't like I could help it; I'd been teased about my own teeth throughout high school. When I'd moved to Baton Rouge for college, I'd decided I was going to become someone better than a mousy nobody from Sunnyside Trailer Park in Holden, Louisiana. My smile had been one of the first steps of my transformation.

So yeah, smiles caught my attention, and this man's was as perfect now as it had been the first time I'd noticed it at the bakery. Sometimes the universe had a real sense of humor.

My date continued looking around, flashing those too-perfect teeth—a real Officer McSmiley. I ran the tip of my tongue over my lips, watching as he fiddled with the pastry box, his expression growing strained.

Jeremy set the bill in front me, and I handed him my card.

My gaze remained on McSmiley.

Was he? No. He checked his wristwatch. As if *I* were the late one. As if *he* hadn't kept *me* waiting.

"Here you go, Ms. Black." Jeremy slid my card back across the bar, along with the slip for me to sign. "Same time next month?"

"Not if I can get out of it."

I stood and considered leaving, but someone needed to put McSmiley in his place. Teach him some manners. Someone needed to make him understand that no matter what he'd been taught, the world did not actually revolve around him.

Who was better suited to the job than me? There was a reason cats played with mice before devouring them, piece by still-wiggling piece. It was fun.

Wasn't that what Diane said I should be doing? Wasn't that *why* she'd made me sign up for Fumble in the first place? *Cor, you'll have a great time! Meet some good men. Trust me—it'll be fun!*

The experience had been lots of things, but fun? Nope.

I crossed my arms and watched McSmiley fidget nervously in his seat.

Maybe that was about to change.

He was staring at his phone as I approached. I cleared my throat and waited for him to glance up.

"Cordelia?" His toothy smile never faltered. I glanced at the pastry box. *Likes to bake,* my flat ass.

I nodded. "And you're—" I did a quick mental search for my date's real name. "Christopher?"

"That's me." He looked pointedly to his wristwatch. "Better late than never, I guess."

Oh yes. This would be super fun.

"You been here long?" My voice was silk. I pulled out my chair and sat down, making a show of crossing my legs.

"I did rate punctuality as a ten." His implication was clear.

Tinder. Grindr. Match. Plenty of Fish. Jdate. Christian Mingle... They all had something that set them apart from the others—at least on paper.

Fumble's big thing was minimal communication before meeting. Only likes and dislikes and the pièce de résistance: their rating system. Two hundred qualities you were expected to rate—things like punctuality, cleanliness, kindness—things any sane person would rate high.

"Yes," I said. "It's one of the reasons I clicked on your profile."

"Is that why you're late, then?" His voice was flirty, and he chuckled.

Then I chuckled.

Suddenly, we were both chuckling as if we were both in on the same hilarious joke. Only, he didn't know the punchline.

I stopped laughing all at once. "I've been sitting over there." I pointed to the bar. "For about half an hour now."

Christopher blanched. "Oh."

"Yep. Punctual. Which, like you, I rated a ten."

"Then you know..."

"That you're late? Yes. And that you were going to sit here and lord my tardiness over me? Uh-huh." Crossing my arms, I leaned back in my seat and looked into his eyes, waiting for the spark of recognition to light his face. The corners of his grinning mouth tightened, and I let him stew a moment. When he still didn't recognize me, I pointed to the pastry box sitting between us. "What ya got there?"

"It's for you." He nudged the opened box toward me, obviously relieved I'd let his little fib slide. Maybe he'd salvaged the date after all.

Bless his heart.

"Oh, that's right. You're a baker." I leaned forward, resting my elbows on the table, giving him a good look at my face. When he said nothing, I frowned at the cupcake. "The icing is a little—I don't know. A little lopsided?"

At least he was original. In my experience, men—especially Fumble dates—compensated for their shortcomings in lots of ways: wearing expensive watches, ordering expensive wine. But baked goods? This was a first.

McSmiley—Christopher—shrugged sheepishly.

I pretended to examine it further. "It looks like you dropped it. Maybe when you bumped into someone at the bakery?"

"Oh no." He paled. "It's you. I thought it maybe could be...but no way the universe would be that cruel. And when you didn't say anything—I thought I was wrong."

"Cruel, huh? Wow. You know how to sweet talk a girl." I traced a finger through the icing. "Your profile says you *love* to bake things from scratch for the ones you care about. Was I supposed to believe that you hand made this, for *me*?" I looked him in the eye as I licked the frosting from my fingertip. "Hm. Buttercream."

Christopher buried his face in his palms. "This is bad." He blew out a deep breath as he peered from between his fingers. "You should shoot me and put me out of my misery."

"Nah. I hate guns. Besides, where's the fun in that?" I picked up the menu, making a show of sliding an index finger down the columns of entrees and appetizers, even though I knew what I was having. Last time, my date had ordered the redfish and I'd suffered plate envy the entire meal.

The weight of Christopher's gaze settled on me. I glanced up.

His chin was cradled in his palm, and he bounced his fingers over his angular jaw. "I…I," he began, finally. "I feel like a complete jackass—it's, well—I'm new to all this… It's my sister's fault—she made me do online dating."

I set the menu aside. "Are you seriously blaming your bad behavior on your sister?"

"No. That's not what I meant. It was her *idea*, not her *fault*. It seemed like maybe it could be fun, but Fumble asked all these questions about hobbies, and I'm a cop—oh yeah, I'm a cop by the way—"

"I know. I saw your uniform. At the bakery."

"Oh. Right. Well. That's one of the reasons I went with Fumble instead of one of the others. I don't have a lot of time for hobbies, and it didn't require me to list my career. People either immediately hate me or want to sleep with the uniform."

I raised my brows. Or attempted to. Onabotulinum toxin A was worth every penny. Giving up, I tilted my head.

"I know that sounds weird," he said. "But there are all these creepy true crime fanatics."

"I love true crime," I said.

"Of course you do." Christopher again raked a hand through his hair. A nervous habit, maybe.

He was saved by the waiter, who appeared and took our drink orders. He ordered a beer and an appetizer of brie and bacon oysters. I had a water with lemon.

"What was I saying?" he asked.

"You were explaining how your little cupcake of deception played into your date-night scheme."

"Cupcake of deception? Scheme?" A glint lit McSmiley's eyes.

I shrugged. "Kind of catchy, right?"

He leaned back into his chair, his tight grin relaxing into something more boyish. Goofy. "You're giving me too much credit."

"Prove me wrong, then," I said.

"The cupcake wasn't supposed to be that big of a deal." Christopher shook his head. "Fumble had all these questions about hobbies, and, like I said, I don't have time for hobbies because of my job. I mean, I do stuff, but nothing that looks good on a dating app. Who wants to see another picture of a man holding a fish?"

"There are no photos on Fumble," I reminded him.

"You know what I mean."

I nodded—because I absolutely did.

Christopher continued. "My sister—who I adore, okay? She suggested the baking thing and told me to get a cupcake. Her actual words were, 'Buy a damn cupcake, Christopher. No woman is going to care if you bought it or baked it. It's *just* a cupcake.'"

"Sugar *is* our kryptonite." My words were flat, but as I spoke, I took another swipe of frosting. It was delicious.

"Yeah. I see how dumb it was, now." His palms splayed on the table in front of him. "Maybe you can cut me a little slack, though?"

"Why would I do that?" I propped my chin on my fists, biting lightly at my bottom lip. Christopher's eyes narrowed on my mouth. This was too easy. When Diane inevitably asked if I'd had fun on my date, I could finally tell her the truth.

"I'm sure you've seen the news." His eyes didn't leave my lips. "Things have been tough at work—maybe stress has scrambled my brain a little. That's the only reason I can think of for why in the hell I took dating advice from my sister." He thrummed his fingers against the wooden tabletop and blinked hard, as if coming out of a trance. "She's been married since before dating apps were really a thing. She has no idea what it's like."

Things have been tough at work... He was a cop. He'd mentioned the news. My mind flashed to the segment I'd seen at Diane's. *Could there be a serial killer in the Red Stick?*

"What do you mean?" I asked.

"She and her husband were high school sweethearts and—"

"That's sweet," I cut him off. "But I was asking about the news?"

"Oh." His brows steepled, and the *gotcha* tone of his voice was irritating. "You don't keep up with the local news?"

"Yes, I keep up with the news," I snapped. Then gentler, because the beginnings of a plan were taking shape. "I meant specifically, what has your brain fried?"

McSmiley paused, giving me a look that asked how long I'd been living under a rock. I shrugged, going for sheepish. I must've pulled it off because Christopher shook his head and continued. "There's been a spike in crime, but I'm talking specifically about the missing men."

I'd known exactly what he'd meant, but I couldn't let him know that. He'd already said he was put off by true crime fanatics, so I had to be careful. Let him connect the dots for me. If I played my cards right, I could find out if I should actually worry when I heard *serial killer*.

An inside source to my greatest threat—the BRPD—would be

invaluable. All I had to do was figure out who Christopher wanted me to be—and be her. It wasn't hard; it was how I hunted monsters. Using the proper window dressings to become their bait.

Christopher seemed like the type who'd want a soft woman—someone delicate. Someone to protect.

I doubted he could handle Cordelia Black, but he was likely the type of man who'd love the watered-down version—the doting version. The *sweet* version.

I could give him *Sweet Cordelia*, if it granted me the access I needed. It wasn't the first time I'd trotted her out when it served me. And finding out what the police knew about a serial killer—that didn't only serve me; it served all the women and others who were vulnerable to bad men. When I was safe, I could help keep them safe too.

It was settled, then. *Sweet Cordelia*. Locked and loaded.

My smile softened from razor wire to something gentle, and I gazed at McSmiley through my lashes, fluttery as moth wings.

"Oh yes, I remember that." I pretended to shiver. "It's terrifying—what in the hell is happening in our city?"

At that moment, the waiter slid our drinks in front of us, interrupting my performance. "Y'all ready to order?"

Christopher picked up his menu and opened it. "I think I need a minute more, please." He smiled. *Again*. Or maybe he never stopped smiling. Maybe he flashed those perfect teeth, smiling forever and ever until he died.

The waiter hurried away and Christopher shined his hundred watts toward me.

I snaked my hand across the table and caressed his arm with my fingertips. "Christopher." Men loved hearing their names. "On television the police chief keeps saying there's nothing to worry about...but how could that be true?" I pulled away from touching him as I uncrossed and recrossed my legs. Christopher's gaze dropped, before crawling back to my face. "The city can be a dangerous place...for a woman."

Those were the magic words. It was as if I'd flipped an invisible switch. McSmiley's demeanor softened so quickly, it wouldn't have surprised me if he sat in front of his bathroom mirror and practiced his facial expressions. "I know." He sighed. "It's one reason I became a police officer—to protect and serve."

"You're so brave." I blinked my lashes delicately. Because that was me—delicate and small, small, small. Thinking small thoughts. Not taking up space. An innocent flower—nothing to fear.

Yes. An innocent flower. Same as deadly nightshade.

Christopher shifted in his seat. "There's something sinister happening—but you don't need to worry."

"I don't?" As if I didn't know. As if the dried blood of monsters wasn't spread artfully across canvases, decorating the walls of my home.

"Obviously, you should be careful. Take precautions." He traced an index finger over the top of my hand. "But the string of disappearances doesn't suggest women are being taken. Only men."

"Taken?" My eyes widened. *Golly gee.* "I read that interview with the police chief, the one where she said there's no reason to believe anyone was *taken* or..." My voice trailed off as if I couldn't fathom saying the word *dead*. "She said that there was no reason to panic—there is no indication the disappearances are connected."

"I shouldn't comment," Christopher said, though we both knew he would. "But if you want my opinion—and this is between us—the missing men aren't relaxing together on a beach somewhere."

No shit.

"What do you mean?" The fear forced into my words turned my stomach. *Sweet Cordelia*—helpless, hopeless femme. Future final girl.

Christopher's gaze swam with concern.

He spoke evenly. "What do you think I mean?"

"Everyone—the police, the reporters—keeps saying there aren't any, you know"—I leaned forward and whispered—"bodies. Is that true?"

He drummed his fingers against the tabletop. "No bodies doesn't mean no foul play."

McSmiley was about to say more, I could feel it, but at that moment, our appetizer arrived and the spell—cast by long legs and a breathy voice—was broken. Christopher blinked, then smiled (of course) at the waiter as we ordered our entrees.

He cleared his throat. "That took quite a turn. I hope...I hope I didn't upset you or ruin your evening?"

"Of course not. I'm the one who asked. You're helping by making me aware."

That was another thing men liked—when you told them how

helpful they were.

"I guess now...well. You see what I mean? Perhaps you can grant me that slack I was asking for?"

"Hm." Sweet Cordelia smirked. "As long as there are no more cupcakes of deception."

"Deal." He took another swig of beer.

Christopher was going to be useful, indeed.

The rest of dinner was a flurry of small talk and flirty smiles. The redfish was decent, and we halved the cupcake. Also decent.

I didn't protest when Christopher reached for the check. The gold flecks in his honey-and-tea eyes caught the lamplight. "You want to get out of here? Go grab a drink somewhere?"

I looked down as if I were considering his offer. A drink with Christopher could be useful, but not tonight. "Rain check?"

"You turn back into a pumpkin at midnight?" he teased.

"Yeah." I pretended to chuckle. "Something like that."

The truth was—I already had other plans. Gerald would be waking up soon, and it would be rude to keep him waiting.

THE UNITS AT MARLIN'S SELF STORAGE, WITH ITS BUSTED gate and long-broken security cameras, housed things people locked away to forget. Stuff you couldn't dump but didn't want. That ugly armoire your dead mom had insisted was a family heirloom. The load of overpriced camping gear you didn't give two shits about but couldn't let your ex have in the divorce. The tacky sofa from your first apartment—the one with memories attached but doesn't fit your swanky new home.

A workshop for killing monsters.

Marlin's was invisible—out on the edge of town where no one gave it a second glance.

I pulled my car past my unit, B-37, and shifted into park.

Stepping carefully across the cracked pavement, I unlocked the unit, then heaved the rolling door upward. Once inside, I yanked it closed behind me, then flicked on one of the nearby floor lamps. Floor-to-ceiling shelves split the space in half, with a dark sheet tacked like a curtain covering the entry between them. Even if the door were left open and someone glimpsed inside, they'd witness nothing out of the ordinary. Shelves lined with junk. Boxes stacked against the walls. Bland. Boring. Not worth a second look. People see what they want to see.

When I pushed past the curtain and stepped through those shelves, everything changed.

It started with the crinkle of thick plastic beneath the red bottoms of my date-night Louboutins. The sound was a melody that never got old. The plastic sheeting hung from the walls like tapestries and stretched across the floor, encapsulating the small space in a shiny chrysalis, one designed to trap blood and keep things tidy.

Taking time to hang the plastic sheeting may seem like overkill, but this attention to detail made me great at my job. If you're going to kill bad men and get away with it, you have to be great, because being merely good leads to—well—nowhere good. I'd had my fill of *nowhere good*, thank you very much.

I closed my eyes and inhaled. The familiar feeling of peace began in my lungs, my stomach, my chest, and radiated outward until it ran through my veins, settling on my skin like sweat. I exhaled, slow and controlled. This peace...it might've been my favorite part.

Slipping on a pair of nitrile gloves felt like a ceremony, the simple action conjuring images of my later ritual. I pulled on the heavy apron over my dress, then stepped out of my heels and into my rubber boots.

The squeak of the boots against the plastic was satisfying, but it wasn't a song—not like the Louboutins. Sometimes sacrifices had to be made because no way would I risk ruining my favorite heels. That would be crazy.

And I was not crazy.

I snapped the gloves for effect and whistled as I waltzed to the table where Gerald was splayed out. I pulled back one of his eyelids and peered inside. *Smoke.* His eyes were hazy with it, curling and clouding as if I were peering through the window of a burning house. I liked to think the smoke was reflection of a monster's soul—dark and dirty and toxic.

I let go of Gerald's lid, and he blinked as if he might fall back asleep. "No you don't," I mumbled and tapped his cheek.

Getting the Bosephan dosing perfect for knocking out bad men had been a work of trial and error—but I'd gotten good at it. One pill would knock out an average sized person for about four hours. Gerald had gotten three and a half dissolved into his mimosa at brunch and spent the rest of his day tied and gagged and none the wiser.

It was a shame Bosephan was being pulled. The drug was truly glorious—and the poetic justice of using a pill that caused erections to bring vengeance on the kind men who believed their dicks granted them authority to harm and abuse, well, it was top-notch.

And, *okay,* hilarious.

I still had a few sample packs on hand, but I'd have to ration them when hunting. No more wasting high doses and letting monsters sleep away the day strapped to my table.

Gerald blinked his crusty eyes into thin slits and sniffed as he came back to his senses. He tried to sit up, and my heart warmed as he realized he wasn't at home in his bed. That something was wrong.

Very wrong.

Zip ties gnawed the tender flesh of his wrists, too tight for him to ever get loose. Yet, he tried.

They always tried.

I smiled my brightest smile because the real fun was about to begin.

"Oh good. You're awake," I sang, then reached over and thumped Gerald's bulging crotch. His eyes popped fully open, rolling wildly in their sockets, like an animal caught in a trap. Which, I guess he was. The table shook as he jerked against his straps first one way and then the other before attempting to scream.

They always tried that too.

His lips were stuffed with a rag and sealed with duct tape, turning the cry for help into a muffled choking sound.

"What's that Gerald?" I leaned close, inches from his alcohol-bloated cheeks. He smelled musty, in a damp sort of way—like the cow pasture near where I grew up, after a heavy rain. It was disturbing to think this monster smelled like home, but it was true. "I can't understand you—speak up."

Gerald's tacky tropical-patterned shirt rose and sank rapidly as his breathing shallowed.

"It's okay, Gerald. There's no one around to hear you, anyway." I stood to my full height and, with my index finger, booped the end of his nose. "Don't stress, I'm here to make sure everything works out exactly as it should."

Gerald sobbed from behind his gag, and for the briefest second, everything felt okay in the world.

Diane would've said it was because in that moment, I was living my best life.

And...maybe she was on to something. Because if you peeled away my expensive clothes, my makeup, my six-hundred-dollar highlights, and exposed who I was on a primal level—it was this.

When I held a blade and stared down at the bad man tethered to my table, stress melted away—it was only me and my monster, and a single goal: justice.

Here in my workshop, I was my authentic self.

The world may do nothing for women—but within these four walls—*Cordelia Black did.*

Gerald was now fully lucid, with pleading eyes.

Lucidity was important. Monsters didn't deserve anesthetic—they deserved fear and dread. Rapists, child abusers, woman beaters, the occasional murderer...the terror and helplessness that flooded their systems was their due. Sweat broke across Gerald's forehead as he struggled—tugging left then right. I thumped him again, and he cried out from behind the tape, squeezing his beady eyes closed.

"If you don't stop, I'm going to keep thumping you." He froze. "Good boy."

I grabbed the box of shower caps from a nearby shelf and tugged one free.

Diane had worked so hard curling my tresses into beachy waves that I considered skipping the cap, but blood was a real bitch to get out of bleached hair, and I'd spent too much money on highlights to let Gerald ruin them, so on the cap went.

The monster's dilated eyes tracked my every move as I picked up my razor knife, relishing its weight in my hand. The metal was cool even through my glove, and the way its familiar grooves perfectly aligned with my palm was comforting. I'd had it since junior high, when I'd stolen it from Tim, the one man Mama dated who wasn't a creep.

Gerald's breathing turned into sloppy gasps as he fixated on the knife. I pressed the button and inched out the blade.

Stepping oh-so-slowly, I sidled up to him and again leaned close.

"Do you recognize me yet?" My smile turned cruel.

He whimpered.

"No? I look a bit different without the wig or glasses." After our brunch, I'd dumped the costume—a puke-colored polyester sack dress, black wig, and red plastic frames, and changed for work. Like most women, I wore many hats. While Gerald enjoyed the last nap he'd ever take, I'd worked my sales job, delivered birthday cupcakes to a middle school, had a conference with my boss, visited the hospital, and even gone on a date. Girl power, I guess.

Gerald still appeared clueless.

"Come on." I groaned. "Think. Where do you know me from?"

Sometimes it took a while, but recognition always lit the predator's pathetic eyes, and they'd recall a mom on a park bench, or a fan from the stands at a ball game where they coached. Maybe a working girl from their late-night haunt, or a sloppy, drunk woman from their favorite club. From saint to stripper—I'd played every role, because monsters didn't discriminate.

"What if I talk like this?" My tone pitched high and nasal.

The whites of the monster's eyes grew, and his breath quickened. Recognition lit his pathetic face.

I've waxed poetic about the peacefulness of my workshop being my favorite part of the process, but I was wrong. The peacefulness wasn't my favorite.

This was. The perfect moment when monsters realized that while they'd been hunting, so had I.

"Ah," I said. "There we go. You know, it would've been fine if you didn't recognize me—because the important thing is, I recognize you. Being a social worker provided you with a buffet of broken women to gorge your depraved appetite. Nobody looked twice, did they? Not at a quiet, buttoned-down professional with a penchant for ugly shirts. They trusted you, Gerald."

I held the razor knife close to his face and leaned low to his ear. "Guess what? I looked twice. I know exactly what you are. It's only fair that you know what I am too."

I pressed the razor into his cheek. A single droplet of blood bubbled to the surface of his pasty skin and slid down his face before stalling at the edge of the silver tape. I swiped it away and rubbed it between my gloved finger and thumb.

The first time, it was the slickness of blood that surprised me. More like oil than water—until it began to dry. Then it had an acrylic quality to it, like paint. There was an art to what I did, not that different than putting a brush to canvas.

Which was another hobby of mine, actually. And also why two oversized roasting pans were currently positioned beneath the edges of the worktable.

Gerald cried through his gag, trying to talk, trying to beg.

They always begged.

"It's too late for tears. This is a decision you made with your actions. You knew you'd have to pay the piper." I cocked my head to the side. "What's that? You didn't? Oh, Gerald...why is that? Why is it that men like you think they'll never be held accountable? Probably because—"

My phone vibrated from where I'd set it on a nearby bench. I held up a finger. "One sec."

A text flashed on the home screen.

"It's my best friend." I shrugged. "She wants to know how my date went. Normally I'd never make her wait—especially not for someone like you—but what do you think? These are extenuating circumstances."

Gerald continued to whimper, but no more tears fell from his eyes. My monster was all cried out.

"I think you're right. She'll understand." I tossed my phone back onto the bench. Gerald tried to pull away as I stepped toward him. "Now. Where were we?"

The artery in Gerald's neck pulsed harder against his flesh, and I sighed, imagining what art I'd create with his blood.

I double-checked that the pans were correctly positioned beneath the table. Not a single splatter of Gerald's blood would go to waste.

None of him would go to waste, actually. Clarence would pay me a pretty penny for the body.

Gerald's eyes were saucers.

"Shh. Shh." I traced a finger over his nose, his cheekbones, his brows, committing every crevice and curve of his face to memory as his fear charged me like a battery.

Without ceremony, and with a flick of my wrist, I finished him with a single slice across his jugular.

As blood slid from his body, the smoke faded from his eyes.

There was something beautiful about death—something so calm.

Something so final.

THE THING ABOUT ME IS, MY MANICURE MAY BE FLAWLESS, but I've never been afraid of rolling up my sleeves and getting to work. Gerald's clothes stank of sweat but were easy enough to remove. Cleaning him up required an entire pack of wet wipes.

The next part had taken me a while to perfect, but now was artful in its execution.

After moving the pans of blood, I spread out a fresh tarp next to the metal worktable. When researching the kind of table to use in my workshop, this model had proven the best for one reason: with the press of a lever, the hydraulic legs could be raised or lowered, which made it perfect for dressing down a body. With everything in position, I rolled Gerald off the table, where I cocooned him in the tarp, then taped it closed.

In the front part of my unit, there was a stack of scrubbed-clean paint cans. I grabbed one. With a baker's spatula kept for this specific purpose, I scraped Gerald's blood from the roasting pan into the paint can, humming to myself as I worked. A tingle of creativity grew in me, and my mind wandered to the art I'd later create—the shading and light, the splashes of color and negative space. It was an important part of my ritual. A part born of necessity after an accidental kill, back when I was a college art major using a more traditional medium to create.

After that first kill, painting, which had always been a way of escaping my life, allowed me feel clean again—every stroke of the brush released pent-up trauma. My instructor said she didn't know I had it in me—to create something so raw. So packed with feeling.

Much later, I'd come to understand the importance of the blood. How using something vile to create something of beauty was not only cathartic, but offered closure—for me and the monster. Closure for the monsters' victims, I knew from experience, was trickier. But I hoped that sliding my blade across his throat, delivering both karma and justice while ensuring they'd never have to see him again, helped.

The broken girl who'd painted to escape was now only a memory. Because I, Cordelia Black, didn't need to escape anything. I loved the life I'd created.

I smiled as I hammered the paint can closed, then set it aside as I gathered everything—bags of wet wipes, Gerald's clothes, the spatula—together into a tidy row. By now, I could've done this part with my eyes closed, but following a plan—methodical and orderly—was important. A plan meant nothing was forgotten. Plans kept you safe.

Each and every item was double bagged then shoved under the

passenger seat of my car. The closed paint can was wiped clean one more time and placed on the car's floorboard, before I hopped behind the steering wheel and backed into the unit.

Next was the hardest part of the night. Rolling tarp-wrapped monsters back onto the lowered table was one of the reasons I hit the gym regularly. Even with my rigorous Pilates routine, lifting deadweight still left me breathing heavy. I panted as sweat beaded across my lip until, finally, Gerald was back in place. I fidgeted with the table settings before I tugged the makeshift curtain aside and wheeled Gerald through the narrow opening between the bookshelves, then slid him and his blue-tarp cocoon into my waiting trunk. I dusted my hands together. *Easy as pie.*

Half my car stuck out of the open unit, but I never worried about anyone catching a glimpse—like I said before, people saw what they wanted. A cute woman in a killer black dress couldn't be hauling a body into her car. Never! A rug? Yes. Must be a rug.

My trunk shut with a satisfying click; then I pushed the worktable back into place and arranged the boxes in front of the narrow opening between the shelves.

Once I'd pulled forward and my unit was securely locked, I swelled with pride. With satisfaction.

In movies, the kind of women who wore heels and lipstick could only be the kind of women who giggled and waited around for a big strong man to help them with their task. That, or they were the kind of women who failed miserably—but in a *cute* way. Or they learned a lesson.

Usually that lesson was women shouldn't be feminine if they

wanted to accomplish anything. We were allowed to be strong *or* feminine, but only if we folded ourselves into a very specific idea of what either of those things meant.

In a man's world, strong and feminine were rarely synonymous.

Fuck that.

Not only did I kill monsters, but I turned a profit doing it.

There could be no redemption for my monsters, but I liked to think I offered a form of postmortem atonement—they ruined lives, so theirs were taken and recycled in a useful way.

It didn't excuse their behaviors, but Clarence was able to parcel them off to medical professionals, which was better than dumping them in a swamp somewhere. Like Sweet Cordelia had told Christopher earlier, no bodies for the missing men had been uncovered.

Because there were no bodies to find.

The drop-off point was located down an old back road that eventually turned into little more than a gravel path. My tires crunched over loose rocks until the road dead-ended at an unused portion of a state park. The swampy land was only accessible via four-wheel drive if it rained more than a day or two, which wasn't uncommon in Louisiana. Lucky for me, it had been a dryish season. I shifted to park and took a deep breath, readying my nerves to get out of the car. There was nothing enjoyable about this part of my process—fulfilling? *Definitely*. Enjoyable? *Never.*

The woods hugging the small clearing were overgrown. Spiny palmettos, with stalks sharp as knives, yawned across the forest floor ready to slice skin or tear clothing, while brambles and briars stretched like barbed wire between cypress knees and loblolly pines.

Here, there were no quaint camping spaces, no picturesque nature trails, no sweet picnic tables or bulletin boards touting hiking maps. Only trees, briars, and soggy ground that stunk like swamp mud and mosquitoes. So many mosquitoes.

It was ugly, unwelcoming, and perfect for my cause.

The cab light blinked on as I pushed open the car door and stepped into the muggy night. The humidity meant sweat was almost instantaneous.

Nearby an owl hooted while gnats and mosquitoes zeroed in on me, attracted by the sweet aroma of coconut-scented dry shampoo. I swatted at the small swarm.

I loathed the woods. When I was fourteen, Mama's ex-boyfriend Tim had been the closest thing I'd ever had to a dad—or parent, for that matter—and I'd become his fervent apprentice in learning to use a Bowie knife and tracking a blood trail. For a while there, I'd thought maybe that was who I was—an outdoorsman. But once Tim took off, it hadn't taken long to figure out it wasn't the forest I'd liked, but spending time with someone who wasn't high, drunk, or perverted. When he left, so did my brief desire for the great outdoors.

A few feet away, a rotting, upside-down pirogue blended into the scenery. With no lake or creek close by, it was an odd place for an old boat. Then again, the swamp held lots of old things. Lots of rotting things. This pirogue served my purpose just fine.

Donning a fresh pair of gloves, I popped my trunk and grabbed the four corners of the blanket spread beneath Gerald's cocoon and gave it a good hard tug. On the third try, Gerald and the blanket slid over the lip of the car's trunk and landed on the ground with a near-silent thud. The monster's weight cut a shallow path across the soft dirt as I used the blanket to pull the body over to the pirogue (a trick I'd picked up from listening to nurses at the offices I serviced in my day job). I then rolled the cocooned body off the blanket and covered it with the boat. I slapped the hull and inhaled a deep, calming breath, sucking one of the gnats down my windpipe. *Damn it.* I wheezed, beating a fist against my chest.

Despite the bugs and briars, my time here was worth it, because I knew deep down to the marrow of my bones that I was doing good. I was helping to heal a sick world. Even Joanie—with her love-me-please smile and timid demeanor—would've been proud. Though, like Diane, she'd hated violence even more than I hated insects. For the second time that night, I pushed away her memory. This was no time to get sentimental.

I shook out and folded the blanket, then threw it back into my car. My fingers were on the door handle when a sound from somewhere in the trees made me pause. There was a rustling of leaves, as if feet were kicking them across the forest floor. I strained to listen, but for a while it was silent.

Too silent.

No bullfrogs. No cicadas. I should've heard *something*.

Then, more rustling.

My skin prickled with the feeling of someone watching me—the hairs on my neck raising as the voyeur's eyes cut a trail over my body.

My heart thrummed, but there was no need to panic—I had a plan.

I always had a plan.

A knife was tucked into my car's glove box. I'd yet to need it and hoped that wasn't about to change.

Whoever was watching me from the trees likely had their own secrets. This forest, this time of night, wasn't the kind of place where you hosted wholesome church potlucks.

Slowly, and with a steady hand, I reached first into the glove box and unsheathed Tim's old hunting knife, then opened the middle console and pulled out my flashlight. With my left hand gripped tightly on the knife's hilt and my right hand wrapped around the cool metal of my Maglite, I took three steps in the direction of the rustling sound. I clicked on the bulb and swung it upward, its powerful beam slicing the darkness like a sword.

The light pierced the trees and slid over two iridescent eyes. The animal froze, watching me curiously.

A bobcat.

I dropped my arm to my side, letting the light fall away from the feline, and looked toward the inky sky as I sucked in a deep breath. My left hand clasped so tightly to the weapon that my fingers had grown numb. I relaxed my grip. Ridiculous.

What had gotten into me? Cordelia Black doesn't get scared.

Damn it, Cordelia Black was scary. Transforming from that throwaway girl into who I was had taken growth. *Meticulous, painstaking growth.*

Every sacrifice, every choice, every difficult action—it had all been calculated to lead me to where I was now and had been damn worth it.

Even killing Joanie.

Joanie hadn't been a monster—but she'd made me sick—always whiny and quiet and letting people use her up. She'd followed me from Holden, and with her in my life, change would've been impossible. She would've spilled my secrets to the world, ruining everything. Her death had been painful—after all, I loved her in my own way. She'd been in my life longer than anyone except Mama. Sometimes at night when I was alone, I hated myself for what I'd done, but it had been necessary for my metamorphosis and I never, not one single day, regretted it.

When it was done, I'd buried her deep, where she'd never be found. Then, I'd committed fully to the change—Joanie's death couldn't be for nothing. Everything I did—every monster I killed, every life I avenged—it was tied irrevocably to Joanie's memory. To her honor.

"Go on now." I stomped my foot at the bobcat. "Get." The animal startled and scampered into the woods.

I'd had enough of the forest for one night and slid into my car. Time to alert the body snatcher.

HEADLIGHTS OFF, I MELTED INTO THE ROADSIDE SCENERY, another shapeless shadow of the forest, not worth a second glance. Even with the moon peeking from behind the clouds, I was invisible unless you knew where to look—which Clarence did not. Like most shady types, skirting around the edges of the law, he understood the importance of discretion.

I flipped open my burner phone—the one I used for a single purpose—and dialed. One ring. Two.

I hung up.

My first encounter with Clarence was at the Red Stick Pharmaceuticals Convention, where he'd been manning the booth for his company, Spirited Gifts. On its pamphlets, Spirited Gifts touted itself as a company that believed, "*We can all donate to a better future.*" But really, they were in the business of selling bodies. Or rather, body parts.

Clarence's business model was disgusting.

Unethical.

Morally gray.

But illegal? That's where it got murky.

There's no governing organization that regulates the sale of one's body to science. People on their deathbeds, usually underprivileged people not wanting to burden their family with funeral costs, were desperate. In waltzes Clarence with his shiny literature and promises of *their donation* making a difference. Of helping others. Of training the doctors of tomorrow. The desperate patients sign away their literal selves on the dotted line, thinking they'll end up at a medical school or university, when in reality, they're divvied into pieces and sold off part by part, like a junkyard car.

A pharmaceutical company needs twenty-five elbows to try out a new product at an orthopedic convention? Call Clarence. Fifty-four femurs? Spirited Gifts has what you're looking for.

That wasn't even the worst of it.

That deathbed *donation*? It was the only part of the transaction that was free. While technically the corpse would still be used to further medical studies, the dying person was being fooled. They weren't donating their body to science, but to a sleazy broker who would profit tens of thousands off each corpse. Clarence was a wealthy man.

There was enough money to be made from each body that *of course* Clarence wouldn't look a gift horse in the mouth. *Contacted by a stranger on a burner phone who won't disclose themselves, but offers you an intact body in the middle of the dark woods in exchange for five hundred dollars, when there are thousands to be made?* Sure. Why not? Seems legit.

I didn't like Clarence. In fact, I strongly disliked him for what he did—misleading the dying and their families. But he was a necessary evil in my plan—a cog in the sprocket of the greater good. Each time I saw him at a convention, standing in his booth dressed like Mr. Rogers and smiling behind his thick glasses, my stomach twisted with revulsion. But never, not once, had there been smoke in his eyes.

And I *always* checked.

No matter how necessary his services, I'd never do business with that particular kind of monster.

Friday was my kill day, and the day I met Clarence. Not every week, and not always at the exact same time. But *always* on a Friday, and *always* late at night. And Clarence *always* came within an hour of the call.

Once, he'd made me wait, so to teach him a lesson, I'd left him hanging for four months. After that—he was always on time.

Which is why, thirty-five minutes later, headlights glared in the darkness like a train barreling through a tunnel.

Clarence's beige, early-2000s SUV was boring. Not the vehicle you'd expect from a wealthy, self-made body broker. Which, I'm sure was the point.

Moments later, Clarence had replaced the body under the pirogue with a plastic sandwich bag of cash and driven away. I gave it another twenty minutes before returning to the clearing and retrieving my payment.

"Pleasure doing business with you," I said aloud after counting the bills—five hundred dollars—then shoved the money into my purse.

As I got back into my car, my phone chirped, reminding me I'd never responded to Diane's text.

DIANE: Sooo...dish. How was the date? Was he 🔥 ? Does he have a good job? Does he bake, like his profile says? I want to hear all the things. Tellll meeee.

Someone had clearly enjoyed the rest of her wine.

ME: Lol Call you tomorrow. I'm in the middle of something.

Diane texted back immediately.

DIANE: 😈 🍆

ME: Not that.

DIANE: 😘 😘 You love me.

ME: Against my better judgement.

DIANE: 😁

I rolled my eyes in the darkness. Diane was right—I did love her. That's why I did this.

When the bad thing happened to her in college, she'd refused to talk about it, to report it, to even acknowledge it. Though I hadn't killed the person who hurt her—not technically, anyway—he'd been the one to show me I could get away with murder.

No, not murder—that wasn't the right word—retribution. That's what I got away with.

I tossed my phone into the passenger seat and shifted into drive. I killed bad men to make the world safer for all women. But especially for Diane and Sugar.

My small two-story was tucked inside a subdivision constructed in the seventies. Most of the homes had been updated through the years—at least on the outside. My neighbors were retirees or couples with older kids. It was quiet. I liked quiet.

I hummed joyfully while unlocking my front door, the paint can and plastic bag both hooked over my arm.

As I stepped inside, something small and furry rushed by me.

Mr. Percival's dog was out. Again.

"Mango," I called, as the demon in a poodle suit zipped into my house for the second time that week. "Mango, come here."

I set the can of gelatinous blood and bag of Gerald's things on the counter. Mango ran to the fridge, her fluffy white body oscillating from head to toe. "No. I'm not giving you cheese."

It was a lie. Not only was the dog Harry Houdini incarnate (she could get out of anything), but Mango was fast—lightning fast. Bribing her with a Kraft single was the only way I could catch her.

I bent forward to scoop her up, but she slipped through my fingers like water through a sieve.

Mango let out a long bark—if you could even call the high-pitched, chortling sound a bark. Before Mango, I'd never heard anything like it—the closest was from a screaming goat in a video Sugar had texted me.

"Mango, I don't have time for this." I glanced to the waiting paint can, eager to get on with my night—to finish the ritual. "Okay. Fine."

I opened the fridge door, and she let out another round of her

Alpine yodel. I unwrapped the cheese, and when she jumped onto my legs, I grabbed her. "Gotcha, you little asshole."

I didn't dislike Mango—what I disliked was the way she ran into my house at the worst possible times, making me late, or jumping onto my legs and leaving muddy paw prints on my cream silk Ralph Lauren trousers—which had not been on sale, by the way. The way she shit in my yard and I always seemed to step in it. And how that one time she managed to knock over my trash can on garbage day. Honestly, I still couldn't figure out how the eight-pound demon had managed that one.

Mango snapped up the cheese in two bites, her entire body gyrating.

I walked her across the street and knocked on Mr. Percival's door. The old man frowned when he saw me holding his pup.

"How'd you get Mango?" He pushed open the screen door, his eyes crusty with sleep and his few strands of greasy hair sticking up from his scalp.

I thrust the Maltese-Poodle mix into his arms. "I stole her," I deadpanned.

He blinked, as if deciding if I was being truthful.

Jerk. Like I'd ever steal someone's dog. I turned and marched back home.

In my kitchen, I stepped out of my rubber boots and finally padded barefoot upstairs for a quick shower. The bathroom doorknob jammed, and while it was on my mind—I opened the Handy Heroes app and booked an appointment; my honey-do list was getting longer every day, and I didn't have time to take care of it myself.

Once the appointment was made, I tossed my phone onto my bed, then pushed the bathroom door hard, throwing my back into it. It flew open. I danced across the tile, the anticipation of closure, of painting something new, growing each minute.

My black dress was covered in sweat stains and swamp dirt. It was a shame it wasn't salvageable. I peeled it off and kicked it to the corner. Bright side—it was the perfect excuse to finally purchase that little Monique Lhuillier that had been chilling in my cart for a month.

Twenty minutes later, I dressed in a pair of my favorite pajamas, with my damp, clean hair hanging around my shoulders.

A yawn built deep in my chest, and I stretched my arms high. It was after midnight and crisp sheets were waiting on my bed, but as tired as I was, I couldn't sleep until I followed through with the entire process. It wasn't a need or a compulsion. No, it's what I imagined a bride or groom felt like the day before their wedding—that sweet promise of finality. A longing for a union settled and secured, not to be undone.

It was almost as good as the night before a kill.

Almost.

I poured myself a glass of wine, then connected my phone to my Bluetooth speakers, filling the room with haunting music and the moody voices of Taylor, Bey, Lana, the and rest of my postkill playlist, as I grabbed my sketchbook and flipped it open. I'd made a few rudimentary drawings of Gerald. On a park bench during his lunch hour. Sitting in his car, waiting to go into his office. Strapped to my table, oblivious to his fate. I smiled at that one.

The art I created for my walls wasn't as clean and straightforward as the sharp sketches in my book—no, my paintings were more about capturing the emotion. The feelings. The terror and hope. Ugliness and light. The blood mixed with paint meant each creation that hung in my home was symbolic of a life I'd taken. And the ones I'd avenged.

I carried my wine, along with the bag of Gerald's things, outside to my fire pit.

Spring in South Louisiana meant heat and humidity. Much too warm for a fire—but not only did I not mind, I couldn't have stopped myself if I'd wanted. The fire burned hot as I settled into my patio love seat with Gerald's belongings nestled in my lap. I took a deep drink of wine and swished the full-bodied cab in my mouth.

I held up Gerald's shirt. The loud print stank of the man who'd died in it. I ran my fingers over each button, over the puckered hem, over the rough, starch-like patches of crusted blood, hoping it would whisper to me its secrets. After a moment, I tossed it into the fire, followed by the hairnet and the gloves. My fingertips traced the waistband of his trousers, when inspiration began to stir.

Gerald was an evil man. A violent man. The revulsion he felt for himself throbbed through the pads of my fingers. His ability to reason away his crime... How he hurt people again and again and again. Gerald was vile, and on a deep level, he'd understood it—and he'd done nothing to stop himself.

I tossed the pants and the rest of the bag into the scorching flame, then turned up my glass, emptying it in a single gulp.

While I could never undo the horrible stain Gerald had left on the world or heal the trauma he'd inflicted on his victims, I could, in a very small way, transform him into a thing of beauty—at least superficially.

Once upon a time, I'd been a broken girl, unable to protect herself from the scary things. Now, I *was* the scary thing. Painting provided closure. Yes, I've said it was a healing ritual. And it was, but it also reminded me that I controlled the situation. That none of this was accidental. That there was beauty in making the world a better place.

Inside my home, I took the paint can and sketch pad upstairs to my studio. I pulled a freshly primed canvas onto my easel, then carefully blended blood with paint.

Gerald would be reborn as art. He would adorn my walls—another reminder as to why the world needed Cordelia Black.

Another reminder of why I mattered.

SUNDAY MORNING, MY EYES POPPED OPEN LIKE CLOCKWORK.

My internal clock was set in childhood, when waking up early and disappearing was the only way to stay safe. For a long time, I'd jerked from sleep to a pounding heart and the primal need to run.

Even though I was now well-adjusted, sleeping in remained impossible. My brain didn't care that I'd spent Friday and Saturday nights at my easel, working on my latest masterpiece into the wee morning hours, breaking only for food. And to text briefly with Diane.

I stumbled from bed and down the hall to the studio, where the sun slanted against Gerald's piece, setting it ablaze. Paint mixed with carefully thinned blood and dripped down the canvas in violent slashes. There were no soft lines. No shading. Not for Gerald. There was white and red. There was the contrast of goodness—the white canvas—representing the world without him in it.

And the violence—his blood stirred together with scarlet paint, darkened with the slightest hint of cobalt blue. I'd taken my time—each slash of blood-mixed paint, each white space—all deliberate. Each droplet represented a life he'd harmed. It wasn't one of my bigger pieces, nor was it one of my more technically difficult, but I adored it.

I stretched my arms over head, yawning in the filtered morning light as I admired my work. The feeling of completeness after a kill—to be creatively sated by the blood of a monster—was itself like a morning. The old day was done and life's possibilities were endless.

It was both the same and completely different from the feeling I'd gotten as a teenager, hiding in the art room at school where, despite the gray murkiness of my young life, I'd spent my lunch hours creating beautiful things. Back then, painting let me imagine I was someone else—someone who wasn't pitied or ignored. And now look at me. Here I was. Making the world better, while living a life I'd only dreamed possible.

Contentment refused to leave my face as I shuffled downstairs, where I settled onto my sofa to sip my coffee and watch the local morning news.

On the television, Tanisha Harris peered seriously into the camera from her post behind the news desk. The anchor, with her brown satin complexion, perfectly styled bob, and—I squinted at the screen—vintage Dior blazer, was something of a local celebrity and, I thought, style icon.

Tanisha's voice was heavy with the perfect amount of concern as she recapped the same story that had taken over Friday night's headlines. *"Are the area's missing men victims of an unspeakable crime? The capitol city could be in the clutches of yet another serial killer."*

Fuck. There were those words again. It was one thing when it was said on the ten o'clock news—a salacious phrase used to rope in late-night viewers. But using it here, on the local weekend morning show? Where everyone from families lounging with bowls of cereal in front of the television to old folks nestled in their recliners would hear? This wasn't going away. And even hearing it—*serial killer*—uttered from Tanisha's perfectly lined lips didn't soften that blow. How long before the phrase was used in print? Or picked up by national news outlets? Because *string of missing men*? Boring. But *serial killer*? That was the kind of narrative that spread.

The screen flashed to show a monster's wife, dabbing her red-rimmed eyes with a tissue. Her young daughter stood beside her, her mouth a tight, silent line. There was no shine of tears in her eyes, only confusion. She was lost, scared...but not sad. It was the same expression that Joanie used to wear, one that would never not break my heart.

The monster on the news—one who was an expert at leaving bruises and cuts and burns on women where they couldn't be seen—would never be found. His art piece hung in my studio, over a shelf of craft supplies. No matter what she admitted to the world, his wife, and especially his daughter, were better off for it.

But the news had it wrong.

The missing men may have died at my hands, but they were *not* victims—not mine nor anyone else's. They were predators who satisfied their depraved needs with the true victims. Victims who, if they came forward, would never make the news. They'd be lucky if they were believed. If their rape kits weren't abandoned in a moldy warehouse. If their bruises weren't brushed off as silly accidents, ignored because the truth was too uncomfortable. If the police even got their names right on their reports. What I did was a service.

The chief of police came on camera, a microphone thrust in her annoyed face. *"I've said it before, and I'll say it as long as it's true,"* she said. *"There are no bodies. There's no crime scene. It would be a far stretch—fictional even—to try and suggest there's another serial killer in our city. Suggesting such is highly irresponsible and sensational. As always, we take missing person cases seriously and continue to monitor all situations. The good people of Baton Rouge don't need to panic."* The screen turned to a shot of the newsroom, and then the weather boy.

I pressed mute.

My mind wandered to my conversation with McSmiley. *They aren't relaxing together on a beach somewhere.* It was a much different sentiment than the narrative the police chief was hammering in each interview. More was going on behind the scenes—I was certain of it.

Sweet Cordelia was possibly my least favorite of all my costumes—but spending more time with Christopher was the right move. I grabbed my phone to send him a text—he seemed like the kind of guy who would enjoy Zippity Zoo Fest.

Simon's truck was parked in my spot in Diane's driveway. *What the hell?* He was supposed to meet us *at* the zoo. My mood soured as I trotted toward my best friend's front door, the skirt of my linen Farm Rio dress swaying around my calves.

Pausing on the stoop, I smoothed my ponytail and forced a pleasant expression onto my face. I could do this. I could make it through the afternoon as the agreeable, supportive best friend who definitely wasn't looking for a way to get rid of her bestie's boyfriend.

If Diane caught me frowning, I could blame it on the odor of elephant shit. There was that, at least. With a final calming breath, I relaxed my shoulders and waltzed into the house.

Simon stood in the doorframe of the kitchen, his hands fisted on his hips, while Diane rushed around, still in her bare feet and favorite paint-splattered overalls. "I'm sorry! I'm sorry," she said, digging through the basket of clean laundry sitting in the middle of her dining room table. "Time got away from me—it's my new project. You know how it is."

"Don't worry, Di." I smiled. "Take your time." Although I was—as Diane put it—a *punctual princess*, I understood how it was when the artistic process took over. "Trust me, I'm not holding it against you for cutting into our zoo day."

She shot me a look. "Hardy-har-har."

Simon shook his head. "I texted you this morning—I knew we would be late if you didn't put away the paint." It wouldn't have been so bad if he'd sounded like he was joking—but the condescending tone of his voice made the muscles in my shoulders tense.

My lips parted into an *oh* as I waited for Diane to tell this guy to fuck all the way off. There wasn't much she hated more than *I told ya so*. Especially about running late. Maybe the Simon problem was going to take care of itself before we even left for the zoo.

Diane blushed beneath her copper freckles. "I know, I know," she said, not meeting his eye. "You're right. I should've listened."

"Excuse me?" I struggled to keep my voice even—because what the hell was going on here? I eyed Simon as I spoke. "Diane. It's seriously no big deal. Take your time."

"No, Simon's right. He called over an hour ago to remind me to get ready, and I said I was." Diane smiled sheepishly, then glanced at Simon. "I'll hurry. Promise."

Simon grinned smugly and walked to where Diane was still digging in the pile of clean laundry. He placed his hands on her shoulders. "Hey. It's okay, babe." She turned to face him, and he dropped a kiss on her forehead before continuing. "Mistakes happen. And look on the bright side—this gives me and Cor—"

"Cordelia," I interrupted.

"*Cordelia*," he said as if humoring a toddler. "A few minutes to chat. We'll be best friends before you've tied your shoes."

Diane's brows arched. "Okay." She pulled a washcloth free from the mountain of laundry. "But don't get too comfortable. I'll only be a sec—and I mean it this time." She smiled—*obviously fake*—and disappeared upstairs.

Diane had dumped people for less, yet she was listening to Simon White as if he were a guru in one of her beloved motivational books.

I looked at Simon—*really* looked at him, trying to see what made a woman like my Diane fall for such an asshole. On the drive over, I'd considered that it was possible I'd missed something when we'd met on Friday, or that I'd allowed my bad day to color my impression. But just now—the way he'd spoken so dismissively. It wasn't like Diane to put up with such nonsense.

So, why?

Simon wasn't *not* handsome, though definitely not *my* type. His hair appeared freshly cut, though still slicked awkwardly away from his face. He had strong, masculine features and bright eyes. The tight muscle that roped his slender frame, his narrow waist and wide shoulders could be attractive, I guess. The way he stood now, shoulders slightly hunched, his arms folded over his chest—he exuded Awkward Nice-Guy. Nerdy. Sweet. *Quirky*.

Diane loved quirky—it's why CrossFit Chad never stood a chance. I continued to stare at him without speaking until he glanced away.

What was it about this man? He set off—not alarm bells, exactly—but something. That dark place inside me, my predator brain, it perked up when Simon was around. The corners of his mouth jerked upward into a smile. Tight. Strained. Phony.

Little things, like the way he'd seemed annoyed on Friday when Diane hadn't corrected Sugar, the way he'd been just now, acting as if Diane being late was some huge affront, made his whole Nice-Guy act—his entire personality—ring inauthentic.

This didn't necessarily mean anything nefarious. Wasn't it possible Simon was making a bad impression because of nerves? Or that he was a regular old run-of-the-mill douche canoe?

Not that it really mattered—no way I'd let Diane settle for a douche canoe. Something in my gut told me to pay attention.

My purse buzzed, and I pulled out my phone.

DIANE: Please be nice.

I snorted.

ME: I always am. 😈

DIANE: No, you're not...

She was right, I wasn't.

Me: This guy, tho? Really?

DIANE: Cor. You promised to give him a chance. He's a good guy. He's handsome. Wants a family. Has a good, steady job. A relationship with his mother. And he is the perfect age—35. I want the unicorn—I never get the unicorn.

Here we go again with the fucking unicorn.

Across the room, Simon fidgeted with the hem of his T-shirt and chewed his bottom lip as he shifted from foot to foot. I shook my head. *Gross.* If this was all it took for a man to be considered a unicorn, I'd happily remain single the rest of my life.

ME: Fine. I'll behave. Now hurry up!

DIANE: 😘

I rolled my eyes and tucked the phone back into my Chanel crossbody.

Simon raked a hand through his hair. "So." He cleared his throat. "Diane tells me you work for Meyer?"

"Yes." I offered the single word with way more eye contact than it required. Making men squirm was a talent of mine. When they squirmed, uncomfortable in a moment, it was harder for them to keep up a masquerade—and I needed Simon to show who he was beneath his JC-Penney-catalogue exterior.

I perched against the countertop and imagined boring a hole through him with my gaze. *A unicorn? This guy?* Simon was a man in his thirties who, according to Di, loved his mama, had a job, and wanted kids. Women who wanted these same things weren't called unicorns; they were called basic.

In college, when she'd ended up pregnant from an academic loser with a Peter Pan complex, Diane hadn't wilted. No. My Diane had risen from the ashes of trauma stronger, wiser, and even more beautiful. Diane was a phoenix—and even if I had it wrong and Simon was a unicorn, well, she deserved so much more than a horse masquerading in a party hat.

Whatever spell he had on Diane, it wouldn't last.

Upstairs, the shower turned on and off within five minutes, meaning Di would soon return.

"I'm glad we're doing this." Simon dipped his chin, but his eyes moved with calculation.

Fake.

"I really like Diane, and anyone who is important to her is important to me."

I pressed my lips closed and nodded, not trusting myself not to call bullshit. Their relationship was too new for this *her friends are my friends* crap. He probably also said things like, "Girls never go for a nice guy like me." Or ranted to his *bros* about another "friend zone." Ick.

Simon continued. "Yeah, I think Diane is right—we can be good friends. But seriously, if you don't want to go to the zoo today, you don't have to."

I looked at him pointedly. "That's so sweet of you." I smiled. Again. "But we've covered this, haven't we? Diane and I have been planning this for a month." Not exactly true, but whatever. "It will be *so great* to have you along on *our day*, though. Like you said—if you're important to Diane, then you're important to me."

The muscles in his jaw ticked. Good. I'd pissed him off. He opened his mouth to reply, but was cut short when my goddaughter skipped into the room, all sunshine and rainbows.

"Hi, CiCi!" Her long braid swung from side to side with each hopping step. She threw open the refrigerator and rifled through the shelves.

"Hey, Sugar." On instinct, I glanced at Simon. I'd been younger than Sugar the first time a man had commented on my looks—how pretty I was, how all the boys probably liked me, and could I be a good girl and give him a hug? Those memories were forever, and made sure I kept an eye on the men in my goddaughter's life.

"Hey there, Sammy. I wondered where you were." Simon's voice was thick with fake cheerfulness.

Sugar froze, her face buried in the fridge, but I understood.

"I think," I said, "she asked you to call her Samantha." I plastered on my own McSmiley-level grin to keep the peace.

Sugar looked over her shoulder and gave me a thankful nod.

Simon shrugged. "Aw, I'm teasing. Sammy is a good girl—she knows how to take a joke." His expression reminded me of one from my own girlhood—one owned and operated by too many men, easily played off as harmless. The look said Simon understood how much power he held in the moment. Maybe the world didn't respect him—but by God this girl would. It was a look that could lead to other things. Dangerous things. The kinds of things that led to my workshop.

I breathed in deeply and held it for three seconds before exhaling slowly. There was no real reason to think Simon was a monster. But no way I'd let him get away with mistreating Sugar. I remembered what it felt like to feel powerless when dealing with adult men.

Only, Sugar wasn't powerless—she had me.

And I left nothing to chance where my goddaughter was concerned.

Sammy knows I'm joking. Sammy's a good girl. Inside I raged. Sugar was raised to be kind and smart, but she never had to be anyone's *good girl.*

In fact, there were no *good girls* in this house—maybe that was the lesson Simon needed to learn today.

Diane's cooking knives were in a drawer only a few steps away. I could grab one and drive it through Simon's heart before he knew what was happening. My breath came shallow as I pictured it—his blood sliding over my knuckles, my fingers gripped around the wooden handle. It would be warm and slick and smell faintly of pennies. Simon would never look at Sugar again. He'd never talk down to Diane. In the moment, I wanted it so badly.

Could you be a monster, Simon? Please? To make things easy? I stared into his gray eyes. No smoke. Not even a flicker. Damn it. I clenched my fist until my nails bit my palm, and the prickle of pain brought me back into the moment.

"Her name is Samantha." I spoke coldly. "You will call her Samantha."

"But—I was only—"

I calmly stepped between Simon and my goddaughter, and he snapped his mouth shut.

"Sweetie," I said to Sugar, once I'd broken Simon's line of vision. "I left my makeup bag in the car. Can you run and grab it for me?"

"Ah, CiCi." Sugar-Bug groaned. "I'm getting a snack."

I pulled a five-dollar bill from the outer pocket of my purse and shrugged. "I guess you don't want this, then." I waved it around like a flag. "You could buy E-Bucks, but if you're not interested..."

"They're called *V*-Bucks, CiCi." Sugar snatched the bill from my fingers. "And I don't need V-Bucks—I don't play that game anymore. I need rupees."

Simon watched as she jogged from the room. I called out, "Look in the glove box," then turned to face this man I hated.

I served him my coldest smile—all knives, and I hoped to hell he realized what it meant. Staring into his eyes, I yearned for a delayed flicker of smoke—for the ease of what that would mean. They remained clear.

Cold, but clear.

Sometimes smoke took a while to show itself. I'd almost given up on Tristan, the Catholic school teacher with a thing for beating up working girls. It had taken finesse on my part—an investment of time and energy. But, as I knew it would, the smoke had appeared and now Tristan hung in my guest bath, a landscape of blood mixed with paint. It could be the same with Simon.

I would keep watching, keep waiting. In the meantime, I'd be damned if he was ever alone with Sugar; he'd never make her feel powerless.

She's a good girl... Sugar was not his good girl. She was not his anything.

"I didn't mean to upset anyone." He shrugged as he spoke, his voice filled to the brim with his Nice-Guy bullshit tone. "I was only trying to—"

I held up a hand. "Stop talking." My gaze dragged from the top of his head to the toes of his sneakers. I'd promised to play nice. Well, he was still standing here, so that had to count for something. "Don't get too comfortable."

I waltzed from the kitchen. Waiting for Diane to come to her senses was no longer an option.

Maybe I should've told Diane about the interaction—about my concern—but if it turned out I was right, and Simon was anything close to the monsters I knew, then he'd have to die.

Not telling Diane was for her own protection. If I had to kill him, it was best for her if there was no gruesome breakup with flung accusations.

Instead, I'd plan it perfectly—orchestrate their eventual separation in a way that wouldn't draw attention. Then, if Simon was a monster, I'd let the distance grow between him and my family, until the time came. When I killed him it would be methodical and perfect. Diane would see on the news that Simon was missing. She'd be the right amount of bewildered and a little sad. If the police investigated, they wouldn't look twice at her. Not like if she was the bitter ex-girlfriend who'd accused him of vile things.

And if, after I broke them up, it turned out he wasn't a monster, that he was simply a creep? Well, I had a code. As much as I'd like to, he wouldn't visit my workshop. Which was fine, because Simon White would be someone else's problem.

Yes, it would work out perfectly. All I had to do was make a plan.

But that was for later. Today, I had a part to play.

I WHEELED MY CAR INTO ONE OF THE LAST ZOO PARKING spots and cut the engine. Sugar sat in the passenger seat, scrolling through the music on my phone, adding songs to playlists and making comments about how some of my favorites were "cringe."

"So." I drummed my fingers against the steering wheel. "I guess we're doing this?"

Simon had insisted on driving—because of course he did—so Sugar and I had ridden separately, claiming we didn't want to be cramped in the tiny backseat of his small pickup. Truth was, there wasn't a vehicle in the world big enough to hold both me and Simon.

Out my car window, he and Diane walked hand in hand toward the ticket booth. My skin crawled at the way he so freely touched her.

"If we have to." Sugar didn't move.

"What if"—I smoothed baby hairs away from my goddaughter's face—"if you're nice to your mama, I'll buy you a chocolate covered banana?"

"And a snow cone?"

I shrugged. "Sure."

Sugar unbuckled her seatbelt. "Deal."

"Wait." I touched her arm. The question I'd been putting off the entire drive, it was now or never. My goddaughter and I talked about everything—she was my mini best friend. But this question...it scared the shit out of me. The world is an ugly place and I'd do whatever it took to shield her from it for as long as possible, but what if I'd failed? What if everything I'd done—what if it wasn't enough? The way Simon had looked at her, the way Sugar-Bug had tensed when he'd called her Sammy...I couldn't stop thinking about it. She'd met Simon before I'd known he even existed. There'd been no smoke in Simon's eyes, but what if it was there...and I'd missed it?

"Yeah, CiCi?"

"Simon—he isn't...being creepy?"

"Creepy?" Her brows pushed together as she considered the question. "Like annoying?"

"No. Like...is he acting—"

"You mean is he inappropriate?" She crossed her arms. "We watched a video on it at school. See something, say something."

I nodded. "Yeah. Like that. You know, you could tell me. You can tell me anything."

She rolled her eyes. "I know, CiCi. But don't worry. If Simon was being creepy, I'd kick him right in the balls." She was so sure of her own fierceness, and I hoped that never changed.

"You're sure?"

"Yeah. He's not creepy—he's just kind of a jerk. He tries too hard, you know?" She shook her head, her braid swinging around her shoulders. "Then he gets annoyed if I don't act like he's the best thing ever."

"Okay." I exhaled. "That's…okay.. But still. You can come to me with anything, you know that, right? Not just about Simon, but about boys. Or girls. You can bring anything to me, and I…"

Sugar grabbed my hand and gave it a squeeze—another reminder that while she was growing, she wasn't grown. "I know, CiCi. And listen, you don't have to worry about me. I'm tough."

"I know, Sug. But if you find yourself in a position where you can't—be tough, I mean. Come to me. That's what I'm here for—to be tough for you when you can't be."

She considered my words, then nodded. "Okay, CiCi. I'll remember that."

Inside Zippity Zoo Fest was a sea of screaming babies, melting toddlers, and snapping parents. The crowd and concrete raised the temperature ten degrees, the heat molding my linen dress to my hips while the soles of my feet grew slick with sweat against the leather bottoms of my Hermes Oran knock-offs (because no way was I risking expensive shoes at the zoo).

Clowns mingled with the crowd, offering photo ops and balloon animals that even the youngest kids didn't want. Probably because their running face paint and wilting costumes were the stuff of nightmares.

"This is great." Diane grinned, taking a phallic-looking balloon animal from one of the nightmare clowns. "Look at us. Making memories."

Sugar rolled her eyes, red blush creeping across her cheeks. "Mom. You cannot carry that thing around."

"What?" Diane thrust and parried the balloon. "It's a sword."

Sugar grabbed the balloon-penis-sword and shoved it into a nearby trash bin. Diane and I giggled while Simon followed along silently.

We passed through the Realm of the Tiger to the monkey habitat, then we stopped to watch a few ducks and pheasants and smaller birds, before pausing under a shady tree next to a statue of Penny, the zoo's first elephant. Simon weaseled his way between Diane and Sugar and draped an arm over each of their shoulders. An act of ownership that left my hackles raised.

I bit my tongue, clocking Sugar's annoyed gaze before she shrugged him off. Best-case scenario, Simon simply didn't care that he was crossing Sug's boundaries, taking up her space—being the type of person who thought if it wasn't a big deal to him, then it wasn't a big deal at all. Worst-case scenario? Well, that's what I had my eye on.

"Where to now?" I asked, forced cheerfulness oozing from each syllable.

Diane tapped the app on her phone. "Hm. Let's make the big outer loop, then play it by ear?"

Playing it by ear wasn't my strongest quality; things worked better when there was a schedule. *Trips to the zoo. Selling medicine. Disposing of bodies.* A time for everything meant everything got done in time.

But this was Diane's day, so I tried to relax. Go with the flow. Be my easiest breeziest carefree self.

"It's so hot," Sugar whined. "CiCi, you said I could get a snow cone. As many as I wanted because of—"

"Sure, Bug," I interrupted before she could mention my bribe.

Diane frowned at the app. "The frozen treat cart is all the way near the petting barn and playground—halfway across the zoo. We can start making our way in that direction."

"I need one now," Sugar grumbled. "It's hot as the devil's ass crack out here."

"Samantha!" Diane's mouth dropped open. Her sunglasses sat on top of her head, and I caught the way she peered at Simon from the corner of her eye, then back at her daughter. "Language please."

"What? You let me say *ass* all the time. We shouldn't change the way we talk just because Simon's here, should we?"

Diane threw me a defeated look.

"Sugar-Bug. Knock it off, brat." I smiled and swatted her braid playfully.

She ducked away, spinning toward Diane, and pulled on her free arm. "Come on, Mom. Doesn't a grape snow cone sound good?"

"I said we're heading in that direction. Chill." Diane untangled herself from both Simon and Sugar and slid her phone into her back pocket.

Simon pulled out his wallet. "Why don't Samantha and I run on ahead? She can get her treat, and you ladies can start walking toward us at your own pace—no need for all of us to break a sweat." He grinned at Sugar. "There are benches we can wait on. It'll give us a chance to hang out."

No way. He and Sugar were not *hanging out.*

"No need." I turned to my goddaughter. "Race you?"

"Um." She pretended to consider, then took off like a comet.

"Cheater!" I clomped behind her in my dress and sandals, without another glance at Simon or Di.

Five minutes later, with sweat dripping down my face, I was paying for Sugar's first snow cone, when I caught sight of one of my best clients pushing a jogging stroller toward the barn door entrance of the petting zoo.

"Dr. Sonnier?" I called out to the young Black woman in athleisure and a sleek bun. "Jessica?" Then louder. "Jessica Sonnier!"

The ob-gyn stopped walking and tossed a look over her shoulder. I waved. We both wore sunshades, but I was sure she recognized me—her brows raised from behind her round frames, and the corners of her mouth curled, as if she were about to smile but stopped herself. Instead of coming over or even returning my greeting, the almost smile dropped from her face, and she sped up, disappearing into the crowd of people.

"Huh," I said aloud. "Weird."

"What's weird?" Sugar took a big bite of her snow cone, her mouth already faintly ringed in purple.

"Nothing." But it *was* something. Dr. Sonnier—one of my best clients—had looked right at me and hauled booty away without a single acknowledgment. A month ago, we'd hit up happy hour at her favorite downtown sushi bar, all comped by Meyer Pharmaceutical. If I was a paranoid woman, I'd say it was almost like she'd ran away from me.

That was ridiculous.

Wasn't it?

I fanned my face with my hands, thankful I'd decided against wearing foundation. There was a reasonable explanation—surely. Dr. Sonnier always talked about how her two-year-old twins kept her busy—and I couldn't blame her if she was in a hurry to get through this obligatory hellscape as fast as possible. That had to be it—no time for niceties. No way it was an intentional snub. Sure, everyone was tense over the Bosephan recall, but Dr. Sonnier was nothing but a complete professional.

We'd have a good laugh about it at her office. Maybe we'd even grab brunch if she wasn't too busy. Without Bosephan I needed to pitch some of Meyer's other medicinal therapies if I was going to make my credit card payments.

Still...why hadn't she at least waved?

I tugged Sugar lightly by the arm as I shuffled out of the way so a family could squeeze by. I'd never understand why the zoo festival was so popular.

Sugar looked longingly toward the nearby playground, which was filled with younger kids. It was also circled with plenty of benches.

And shade.

"You know," I said. "The playground looks like a lot of fun to me."

She sighed. "It's for kids, CiCi. What if someone from school saw me?"

"Sugar." I crossed my arms. "If someone from your class is at this godforsaken zoo festival, they're probably already on the playground having a good time. And if not, you can always say—I don't know—that you are helping babysit or something."

"You're telling me to lie?" She cocked a hip to the side as she shoveled another scoop of frosty grape slush into her mouth.

"No." I grimaced. "I mean—kind of. That was bad—forget I said that. I only meant—who cares what other people think? What if I go with you?"

"You? On the playground?" Her eyes widened in shock.

"Sure," I said. "Why not?"

I hoped she'd say no. God, I hoped.

Diane would join a game of tag or jump on the swings like an overgrown kid. She practically bled excitement when playing with her daughter.

I, on the other hand, had never been the playground type. Even as a child I'd sat on the sidelines at recess, bedazzled by my classmates—the way they ran and yelled with no cares. It was like there was a secret textbook everyone read except me. *How to Be Free and Fun on the Playground: Tenth Edition.*

There was only one place I'd ever captured that weightless joy, that uninhibited bliss—and it wasn't on the swings or merry-go-round.

Still, if Sugar needed me...then I'd try. Even if it meant staining my favorite dress or chipping my fresh seventy-dollar manicure.

My goddaughter sighed. "No. It's okay—that would be so much worse."

Oh, thank god.

"Wow." My hand fluttered to my collarbone as if I couldn't believe what I was hearing. "Your loss."

Sugar slurped down the last of her snow cone, purple sugar-water dripping down her chin. She looked again to the play-ground, the wheels in her head turning.

"Come on." I took a step toward the way we'd come. "If you don't want to play, we should go find your mom...and *Simon*."

Sugar wiped her mouth on the back of her hand and her eyes narrowed. "I'd rather swim in the toilet."

I pushed my sunglasses onto my head, mirroring her phony stink eye. With possibly the most dramatic eye roll in history, Sugar tossed her trash in a nearby bin, then took off like a rocket toward the hippo slide.

Lately, that girl contained more angsty almost teen and less and less free-spirited kid. *This might very well be our last playground visit.* My heart fluttered like bird wings, and for a moment I understood why Diane had gotten emotional over baby teeth.

I dusted off a nearby bench and took a seat in the shade.

That's when I saw him.

I guess the flyer was true—*everyone* really did go wild for Zippity Zoo Fest.

Unlike Dr. Sonnier, this person didn't have to pretend not to recognize me—he had no idea who I was.

I'd been stalking Frank off and on for a while, always carefully hidden or disguised.

I thought I knew of all his haunts. The dilapidated playground near the overpass. That hole-in-the-wall bar downtown. Even his preferred barber. Strangely, he was at the zoo. If Frank was branching out, exploring new hunting grounds, then his behavior might be escalating. He was getting braver.

That wouldn't do.

I couldn't be everywhere—the unfortunate truth was, there were *always* more monsters to deal with. *Always* worse monsters to deal with.

Frank was always there, lurking on my periphery. I'd been on edge lately—*thank you, Simon*—that urgent jitteriness sparking just under my skin. A feeling, I knew from experience, that could only be calmed by action. Maybe it was time to bring Frank into my crosshairs.

I fidgeted with the friendship bracelet on my wrist, staring at the monster as he stared at a child—a girl somewhere around four years old—with a head of dark hair and a wide smile. Frank had no family, and this little girl gave no indication that she knew the creepy man. No side glances in his direction. No grins. No calls of *Watch this!*

She was spunky, arms waving in the air as she chased bigger kids.

My eyes narrowed on the monster. He leaned forward, elbows on his splayed open knees. If he engaged in any way, I'd intervene. I had to.

There was no need. Frank stood and shuffled across the playground, no one noticing how strange it was for a grown man to hang out in such a place without a reason for being there.

Almost no one.

I'd noticed, hadn't I?

The hairs on my arms stood to full salute.

Not enough time had passed since my last kill—I knew this. But I also knew I couldn't wait much longer. Tension built in me; it screamed. Frank was dangerous. I had proof: messages he'd sent to an underage girl online, pictures he'd requested, and then there was the dark smoke clouding his eyes.

It was time he learned that the world could be dangerous for monsters like him too.

Soon, Frank. Sooner than you think.

"You decided to come to the zoo after all?"

Startled, I thwacked my palms against the aluminum bench and looked up.

Christopher stood over me, smiling (because of course he was), silhouetted by glowing sunshine. In that moment, he was a literal golden-boy.

"Jesus. You surprised me." I squinted past him, in the direction where Frank had been heading moments before. He was gone.

Good.

"Sorry about that." Christopher's arms were crossed loosely over his chest. With his black curls and dressed in a white fitted tee and dark jeans, he was one set of black-rimmed glasses away from a Clark Kent cosplay.

I pulled my purse into my lap and gestured for him to sit.

"You sure?" he asked. "I texted you a while ago and you didn't answer—I figured you'd changed your mind." He paused, then added quickly, "Which is totally fine."

"What are you talking about?" I slipped Sweet Cordelia over me like sliding into a perfectly tailored dress and let concern drip from my words. *Had I upset this big amazing man? Oh no. That wouldn't do.*

"That text you sent this morning? Asking if I would be at the Zoo Fest?"

"Shoot. I'm sorry. This morning has been...well it's been interesting." That was an understatement. Simon had rattled me and that text felt like a lifetime ago. "I wasn't ghosting, I promise. When I didn't hear from you immediately, I figured you had plans already."

"Nah," he shrugged. "I was outside mowing the grass and didn't see it until later. I texted you back."

"Oh." I opened my bag to pull out my phone, but it wasn't there. Oh. Right. Sugar had used it to make playlists on the drive over. "I must've left my phone in the car."

"No worries." McSmiley slid onto the bench next to me. "I was already bringing my niece, Olive, anyway. That's her over there." He gestured to the dark-haired free-spirited girl—the same girl Frank had watched. I shuddered. Christopher had no idea how closely a monster had lurked to his family. Frank was officially bumped up my roster.

"She's so cute," I said. "That one's my goddaughter, Samantha."

I gestured to where Sugar was hanging upside down on the monkey bars, shrieking with laughter.

"Looks like she's having a good time."

"Ha." I gave him a conspiratorial look. "I had to bribe her with snow cones and I'm pretty sure she'll freak if she doesn't get a frozen banana. Not that I blame her."

"What? You don't like the zoo?" he asked.

"Oh, come on," Sweet Cordelia teased. "You can't tell me your idea of fun is sitting around sunbaked animal dung and crying babies?"

"I like bringing Olive to the zoo—we have the yearly pass." He watched his niece, who was in line for the slide. "It's worth it to see her excitement, you know?"

Did I know? I hated the zoo, but here I was. And why? Because it was important to Di. "Yeah," I said. "I guess maybe I do."

A breeze brought the odor of the nearby goat pen. "Nope." I coughed against its sour taste. "I lied. This is the worst."

Christopher laughed; I was such a funny little thing. *Score one for Sweet Cordelia.* Soon I'd know all his secrets. And, okay, fine. It was a nice laugh—uninhibited and easy.

"There you are!" Diane appeared behind me. She squeezed my shoulders before circling the bench. Curls escaped her bun and frizzed around her face, and in the sunshine, her freckles stood out like pennies dropped in snow. She didn't bother to hide the smirk on her lips as she openly sized up Christopher, her eyes twinkling.

She was alone. I worked concern into my voice. "Did Simon leave?"

"What?" She slid her plastic heart-framed sunglasses from the top of her head onto her face. "No. Why would he leave? He's over there getting us something to drink." She waved toward the small café that sold sodas and snacks, near the other side of the petting zoo, where Simon stood in line, his back to us.

"We got caught up watching one of the handler shows—did you know this zoo has a ring-tailed lemur? Fascinating, right?" Diane's face swiveled from me to Christopher, who was, of course, still smiling. "I'm sorry. Did you two just meet?"

Diane would've loved that—a rom-com meet-cute at the zoo. "This is Christopher. He was my date. From Friday."

"Wait." Diane's eyes rounded. "*You're* McSmiley?"

Even with her sunglasses, her face flooded with that familiar faraway, swoony look—an expression as common to Diane as sneezing.

Christopher's brow furrowed. "McSmiley?"

"You know." Diane grinned at Christopher and pushed her index fingers into the corners of her smile—a real cheesecake pose. "Mc*Smiley*. Because Cordelia has a thing for nice teeth."

"She does?" Christopher's tone was playful. "McSmiley, huh? I like it."

"Cool it, cupcake kid," I said.

"Oh, that's right. The cupcake." Diane shook her head while Christopher pretended to groan.

"For what it's worth,"—Diane shot me a look—"*I* thought it was cute. I'm Diane, by the way. Cordelia's best friend, though you probably can't tell since she still hasn't introduced me."

Diane wiggled between me and Christopher on the bench, her gaze still pivoting back and forth as she grinned at each of us. She was loving this.

"Nice to meet you." Christopher nodded to where Diane's hand squeezed mine. "Okay. It makes sense now."

"What does?" I asked.

"The bracelet. I noticed it at the restaurant."

Diane's eyes crinkled and she mouthed, *So cute.*

I ignored her. "What about it?"

Christopher shrugged. "I haven't seen a friendship bracelet since cub scouts, is all."

"You were a cub scout?" My bestie's hand flew to her heart. She should've met Christopher first—the cupcake thing would've totally worked on Diane. And Christopher, despite being a know-it-all cop, and a tad annoying, seemed like an *actual* nice guy—not a phony like Simon.

The two of them sat on either side of me, grinning like they were in on a joke. Yeah. They'd be kind of perfect together. Too bad *girl code* was Diane's religion. She'd never go out with someone after I'd dated them, even if I insisted it was fine.

An ear-piercing scream came from the playground. We all looked toward the sound in time to witness Christopher's niece landing on her butt at the bottom of the slide, tears streaked across her rosy cheeks.

Without a word, Christopher jogged over and scooped her up. He held the tiny girl over his shoulder and patted her back as he whispered in her ear.

"Stop it." Diane clutched my arm. "I think my ovaries exploded."

"Do you even want another kid?"

"Doesn't matter. Something about a huge good-looking guy, taking care of a little child. It just—" She fanned herself with both hands. "And he was a *cub scout*. That's so adorable."

"If you say so." My ovaries were perfectly safe, thank you very much.

"I don't remember swiping on a guy with a kid, though. Did he not mention her, or?"

"That's his niece, Olive," I said. We watched as Christopher jostled the tiny girl up and down in his arms as he walked toward the frozen concession cart.

"He brought his niece to the zoo? That's too much. He's not real."

"You want him?" I said it like I was joking.

She swatted my arm. "Stop it. Christopher's adorable, but you know I like 'em a little nerdy."

Sugar jogged over, stopping the conversation. The corners of her lips turned down as if she'd rather have been anywhere else. The child who'd hung upside down, shrieking on the monkey bars had once again been replaced by a moody tween. Talk about whiplash.

"Hey, sweetie," Diane said. "Having fun?"

"It's fine," Sugar grumbled. "It's just so hot."

I looked to the concessions cart, where Christopher was paying for a frozen banana. Olive's face was buried in his neck as he walked back over, approaching at the same moment as Simon, whose arms were full of paper cups. Simon passed one to Diane and one to me. When he tried to pass Sugar a drink, she shook her head. "No thanks. I don't want anything right now."

He frowned, first at Sugar, then at Christopher, but said nothing, clearly annoyed his soda run was being overshadowed by another man exploding his girlfriend's ovaries.

"Sorry about that. Evel Knievel here took a tumble." Christopher bounced Olive on his hip. "If I don't get this one back home to her mom, this could turn into a code red. Code red is not the second date experience I want to give you."

"Date?" Sugar's eyebrows shot up. "Wait one minute..."

"And you must be Samantha." Christopher looked down at Sugar and held out the banana. "A little bird told me you could use one of these."

"Yeah. That's me." Sugar grinned and took the treat, chomping off a mouthful. "Thanks!"

"Thought you didn't want anything right now?" Simon said. He spoke as if he were teasing, but once again, the slight tic in his jaw gave him away. He was pissed.

Sugar rolled her eyes, then said to Christopher, "And thanks for getting my name right."

The dig was subtle, but no way Simon didn't register it.

Diane bounced to her feet and grabbed Christopher's free arm—the one not full of whimpering preschooler. "Christopher, Samantha here is the one that made these incredible pieces of jewelry you like so much." She waved her wrist through the air.

"Yeah. When I was a baby," Sugar mumbled, straightening up. "So embarrassing."

Diane nodded toward Simon. "And this is my…um…boyfriend, Simon."

Christopher adjusted his niece in his arms and held out his hand. "Good to meet you."

Simon looked at Christopher's outstretched hand, but nodded without a word. Christopher let his arm drop to his side, ignoring the snub.

"I know how it is when the baby gets tired, so I won't keep you," Diane said, trying, and failing, not to sound embarrassed. After a beat of awkward silence, her smile brightened. "Oh. I know. I'm planning a…uh…a barbecue! Yes, I'm planning a barbecue for next Sunday."

"You are?" I asked.

She nodded. "Sure am. I told you about it, remember?"

I was certain Diane had never mentioned a barbecue. Normally I'd be annoyed at getting railroaded into hanging out with a man I barely knew, when it wasn't my idea. But this…this could work—another opportunity to pick McSmiley's brain, and also watch Simon.

Sweet Cordelia grinned. "Oh yeah. Sure."

Diane patted Christopher's arm. "You're invited—and I'll take it personally if you don't show. Don't let our Cordelia here off the hook."

Simon cleared his throat, and when no one paid him attention, he slipped his arm around Diane's waist, tugging her toward him. Hard.

Christopher's brows steepled. Diane stumbled into Simon's

side, almost toppling over. I opened my mouth to say something, but Diane rolled her eyes and laughed. "Babe. What's wrong? You don't know your own strength?"

Simon's gaze landed on each of us, gauging our reactions, before locking on Diane's. He dropped a kiss on her head. "Sorry. You're just so tiny and cute."

Bullshit. The way he'd pulled her—it had not been an accident.

But Diane was smiling. She was laughing; it was her real laugh. Her arm was looped around Simon's waist.

Had I only seen what I wanted to see? A monster behind every bush?

"A barbecue sounds great." Christopher recovered the awkward moment. He patted his niece's back. "And it was nice to meet all of you, but I think it's time for us to go."

He faced me, his brown eyes looking intently into my blue ones. "I owe you an actual decent date. Let's get together soon. No phony cupcakes. No—how'd you put it?—screaming babies and baking animal poop?"

"Dung," I said. "Animal dung. And yeah, sure. You have my number."

Sugar shook her head. "I cannot believe CiCi's on a date right now."

"So's your mom," I teased.

My goddaughter doubled over and pretended to gag. Christopher laughed, but my eyes were on Simon, whose expression remained plastic—all smiling Nice-Guy. Curated.

"Great," Christopher said as Olive whimpered, gearing up for another round of tears. "I'll call you." He turned to Diane. "It was great meeting you." Then to Sugar. "Ms. Samantha. It's been a pleasure." The way he completely ignored Simon made me like him a little more.

Sugar grinned as he walked by, heading down the sidewalk toward the exit.

Once he was out of sight, Diane spun toward me. "Cordelia Renee Black—I *like* this guy."

"Renee? Who the hell is Renee?"

"The moment called for three names. Renee fits—I like Renee."

"You know I don't have a middle name." I wrinkled my nose. "And Diane. A barbecue? I thought you were vegetarian now?" She'd sworn off meat after a blind date forced her to watch a particularly gruesome documentary.

"I haven't been a vegetarian for months." Diane shook her head.

"Mom, you were *never* vegetarian." Sugar sighed dramatically. "Once, after dinner with the weirdo, Mom took us to get Taco Bell."

"Hush. Kate wasn't a weirdo. She, you know, had her convictions." Diane shrugged. "But I'm not giving up steak quesadillas for anyone."

Diane pulled away from Simon's embrace, then passed him her soda. "Here ya go, babe." She held out her hands, and I set my own cup aside and looped my purse over my shoulder, then let her tug me to my feet. We locked arms—the three of us—me, Diane, and Sugar.

Simon's hands clutched the giant cups of soda so tightly it was a wonder his fingers didn't pierce the paper.

"You okay?" I asked him, *sweetly*. Maybe my question would direct Diane to notice the way the bands in Simon's neck tensed or the way the corners of his mouth hardened. It was overkill to be this upset over a conversation with another man—over Diane, who was a self-professed flirt, simply touching another guy's arm. It didn't make him a monster, but the red flags were piling up.

For the second time, I wondered if I wouldn't need to break them up after all—maybe it would take care of itself. Nothing was less attractive than a sulking man-baby.

Simon blinked away the sour expression. "Sorry. Thanks for asking. This heat has me a little off."

Simon turned his mask of a smile toward me, and I met it with my own.

Was it me? Was I delusional? Was my history, my calling, my jealousy of anyone who took up my best friend's time—were these things making me see something that wasn't there? No. He'd completely snubbed McSmiley, not to mention the way he'd tugged Diane.

There was no smoke...

What about Tristan? The smoke had come late with Tristan.

But Simon wasn't Tristan, and I had a code.

The rest of the day passed as expected—slow and sweltering. Simon and Diane meandered through the zoo, their arms draped over each other, while Sugar skipped ahead. Simon was on his best behavior. He was overly gentle with Diane. There were no side glances at Sugar. No rude remarks or leapfrogging over boundaries. When I brought up Christopher, hoping to get a reaction, he was polite.

He was nothing but a forgettable man dating a woman out of his league. Annoying? Yes. But annoying got a broken heart—not a death sentence.

"Mooom." Sugar froze, yards in front of us near the bank of bathrooms. Her voice shrill with panic. "I need you. Bring your purse."

"Oh." A knowing look crossed Diane's face. "One second."

She hurried after Sugar, leaving Simon and me alone. His hair—earlier styled—now hung limp from sweat.

Without Diane around to impress, Simon's Nice-Guy mask dropped, and his mouth puckered into a frown.

I stared at him. My mind reeled—*there was no smoke, I had a code, my instincts are never wrong.*

"What?" he snapped. "Why do you keep looking at me like that."

Fuck it. There were too many warning signs. I couldn't risk it. Not when it concerned my family.

I closed the gap between us, standing inches in front of him. I stood on my toes, leaning close and peering directly into the gun-metal depths of his eyes. "Be still."

"What's wrong with you?" He stumbled back, a snarl twisting his mouth. "Get away from me."

I bit my bottom lip and looked harder.

"Cordelia? Did you hear me?" His voice was a dagger, steely and sharp.

"Hold still." My tone was sharper. "I'm checking something."

It had to be there. All the signs said it *should* be there—the way he treated Sugar, the way he'd harshly tugged Diane, how he'd gotten so pissed that she'd dared to talk to another guy that he wouldn't shake Christopher's hand. And there was the feeling in my gut.

Simon shifted his weight from one foot to the other. "Well, stop. You're acting crazy."

I frowned.

There was still no smoke.

ON MONDAY, I PICKED UP TWO DOZEN GOURMET DONUTS and delivered them to Dr. Sonnier's office. The swanky women's health clinic was an oasis, scented with lavender essential oils and vases of fresh roses on every table of the waiting area.

I hummed as I waltzed through the heavy front door, arms full of hot-pink boxes containing flavors such as Sweet Swarovski, Tiffany Blueberry, and Million Dollar Maple.

Before I made it to the nurse's office with my gourmet pastries, the staff bombarded me with questions.

"Did you know the side effects? Is it true people are dying? I heard it was hundreds... Oh, Cordelia—did you really not suspect a thing?"

My heart pounded in my ears as I smiled and nodded and assured the gaggle of nurses that everything was fine—everything was blown out of proportion, and here—have a donut.

That wasn't the worst part.

Dr. Sonnier couldn't see me.

Or rather, she wouldn't.

She was overbooked—*a mistake*, I'd been assured. And *No, she doesn't want to reschedule for a later time.* Not until *we see how this whole Bosephan thing shakes out.*

At the zoo, Dr. Sonnier hadn't waved. I wasn't paranoid. She *had* run from me.

My eye twitch held off until my second appointment of the day called and cancelled. They also weren't interested in rescheduling until *things settled down.* When I pressed for a more concrete time—Would *it be days? Weeks? Months?*—the doctor's assistant was snippy. *You'll have to wait and see, won't you?* The line clicked silent before I could respond.

Once could be a fluke. Twice was a pattern.

As if I had anything to do with the double-blind studies or the FDA or anything outside of selling the pills and cashing my checks.

I parked my car and stomped toward my office building, my eyelid practically tap-dancing on my face. The folder holding the forged documents was cradled beneath my arm.

Meyer took up the top three floors of the modern steel-and-glass structure, which stood out against the dark stone that made up the rest of the downtown Baton Rouge skyline. By the time I got on the elevator, I'd worked myself into a mood. I should've been made aware of what was happening in real time—not subjected to half stories at the same time my clients heard gossip.

Meyer made me look like an idiot. There wasn't much I hated more than appearing like someone who didn't matter. I'd spent half of my life as that person, and I was never—*never*—going back.

I pressed the button for my floor a little too forcefully, chipping the nail on my right index finger. *Great.*

Work was busy, even for a Monday. Sales staff crowded offices and cubicles, taking calls. Everyone shuffled around, speaking in hushed tones, while an air of panic crackled through the space like electricity.

"Do you have your logs for me?" Margery appeared as if from nowhere, hand clasped tightly to my elbow, tilting her face upward to meet my gaze. Her stony expression was unreadable, but the way her fingers dug into my arm said she was more concerned than she let on.

My teeth clenched into a smile so tight my jaw ached.

I liked my boss. She was tough; she'd fought her way up the corporate ladder and kicked ass in her role. I did not, however, like the way she grabbed my arm. Especially after making me a fool.

"Of course." I pulled free.

She glanced around the room. "Come on."

I followed her into an unused office, closed the door, and handed her the yellow folder. She opened it and thumbed through the papers. Her dark brows furrowed.

"What?" I folded my arms over my chest. "Is there a problem?"

"I expected a PDF. But paper forms?" The older woman took a deep breath. "And they're signed by *Robin Ezelle*?"

"She prefers paper." I shrugged.

"The thing is"—Margery pushed her bifocals to her head, pulling her hair from around her face—"she died this morning."

"What?"

"Robin Ezelle died this morning."

"No. I mean—I heard you...but. God." I swallowed. "I knew she'd had a stroke, but I hadn't heard that she'd passed away. That's...sad."

Thank god I'd handled the forms myself—that I hadn't waited and I'd brought them in today.

A cocktail of relief and adrenaline weakened my knees, but I stood rigid, my face expressionless. Maybe I should've squeezed out a few tears for the passing of a client, but at that moment I didn't have it in me. "She'll be missed."

Margery thumbed through the documents. "When did you get these signatures?"

"I've collected them over the past several months, I guess. You know Dr. Ezelle—she still uses, I mean she *used*, an old-school charting system. She wasn't comfortable with the e-forms or the iPad. There are several older doctors like that. I keep their folders in my car and turn them in when I think of it."

That part was true. Ezelle's office hadn't been updated since the Bush administration. Any rep from another company who'd met with her could back me up on this.

Deep creases spread across Margery's forehead. "She had a stroke... I guess that's why her signature looks a bit off. Perhaps she was having some preliminary symptoms?"

"Excuse me?" I did my best to ignore my eyelid, which now twitched worse than Sugar that time I let her have some of my espresso.

"On this first form, her signature is a bit different than these last few. A bit loopier. A bit darker; you can tell she'd pressed down harder with the pen. By the time she signed the rest of the forms—she must have had *preliminary symptoms*. She must've grown shaky." Margery eyed me like a hawk gazing at a field mouse.

I, Cordelia Black, was nobody's prey. I straightened my shoulders. "Must have."

My boss walked to the desk in the middle of the room and propped a hip against it. She pulled her eyeglasses from her head and twirled them in her hand. "I need to know without a doubt this isn't going to come back on me. That everything is squared away. Personally, I don't care one bit about these forms. I do, however, value my job." She paused, her eyes piercing me like hot needles. "You should value yours too."

"What are you suggesting?" My cheeks flushed. Margery was good at something most people weren't—getting under my skin.

"I don't think you understand. Shit is hitting the fan. And—"

"If I don't understand, it's because you didn't clue me in. Not on any of this. I looked like a fool this morning. All I knew was my medicine was being pulled. I didn't know that every doctor's office in this whole godforsaken city would suspect it's because of something unethical. They assumed I knew about it. Margery, I will *not* be the bad guy here. This is my *career*—a career I've worked my ass off for."

Margery huffed. "You think this is about you? This is about all of us. We could all be fucked. Royally and completely fucked."

"Bad medicine is part of the process," I said. "I don't understand how this is such a huge problem. What the hell's going on? Keeping it from me makes zero sense."

She looked me in the eye for what felt like days, the silence softening the edges of the hostile vibe. When she spoke, her words were clear and succinct, like someone reading a list of facts that held no emotional bearing on them whatsoever. "After a string of deaths, evidence was uncovered that Meyer may have fudged some of the trials."

"You believe that?"

"Doesn't matter. It's a PR nightmare. I've heard rumors of a class action lawsuit." She paused. "We had a meeting and Robert Denison himself spoke on the matter. VP of the company, Robert *Fucking* Denison. I've worked here my entire career—thirty years—and have never so much as seen the guy."

"Did he mention a lawsuit? Or deaths?"

"He didn't have to—his point was implied. That we're all expected to do our part for the company. If anything comes back on *you*, that means it comes back on *me*. So listen good. I'm merely suggesting to you that if someone asks why these signatures appear a bit different, that possibly the poor doctor was having preliminary symptoms of the stroke." She shook the folder at me. "The stroke that later killed her."

"That must be it." My eyes narrowed as I fully committed to the lie. "Because the records are one hundred percent legit. Jesus, Margery, listen to yourself."

Margery pressed her fingers against her temples and tilted her face toward the ceiling. "You're right. Of course. You always do a good job. There's no reason not to trust you. But remember, if anyone asks, Dr. Ezelle—"

"She had a stroke. Preliminary symptoms. Got it." Margery was full of shit. She didn't believe me...but it didn't matter. It was in her best interest that my forms were real—so they *were* real. "Now, is that all?"

My boss let out a controlled breath, pinching the bridge of her nose between her thumb and index finger. "No more fancy donuts or expensive sushi happy hours on the company card. Not until we get through this."

"What? That's the price of doing business," I said.

Margery shook her head. "And until business is stabilized, knock it off. Let's get your forms turned in, make sure everything goes...smoothly."

My control over the situation was slipping and that wasn't okay. This wasn't how my life was supposed to go.

I turned to leave when Margery called out once more, "And, Cordelia?"

"Yes?" I didn't bother to face her.

"You should see a doctor. About your eye."

Heat flooded my face, and I huffed. "I don't know what you're talking about."

I rushed through the cubicle farm, down the hallway, past the bathrooms, all the way to the elevators. Once the doors closed, I pressed my palm to my twitching eye.

I was fine.

I was strong.

I was in trouble.

Once upon a time, I'd been a little girl living in squalor with a track-marked mama and whoever was feeding her habit that week. I'd been born into a life with no hope of agency.

Getting out had taken everything. Moments like this—moments when my curated life spiraled away from me—reminded me of my past. Of the girl who always smelled of mildew, with chronic stomach aches from anxiety and hunger. These moments reminded me of Joanie and huddling under my bed, dead still, waiting for the adults to pass out, because only then was there safety.

The chaos of these memories made me crave control.

There was one place where I could find it without fail. The place where I held literal life in my hands. Where I made all decisions and controlled all outcomes.

Gerald was still drying on the easel in my studio, but the timing couldn't be helped. The desire for my workshop was an itch that wouldn't go away without a good thorough scratch.

The 7-Eleven where I parked offered the perfect view of the run-down playground across the street. The air was heavy with the smell of exhaust, and the sounds of traffic from the nearby overpass whirred louder than the laughter of kids spinning on the rusted merry-go-round. The whole space was more tetanus trap than park.

Still, there were moms smiling with tired eyes as their preschoolers burned off energy.

The first time I'd discovered Frank was at this playground, where I'd watch him watch others.

Ever since then, Frank's face featured prominently in my daydreams: His graying temples. His soft chin. His short hairy, gnomelike arms and legs. The way no one questioned why he was at this park.

Alone.

Exactly how he'd been at the zoo playground.

That was the problem; most people didn't see monsters because then they'd have to admit monsters haunted the people they loved. That sometimes the monsters *were* the people they loved. It's why the world needed Cordelia Black—why I could never give up hunting. Why I couldn't risk losing control.

Five minutes watching Frank, and already my eye had eased its twitching.

Once I'd discovered Gerald—the social worker preying on the invisible—he'd taken center stage of my synapses. Though all monsters were disgusting, Gerald's actions felt personal. I saw my childhood in his victims and became obsessed, and my attentiveness to Frank had admittedly waned once Gerald took the spotlight. I guess Zippity Zoo Fest wasn't a total bust—it had rekindled an old interest.

Frank was slumped on a bench, knees spread, his hands resting in his lap. Like at the zoo, he didn't bother pretending to read a book or play on his phone. He only sat. And watched. And, *I knew*, planned.

I grabbed my phone from the passenger seat and double tapped Frank's preferred social media app, then clicked open his latest message request to JessicaLovesIceCream14—the profile I'd created. The profile whose icon was a cartoon princess. Whose bio said I loved hanging out with friends, video games, and rolled ice cream. Photos and videos posted by JessicaLovesIceCream14 were of things like clips from Sugar's video games, close-ups of kittens, and a pair of pink Converse doodled with hearts and stars.

It had been easy enough to find Frank—monsters aren't as smart as they think. I'd liked a video he'd posted of a frou-frou dog wearing a rainbow-glitter sweater, and that was all it had taken for the man to zero in on me. He begged for photos, and when I didn't send any, he sent his own. There were parts of Frank I could never unsee.

His latest message asked if I liked to go swimming. If I had any photos of me in a bathing suit; he bet it was so cute.

Of course you did, Frank.

I closed the app with a sneer and leaned close to the window, so engrossed in what was happening across the street that when my phone rang through my speakers, I smacked my forehead against the glass.

Diane. I hit the answer button on my steering wheel while flipping down the visor mirror to inspect the tender spot on my forehead. "Hey, you. You ready for our lunch?"

"Hey yourself. Actually, that's why I'm calling. I need to reschedule."

"Oh." I pulled my compact from my purse and dabbed powder over the red splotch. "For when?"

"How about next Monday? I know this is a last-minute change, but the whole hospital is in a tizzy over this financial audit.

Especially since they obliterated the budget by purchasing the waste incinerator—"

"That's fine." Diane could really get going about the audit. I set my compact in the passenger seat and flipped the visor closed. "I wouldn't be much fun today, anyway. It's been a total bust."

"About Bosephan?" she asked.

"How do you know about it?"

"I overheard some of the nurses. Sounds like a nightmare."

Across the street, Frank struck up a conversation with a little boy near the seesaw. My breathing hitched as I waited for the child's grown-up to realize he was talking to a stranger.

"Listen, I know you think it's depressing, but do you mind if we eat at the hospital café?" Diane asked. "Leaving won't be an option until we get through this shit-show at work."

Diane's words were a dull buzzing in the background.

Frank was smiling, hands outstretched.

If I intervened, I couldn't kill him, because the police would definitely investigate the irate lady from the park. But I wouldn't let him hurt a child if I could prevent it.

"Cordelia? You there?" Diane sounded annoyed.

A young woman intercepted the boy, guiding him away from Frank. *Good.*

"Cordelia?"

"Oh. Sorry. What did you say?"

"I asked if you're okay with the Mercy Hospital café? I know you don't like it, but with the audit, I'll only have forty minutes to eat. Work's piling up."

"Sure. That's fine."

The monster looked around the playground. What was he going to do next?

"So, I'll see you Monday?"

"It's a date," I said.

We said our goodbyes and ended the call. Across the street, Frank loaded into his brown pickup truck, but he'd return, same time tomorrow. Twelve to twelve forty-five, four days a week. The idiot would eventually get caught by someone. But a lot could happen between now and eventually.

Anticipation coiled in my stomach. It wasn't time to kill. Not today.

But I wasn't sure how much longer I could wait.

AGREEING TO LET CHRISTOPHER PICK ME UP FOR DIANE'S barbecue wasn't the smartest idea, I admit. I should've been nervous, having a cop coming to my house.

I wasn't.

Christopher was looking for a serial killer, a big bad guy who was snatching up Baton Rouge's men and making them disappear. He'd warned me to be careful, while everything about him—from his body language to the way he spoke—said he wanted to protect me. It was cute, how physically close he was to the answer he sought, but he couldn't see it. He'd never see it.

When he'd insisted on giving me a ride, I'd agreed. Not only because it's what Sweet Cordelia would do. In fact, I'd hardly considered her at all. No—I agreed to let Christopher come to my home because the thrill of being smarter, of being several steps ahead, it was intoxicating. And, okay. Maybe he was fun to talk to. In another life, we might've even been real friends.

I waited on my front stoop because, as exciting as it was to be the cat to his mouse, why press my luck? He didn't need to come inside.

McSmiley arrived five minutes late (of course), with his signature smile in place (also, of course), and thrust a bouquet of sweet-smelling lilies toward me. "For you."

"You didn't have to get me flowers." I buried my face in the blooms and inhaled.

"Are you kidding?" His eyes lit with mischief. "I dug myself into a hole on our first date; then we met up at your favorite place—the zoo, where I bailed early. I'm kind of starting at a deficit. It's only my A game from here on out."

"You'll get no argument from me, then. I'll put these in water before we go. Wait here." I opened the door to step inside when Mango came out of nowhere, zipping through my legs.

"Damn it." I set the bouquet on the side table near my front door. Mango rushed to the fridge and spun in tight circles, yodel-barking louder and louder.

Christopher stepped inside behind me and nodded toward Mango, one eyebrow raised. "What's wrong with your dog?"

I froze. He was standing inside my home. A few feet away, one of my favorite paintings hung on the wall—*Ethan*. It was a beauty. Ethan had been a fun one to hunt. He'd hurt elderly women, so I'd hurt him. And now he decorated my foyer.

My heart thumped—*There is a cop in my house!*—while the delicious pang of excitement grew. McSmiley had no clue where he was, what happened here. Who I was. My skin prickled.

"Cordelia?" Christopher cocked his head to the side. "You okay? You look a little flushed."

"Yeah. I'm great." I pulled Sweet Cordelia back into place. "But this dog? Well, since you asked, *everything* is wrong with this dog." Mango barked at the fridge, demanding her cheese. I ignored her and retrieved a vase from underneath my sink and filled it with water before passing it to Christopher. "Put my flowers in here, please."

I scooped up Mango and unwrapped a slice of American from the fridge. "Here ya go, ya little terror," I whispered. The dog vibrated in my arms, snapping up the treat.

Christopher arranged the lilies in the vase and set them on the entry table. His arms were crossed over his chest as he studied the painting hanging above it.

"You like it?" I walked over, holding Mango. "It's one of mine."

My chest was buzzy, as if my ribs protected a beehive instead of a heart and lungs. How long had McSmiley searched for this monster? Was the case still open? How many nights' sleep had he lost, going over evidence, listening to theories? And yet here he was, feet away from proof that could close the case for good... That was the power I held.

"I forgot you're a painter," he said. I'd mentioned it on our date. "And yeah. I like it. Something about the dark red—it has a... I don't know. A depth. Do you sell your work?"

"No. I paint for myself. I'm glad it speaks to you, though." I shifted Mango from one arm to the other, her tiny claws scratching my goose bumps. "What do you like about it, particularly?" Sweet Cordelia looked up at him through her lashes. "If you don't mind me asking."

Christopher peered with a quiet intensity at the slashes of red and blue paint mixed with the blood of a predator. "Don't take this the wrong way—but it feels almost violent. Like it contains a rage, but also peace."

"Really?"

"I'm sorry." Christopher's brows shot upward. "Was that rude? I know nothing about art. Ignore me."

"No. No you weren't rude at all." The sentence trailed lightly from my lips, almost a breath. Christopher's eyes flickered onto mine. I recognized the look. He wanted to kiss me.

Sweet Cordelia would never kiss someone so soon. But I—Cordelia Black—almost wanted to let him. To see what it would be like. He'd described my painting—Ethan—perfectly. The violence. The rage. The peace too. Could there be more of a depth to McSmiley than I'd given him credit for?

The corners of Christopher's mouth ticked up into the slightest smirk. He leaned closer, his dark fringed eyelids lowered to half-mast. *Maybe...*

No. It wasn't the right move. I was looking for information—not a good time.

I cleared my throat and stepped back. "Let's get this devil dog home so we can leave."

Christopher followed me up the pathway to Diane's front steps.

My hand was almost on the knob when the door flew open. "Mooom! CiCi and her boooyfriend are here!" Sugar narrowed her bushy eyebrows and smiled, her incisors peeking through lips, sharp as puppy teeth.

Christopher stood behind me as I glared in mock anger at my goddaughter.

She giggled, stepping back and letting us inside. The house was messy, as usual, but we were met with the aroma of savory grilled meat and baking sweets.

Sugar peered up at Christopher. "How's Olive?"

"She's great," Christopher said. "Next time maybe I can bring her with me."

Sugar—only child that she was—loved bossing around smaller kids. She beamed. "That would be fun."

"Where's your mom, anyway?" I asked.

"She's out in the backyard." She glanced toward the television. "I need to go. I'm in the middle of a new game." After a quick hug, she stomped away in her pink Converse.

"Come on." I led Christopher through the house, navigating around Diane's doom piles and half-finished craft projects, toward the patio doors.

In the backyard, a folding table was covered with a lavender sheet. Mason jars filled with short fat candles made up the centerpiece, while overhead, fairy lights were strung between two posts, twinkling in the dusky evening pinkness.

"Good, you're here." Diane drawled out her vowels in the way that meant the beer she held wasn't her first. "Like my table? Looks good, huh?"

"It's gorgeous."

"Don't sound so surprised." Diane threw an arm over my shoulders. "Also, I told you this was casual." She eyed my Stella McCartney midi dress.

"I *am* casual." I'd paired the cotton frock with low-heeled sandals and tinted lip balm—what else did she want from me?

Diane was barefoot, wearing her usual painter's overalls over a cropped white tank.

"Your dress cost as much as my entire closet—there's no way you really think that's casual." Diane eyed Christopher as if noticing him for the first time. "Not to say our Cordelia here is high-maintenance or anything."

"What's wrong with being high-maintenance?" I asked.

Christopher squeezed my hand. "I like high-maintenance. Who doesn't want to walk into a room with the best-dressed woman in the place?"

"Damn straight." Diane nodded her approval. "Cordelia Renee—"

"Still not my name."

She ignored me. "Cordelia Renee Black. I like McSmiley."

I turned to Christopher. "My name isn't Renee."

He held up his hands. "She likes McSmiley." He mimicked Diane. "So McSmiley isn't saying a thing."

Not rolling my eyes was a struggle, but I reminded myself that tonight I was Sweet Cordelia, the damsel McSmiley could tell all his case secrets to. I dipped my chin demurely.

"Is your boyfriend here? I was hoping to get to know him a bit," Christopher asked Diane.

"Yes—"

"Why?" I interrupted Di, the word crossing my lips urgently before Sweet Cordelia could choke it back. Why did Christopher want to get to know Simon? He'd recognized the darkness—the violence—in the brush strokes of my artwork. Was it possible he'd recognized some darkness in Simon as well? Did he agree that I wasn't crazy? That the way Simon pulled at Diane wasn't so accidental, and the way he treated Sugar wasn't funny?

Christopher looked at me quizzically, and I forced myself to smile. To flutter my lashes. To be fucking normal. I cleared my throat. "I mean—I didn't realize you guys hit it off so well."

What a stupid thing to say; of course they hadn't hit it off.

Christopher shrugged but sounded uncomfortable when he spoke. "Nah, I was just wondering if he was here or not..."

"He's here somewhere." Diane looked around the small yard, unflustered as always. Maybe she didn't notice the uncomfortable shift in Christopher's tone. Like my question had hit a nerve. "He must've gone inside right before y'all got here. Let's go find him; it's time to bring out the food."

Diane walked ahead of us toward the house, and Christopher slid a hand to the small of my back. "You okay? You got this weird look on your face."

"I'm fine," I said. "Just...thinking."

Christopher was quiet as we followed Diane through the backyard. He tugged my hand, and we slowed, letting her walk ahead.

Once she'd disappeared through the patio doors, I turned to him. Christopher sighed. "I want to say something, but I don't want to upset you."

Sweet Cordelia tilted her chin, and looked up at McSmiley, her lashes batting like butterfly wings. Fingers sliding through his. Internally I was a mess—confused about Simon, worried I might be right, frustrated I might be wrong. But outwardly, Sweet Cordelia was cool and calm and ready to collect McSmiley's secrets. "You won't. Upset me, I mean."

Christopher's lips pressed into a hard line, which looked out of place on his eternally happy face. His heavy brows knitted together. "I'd never say something in front of Diane, but...something about this Simon guy, I don't know; he just got my antennae up at the zoo. It's probably nothing, but I see a lot of guys who can get...possessive."

My heart rate sped. Christopher did feel it, then? That...*that thing* about Simon? That offness. Sweet Cordelia's voice was neutral. No excitement—because why would she be excited? Sweet Cordelia certainly wasn't celebrating that her best friend's boyfriend was being described as possessive. "What do you mean? Should I be concerned?"

"I'd just...keep an eye on things. Maybe I can check him out at the station? Honestly though, it's probably nothing. With all this work stress going on, you start seeing bad guys everywhere, you know?"

When I didn't immediately respond, he added, "I've made you mad."

"What?" I squeezed his fingers in mine. "No, you didn't, I promise. I don't care for the guy, either." *Understatement.* "But I'm not worried. He won't last long."

That last part? That wasn't Sweet Cordelia. That was me. And it was true.

Because one way or another, Simon wouldn't last long.

I'd make sure of it.

The sun was sinking by the time we made our plates and poured wine and sat down to our meal. Diane insisted I sit next to Simon and across from Christopher, and she the opposite, explaining with slurred speech that it was so everyone could get to know each other. This made no sense to me, but it was Diane's party, so I went with it. Sugar sat at the end of the table, swiping her mom's phone.

The sky was a watercolor of pink and orange bleeding into muted blues that reminded me of lips and fingernails and my workshop. Calming and perfect. The rosy light bathed everything in a soft focus and set Diane's copper hair ablaze. It was difficult not to stare—she was beautiful in that light. But she was beautiful in any light.

"Tell him, Cordelia," Diane urged.

"I'm sorry. What were we talking about?" I looked in each of their faces. Diane's brows raised in question. Christopher wore an amused expression. Simon's mouth curled into a smile.

Diane rolled her eyes. "Don't play dumb, Ms. Uptight Rule Follower. You can't get in trouble for it after all these years." She turned to Christopher. "In college, at night we'd jump the gate to this one house in this snooty neighborhood and use their pool. We never got caught."

The skinny-dipping story—Diane's favorite. "Yeah," I said. "We'd strip down—"

Diane's eyes flicked urgently to Sugar, who was all ears.

"We'd strip down to our *swimsuits*," I course corrected, "and float all night, staring up at the stars."

"Sound's amazing, babe." Simon reached across the table, and Diane slid her fingers into his.

"It was." She smiled longingly. "Sometimes I think I'll spend the rest of my adult life chasing the peace we captured in those moments."

"Ugh," Sugar groaned, her wide eyes staring daggers at her mom's fingers tangled in Simon's, her cherubic lips pursed into a frown. "Y'all are so gross."

"Manners." Diane pulled her hand away from Simon's grasp as she spoke.

The smallest almost smile flickered over Simon's lips before he tucked it away, leaving his face blank. He'd enjoyed the way Diane had corrected Sugar—but he knew better than to show it.

I bit into a dinner roll to keep from saying something I'd regret.

Simon shoveled a piece of rare beef into his mouth, chewing loudly, red juice dribbling from the corner of his lips, down his chin.

How I ached to drain those lips of their rosiness. That mouth would fade to a perfect icy blue, the same color that streaked the evening sky. I imagined how he'd spread across my canvas, smooth as silk. *Where would I hang him? Somewhere prominent...*

I took a deep drink of my wine, careful to keep the delight of my daydreams from appearing across my face. *Sweet Cordelia* was a gracious guest. A good friend. She didn't have deadly fantasies of her bestie's boyfriend over dinner.

I refilled my wineglass. Simon laughed at something Christopher said. I smiled along, even though I wasn't hearing any of it.

I took another sip of my drink.

Across the table, Diane leaned toward Christopher, who nodded along as she started on her favorite subject—the financial dangers facing Mercy Hospital. My head swam from the alcohol, and my belly was full of red meat and buttery yeast rolls. The evening air was a warm hug against my skin. Sugar played quietly with Diane's phone.

No one was watching. No one was listening. I leaned close to Simon, staring into his face, until he was forced to look at me. "Not again." he rasped quietly. "What do you want now?"

Did he think I was crazy? Maybe I was. I felt crazy. My mind felt light and bubbly and I didn't care.

"What's your game here?" I propped an elbow against the table, leaning the side of my head against it, never dropping my gaze. I wouldn't risk looking away—missing a flicker of smoke hidden in the depths of his irises.

"My game?" He sounded bewildered. "I've been nothing but nice to you, and you're asking what *my game* is? My game is dating Diane. I care about her and Sammy—"

"Samantha," I said. "And I bet you do."

He ignored the jab. "I care about Diane and for some reason she cares about you. Which is why I didn't tell her about your little stunt at the zoo. But this is getting ridiculous."

Simon's eyes widened and I leaned forward, trying for a better view.

"Are you drunk?" He wrinkled his nose in disgust and scooted away. "It's not fair. Women can drink and act as crazy as they want, but a man can't do anything or he's—"

"He's what, Simon?" I pretended to pout. "Tell me about all the poor men, treated unfairly."

"This is what I'm talking about. You've lost your mind, and I have to sit here and behave, or you'll call me a misogynist and tell Didi I'm some kind of woman hater. One day, when we are—"

"Wait. Who the hell is Didi?" I crossed my arms over my chest. This jerk was desperate to give someone a nickname. "And when you're what, exactly?"

"Oh good, you two," Diane said. Simon and I froze. "I don't know what you're talking about over there in such deep conversation, but I knew you'd be friends."

Simon and I both pulled our masks into place—he, Nice-Guy, and I, Sweet Cordelia. We beamed at each other, all teeth and eye crinkles. Best friends forever.

"Sure thing, babe!" Simon said.

Diane gave us a thumbs-up, relief playing over her face, then returned to her conversation with Christopher, who was learning more about the hospital audit process than he probably ever cared to know.

"Leave me alone," Simon whispered. "You're insane."

"You're probably right," I whispered back. "But I won't leave you alone, Simon. I can't."

The rest of the night, Simon ignored me. He spoke with Christopher. He laughed with Diane.

I nursed another glass of wine and watched him intently.

But there was no cold stare. No cruel gaze on my goddaughter or jealousy when Diane laughed at Christopher's corny jokes.

No matter how long I peered into those wide gray eyes, smoke never appeared.

MERCY HOSPITAL'S CAFÉ WAS NOISY, YET SOMBER. HUSHED conversations from families taking respite from their campsite next to loved ones' beds mingled with the serious monotone of staff settled at other tables. Near the corners of the room, laughter rang out. People paid at the register, filled paper cups, and shoveled rubbery chicken à la king into their mouths.

There was something heartbreaking about witnessing one family's trauma playing out, while a table over, people chatted about sports.

"So." Diane doused her wilted salad with Thousand Island. "Bosephan causes strokes—is that what they're saying now?"

"Can we talk about *literally* anything else?" I was exhausted. After the barbecue, I'd been too keyed up to sleep. It occurred to me while lying in the dark of my bedroom—if Christopher could sense something strange about Simon, then what about me? Did he know I was different too? I'd thought I was the one in charge of our little game—trotting out Sweet Cordelia—but what if he was doing the same? What if McSmiley wasn't real?

I know—ridiculous. But last night, I couldn't shake the idea.

So, after a couple of hours of tossing and turning, I'd gotten out of bed and indulged in some light stalking—always calming. I'd followed Frank from one late night haunt to another, staying out longer than I intended.

My morning meetings were brutal. Not only was I exhausted, but there were no real answers on how things were going—not from my boss, Margery or the higher-ups. The entire office was in a tizzied state, and I desperately needed a break from thinking about it.

I desperately needed a break, in general.

Diane chewed her lunch thoughtfully. "Sure. *Anything* else, huh?" Her eyes gleamed. "McSmiley is a hottie. I had fun chatting with him at dinner. He likes you; I can tell." She stabbed a cherry tomato, then pulled it from her fork with her front teeth.

I groaned. "You were right. Bosephan's in trouble."

"Nope. Too late. You said we could talk about *literally* anything else. I've moved on. I want to hear about McSmiley."

"Fine." I slumped in my seat. "What do you want to know?" What's that saying? The fastest way around is through? That was true when talking to Di about my love life.

"For starters," she said, "what happened after y'all left my house?"

"Nothing. He took me home."

"No kiss good night?"

"No," I said honestly. I hadn't told her how when Christopher came to pick me up for the barbecue, he'd given me a dopey look, leaning close with his lips parted, and I'd bolted, or how when he'd walked me to my front door after bringing me home, I'd disappeared inside before he had the chance to try again. How I'd then spent the night wondering if it was all an act—which by the light of day seemed highly unlikely but, okay, maybe not impossible.

Diane took a sip of water, then smiled wryly. Somewhere on the hospital floor, a siren sounded a code. She asked, "He's a cop, right?"

"You know he is." Diane loved a uniform. Like, *loved* them. She nursed a long-standing crush on her mail lady. She was the only person I knew turned on by knee socks and a sleeve patch.

I plucked a cucumber slice from the last dregs of my salad and popped it into my mouth.

"Cordelia—what do cops have?"

"Big egos?" I answered. "Tempers? God complexes?"

"No." Her eyes shone with a wicked glint. "Handcuffs."

I tossed a salad cracker toward her, and it stuck in her curls.

"Hey. I'm going back to work after this. I don't want crumbs in my hair." She pulled the cracker free and crunched it loudly between her teeth.

I shrugged. "You started it."

"How? By stating the obvious?" Her gaze darted to her watch as she chewed the final bite of her lunch. *Weird.* Diane never looked at her watch. For her, watches were like bracelets—decoration.

Come to think of it, she'd been acting a little off the entire meal. Pensive. Nervous. Even joking about Christopher's handcuffs, she'd seemed as if her mind was elsewhere.

I asked, "What's wrong?"

"Nothing's wrong."

"Okay. Let me rephrase. What's on your mind?"

She bit her bottom lip. "You want to know?"

"Is it about handcuffs?"

"No."

"Then, yeah," I said. "Of course."

"I want to talk to you about something, but I'm sure you're going to freak out." She folded her paper napkin into a tiny square before immediately unfolding it again.

"Is it Sugar?" My mind flooded with possible scenarios. "Is she okay?"

"Yes. Samantha's fine. Chill. This is nothing bad."

"Okay." I took a breath. "What is it?"

"Don't freak out."

"You already said that," I reminded her.

"Yeah. And you immediately freaked out. Maybe I should wait until later."

"No," I said, a little too aggressively. I set my plastic fork on the table, giving her my full attention. "What's up?"

She straightened her spine and looked me in the eye. "Simon is taking a travel nursing job."

"And?" Good riddance.

"And." Her hazel-green gaze dropped to her plate. "I'm considering going with him."

My heart fell hard as a stone from my chest and landed somewhere in my guts. I opened my mouth to speak but my tongue was gummy. Dry. *Say no. Say it's a bad idea. She'll listen.*

But she wouldn't—I knew she wouldn't. Diane was a wildflower. The best way to make sure she leapt without looking was to tell her not to.

Fucking Simon.

Diane held up a palm. "Before you tell me I'm crazy, I don't mean go with him as in *move*. I mean for the summer. When Sugar is out of school. It could be fun—a little adventure. God knows I need some adventure in my life."

No.

My head spun. I had to make her realize this was stupid—for a million reasons. Simon could be a monster—hadn't Christopher also noticed his strangeness? Why couldn't she see it too? Simon could be the worst decision she ever made. He could be dangerous. But even if he wasn't, she couldn't go. I needed her.

I croaked, "What about work?"

Diane shrugged. "It's not like I've ever taken a vacation. They need me here; I have the upper hand. Simon said they'd be crazy not to work with me." She paused, sitting her fork in her bowl. "I can find another job if they don't."

"Did Simon tell you that too? That you could *find another job*?" This was so much worse than the Bosephan recall. This was worse than getting chewed out by my boss. This was worse than being ghosted by my top clients and no longer being able to afford my shoe addiction.

This was worse than everything. Than *anything*.

Simon was going to take Diane and Sugar away from me. He could hurt them.

And I couldn't tell Diane that. Not if there was even a smallest possibility I'd need to kill Simon. I had to make her understand. I had to appeal to her in a way that she'd come to the right decision on her own. I knew my best friend better than I knew anyone, and that was the only way to convince her of anything.

"You love your job," I said. "You *love* working here."

It was true. Diane made a good living. She got along with her coworkers. Her boss loved her. And her schedule was flexible. Not bad for an accountant.

"It'll be fine." She frowned. "Anyway—it's not like I've said yes. It's something to think about, and I wanted your opinion."

"My opinion?" My voice was raspy. "Is you barely know him. You'd really take Sugar and follow him across the country?" I shook my head.

"I know him better than you think." Diane crossed her arms over her neon purple T-shirt. "Give me a little credit."

I picked up my fork and dragged its tongs through the Catalina salad dressing puddled in the bottom of my plastic bowl, creating orange rainbows. There was nothing I could say.

If Simon was a monster, I could fix this—all of it—permanently.

Except there was no smoke.

And no matter how badly I wished otherwise, I had a code. I only killed monsters.

"You're mad at me." Diane snaked her hand across the table and touched my arm. The pads of her fingers were cold—her hands and feet were always cold—but Diane's touch sent familiar warmth through me. I met my best friend's gaze. "I really like

Simon," she said. "A lot. I feel like he could be the missing piece, you know?"

The missing piece. My stomach clenched. Diane was always talking about the damned missing piece. She had this idea of how her family was supposed to look, and it was very specific. A partner with a good job who could coach Little League if they chose to have another kid. She could work part-time to have more opportunities to volunteer at Sugar's school. They'd get a bigger house. A nicer car. They'd go on vacations to Pensacola and take pictures in white shirts on the shore. It was a whole fantasy she'd created for herself—one she'd grown up in—and it was so incredibly sweet how badly she yearned for it.

But Simon? He was *not* the missing piece. I couldn't let him steal her from me. *Think, Cordelia.*

I pressed my lips closed, biting my tongue between my molars, afraid I'd say the wrong thing. Something that would make this so much worse. Because when Diane mentioned the missing piece, her heart was on her sleeve. I couldn't be the one to break it. "Di, I can't stand the idea of losing Sugar. Of losing either of you."

Diane's eyes softened and she clasped my wrist, looping her index finger through the friendship bracelet. "You'll never lose us. It's me and you and Sugar, right? Vintage."

"How can it be me and you if you go away?"

"And you call *me* dramatic." There was no animosity in her words. "You're overreacting. If—*and it's a big if*—I go, it'll be for two months tops. Nothing will ever come between us. We are Cordelia and Diane. Di and Cor."

Two months? Lots could happen in two months. Lots of bad things.

Diane was flighty; she lived in her daydreams and was optimistic to a fault. But this—this *stupid absurd ridiculous* idea—this wasn't her. This was Simon. All Simon.

Fucking Simon.

"I'll miss you," I said. "A lot."

"Oh, babe." She squeezed my hand. "I didn't mean to make you feel bad. Listen, this is not worth worrying about—not yet. Forget I mentioned it."

But Simon had upped the stakes.

Forgetting was one thing I could not do.

MY NEED TO KILL GREW UNTIL IT THRUMMED IN MY BONES as if it were its own separate living thing curled inside of me. A parasite with a beating heart. Who was I to ignore it?

So yes, it was earlier than usual, but Friday was Frank day.

Becoming Frank's type of woman was easy. My stringy brown wig sat limply on my head, its fringe parting in the middle so my seemingly beady eyes could peep through. Cheap dark leggings paired with a loose top and ballet flats completed the ensemble. Nothing had ever felt more like a disguise.

As for my face—well, thank you social media tutorials. A little highlight. A lot of contour. My chin receded, my nose grew, my cheeks filled out. It wouldn't fool someone who knew me as well as, say, Diane, but to anyone else I was a different person.

The look was carried all the way through to the smallest details. My socks (yes, socks with ballet flats) were mismatched, and my handbag was one I picked up from the thrift store that same day. The whole ensemble cried "tired mom." I named her Margo.

I *accidentally* ran into Frank at his park, where I was watching my daughter play with her friends. I never actually had to point out my (lack of) daughter, because all a man like Frank cared about was that there was a daughter. Despite what Diane believed, I'm a *great* liar.

I'd settled next to him on the park bench and chummed the waters with stories of how I was overworked and underappreciated at a local call center. Of how I desperately needed help since my deadbeat ex moved away. How doing it on my own was exhausting, and nothing sounded sexier than a good cuddle followed by a nap.

Frank couldn't resist Margo.

Margo let him choose the restaurant—a chain bar and grill with fake flair and crowded tables. Exactly the kind of place I'd have picked for us—not somewhere so empty that we'd be noticed, nor trendy enough for a frumpy couple like us to stick out. This was the kind of place where we could blend in, and no one would pay any attention if Frank was a little wobbly on his feet as we left. *Another husband who can't handle his booze. What a shame.*

Margo could never be too careful, so Frank agreed to meet her at the restaurant. I arrived early, as usual, and got us a table. The devil's in the details, so I hunched forward in my seat as I loudly slurped the last bit of my daiquiri—Margo's favorite, I decided—then twisted the straw between my fingers. Margo checked her phone every ten minutes, because she'd been stood up often.

Across the room a flash of blond caught my eye. I didn't recognize him at first, out of context. Simon didn't look that different—his hair was shiny with product and even more slicked away from his face than usual, transforming his cheekbones to razor blades. He was dressed differently—his jeans replaced with tailored slacks and a slim-cut charcoal button-down showed off his lean frame. And there was no mistaking his steel-gray eyes.

The woman with him was not Diane.

Did he have another girlfriend? The betrayal I felt on behalf of my best friend surprised me. So this was it, then. The way he'd ignored Sugar's boundaries. Been annoyed that Diane had laughed with Christopher at the zoo. And now this. The reason he'd pinged my Spidey sense from the beginning. He wasn't a monster—just your average controlling, two-timing creep.

Fine. This wasn't as satisfying as a trip to my workshop, but it could be a lot easier. I'd expose him, and Diane would dump his ass. I dug in my purse to get my phone to snap a photo, then remembered; Cordelia wasn't here—Margo was. It was fine. Now that I knew his secret, another night I could trail him and get the evidence I needed to break them up.

He'd soon be gone from our lives forever.

I expected to feel glee—*because wasn't this perfect?*—but a different emotion took hold of me. Anger. How dare he hurt Diane?

I seethed. Simon needed to go, true, but emotions are complicated. I'd hoped for Diane to dump him without getting hurt herself.

My eyes bore into him as his hand trailed to the small of his date's back, his large palm sliding over her perky ass.

Simon turned and I quickly averted my eyes, holding the menu in front of my face. After a moment, I peeked over the top—a very Margo thing to do.

The woman threw back her head in a boisterous laugh and touched Simon's cheek—not first-date body language.

He tenderly traced her full lips with the tip of his right index finger. She caught the digit in her teeth, and the couple fell into more laughter, completely engrossed in each other.

Did she know he was going to travel nurse? Had he invited her to visit him too? Was that his plan? Have Diane visit a few months, and when she left, another woman could take her place?

My eyes narrowed on the two.

I'd read about—and dealt with—malignant narcissists. How they love bomb, then destroy. Was that what I was dealing with here? Margo bounced her nails against the tabletop with one hand and cradled her chin with the other.

Simon wasn't the image conjured when I thought of a narcissistic cheater. He was too forgettable—nothing about him special. That was probably the point. Rude how there was no single aesthetic for fuckery. How much easier would life be if men always looked as horrible on the outside as they were on the inside? That was rarely the case, though.

Simon's fingertips lightly grazed the woman's collarbone, then tugged playfully at the scoop neckline of her dress. My stomach knotted. I forced my gaze away before I could be caught staring.

Fucking Simon.

I slurped the last of my daiquiri and the cocktail went straight through me. Cordelia would never leave the table while waiting on a monster, but Margo would. I hurried across the dining room floor toward the bathroom. Less than ten minutes later, I was back in the small hallway that housed the restrooms. Simon stood outside the men's room, his long limbs and broad shoulders filling most of the tiny space. There was no way to avoid brushing against him as I passed by.

"Excuse me," he said, smoothly. No awkward Nice-Guy here. No rolling question mark spine. This Simon? He stood straight, his arms folded effortlessly across his chest. He was confident as his gaze lingered on Margo a little too long. It was startling—how both familiar and strange he was. *Is this how my monsters felt when they saw me out of costume? Unsettled?*

A smirk toyed with the corner of Simon's mouth as he watched Margo. Hate—searing and alkaline—barreled through my veins. This man, so beneath her, was going to hurt Diane. I couldn't kill him for that, but I would make him wish he were dead.

Later. Margo returned his smirk with a bemused, uncomfortable smile.

Simon was a job for Cordelia Black. Right now, I was Margo No-Last-Name. Now that I knew his secret, there'd be plenty of time to create a plan. A perfect, delicious plan, designed to bring the most pain to Simon, and the most joy to yours truly. A plan that would—above all else—help me salvage as much of Diane's heart as possible.

Simon's smirk stretched across his face, until it was the full-blown smile of someone who knew exactly how much space he took up in the world. Of someone who believed the world owed him that space to begin with.

"Do we know each other?" Simon tilted his head to the side.

"No," Margo said. "I don't think so."

He nodded toward my wrist. "A friend of mine has a bracelet like that. But hers is orange."

I looked down. *Shit.* Sugar's bracelet had slid from beneath the sleeve of my tunic top. Its fluorescent pink shown brightly next to the deep brown sleeve of Margo's favorite tunic.

I swallowed my worry and rage. With a shrug, I tucked the bracelet out of sight and mumbled, "Kids."

Before he could draw me into a full-fledged conversation, I pushed past and hurried back to my table.

The interaction lasted the shortest moment—only a few words—but everything about it was wrong. The way he stood. Moved. The way he spoke.

That manipulative sonofabitch.

And his *friend* had a bracelet like this? The *friend* he invited to travel with him. The *friend* he told to *just find another job*.

He would pay for this.

I picked up the menu, pretending to peruse its contents. I inhaled deeply—then breathed out the rage. I'd make a plan to deal with Simon.

Tonight was for Frank.

Short. Furry. Smoke-filled Frank. A monster who deserved his fate without question.

I closed my eyes and reset my intentions. In my mind's eye, I saw Frank as he slouched on the rusty park bench, eating lunch from a brown paper sack. Frank grinning at the crowded zoo playground.

The photos he sent to JessicaLovesIceCream14. Frank, whose smoke was so deeply gray that it was almost plum.

Frank, who had to die tonight.

When I opened my eyes, Frank was at the hostess's station as if I'd conjured the squat troll of a man into being. *Fee-fi-fo-fum, Frank.*

He scanned the restaurant with his green eyes, and when they landed on Margo, I wiggled my fingers in an eager wave.

The monster sank into the seat across from me with pink cheeks, polluting the air with his dollar store cologne. "I thought you might not show," he said.

I caressed the top of Frank's hairy arm with my fingers. He looked down to where I touched him, then back into my eyes.

I said, "I've been looking forward to this all week."

It was the truth.

Less than an hour later, I had my opportunity. Frank went to pee, leaving his drink unattended—the number one thing on a long list of *nevers* that moms drill into their daughters' heads before they're old enough to date. Never leave your drink alone. Never get into his car on a first date. Never walk alone into a dark parking garage. Never ignore your gut.

Men weren't imparted these pearls of wisdom. Lucky me.

Unlucky Frank.

Bosephan was designed to dissipate quickly under a patient's tongue—so the next part of my process required skill. I discreetly dried my incisors with my cloth napkin, then pretended to cough into my palm and slid the Bosephan between my front teeth, where I hid it carefully behind my lips. I had to act fast. Frank's beer sloshed in his half-full glass as I slid it across the table and pretended to take a sip, instead spitting the pill from my mouth. It sank to the bottom, fizzing into the amber liquid without a trace.

There was nothing to see at our table, only a lady taking a drink of her date's beer while he was in the john. I slid the pint glass back into place.

Half an hour later, Frank's speech slurred as his chin dipped to his chest and his shoulders rolled forward. I paid our bill in cash and led tipsy Frank out of the restaurant.

Everything was going according to plan.

THE BULLFROGS AND CICADAS SCREAMED IN THE NIGHT-time, their calls shrill and demanding. My car was backed into my roadside hidey-hole, where I sat feeling jumpy as I waited on Clarence. Cicadas are romanticized in movies and books, but let me tell you, there is nothing romantic about their reckoning shriek. It only added to my nerves.

I was unable to shake the feeling something wasn't right, but that was ridiculous—I'd followed my plan to the letter. I went over the kill mentally. Frank had been easy. He'd woken on my table, his terror jerking him from the fog of Bosephan, once he'd discovered he wasn't at home, tucked away and dreaming in his bed. Like all monsters, he'd sobbed. And, again like all monsters, Frank grew hysterical when he saw my blade—felt it pressed against the doughy flesh of his neck. I'd given him the chance to confess his crimes and go free, but it's difficult to talk when you're gagged, with your lips duct-taped closed, so on my table he'd remained.

Then, because he's a coward, he'd tried to squeeze his eyes shut during the final moment as I delivered his sentence. That wasn't fair. Why should he get to look away, when his victims had to live with the images of his crimes seared into their young minds? Another strip of tape ensured he'd watched his death—the sum of his putrid actions—with eyes wide open.

All in all, it was pretty straightforward.

There was no reason to feel so jumpy, yet my fingers twitched with anxiousness working its way out of my body.

Each minute lumbered by slowly, and I couldn't breathe easy until the body snatcher finally passed with a cocooned monster packed away in his SUV.

I waited the usual twenty minutes then drove back to the clearing to collect my payment from beneath the pirogue.

One hundred. Two hundred. Three. Four. Five.

Easy money.

That's when I saw it.

Further back in the trees, where scrubby underbrush grew thick, a tiny pinprick of blinking green light.

The anxious twitch of my fingers grew into full-blown hand trembles as I stepped toward it, into the forest. Even from far away, I knew what that little light meant.

Tim, Mama's old boyfriend, owned trail cameras. I'd even researched them myself when deciding what to use outside my workshop.

Newer expensive models gave live feed to apps or computer programs. Others saved data to upload to the cloud as soon as they had a signal. Still yet, older or cheaper ones recorded the data onto the device and couldn't be accessed until manually uploaded to a computer.

Please let this be the latter version.

Even in the best-case scenario, someone had taken an interest in my secret patch of land.

Hunting wasn't allowed out here—and I periodically performed perimeter sweeps to make sure this section of forest was as isolated as I needed it to be. It always was. Always had been, anyway.

When was the last time I'd done a check? Too long. Just like with the Bosephan forms, I'd grown complacent—and that was dangerous. Cordelia Black knew better.

Rogue tree limbs yawned towards me as I hurried toward the blinking light. Briars grabbed like talons at my arms and legs, tearing at Margo's cotton leggings.

How had I, Cordelia Black, been so careless? I'd have to go back over the pirogue with a fine-tooth comb. Wipe it down. Make sure I left nothing of myself behind. I'd have to find another place to meet Clarence. I'd have to thoroughly go through the woods and make double sure that this was the only camera...

My thoughts jumbled together.

How long had the camera been there, its watchful green eye recording the forest? It wasn't there when I'd disposed of Gerald. No way I'd be walking around free if it was.

I made it to the tree before I realized I'd left my knife in the car. *Fuck.* By the time I retrieved my blade from the car, then returned to the tree and freed the electronic device, angry cuts covered my arms like scarlet tic-tac-toe boards. God, I hated the woods.

Back in the clearing, I resisted the urge to flee, because running would do no good. If it was a live feed—then whoever was on the other end of the camera had already gotten clear shots of Margo's face and possibly Cordelia's car.

The camera itself was boxy and black, instead of smaller and sleeker, like the newer models I'd considered purchasing. Its plastic casing was faded and worn, there was no playback screen on the device, and its strap was frayed near the edges. The back of the camera was stuck tight with grime. All of this gave me hope. I slid my knife along the seam of the plastic until it separated into two parts.

With shaky fingers, I pulled the batteries free and chucked them into the woods. Once the green light was out and I was sure it was no longer recording, I could breathe.

Think, Cordelia...

I needed a plan. Plans gave order. Plans made sense. A plan *always* made me feel better.

The swamp air pressed thick around me. My awful leggings were wet from sweat and humidity, and shredded from the sea of scrubby thorns. My makeup smeared and ran, and my arms ached from the cuts.

How had I screwed up so royally? Suddenly, I felt small in a way I hadn't since I'd been the nobody daughter of a junkie mama in Holden. Adrenaline ebbed, and my knees barely propped me up.

If I were caught, who would hunt the monsters?

Worse, Diane would hate me. Sugar would forever be labeled as the goddaughter of a killer. They'd have to leave—disappear somewhere new. I'd never see them again because I'd be in prison. Simon would gladly step into the space I left behind.

Breathe. You aren't caught until you're caught.

This was just an old game camera.

Yeah. *Just* a camera.

And I *just* needed oxygen to breathe. Fire was *just* hot. Dolce was *just* a label.

I needed to get home and find out what I was dealing with, instead of waiting around for someone to discover me sitting in the forest with a bucket of blood on the floorboard of my car. There wasn't an excuse in the world that could explain that away. I tossed the camera onto my passenger seat, needing to do one more thing before leaving.

Armed with Armor All wipes and a twitchy eye, I wiped down the pirogue, not leaving until I was satisfied there were no fingerprints. I scuffed away any footprints I'd left in the dirt, then crossed my fingers. There was nothing to be done about tire tracks except hope for rain.

On the main highway, I glanced into the rearview mirror. My eyes were hollowed from my pooling mascara, and my skin was sallow from the too-light powder that was part of my disguise. The contour cream I'd used to create Margo's face was smudged like dirt across my cheeks. I straightened my spine and set my jaw tight. "You are Cordelia Black," I said. "Stop panicking. You're *strong*. You're *capable*." My voice cracked. "*Stop it*. You're Cordelia!"

I gasped. The woman in the mirror didn't look like Cordelia. She looked like someone I used to know long ago.

No.

I shook my head and jerked my gaze back to the road, but at the next red light, I couldn't stop myself from peeking.

It was only me, but in my reflection, behind the fear that settled in my eyes, were everything and everyone I'd worked so hard to leave behind—Mama, Tim, Joanie, everyone. My jaw clenched firm. I was not my past.

I was Cordelia Black.

I was.

MY ARMS WERE WEIGHED DOWN BY MY PURSE, THE PAINT can, the camera, and the plastic bag of Frank's clothes. It took three tries to fit the key into the lock of my door. Once inside, I set everything on the table, then peeled away the sweat-dampened tunic and leggings like a snake shedding her skin, kicking them to the corner of the dining room. I was splashing cold water on my face at the kitchen sink when I noticed.

My wrist.

"No. No, no, no." I ran to my pile of dirty clothes and dropped to my knees and dug through them. Maybe it had gotten snagged when I'd undressed.

It wasn't there.

The bracelet Sugar made me—the one I'd sworn to never take off—was gone.

When was the last time I'd noticed it? It had slid from beneath Margo's sleeve in the restaurant, where it caught Simon's attention.

After that…it could've come loose when I'd pushed through briars to get to the camera.

The camera!

Things kept getting better and better.

I sank onto a barstool at the island as my mind sprinted ahead to a crime scene where the hot pink bracelet was picked up with a gloved hand and placed in an evidence bag. This was a wild leap—losing the bracelet wasn't that big of a deal, was it? How many homemade friendship bracelets were there? It was a common craft for kids at day camps and art classes, and recently, even teens and adults made them for concerts.

Except…

Except for the game camera sitting on my table.

Except Simon had noticed the bracelet.

Each of these things on their own—*the missing bracelet, the camera, Simon*—were not great. Together, though?

If the camera fed to an app or the cloud and whoever accessed the footage reported suspicious activity in the clearing and the bracelet was found nearby, if Frank was reported missing, and then somehow the news found out about the bracelet and leaked the information, Simon would see it and easily put it together. He'd seen Margo wearing the bracelet on a date with Frank the last night he was seen alive. Footage of Margo dropping a suspicious body-shaped package at the dump site, coupled with the image of my car…that's all she wrote.

Fuck.

That was a lot of "ifs," but, it didn't matter. The fact was, Cordelia didn't make these types of mistakes—I was meticulous.

Except I'd lost the bracelet and missed the camera until after the body disposal. That was *the opposite* of meticulous.

I inhaled a deep breath, steadying my hands.

Everything hinged on the camera; it was the smoking gun. If it uploaded to an app or cloud, giving whoever placed it in the woods instant access into the night's events, I was in trouble. I imagined a poacher hunched forward in his truck, squinting at his smartphone, watching a mousy woman unload a package that looked suspiciously like a body.

I couldn't control the camera. All I could do was cross my fingers and hope like hell it was a dated model.

What could I control?

The bracelet. I needed to find it before Frank was reported missing. If by some miracle, there was no camera footage—the bracelet was the only clue tying Margo to me. And, if it was lost at the swamp, me to the crime scene. *Calm down, Cordelia.* I was getting ahead of myself. Without the camera, the swamp wouldn't be known as a crime scene.

Everything was so tangled in my head, spinning in circles. I fisted my fingers through my hair and pulled, squishing my eyes closed. The tiny prickles of tugged hair helped me focus. The bracelet could give me away. The camera could send me to jail. Simon would love it.

No. Stop. Another shaky breath. *You're not caught until you're caught.* It would be fine. First, check the camera. Then, for the bracelet, retrace my steps. No need to panic.

My gaze landed on the clunky camera. I picked it up, and it

was heavy in my hands as I turned it over and over, searching for a serial number or brand or make or model—anything that would identify what I was working with.

The camera shell was faded, and the dirty plastic was gritty under the pads of my fingers. In the back right corner, it was extra bumpy beneath a patch of dried dirt. I scratched it, manicure be damned, before remembering the screwdriver in my junk drawer. I grabbed it and began scraping. I sat on a barstool at the kitchen island as I worked, scattering dirt over the countertop, until finally, I could make out a brand name stamped into the plastic. Underneath was a model number.

Ten minutes and a panicked google search later, I heaved a sigh of relief. The camera didn't give a live feed.

It was outdated, relying fully on a memory card. This made sense, didn't it? That stretch of forest was protected, and the camera was likely placed by a poacher who wouldn't want to leave a digital trail to their identity.

Using the example on the website along with the screwdriver, it was easy enough to locate the slot and pop out the small plastic memory chip. I considered snapping it in two and tossing it in the trash, but maybe it held important information. Considering my current situation, the more I knew, the better. I grabbed my laptop from the coffee table.

The memory card didn't fit; it required an adapter, because of course it did. Five minutes and several websites later, I clicked add to cart, the weeklong shipping time making me groan. I tucked the tiny piece of plastic safely into a kitchen drawer.

Was it ideal? Hell no. It also wasn't worst-case scenario. The camera's lack of technology bought me time to find the bracelet.

This was too close. The tsunami of adrenaline that had crashed over me in the swamp ebbed with the realization that everything was going to work out. Tomorrow, I'd check for more cameras, find the bracelet, and spend the rest of my time going over my plan, looking for holes, making sure this never happened again.

Crisis averted, I was suddenly aware of the sweat, blood, and swamp grime that covered my skin like an animal's coat. I sniffed. Never good when you could smell yourself.

I headed upstairs for a quick shower, eager to sink back into my ritual. To close Frank's chapter by spreading blood and paint across canvas, completing the process would center me. And God did I need it.

When I was a teenager and seeing the school counselor, she'd taught me after a panic episode, it could be helpful to focus on the positive in a situation. Well. The night wasn't all bad—maybe it could even be considered good. Mini emergencies to show me where I'd grown complacent, even lazy. Like a fire drill, except for body disposal. And I'd almost forgotten Simon's creepy cheating ass would be gone soon. That was a good thing.

A great thing, actually.

Halfway to my bathroom, three succinct raps sounded from the front door.

Who in the hell was coming over this time of night?

The oversized tee I threw on hung to the middle of my thighs, covering everything that needed covering. Good enough for surprise visitors.

I was wrangling my wig-and-sweat-flattened hair into a topknot when three more knocks sounded, followed by, "Knock, knock. I know you're home."

I froze.

What was he doing here? This time of night?

My stomach burned as if it were filled with gasoline, and I'd swallowed a match. Without a word, I padded to the door and swung it open.

He grinned, gunmetal eyes flashing. "Oh good." He stepped toward me and without thinking, I shuffled back, letting him into my home. "You're still up."

"What the hell are you doing here, Simon?" Better yet, *how* was he here? Had Diane pointed out my neighborhood to him once? Had he spotted my car in the driveway? Both seemed unlikely—but I didn't want the answer—not tonight. All I wanted was for him to leave, so I could finish Frank and relax.

"What am I doing here?" Simon sauntered into my kitchen and pulled a barstool toward him, its heavy legs scraped against the tile in a loud *scraaatch*. He propped against it. "That's not the question you should be asking."

"I'm sorry?" I tilted my head slightly. "I don't understand. You know what? It doesn't matter. You need to leave." Frank's blood, Margo's wig, the bag of ruined men's clothes, all sat nearby—a flashing beacon broadcasting the details of my perfectly planned, then perfectly ruined, night. I was careful not to look. "Now."

The size of Simon struck me for the first time. Could he be dangerous, alone with me in my home? What if he attacked me? It was a weird place for my mind to jump, but it wasn't surprising.

I could smell the hate on him. Maybe he'd never hurt anyone, but something told me he'd thought about it. The lizard part of my brain—that gut feeling all women have—said he'd wanted to. The way he'd looked at Sugar, talking down to her. The way he'd grabbed Diane. No. It wasn't surprising.

But if he tried something tonight, in my home, with me...

I swallowed my eager smile, imagining the scene that could play out if I was forced to defend myself. This could be fun. He was bigger than me, sure. But I knew where the knives were.

My heartbeat quickened.

His eyes flashed. "I'll admit, *Cor*, you almost had me fooled. With that whole getup. What was that about anyway?"

"It's *Cordelia*." A strange mix of fear and hope curdled in my stomach. I did not want him here—he needed to leave. But since he *was* here maybe I could... *No*. No matter how badly I wanted it, no matter how good it would feel, Cordelia Black had rules. "And what the hell are you talking about?"

"Cut the shit." He sounded so smug. "I saw you. I saw all of it."

"All of what?" My tone was flat despite my hatred. "Simon, I need to shower and get to bed. Maybe you can get to the point?"

"Damn it, I said knock it off." Simon's voice came in a roar. It wasn't the affable Nice-Guy tone, nor his sleazy wanna-be-pickup-artist growl from the restaurant. This Simon sounded...raw. He took a step toward me, chin raised, eyes narrowed. I remained planted in place, refusing to be intimidated in my own home. If he attacked me, he'd get a fight he wouldn't forget. Simon was taller, but I was strong. And like I said: *knives*.

He raked a hand over his hair—over, not through because, as usual, it was slick with product—and peered down at me. Long seconds ticked by. "I'm not here to play games, *Cor*. I'm here to make a bargain."

"A bargain?"

"That was you tonight at the restaurant." He nodded to Margo's clothes and shoes in the corner, and then the wig on the counter. "No need to deny it."

With an exasperated sigh, I lifted my chin. "What restaurant? What are you talking about?" So that's what this was about. He'd figured out Margo was me. That I'd seen him with another woman, and he was worried. Well, good. He should worry.

"Still not going to admit to anything are you?"

If he expected a confession, he'd need more proof than some literal dirty laundry and a brief glance at a piece of hot pink yarn.

I shrugged. "You've lost your damned mind."

"Yeah. I thought so too, at first." He shook his head. "Doesn't matter—the point is, you looked familiar, and I couldn't let it go."

I clutched my hands in front of me, and bit down hard on my bottom lip. The pain kept me alert—kept me in the moment. The tiny drop of my own blood across my tongue reminded me who I was and what I was capable of.

"I didn't know what I was seeing at first. Did you have a secret OnlyFans? Were you cheating on your cop boy toy? Did you have a thing for costumes and gross old guys? But, I thought, you know what? Doesn't matter. Whatever you were up to, it was clear you didn't want anyone to know about it. I figured if I snapped a photo, then you'd keep your mouth shut to Diane about seeing me with another woman."

"You were with another woman?" I opened my eyes wide, but the shock I forced into my words didn't land, not even to my own ears.

"Cut the shit." Simon grimaced. "God, you're the most annoying bitch I've ever met." He pinched the bridge of his hawkish nose and shook his head. "I know it was you. Don't you want to know how?"

I crossed my arms over my chest, saying nothing.

"See, I put my date in an Uber and waited. Don't get me wrong—I thought I could be losing it. That maybe you'd gotten into my head and I was literally seeing things."

He waited for me?

"Simon, what are you talking about?" My perfected calmness was waning. *He waited for me? Why?* And damn it—*how did he find my house?* It was suddenly a much bigger issue. I narrowed my eyes at the smug bastard. Simon was walking a tightrope, and he didn't even realize it.

He shook his head. "Now I have your attention."

I opened my mouth to speak, but he held up his hand. "Before you say anything, you should know I followed you to your car, watched you load that old man inside. Until that moment, I still wasn't sure. I thought that...that I was going crazy."

"You sound crazy."

"Maybe." He shrugged. "That doesn't mean I'm not speaking the truth."

"What's your game here?" I asked. "What is it you want?"

Simon paused, enjoying the power he thought he held. "Look. I like Diane. I like being in her life. I like everything she has to offer."

Everything she has to offer? "And what exactly does that mean?"

I thought of that moment in Diane's kitchen, when Sugar skipped into the room, sunny and coltish. Simon's eyes had slid over her—a child—he'd called her his good girl. But there'd been no smoke, so I'd convinced myself it was nothing. I'd misread the moment. *A monster behind every bush.*

But now? *All she has to offer.* I shivered.

Simon's cold eyes shifted. I squinted. Could there be something there? Finally? Movement behind his irises.

I shifted forward on the balls of my feet. "Go on." I fixated on his face—on those gunmetal orbs. *Desperately.* That's how bad I wanted to end Simon White. Monster or not.

I won't. I can't. I only kill monsters.

"The thing is"—he scratched the back of his neck and let out a slow breath—"I can't have you telling Diane you saw me on a date with someone else. That wouldn't go over well. That's where me and you—we can help each other out."

The sound of blood thrummed through my ears with each heartbeat. The smart move was to play along with his demands and learn what he knew, or what he thought he knew.

But I didn't have it in me. I was too angry. Furious. He would get nothing from me—not a damn thing.

"You can't stop me from telling my best friend her loser boyfriend is a cheater." My nose wrinkled in disgust. "How the hell did you do it, anyway? Convince Diane you're worth her time." I shook my head. "I don't get it."

He smirked, not nearly as bothered as he should've been. "Who was that man and why did he get in your car? Why was he barely able to walk?"

"He's a work friend. He was drunk. I gave him a ride home. Any more questions?"

"Okay." He nodded. "Sure. That would make sense." He paused and stared straight into my eyes. "If he lived in a storage facility."

Internally I screamed—I wanted to kill him. I *needed* to kill him.

But I couldn't. I was an executioner, not a murderer. No matter what the news said.

Simon continued. "That's right. I followed you. I parked down by the main road and watched you take that poor man into that unit. Then I watched you load him out."

Shit shit shit...

"Load him out?" I scoffed. "I went by my unit to pick up a rug for his apartment. He waited in the car."

"Stop it." Simon waved a hand through the air. "I don't know why, and I don't care. But I know you killed him. I trailed you to that back road, and I pulled off and waited. I was about to give up, when you came flying back like a bat out of hell all the way to your neighborhood. I drove past your house, hid my car down the street, and here we are. I have to say, I'm impressed. I thought you were a psychotic bitch, but this is next-level, *Cor*. You're a murderess."

I didn't flinch. Why should I? I'd done nothing wrong. And who says *murderess* with a straight face, anyway?

"You're a sicko. A *monster*," I said, testing out the word, relishing how it rolled off my tongue when talking about Simon. *Was he, after all? Could he be?* I wanted it so badly, now more than ever.

"Monster? Really? That's what you think? Monsters *kill* people, *Cor*. I've never hurt a soul." He walked around the island, all catlike strides, no Nice-Guy awkwardness. None of the fake timidness from the first time we'd met.

No fakeness at all. This was the real Simon. I watched every silky step, anticipating his next move.

My feet were planted squarely into the tile floor, holding me in place, keeping me from bounding over the island and tackling him.

"Don't worry." He shrugged. "I won't even ask you why you did it. I don't care. Maybe he deserved it. Maybe he didn't. The only thing I care about is you keep my secret and I'll keep yours."

Where was the smoke? Was I wrong?

He sidled closer to me, now six inches away. "You're going to keep your mouth shut, and you're going to stay away from me and Diane. Let us have our life together, or I'm going to tell the police *everything* I saw."

"Why do you even want her?" I hated the desperation in my tone. " Please. Leave them alone."

He knew I'd killed a man; he could feel the rage wafting from me, yet he wasn't afraid. To him, I was a joke. A *silly little woman*. Nothing to fear.

My heart thumped in my ears. My blood whirred through my veins. I wanted him dead.

More than I'd ever wanted anything in my life.

"Aw. You don't have to worry about Diane and Sammy." He tsk-tsked. Nice-Guy was back. "I'll take excellent care of them."

I angled my body toward his and closed the minute gap between us, working hard to keep it together, to remain calm. I could break my code for him. I could do it.

As good as it would feel, I was not a murderer.

I could be, though. For my family, I could be.

The way he'd leered at Sugar—calling her his good girl, his eyes all need and longing. Because I hadn't imagined it.

The way Simon's long fingers had closed around Diane's arm like a vice as he'd yanked her close to him, jealousy burning in his glare.

The way we'd ignored both.

He can't have them. He won't.

There was no smoke. No divine proof. Only a gut feeling. Uncomfortable looks and awkward moments didn't deserve a death sentence. There was blood on my hands, but Cordelia Black was *not* a murderer.

There had to be a way. Perhaps if Simon struck first? My spiraling mind circled back to the first thought I'd had when Simon pushed into my home. *If it was self-defense—that wouldn't break my code.*

I pressed my eyes closed and shook my head, biting hard on my lip until I tasted sweet copper. Digging my nails into my palms until the pain brought me back.

How long had Simon been talking? What was he saying?

"There's just one thing I've been wondering, Cor." He sounded far away. Muffled.

My eye twitched. My hands trembled.

His eyes flickered.

I was sure of it.

"Why do you call her *Sugar*? Is she really that sweet?"

I'd given Samantha the moniker of *Sugar* when she was a little gumdrop of a baby. *Bug* had been added later, because she was a chubby little bug toddling around on dimpled legs. They were precious names. Special names. *Sacred* names.

Sugar's name was twisted and wrong coming from Simon's foul mouth. I was still with rage—the kind of fury that traps you in place.

"I guess—" His voice trailed into laughter, the sound barking and sharp, like a man gasping for air. "I guess I'm going to find out."

The flicker in his eyes was undeniable. It caught like a spark lighting the wick of a candle.

I blinked. Time stopped.

I wasn't imagining it; I couldn't be. Tongues of gray leapt from behind his irises, flicking up and over the whites of his eyes.

There was no sound but the rasp of my breath and the whoosh of my pulse. My vision blurred around the edges, wavy and distorted like heat rising from summertime concrete. All I could see was Simon's face—his eyes. His smoke.

My blood, salty and metallic, dribbled from my lip, down my chin.

Time began again, but everything swirled in slow motion.

And then, inside myself, a switch flipped, unspooling a peacefulness.

I smiled big. My charming smile. My feline smile.

Tonight, my blood smile.

Like every other man, Simon smiled back. It was automatic.

"You don't get to call her that." The words came without venom—spoken so clear and nonchalantly, I could've been asking about the weather. "You don't get to call her anything."

His brows knitted, and he opened his mouth to respond, but I'll never know what he was going to say.

I swiped the screwdriver from the countertop, the one I'd used to scratch away the dirt from the game camera, and lunged forward, thrusting it into Simon's neck. He howled in pain as confusion waltzed with the smoke in his eyes.

I wrenched the screwdriver free and plunged it into his chest. He dropped to his knees, gurgling from the back of his throat, as I planted my foot in his abdomen and pushed him backward. In a flash, I pounced on top of him, again yanking free the tool. Blood spurted from the neck wound with each beat of his monster heart, landing around us in fat red raindrops. He grabbed at me, but he was weak and slow—and too late. I plunged the tool into his throat, once, twice, three more times.

He would never hurt my family. *Never.*

Out of breath, I collapsed onto his chest. The warmth of Simon's fresh blood was slick against my cheek.

A shiver rolled through me.

As quickly as it appeared, the monster's smoke was gone.

SIMON'S BLOOD SMEARED ACROSS MY FACE AND DRIED ON my thighs in crusty streaks. My fingers curled around the screwdriver, while my knees were splayed on either side of the monster's chest.

Diane thought she might love this man. But the person she'd fallen for wasn't real—he'd been created to infiltrate her life—a cuckoo in the songbird's nest.

I'd killed him in the moment, no plan, no waiting.

So unlike me.

So dangerous.

So...*extraordinary*.

I held a deep breath until my lungs burned. When I'd plunged the screwdriver deep into his neck and chest, I'd left my body. I'd hovered above our fight and watched as I stabbed Simon over and over, and was only now settling back into myself, fully aware of every muscle, every bone, every tendon clicking inside me.

I'd never killed twice in a single night and the buzz of the unbridled electricity of it was intoxicating. But as the primal, emotional part of me settled and the thinking bits of my brain snapped on, there was also panic.

There'd been smoke—I'd seen it. It was real.

So why had it disappeared? Why had it not wafted away, unspooling slowly like every monster before him? Even Tristan's smoke had lingered, purple and foul as sulphur.

I'd needed there to be smoke so badly... People see what they want to see...a monster behind every bush.

No. I clenched my jaw. *It was real. It had to be real. I have a code.*

Simon's blood was everywhere.

I'd not planned this, and I knew—*I knew*—that killing required planning for good reason. Sloppiness got you caught. Rules kept you safe. I'd broken every single one of my rules.

Not all of them—there'd been smoke. It was real. It had to be real.

I slid from atop the corpse and tried to stand.

The thinking part of my brain—the reasonable part, the Cordelia part—shifted into high gear. There was work to do.

Blood spray fanned out like a hurricane with Simon at its eye. My knees went weak, and I sat down hard on the sticky floor.

It was Friday. From what Diane had said, Simon had stopped working weekends to have more time to hang out with her, so that bought me a little time before the hospital would notice he was gone.

When Diane couldn't get in touch with him, would she worry? Or be pissed? What about the woman from the restaurant? It struck me how little I knew of the monster—*because he was a monster, damn it.* Usually I committed to memory my prey's routines, their families, everything down to the most boring detail. It was a prerequisite to finding their way to my workshop. This—killing in a moment—was new and dangerous ground.

Simon told me he'd followed me—he'd watched me. Had he snapped pics? I shoved a hand in one of his pants pockets. Empty. The next one was empty as well.

"Simon, you sonofabitch, where is it?"

His left arm slapped against the tile, slick with blood, when I heaved him onto his stomach. His phone was in his back pocket.

It was locked. I took Simon's hand and mashed his index finger to the cracked screen, and it clicked open.

I scrolled through the photos, until I found it—the hidden album. Monsters thought they were so smart—there was always a secret album.

There were no photos of me or Margo or Frank or the night's events. What I found was worse.

Simon was sick and if I'd let him live, my family wouldn't have escaped unscathed. I silently cursed myself for ever doubting my intuition.

Simon had a fascination with hurt women and girls. His appetite was for the bruised and broken. Photos of sleeping patients—women and girls mostly, but a few boys too—in their hospital beds, IVs burrowing into their arms as they lay deathly still. Simon was a nurse—the horror of it hit me all at once. What had Simon done with these images? My skin prickled and crawled, but I kept scrolling. Screenshots of photos that appeared to be from message boards—photos of college girls passed out in different places and positions—some with busted lips or black eyes, others with vomit crusted in the corners of their dry mouths. The photos also captured the comments posted below each picture, rating the women, degrading them. *The things I could do to that cunt! I could make her scream...make her cry...make her like it.*

From there, things grew darker. Grimier. Women shackled and harmed—their bodies smeared with blood. Maybe it was consensual—a disgusting violence kink that I could never understand. Flipping to the next page, it was obvious that wasn't true. More shackles. More harm. No more women. *Girls*—young as Sugar. Adolescent bodies and terrified faces. Simon may or may not have ever enacted on his fantasies, but these pictures made him complicit. The internet is dark and deep and Simon had made full use of it.

My chest writhed as if it were full of a worms trying to climb up my esophagus. I swallowed hard. From the very beginning, I'd been right. Simon was a monster. A cruel, disgusting monster.

I closed the app.

He couldn't hurt Sugar. He couldn't hurt Diane. He couldn't hurt anyone ever again.

I turned off the phone and removed the SIM card, then put both in the drawer of my buffet. Like I did with the phones of all my monsters, I'd destroy the evidence before I got rid of the body.

Which would be when, exactly? And how?

My body snatcher was motivated by greed and greed was reliable. But two bodies in a single night was pushing it. I'd only killed Gerald a week ago. Even Clarence must have limits on what he chose not to see.

My gaze traveled to the island where the game camera sat, chipped open. Taking Simon to my usual dump site wasn't an option, anyway. Not until I swept the area—and possibly not after. I couldn't risk getting caught by some Bubba poaching deer on public land.

It had taken a long time to discover the off-road, forgotten stretch of forest. Even longer to scout it and assure it was indeed unused. Simply choosing another parcel of property at random was not the move.

This required research. Meticulous care. First, I'd revisit the old site and I'd find the bracelet. Search for cameras. Then make my decision.

As far as when… Well, Simon had an expiration date. I pressed my palm against Simon's slack-jawed face. Bodies bloat. They smell. They lose their beauty. I had a week, tops.

I'd call Clarence next Friday. That would give me time to figure everything out.

This delivery was sooner than usual, but it would be fine. It had to be, because what other choice was there?

I patted Simon's cheek. Dealing with a corpse for a week wasn't so bad.

Nothing to it.

If I were going to do this—*like I had a choice*—then I needed supplies.

And a plan. *Always* a plan.

First things first: getting through the night. I began a mental list.

Move Simon's car. Clean the mess. Store the body.

Where?

"The bathtub!" I blurted. He could stay in the guest tub until body-dump day. Then I'd cocoon him up, same as always, and sell him to Clarence. No big deal.

Right.

My phone buzzed on the counter. Who in their right mind would be calling me this late?

I looked to where Simon was splayed in his own blood. Well. I knew who it wasn't.

I checked caller ID. Christopher. Last we'd talked, he'd mentioned working a few nights this week, and I'd joked about me being a night owl. At the time, I'd imagined late-night conversations where I lulled him into a comfortable rhythm and he let important information slip.

Now was not the time. I sent him to voicemail.

Immediately a text came through.

CHRISTOPHER: You awake? You said you were a night owl. 

ME: About to shower. Call you when I get out.

CHRISTOPHER: I was picking up food for myself and remembered you said you've never had Lotus Chinese.

Christopher sent a pic. An open bag filled with orange and white striped take-out containers were nestled in the passenger seat of his patrol unit.

I huffed and stared down at Simon. The hollow spaces beneath his eyes had darkened into purple pools. Things were settling, and the longer I waited, the harder it would be to move him. This conversation with Christopher was dragging out too long.

ME: Sounds amazing. Enjoy, gotta go!

There was no time for Sweet Cordelia. Not now.

The second I set my phone on the island, it buzzed again.

CHRISTOPHER: Surprise! I'm coming over to drop some off.

Oh dear god. What was it with men and thinking they could pop by whenever they wanted? And night owl or not, who dropped food off this late?

ME: Rain check? It's late. I'm exhausted.

I looked down the length of my body at the smears of crusted blood.

ME: And kind of funky. Aren't you working?

...

...

CHRISTOPHER: Yes. Slow night. I won't tell if you won't. I'm in your neighborhood. Won't take long. Promise.

CHRISTOPHER: If you're feeling funky, I can hang out for a bit and take care of you. You need anything? Besides food?

I rolled my eyes. Why did men think it was cute to pester you into changing your mind? This always happened to Sweet Cordelia. Well. Not *exactly* this—*this* was a first. But when I was nice, my boundaries were treated as suggestions.

ME: No. I'm fine. I want to sleep. How about we get lunch tomorrow?

CHRISTOPHER: Too late! I'm practically there. Hey! I can't

get your painting out of my head. Maybe when I'm dropping off the takeout, I can see more of your art? You're so talented.

I looked around. He wanted to see my art?

Well, my art was splattered all over the room, and something told me that Christopher wouldn't appreciate it.

I YANKED THE BLOOD-SOAKED TEE OVER MY HEAD, THEN peeled off my bra and panties, and hotfooted it up the stairs to my bedroom, butt-naked and hoping like hell I wasn't leaving red footprints in my wake.

Fuck me for letting Christopher pick me up for Diane's barbecue—for letting him know where I lived.

Of course, at the time, if anyone would've told me I wouldn't want McSmiley to come over because I had a corpse in the middle of my floor, I'd have laughed in their face. Because Cordelia Black wouldn't take that kind of risk. Killing in my own home? Never.

Where did Christopher get this stupid idea anyway? Who wants food delivered this late? Damn Sweet Cordelia and her irresistible ways. She was cute and helpless and patriarchal catnip.

I slid into my bedroom and winced at my reflection in the floor length mirror. Strands of my bleached hair were crimson with

Simon's blood. My hands were covered. My arms. My chin was slick with it, as if Simon was the world's juiciest piece of watermelon and I'd taken a big bite.

There was the sound of a vehicle—*Christopher?*—pulling into my driveway. I froze. The front door—had I locked it? Of course I had; I never forgot. But then again, I was never followed by a monster, either. I never left evidence behind at the dump site. Never got caught on camera. Never killed without a plan.

It was an evening of firsts.

Shit.

I yanked my oversized robe—threadbare and ancient—from my closet, and its hanger rattled to the ground. Terry cloth stuck to my blood-dampened skin as I slid it on while sprinting into my attached bathroom. I grabbed a washcloth and cleaned up as well as I could, but it was no use—the blood smeared across my face, stuck in the creases of nose and crusted near my hairline. This was going to take forever.

I didn't have forever. *Think, Cordelia.*

A million bottles and tubes lined the counter around my sink. My fingers walked over each one, knocking some to the ground, before grabbing a tube of violet-pigmented hair conditioner to keep those blond highlights bright! *This could work.* I squeezed enough for three heads into my palms, then yanked it through my bloody tresses, covering the crimson splotches and streaks. I knotted my conditioner-caked hair into a bun on top of my head and covered with one of the disposable shower caps I kept on hand for deep-conditioning treatments.

I leaned close to the mirror. The blood in my hair wasn't noticeable beneath the mess of purple conditioner. Perfect. My face, however, was still a problem. Time was running out. Christopher would be at my doorstep. Probably I hadn't locked the door. Probably he'd walk right inside. Probably I'd spend the rest of my life in prison with Diane hating me and Sugar ashamed that her godmother was a murderer.

Fucking Simon.

That couldn't happen. How did I hide the evidence on my face? Cover it up—same as I had with the conditioner and robe.

I tore through the products on my counter a second time, this time picking each one up and tossing it aside. Toner? *No.* Serums? *Not helpful.* Snail mucus? *What was I supposed to do with that?*

Algae facial mask? That...okay, yes. I squeezed a glob into my hand and smeared the deep-green goop across my cheeks and forehead until only my eyes peeked through. Did I look great? *No.* In fact, I looked horrible. But neither did I look as if I'd soaked in enough blood to make Elizabeth Bathory jealous.

I found a few abandoned self-tanning mitts in one of the drawers, left over from my oompa-loompa era. Hey, we all make mistakes. I pulled on a pair. They were out of place, but were so much better than bloody fingers. Christopher didn't seem like the guy who'd notice. Hopefully.

I ran to my bedroom to grab slippers, but outside a car door slammed. I peeked out the window. Christopher was strolling up my walk, his arms filled with bags of Chinese food—enough for an army. Leaping down the stairs and racing past Simon, I made it to the front door and slipped out. Christopher wasn't close enough to see inside, nor to insist I let him in. But Mango was.

The dog appeared from nowhere and scampered between my legs. Of course she was outside this time of night. Made perfect sense.

I paused before the glitch in my brain worked itself out, and I pulled the door closed. If Mango was traumatized from what she'd find in my kitchen, it was her own nosy fault.

"Hey," Christopher said. "You okay? What's that on your face?"

I frowned. "It's a facial mask. Self-care, you know? I've felt sick all day."

He held up the Chinese takeout. "Then let me take care of you. I have a window of time where I won't be missed." He tried to scoot past me, but I sashayed in front of him, pointedly.

"You're sweet, but not now, okay? Thanks for the food. Really. I'll call you tomorrow." How else could I say it? *Leave.*

"You sure?" His brows furrowed. "If you're sick, let me help." Oh right. He was a cub scout. Of course he'd want to fix things.

"I, um." *Think, Cordelia... Get rid of him.* My gaze dropped demurely, one of Sweet Cordelia's best moves. "It's just..." I almost gasped at what I saw. Thick flecks of blood dotted the top of my feet. I'd forgotten the slippers. I'd ran into my bedroom, but instead of grabbing them, I'd looked out the window. Christopher had been so close.

Shit. I looked up before he could follow my line of sight.

What would McSmiley do if he noticed my bloody feet?

Bloody feet. Blood.

"I'm cramping." I frowned. It was the ace-in-the-hole to get rid of most men—even former Boy Scouts. "I'd rather not get into the details of my *cycle*, if that's okay with you."

Panic spread over McSmiley's face. "Oh. Uh—"

"All I want is to lie on the couch, *by myself*."

Inside the house, Mango chortled loud enough to wake the dead—not literally, thank god.

"At least let me get the neighbor's dog and take her home. Then I'll get out of your hair. You can stretch out and eat Chinese while watching all the ID channel you want." He moved to step past me again. Again, I blocked him. It was an awkward dance.

"You know?" I couldn't believe what I was about to say. "I think I want to...cuddle...with Mango."

Another round of barking sounded from inside, like Mango had overheard and also hated the idea.

"You must be feeling rough." He chuckled. "You sure? About Mango? I thought you said she was a 'devil dog'?"

I closed my eyes and inhaled deeply, then nodded. "Yes. Mango cuddles sound...great."

He passed me the bags of takeout, and I took them in my clumsy mitted hands. Christopher sighed. "I'm sorry if I'm annoying you with this. Diane said you were—"

"Diane put you up to this?" *Of course.* I shook my head.

"Well, yeah. She said you were having a rough time at work, and I should do something nice."

Aw. That tracked. This was exactly the kind of gesture that swept my bestie off her feet. I smiled. My face was beginning to itch from the algae and blood. "That's sweet. I didn't know you and Diane talked."

"We don't really. We traded numbers at the barbecue so we can make future plans for all of us. This is the first time she's texted me, though. I thought maybe you knew about it?"

"No." I shook my head. The dried facial mask cracked from Sweet Cordelia's forced, overly bright smile. Because if Diane would like it, then Sweet Cordelia would too. And, okay, it was a nice gesture—just incredibly bad timing. "I didn't tell Diane to tell you to surprise me with food."

"Oh. Okay." He frowned, disappointed. "Well."

"Well," I echoed.

"Guess I'll see you later then?"

"Sure." *Wait. No. Be sweet.* Inside information would be more useful now than ever, all things considered. I cocked my head to the side, batting my lashes—probably not as effective considering my current cosmetic situation. "Yes. We'll make plans when I'm feeling better. And thank you. For the food."

"Don't mention it." For once, McSmiley didn't smile. He stood awkwardly a moment longer, like he wasn't quite sure how to end the encounter. *Leave! Just leave!* my inner voice yelled, until finally, he walked back to his car, his strides long and confident.

I waited until his cruiser disappeared from my neighborhood before I returned inside and set the food on the table, then slid off the mitts. My bloodied hands looked like I'd been in a horrible accident.

Oh god—what if, after listening to my excuse about my period—Christopher had pushed his way into the house and saw all the blood splattered around the room? What would he think? I chuckled, remembering the story of how NASA sent a hundred tampons for Sally Ride on her six-day space voyage. The horror that would've played over Christopher's face would've made it almost worth it...if Diane's dead boyfriend hadn't been lying in the middle of it all like a macabre centerpiece.

Fucking Simon.

Mango whined from her post near the fridge.

I got her cheese, which she snapped from my fingers, but before I could grab her, she darted toward Simon, her nails tapping against the kitchen tile. She slid into the corpse and rolled onto her back, wiggling through the blood as if she were checking something off her bucket list. "Oh, no. Mango, you bitch."

The white poodle mix looked as if she'd been attacked. This night kept getting longer and longer, because there was no way I could return Mango like this. Sticky crimson splotches matted her long curly fur in streaks and globs. Great.

My own shower had to wait. I quickly splashed water on my face at the kitchen sink and wiped off most of the itchy mask, then scooped up the dog, who now lay on top of Simon's stomach. To the downstairs bathroom we went.

I ran her a bath, then tossed her collar onto the counter. When I plunged Mango into the water, it bloomed the hue of strawberry puree. Everything felt surreal; there was a corpse in my kitchen, yet here I was, bathing my neighbor's dog. Wild.

After two shampoos, Mango no longer looked like she was bleeding out, but she still couldn't go home. On ID channel, it was always something dumb that got people caught—some oversight or random screwup.

Mango would not be my random screwup.

Her hair was matted and stringy with stained splotches of Simon's DNA. There'd be no explaining that away—not to nosy Mr. Percival.

She'd have to be shaved first—all evidence of Simon removed. I could tell Mr. Percival she got into an open container of paint and a haircut was the only way to get it off. It was almost the truth, actually. Maybe after this he'd do a better job of keeping her away from my house.

Mango yelped, and with her big brown eyes and pathetic wet face, she was almost cute. Almost. I gave her a pat on the head. "You need professional help."

I'd find a groomer first thing tomorrow. Last time Mango escaped late at night, Mr. Percival hadn't realized she was gone until morning. Fingers crossed history repeated itself. Last thing I needed was that grouchy old coot knocking on my door when I was dealing with...everything.

"Come on." I scooped the damp dog into my arms and we trotted upstairs. After moving my shoes to the top shelf, I plopped Mango in the most muffled room in my home—my walk-in closet. She'd be fine.

There were more important things to worry about than the minor comforts of the devil dog.

Things like the corpse in my kitchen.

With Mango handled, I intended to jump in the shower, but was overtaken by the urge to recheck to front door's lock. Paranoid? Yeah, okay, maybe. Who would've unlocked it? Definitely not Simon. But after a night like I'd had, I think I earned the right to a little paranoia.

I unlocked, and relocked the door, then jiggled the knob. Satisfied that no one could open it from the outside, I bounded back upstairs and took the hottest shower of my life. Under the scalding spray is where my best ideas happened, and by the time I shut off the water, I knew exactly what I'd do.

My stomach rumbled as I dressed. Might as well eat. My night was only getting started, and I could use the energy boost.

I took the Chinese food to my sofa and sat cross-legged, shoveling noodles into my mouth and staring at Simon in the kitchen. His head peeked out from behind the island. The entire kitchen was a mess—footprints and blood spray everywhere. If Simon had shown his smoke in the beginning, this could've been avoided. He could be wrapped in a tidy cocoon.

Oh well. He was gone. That's all that mattered.

One last bite, and I set the take-out container on the coffee table and dusted my hands together. Time to get to work. I had a body to move.

A monster to impersonate.

First things first, I loaded Simon onto an extra blanket from the linen closet, and thanks to years of practice, moved him to my guest bathroom, smearing only a little blood in the process. Lifting him into the tub was harder, but I managed. Next, I stripped him and tossed his clothes into my washing machine. I'd need them for my plan.

I changed my own clothes, pulling on some tights, a sweater, and a pair of sneakers before heading to the store. If Simon was going to be my roommate, then I had some shopping to do.

MY FIRST KILLS WERE MESSY AFFAIRS, BUT THEY'D EACH taught me an important lesson. For one thing, it didn't take as long as you'd imagine for decomposition to begin.

The memory of those first monsters with their lolling heads and empty eyes, their stench growing worse each day as I kept them hidden in the woods, or an abandoned building, or even, one time, their own home—it sent a chill up my spine. I would not share my house with a decaying monstrosity. Simon must be kept fresh until he was delivered to Clarence.

I needed ice.

Probably all the ice.

The fluorescent bulbs of the twenty-four-hour market hummed and washed everything in its sallow, sad light. I preferred Sasperella's on the other side of town. It was quaint, carrying farm-to-grocer meats and locally sourced produce, as well as organic cleaning products scented with essential oils that left my home smelling like a lemon orchard on the Amalfi coast.

Organic floor cleaner couldn't help me now. My situation required bleach. Lots and lots of bleach. And mops and rags and buckets. A new tarp.

Bleach. Mop. Rags. Buckets. Tarp. Ice.

The list kept growing.

My shopping cart squeaked and wiggled from a faulty wheel as I hurried down one aisle and then the next, tossing in supplies with abandon. I took a sharp turn down the pet care section to grab a small bag of dog food. Mango was going home right after her haircut, but she'd need breakfast. Not that I cared. *Dumb devil-dog.*

I jerked my cart to a stop to keep from plowing into an elderly woman with cottony-poofed hair. Her hunter green sweatshirt was baggy, hanging almost to her knees, and was emblazoned with a giant sequined cat on the front.

She strained under the weight of a hulking bag of kitty litter and smiled at me as she plopped it into her cart, which held three more bags of the same brand. "It's the best, you know. I have six cats, and you can't smell a thing. I know all cat owners say that, but it's true at my house." She beamed, her perfectly straight, milky-white dentures on display. "It clumps up all the moisture and traps the odor, exactly like the commercial says. You know the one? That commercial with the singing kitties? They're so precious and—"

"You can't smell anything? Not with six cats?"

She shook her head, and her earrings—gold cats with green gemstones for eyes—bounced against her wrinkled cheeks. "Nope. Not a thing."

Genius.

I pushed past the woman and heaved a bag of the kitty litter into my cart, on top of my cleaning supplies and dog food. The woman's squinting eyes turned to saucers as I pulled the entirety of the remaining bags from the shelves, stacking them under the cart and in the child seat.

"I'm Betty, by the way." She pushed her glasses higher on her pug nose. I gave her a smile—the one I saved for old ladies and children—but ignored the cue to introduce myself.

"I hate to be nosy, dearie." Betty didn't sound like she hated it at all. "But you must have a real predicament on your hands."

I froze. "Why do you say that?"

"You have nine bottles of bleach and now you're stacking kitty litter into your buggy like you're stockpiling for kitten doomsday. What happened? Your cat eat a frog?"

"Huh?" I didn't have time for this.

"You know…a frog? Nothing will give your cats a tummy problem like the wrong frog." She rubbed her own round paunch.

"Oh. Yeah. A frog," I said. "Lots of frogs. A whole mess of frogs." I began to push my cart away.

"How many do you have?" Betty asked.

"What?" I stopped. "How many frogs?"

"No, dearie. Cats. How many cats do you have? Buying that much kitty litter, it must be a ton. Is it more than six? It must be more than six." She rocked back and forth on her sensible flats, vibrating with excitement at the idea of a ton of smelly shitting felines. "I hope that dog food isn't for them. Dog food isn't good for kitties, you know."

"No, it's not. And I have...um...twelve. Twelve cats. One dog. Now, I'm sorry, I have to run. You know—that frog situation."

"Oh, of course." Betty's voice grew solemn. "I shouldn't have kept you. You go home to your poor kitties. They need you now more than ever."

I shook my head. Only freaks came to the market after midnight. But I couldn't be annoyed with the shitty-kitty Betty. I didn't have cats, but she'd helped me out, regardless.

Kitty litter was going to work so much better than ice.

The thing about blood is, it travels.

I squatted on my kitchen floor with a scrub brush and a pail of bleach water, cursing Simon all the while. This should've happened neatly, encapsulated by plastic sheeting. Celebrated with paint and canvas.

At least my floors could be salvaged. My manicure, well, blood and bleach do bad things to gel acrylic.

I was already sick of Simon, so I put off dealing with him until last.

The tip of my tongue peeked from between my teeth as I scrubbed. My mind wandered to Joanie. She would've cried herself to sleep. While I was consumed with rage, Joanie would've been soppy with useless tears—making a hard situation harder, same as she always had.

If she were here now, if I'd let her live, she'd turn us in. Maybe her tears coupled with the pictures on Simon's phone would've even bought us mercy. Maybe the judge would've pitied us and only given us a little more time than he'd have given Simon, if Simon would've even been arrested for owning those photos. But I, Cordelia, didn't have to worry about that.

I bundled up any materials holding so much as a hint of death, packing them into my handy-dandy outdoor fire pit, where I was reminded of Frank. Had it only been hours since his execution? It felt like weeks. Months. Yet, it was lacking.

The interruption of Frank's metamorphosis gnawed at me like a vulture picking clean a roadside carcass. I should feel at peace. Happy in the knowledge that I'd once again done a good thing. Instead, I was left with an unfinished sensation. Uneasy, like I desperately needed to yawn and couldn't. It was Simon's fault. He'd stolen that from me—that sense of finality.

I moved Frank's paint can to the back of my fridge, because eventually—I assured myself—I'd finish his art piece. I had to.

I'd almost forgotten about Mango; she'd been so quiet. A good little devil. I poured some of the kibble I'd purchased into a bowl and took it upstairs. "Mango, I have something for yo—" I opened my closet door and my words caught in my throat. Mango was quiet because she was sleeping contentedly.

In a nest she'd made from my prized 1960s Givenchy nightgown.

How? She would've had to jump—no, leap—to catch the hem of the short frock. And why—*why?*—this gown? Clearly the demon had good taste, but other, longer, easier-to-access dresses and skirts and pants were *right there.* Items that were more expensive, sure, but replaceable. The Givenchy was special. Mint condition and thrifted from an estate sale Diane had dragged me to ten years ago, it was one of the first designer pieces I'd ever purchased.

Of course this would happen tonight. Why not? Everything else had gone wrong, why shouldn't the devil rip my soul to shreds?

She never stirred as I set her bowl on the floor and eased the door closed.

I'd mourn the Givenchy later.

Simon's clothes, charcoal slacks and dark button-down, were finished washing and drying. They were stained, but not in a way that screamed, *This is blood! Look at me! Murder, murder!* His pants were too long, and his shirtsleeves swallowed my wrists, but I was confident I wouldn't draw a second look from a stranger. With my hair shoved under a cap and Simon's keys in my pocket, I left to find his truck. It didn't take long in my smallish neighborhood; it was parked down the street, exactly as he'd said.

I took a quick joyride to a rougher part of town, where I left Simon's windows down, and the keys and a wad of cash on the driver's seat, then walked half a block and caught the bus. By the time I arrived home, exhaustion had set in, but my night wasn't even close to being over.

The idea of pulling Simon out of the bathtub made my muscles scream, and for a second, I wished I'd simply bought the damn ice. It would've been easier—plug the tub and pour it in until Simon was chilled like a bottle of champagne on New Year's Eve. Too late now. Shitty-kitty Betty said the litter wicked away moisture and stench. I was banking on it being the better choice long-term, since I didn't have to deal with melting.

I hauled Simon over the tub's edge, onto the cold ceramic tile, then spread a new tarp over the bottom of the bathtub, because while I was no plumber, I imagined kitty litter and drainpipes didn't mix. Then, back into the tub Simon went, landing with a thump, his body twisted at odd angles. He stared at me as I tore open the bags and buried him in kitty litter.

"What do you think you're looking at?" I tried to push his head further into the tub, to cover it as well. No use, Simon was too tall. Well. He wouldn't be here long. It was fine.

It had to be.

The last of the night's garbage—*empty kitty litter bags, Frank and Simon's clothes, my receipt from the late-night purchase*—were added to the fire pit, and I watched as the evidence went up in smoke.

After another shower and fresh pajamas, I finally slid into bed. I was drifting off when there was a noise in the closet.

Scritch-scratch. Scritch-scratch.

I'd forgotten about the dog.

Mango scratched again, this time adding a high-pitched whine.

"No," I called. "I hate you. Go to sleep."

She whined louder. I pulled a pillow over my head, but it was no use. Her moans were nails on a chalkboard.

"Fine." I threw back my covers and got up. "You win. The Givenchy wasn't enough—I guess you need my bed too." I yanked open the closet door, and Mango stared up at me in the filtered blue moonlight.

She yipped.

"Come on." Mango followed on my heels as I fell back into bed, then she burrowed beneath the duvet and snuggled next to my legs. There was something oddly comforting about the slow, rhythmic rise and fall of her tiny sleeping body. "I still hate you," I whispered, but stroked the back of her head, which, despite being washed twice, was crusty with beads of dried blood.

Diane was free. Sugar was safe. Mango would go home tomorrow with a fresh haircut.

And Simon was sitting in a human-sized cat box like the piece of shit he was.

Everything was working out.

I was almost a sleep when I thought I heard someone outside calling, "Mango! Where are you? Mango."

The little dog snuggled closer to me, a growl vibrating her tiny body. I strained to listen, but I didn't hear it again. It was probably nothing. Maybe paranoia.

That night I dreamt someone was banging on my door.

SOMETHING WARM AND WET SLID OVER MY LIPS. MY EYES popped open. Mango was sprawled on my pillow, peering into my face. Her pink tongue hung from her mouth, and her breath was meaty and wet. "Ick." I wiped dog spit from my face with the hem of my pajama shirt and sat up.

Mango yipped, then spun in tight circles across my bed. "Okay. I'm up. And don't worry—you're going home today."

She hopped into my lap at the same moment someone pounded on the front door.

Her ears perked, and I clamped my hand lightly over her snout. "Shh," I ordered, as if she could understand. Scooping Mango up, I hurried to the window.

The front stoop wasn't visible from my bedroom, but it didn't matter. I knew who it was.

Mango squirmed in my arms like she'd been struck with a bolt of electricity. Another low growl rumbled through her.

"Calm down." I plopped her back into the closet. "Keep quiet and I'll give you all the cheese you want." I shut the closet, then hurried downstairs.

I slid through the kitchen. Last night, under the soft glow of the sixty-watt bulbs, it appeared I'd done a fair job cleaning. Now, the unforgiving streams of sunshine puddling across my floor told a different story. Stray splatters speckled the bottoms of cabinets and caked into the tile's grout. There was even a crimson splotch or two on a couple walls.

More booming knocks. What was wrong with this man? "Coming," I called out.

I plastered on my brightest smile and answered the door.

"Where is she?" Mr. Percival glared at me.

"Who?" My voice came out dismayed. I'd hoped to avoid Mr. Percival until Mango was clean, then drop her at his house, claiming she'd gotten into my studio and covered herself with paint, and *Yes, I did have her shaved for you because I'm such a great neighbor.* So much for that.

"I know Mango's in there." He craned his neck to peer past me.

I stepped onto my front stoop and pulled the door closed. "Mr. Percival, what in the world are you talking about?" So far, I hadn't even needed to lie. "I woke up to you banging on my door because you think...what? That I have your evil dog?"

His eyes narrowed behind his wire-rimmed spectacles. "That's exactly what I think." Mr. Percival held up his phone with a liver-spotted hand. His fingers wrapped around it like gnarled tree roots. "I know you have her. It says so right here."

"What's this?"

"Mango keeps getting out no matter what I do, so I ordered her this newfangled collar. Has a GPS tracking built in. Shows her at your house, right now."

Shit. I thought old people were supposed to hate technology. "I don't know what to tell you. She's not here."

He pressed his lips together, his eyes narrowing into slits. "Young lady, if it's all the same to you, I'd like to see for myself."

There was blood splatter across the kitchen. A body in the bathtub. Not to mention I actually did have his furry demon. "No."

"No?" His voice ticked upward in surprise.

I shook my head. "No, you can't come into my home. Not right now."

"Why not?" He shifted in his orthopedic sneakers. "If you have nothing to hide?"

I widened my smile, but could feel the tremble building in both my fingers and eyelid. "Why am I not going to let an angry man accusing me of dognapping into my home first thing in the morning? Oh, I don't know. Because I don't want to?"

He stared a moment more. "I paid a lot of money for Mango. She's a designer breed and I'm going to make a good return on her investment."

"Investment?" I asked.

"Puppies," he said as if I were the dimmest person alive. "She's going to have lots and lots of puppies for me to sell. You can bet your butt I'm not about to let someone steal her. This device says she's here. You won't get away with this."

Lots and lots of puppies? *Poor Mango.* I'd run away too.

I nodded to the phone, still held in front of him like a weapon. "Have you considered this doesn't mean Mango's here—only that her collar's somewhere around? She could've come in the yard and gotten out of it. You know she's a regular Houdini."

He considered this and nodded. "Maybe."

"I shouldn't do this, since you barged over here and accused me of being a thief, but why don't you look around the front yard for her collar, and I'll check the back."

Mr. Percival opened his mouth to speak, seemed to think the better of it, and snapped it closed. He nodded.

I left the old man on my stoop, locking the front door in case he decided he wanted to have a look around after all. I snatched Mango's collar from the bathroom counter, careful not to look at Simon, and ran to my backyard.

My yard wasn't big, most of it taken up by my patio, which held my fire pit, an outdoor lounging set, and some Adirondack chairs. Flowerpots sat empty, or with brittle plant skeletons, because I'd lied; monsters weren't all I killed. My eyes landed on a patch of soft dirt near the yard's back corner. Perfect.

I rubbed the collar through the soil. Once it was good and dirty, I squeezed through the gate of my backyard privacy fence, leaving it slightly open.

"Is this it?"

Mr. Percival was kicking through the grass under a mimosa tree next to my house. He held out his hands as I approached.

"I found it near my trash bin in the back." I handed him the filthy collar.

His face fell as he inspected the pink nylon. "How did she get back there?"

"My gate was ajar."

"Pretty irresponsible, don't you think?"

I was running out of patience. "Do I think it's irresponsible that my gate was open? *Me*, who doesn't have pets or children? It was *your* dog who got out, who is always pooping in my yard, digging holes, and sprinting into my house." Shredding my beloved Givenchy nightgown. Rolling on a corpse in my kitchen. Leaving bloody paw prints everywhere.

The old man rubbed at the right side of his chest as he considered what I was saying.

"Look." I took a deep breath; I didn't need him keeling over from a heart attack in front of my house. What if one of the first responders wanted to come inside to use the bathroom or something? "I'm sure Mango's fine. She's likely snuggled up in someone's bed. They'll probably look for her owner today. You'll have her back before nightfall."

"You think so?"

"I do," I said.

His eyes perked up. "Maybe I'll make some flyers."

"I'm sure that's not neccess—"

"That's exactly what I'll do." He waved an index finger in the air. "Paper the neighborhood with flyers. That way whoever has her will have no excuse." He turned abruptly and marched back across the street. "Nobody steals from Percival C. Manchester and gets away with it."

Great. Missing dog posters would make everything so much easier.

I set my coffee mug on the nightstand and used my cell to google groomers. Eight were open on Saturdays. I called the first one.

Booked.

Second one.

No answer.

I continued down the list with no luck. Finally, on number eight I was able to get an appointment...in two weeks.

"That... No," I stuttered. "Please, I need something today."

"Hah!" The person on the other end of the phone laughed.

When I said nothing, they added, "Oh. You're not joking. Honey, nobody you'd want to trust with your dog is going to have a day-of appointment on a Saturday."

"It's an emergency," I explained. Mango nuzzled her head under my hand, and I gave her a pat.

The groomer sighed into the receiver. "Tell you what—I'll bump you to the top of my cancellation list and give you a call if something opens up. That's the best I can do."

"Okay." I tried and failed to muster some enthusiasm. "Thanks."

How was I going to keep Mango for two weeks? The prospect of keeping Simon was less daunting; I didn't have to worry about keeping him alive.

I scratched her ears, and she let out a low whine. "You said it."

My phone buzzed. Someone had left a voicemail when I was on the phone with the groomer.

Dr. Ezelle's office.

Weird. It was Saturday—they weren't usually open on the weekend.

An automated message about Dr. Ezelle's death, probably. This wasn't the first time a doctor had died or retired or moved. Sending out a message to everyone in the system was common practice, and the timing made sense. I ignored it.

Normally, Saturdays after a kill were for resting and art—but that wasn't happening. It didn't feel right to work on Frank with Simon's corpse in the other room. I wouldn't be able to give the artwork the focus and attention it deserved. I'd be going through the motions, and it wouldn't grant closure.

Maybe I should knock out another deep clean of my kitchen? I groaned. No—there was plenty of time for scrubbing floors later. What I needed was a break. Maybe Diane and I could catch a movie or something.

It's not like she'd have plans with Simon. Or rather, he wouldn't be keeping them.

The thought made my insides do this weird thing, flip-flopping between emotions. I'd saved Diane from a predator. But she was going to think Simon ghosted her, and it was going to break her heart. I knew that her broken heart would be Simon's fault—not mine—but I couldn't help it. It *felt* like my fault, like I could've handled things in a different way, one where Diane dumped Simon. She'd have been upset but not devastated. Diane had been ghosted before, well into a relationship. The experience had left her catatonic for days. I hated seeing her that way.

Killing Simon had to happen, but hurting Diane was like hurting myself. Worse, actually. I was tough—I'd had to be. Diane was sunshine and happiness.

On the nightstand, I kept a framed photo of us. I picked it up and traced my fingers over our smiling faces.

We were so young, babies practically. We stood on the levee near the Mississippi River, our arms looped over each other's shoulders, wearing big grins and matching LSU sweatshirts. Diane's was tight, her belly round with pregnancy.

The levee was our spot. Whenever one of us was upset or had big news to share, we always ended up there, overlooking the river, with its barges and boats gliding across its murky surface. It wasn't pretty as far as scenery goes, but Diane often waxed poetic about the river. She found comfort in knowing that no matter what changed in our lives, the river was always there. Unyielding and ever the same. "Like us," she liked to say. "The Mississippi will always run to the gulf, and we'll always have each other."

I set the photo down and frowned.

Simon had been a monster, and getting rid of him was for Diane's own good.

So why did I feel guilty?

My phone buzzed again, drawing me from my daydream.

There was a text from my hairstylist, Drewy.

DREWY: Hey—everything okay? You're never late...

Oh no. I'd completely forgotten.

The appointment was pre-booked two months ago at my last root touch-up. Drewy was the best in the city and had the wait list to go with it. I couldn't lose my spot.

ME: Sorry! Had an emergency.

Understatement of the year.

DREWY: You're coming, though, right? I can't fill your spot this late so....

So I'd have to pay whether I showed or not. It was salon policy. Considering my appointments were not cheap, being a no-show wasn't an option. Besides, I looked in the mirror that hung over my dresser and pulled my hair down from its messy bun. Mango wasn't the only one who needed help.

ME: On my way!

After getting ready—a bun, some highlighter, mascara—I peeked in on Simon on my way out. He stared, ghostly and hollow, his head still lolled to the side, sticking up from the litter. The gash in his throat was turning black around the edges. I shivered. He had to go and soon. My monsters, clean and packaged, were one thing. A predator's snarling corpse was another. The doorknob jiggled as I tugged it closed.

I was pulling out of my neighborhood when my phone reminded me I hadn't checked the voicemail from earlier. Without much thought, I pressed the button on my steering wheel, and a familiar roughened voice flowed through my car's speakers.

"Hi, Cordelia. This is Practical Family Medicine on Airline. I'm calling because I need to talk to you about some records I received from Meyer Pharmaceutical."

The woman cleared her throat, not bothering to cover the receiver, then continued.

"They wanted Dr. Ezelle to verify that everything is correct—nothing major, except Dr. Ezelle's no longer with us. It's very sad, you know."

The receptionist didn't sound like she thought it was sad.

"Case manager said that was fine—extenuating circumstances and all—and that as the office manager I could initial and sign. I'm happy to do it, but thing is, some of these signatures seem a little...peculiar. You should give us a call. I'll be at the office today, Saturday, until two o'clock. Thank you." That annoying tickle built in my eye socket, and my fingertips tingled.

I'd left anxiety attacks in my past—in Holden. And yet, these past few weeks, they'd crept back into my life as if they belonged.

Well, they didn't.

I wheeled to the side of the road and pressed my eyes closed, inhaling deep breaths, clenching and unclenching my fists until my fingers felt normal.

I was fine. Sure, my life tried to spiral, but I'd stepped in. I'd fixed it. Simon couldn't hurt me, and without him around, I wasn't as worried about the missing bracelet except for sentimental reasons. The camera wasn't an issue. And work...

Work was fine. Was I really letting some nicotine-stained secretary work me up?

But there couldn't be an investigation. There couldn't be charges or cops looking too closely at my life.

No. I was prepared for this.

Ezelle died of a stroke. If her signature is strange—it's because of preliminary symptoms. Margery made sure I understood.

I practiced saying the words aloud. "She died of a stroke."

I repeated it again, contorting my face into different expressions.

"What are you saying?" I said to an invisible office manager. An invisible lawyer. My invisible superiors at work. I said it again and again until there was no trace of panic in my voice.

My eye twitched. *Sonofabitch.* This was not that big of a deal—forged signatures wouldn't be the thing that caught Cordelia Black. I drew in another deep breath and relaxed my shoulders as I exhaled.

"What are you hinting at?" I turned down the corners of my lips. "Dr. Ezelle died of a stroke. Of course her signatures appear strange. Maybe if we'd noticed it beforehand, she'd still be here." I said the last part with righteous indignation. Then with sadness. Then again with sympathy.

Eventually, the lie rolled off my tongue with ease, no matter how I packaged it.

Satisfied, I deleted the voicemail, then pulled back onto the road. I could only deal with one emergency at a time, and when I glanced in the rearview mirror at the strawberry-pink splotches covering the blondest sections of my hair, there was no denying which emergency took precedence.

There was a monster in my bathtub. A devil in my closet. I'd likely broken my best friend's heart, when all I'd wanted to do was save her. On top of all of that, I was half an hour late—*late!*—to my hair appointment. If I could handle all of this—I could handle anything.

I flipped on the radio for a distraction.

"If you or a loved one wanted a good night's sleep, but instead ended up with a stroke that led to permanent brain damage, you may be entitled to compensation..."

Shit. I turned it off.

This was the first commercial I'd heard for the Bosephan class action lawsuit. Things were escalating, which meant everything was about to get a lot crazier at Meyer Pharmaceutical. Tensions were already high. The higher-ups were breathing down my boss's neck, who was graciously passing along the sentiment to me and the rest of the sales reps. If Dr. Ezelle's office suspected something, they'd have me between a rock and a hard place.

"No," I said aloud. "I refuse. I'm not stressing over this. *It'll be fine.* Everything is always fine for Cordelia Black."

One thing I'd learned in my childhood at Sunnyside was, sometimes you had to lie to yourself until you believed it.

Once you believed it—you could make it true.

MY CAR WAS RIGHT AT HOME IN THE SALON PARKING LOT next to the Audis, Mercedes, and BMWs, all lined up like the colorful gemstones in the Irene Neuwirth bracelet I'd bought last Christmas, then promptly returned because that purchase was a little extra, even for me. Never shop online when tipsy, especially when you're feeling melancholy because of the holidays.

I flipped down my visor and added a coat of lipstick—*Dior number 999 in velvet, thank you very much*. The message from Dr. Ezelle's office was fresh in my mind. Without Bosephan my commission checks were about to get a lot lighter, but if Practical Family Medicine caused a stink, I would lose my job entirely (best-case scenario). People who say money doesn't matter didn't grow up hungry. I'd worked too damn hard to become Cordelia Black.

When I was a little girl, I'd seen her everywhere—those shiny women who I'd imagined smelled like strawberry shampoo and angel food cake. She was in magazines. On television. Even at school, picking up my tidy, starched classmates. She never looked lonely or sad or used, and I'd decided it was because everyone must love her with real, adoring love. Not the kind with claws and teeth that left you hollowed out and alone.

She floated through life with no worries of a track-marked mama who invited men into her trailer all times of the day and night.

I'd been so young when I decided that no matter what it took, I would become her.

Look at me now. This life—it was both my truth and my best disguise. In society's eyes, someone with highlights and luxury lipstick, wearing the right brands and without an ounce of trailer park in their vocabulary, could never be a killer. This belief allowed me to do the dirty work. The necessary, *meticulous* work. This disguise protected me, so I could protect others.

I winked at my reflection and closed the visor.

With a deep breath, my back straight, and my chin up, I got out of my car and smoothed my blouse—last season's Alexander Wang—and marched into the salon to check in. The receptionist brought me a flute of sangria a moment before Drewy Hernandez appeared in the waiting room, a flurry of tattoos, sleek chin-length black hair, and enthusiasm, wrapped up in a petite package. "Cordelia, honey! I hope everything's okay. You've never been late, not even once."

"I'm fine." The lie rolled off my tongue as I followed her to her station and sank into the black leather salon chair. "Only...a minor emergency." I pulled one of the pastel pieces loose from my bun and held it out for her to inspect. "And speaking of minor emergencies..."

She took the strand between her fingers and eyed the tress closely, muttering something in Spanish under her breath. Drewy's golden brown eyes locked on mine in the mirror. "Back at your art projects I see. I told you, if you're going to be this blond, you must cover your hair when you paint. You can get a whole box of processing caps at the beauty supply store." She shook her head and tsk-tsked. "We must be careful, or your hair could break. But don't stress. I have a plan. A gentle lightener. A few honey lowlights. You'll be good as new." She bit her bottom lip, which, admittedly, wasn't the best sign.

"Should I be worried?" I asked.

Drewy shrugged. "You're lucky to have someone with my skills behind your chair or this could've been bad."

Once she'd mixed her product, Drewy started to work, foiling some strands and hand-painting others. She cast her magic in a way that made her worth every high-priced penny.

"Give me one second," she said, her words breathy. "I need to grab a stool. I can't hardly stay on my feet for an entire color process anymore."

"Is something wrong?" I asked. The petite woman had an athlete's body, wide shoulders with muscular arms and legs. I'd met her years ago at the gym and knew that physically, she was a beast.

She smirked, and her dark eyes flashed. "Nothing's *wrong*." She pulled her loose black top tightly against her body to reveal a small bump.

"Congratulations—that's amazing!" I knew she and her spouse had been trying for over a year.

"Thanks." She pulled a lopsided saddle stool from the corner, its legs scraping the marble tile floor. "They really need to call a handyman to make some repairs around here. As much as we pay in booth rent, you'd think the owners would run a tighter ship."

A handyman?

Oh no.

I jumped up from my chair, my foils rustling in my head like a hundred tiny sails. "What's the date? Quick—what's the date?" My voice was frantic.

"It's the twentieth. What's wrong with you?"

I grabbed my purse from Drewy's station and slung it over my shoulder. "I'll be right back. I promise."

"Are you serious? You can't leave with foils in—you already came in late. I'm telling you Cordelia; we're pushing it with this process. I need to keep an eye on it."

Feeling like an asshole, I waved off her words and bounded for the door, ignoring the curious stares from other clients. If I didn't make it home in time, I'd have a lot more than bad lowlights or split ends to worry about. "I'll be right back. You know I'm not running out."

"Cordelia!" Drewy called after me. "*¿Qué carajo?*"

"Sorry. Sorry," I yelled over my shoulder, meaning it.

I slid behind the wheel of my car and frantically scrolled through my phone until I found the number for Handy Heroes, the handyman service I'd hired to complete my honey-do list. It rang three times over Bluetooth before their answering service picked up asking if I'd like to leave a message.

Um yes, can you please tell your handy person that they shouldn't come today because there's a body in my bathtub? No, they shouldn't worry about it. It's fine. Really.

Yeah, I didn't think a message would do the trick.

HAD I LOCKED THE BATHROOM DOOR?

It didn't matter. The handyman was supposed to replace shaky or loose knobs on several of my doors, including the guest bath.

I clenched my jaw and gripped the steering wheel tighter than this season's Dior mistakenly marked half off. *It's fine. It has to be fine.*

The mantra rang hollow. Was it fine? Was anything in my life fine?

It hadn't been twenty-four hours since my surprise killing of Simon, and already things were threatening to fall apart.

The traffic light changed to red, and I punched the brake. *Damn it.* I tossed my head back into my headrest and slapped the side of the steering wheel angrily with my palm. A foil fell from my hair and landed in my lap..

It would be a miracle if Drewy didn't fire me as a client. If I lost my job, I wouldn't be able to afford her anyway. Oh God. I'd probably end up somewhere like Cost Cuts or Discount Doos.

Of course, if Handy Heroes beat me to my house and discovered the surprise in my shower, then none of that would matter—not my job or my hair. My life would be over.

So, no. Maybe I'd lied to myself. Maybe everything was *not* fine.

The red light blinked to green, and I pressed my foot all the way to the floor. I took the next turn at full speed, barely missing a bus stop sign.

If Simon was found, no one would care that he was a predator. No one would care that I'd done our city a favor by taking him off the street. No one would care about the lives I'd protected.

I'd go to jail. Do not pass go. Do not collect two hundred dollars.

It would ruin Diane's life. Sugar's life. They'd be constantly plagued with questions wherever they went. *Did you know your godmother was a killer? Come on, there's no way you didn't know your best friend murdered your boyfriend.* They'd hate me.

The next traffic light flashed to red, but this time, I zipped through, barely missing an ancient Cadillac. Horns blared.

My phone rang through my car speakers. *Oh no.*

I flushed, beads of sweat popping across my forehead and neck as the lump in my throat grew.

Had the handyperson beaten me to the house? Had they found Simon? Had they called the police?

Were the police calling me? Would they do that? Was that even a thing that happened?

My hands trembled.

"Get a grip. Look at yourself—you're acting like Joanie." The words held venom, but I straightened my spine and took a deep breath. I tried to rouse some useful fury as I pressed the button on my steering wheel to allow caller ID onto my console screen. In blue digital letters it read *Practical Family Medicine.*

"I don't have time for this!" My fist beat out my frustration against the horn of my steering wheel as an ear-piercing scream escaped my throat.

I slammed the brakes while entering my neighborhood. My tires squealed.

"What the hell?" Mr. Percival hadn't been messing around; I'd not been gone that long, but lost dog signs with pictures of Mango were everywhere. He'd taped over old political signs and stuck them in the ground. Utility poles were decorated with flyers of Mango's face. There was even one taped underneath the neighborhood's main four-way stop sign. I'd been taking out monsters for years, and there hadn't been a single one who'd garnered as many missing persons signs as this dog. Mr. Percival was unhinged.

If the hired Handy Hero didn't discover Simon but found Mango—well—dog thief was *slightly* better than murderer in the court of public opinion.

I wheeled into my driveway and hopped out, foils flying from my head, leaving a trail of silver behind me as I ran toward the front door. A work van with a faded blue decal on the side was parked in front of my house. No one sat behind the driver's seat.

Across the street, Mr. Percival stood in his front yard, his arms crossed as he watched intently, not even bothering to pretend he was minding his own business.

"Slow down, Ms. Black," he yelled. "You could get someone killed driving like that; then how'd you feel?"

I bristled but ignored him as I raced up my walkway. The flowerpot where I'd hidden a key for Handy Heroes the day after I'd made the appointment was moved from its usual space. How had I forgotten I'd hidden a key? How had I forgotten the appointment? Work stress had taken my focus and made me forgetful; that was the only explanation. Because Cordelia Black would never...

I twisted the knob. It was unlocked.

"Hello?" I hated the quiver in my voice. It sounded guilty.

The orchestrated life I'd painstakingly created was on the verge of falling to pieces, like shards of glass from a smashed mirror. Shards that would stab me on their way down, ending everything in a single, uncontrolled moment.

"Hello? Who's here?" I called again. Muffled barks came from upstairs. Good. At least the handyperson hadn't found Mango.

"I'm in here, Ma'am. Just the handyman you hired from Handy Heroes." His gruff voice called out from the short downstairs hallway.

The guest bath was in that hallway.

"No need to be afraid," he added.

The fact that he was worried about scaring me instead of sounding terrified himself gave me hope. Upstairs, Mango picked up steam.

I ran through the dining room, then living room, and down the short hall. The handyman clutched the doorknob to my guest bath. He twisted, then pushed it open.

"No!" I screamed.

He jerked his face toward me, his navy-blue eyes opened in surprise beneath his bushy eyebrows. "Ma'am? Are you okay?"

His hand dropped from the knob, leaving the door open a crack, as he took a step in my direction. He raised his palms in front of him to show he wasn't a threat. "Listen, ma'am. I'm here to help with light home repairs. Sorry if I startled you, but there's no reason to scream."

I swallowed hard. The small vein in my forehead—the one I hated because I'd inherited it from Mama—pulsed with every heartbeat. The handyman stood in front of me, perplexed, while every muscle in my body tensed. If he pushed the door open a little further, he'd see Simon sprawled naked in a tub of kitty litter. There was no coming back from that.

Upstairs, Mango was going full blast with her screaming-goat barks.

"Stop. Just—whatever you do, don't go in there." I bounded past him, yanking the door closed, and put my back against it.

He shook his head. "Listen, miss." He paused and pulled a printout from the front pocket of his overalls. "Ms. Black. That's you, ain't it?"

"Yep. That's me. This is my house."

"Well, Ms. Black, I don't get paid if I don't complete the job and the homeowner—that's you—doesn't rate my work at least three stars on the app. I've already tightened the door handles on your exterior doors, oiled the hinges on your upstairs bathroom door, changed a few light bulbs in your kitchen and living room,

I saw about your garbage disposal—only needed emptying, by the way—and all I have left is to check on…" He glanced down at the printout. "The doorknob on the guest bath, first door on the right in the downstairs hallway. Says it won't click shut, even when locked. Should be an easy fix; knob likely needs replacing. I probably have one that'll work in the van. Won't take me long, and I'll get out of your hair."

He chuckled.

"What's so funny?" I asked.

"Out of your hair?" He pointed at my head. "Never mind, forget it. Can I do my job or what?" He attempted to reach past me for the knob, but I didn't budge.

"The doorknob's fine. I fixed it."

"You fixed it?" He was skeptical.

"Yes. I fixed it. You're all done."

"If you fixed it, I wish you'd have updated your request in the app. It's on my work order. I have to at least check it out, or I could get in real trouble. I don't want to be rude, but, ma'am, I was hoping to finish this job in time to make the last bit of my grandson's soccer game. But things here are getting drawn out…" His voice trailed off.

"Listen, Mr.—"

"Goodreaux, ma'am."

"Mr. Goodreaux. I should've messaged you, but I forgot. You're all done, so why don't you go now, and you can be at the soccer complex in no time."

He hesitated.

"What is it?"

"It's... Well, I get paid by the job completed. This is one less job. I could've booked something else."

I sighed loudly. "I don't have time for this, Mr. Goodreaux. How about I give you some cash and we pretend everything is perfect, okay?"

He rocked back on the heels of his work boots and gnawed his bottom lip.

"Oh my god, what is it?" My voice came out pinched.

"Thing is, we aren't allowed to take tips, and I don't want to get into trouble. I'm retired, you see, and this is where I make my spending money for me and the wife. If they find out I took your money—"

"How would they find out?" I breathed deep. Upstairs, Mango was in berserker mode, growling and barking and yodeling like an animal ten times her size. Mr. Goodreaux glanced at the stairs, expecting me to acknowledge it, and when I didn't, he shrugged.

He said, "You see, there is that survey on the app and—"

"Listen, I'm super stressed and don't have time for this conversation. I'm going to give you some money, and you're going to go to your grandson's soccer game. Then you can take the cash and go out to eat after, okay? When I take the survey, I'll say you did everything I asked. I won't even have to lie about it. Five stars across the board."

"If you'd let me look at the doorknob—"

"There is no way you're looking at the fucking doorknob." I snapped, then took a deep breath. "Take my money and leave now with a good review, or I can tell them about your terrible customer service and refusal to leave my property. It's up to you, but I'd rather pay you and let you have a nice day. What'll it be, sir?"

He looked at me for a long hard minute. "No need to get snippy, Ms. Black. I'm only trying to do my job."

"I know. I'm sorry—I'm having a day, you know?" My shoulders slumped forward, but I remained planted between him and the door.

The old man stood in front of me for a few more seconds, and when it became apparent I wasn't moving, he shook his head. "Yeah. Okay. I'm not going to sit here and keep arguing to do more work for less money. You give me some cash, and I'll be on my way."

"Good call." I pulled a couple of twenties from my purse and handed them over.

"Pleasure." He nodded, turning to leave.

It was when the front door thudded closed that I remembered he still had my key. I jogged after him, calling out, "Key, please."

He dug it from the pocket of his overalls and dropped it into my outstretched hand. Before going he smiled and said, "Ms. Black, I'm sorry if I came across as rude a minute ago. I like to do things by the book, you know. But I know why you don't want me in your bathroom."

"You do?" My shoulders stiffened.

"Sure I do." His brows drew together. "You're embarrassed. You see, I have a super smeller." He tapped the side of his nose.

"A super smeller?"

"Yep. I can smell things better than most people. My granddaughter says it's my superpower. When I cracked the door, boy did I get a whiff of it. Either that is one nasty litter box, or you have something dead in there." He narrowed his eyes.

"Something...dead?"

"You shouldn't be embarrassed. I don't handle that sort of thing, but you can call an exterminator. It's probably a mouse or squirrel got inside your wall and got trapped. It's not too bad right now—most people probably can't even smell it, yet. Must be somewhat fresh. I wouldn't wait too long."

"A mouse?"

"Yes, ma'am. Or a squirrel. When it starts to turn, it can get bad quick. Especially with how warm it is in your home. Seemed like your air-conditioning might need a little work. Like it's having trouble keeping up."

I blinked but said nothing.

"Oh gosh." He shook his head and rubbed the back of his neck. "I've done upset you. Listen, having something die in your wall doesn't mean you're a bad housekeeper. Just one of those things—life, you know? Could even be a lizard or something your dog brought in and hid. They do like to bring you gifts now and again. I have two myself."

"Two lizards?"

"Dogs. Cocker spaniels. Names are Betsy and Ross." He chuckled. "Now, if you'll excuse me, I have to get to the soccer game. Thanks for the tip." He shook the twenties in the air and hopped into the van with a spryness I wouldn't have expected from someone with gray hair and a paunch. I watched as his van sputtered down my street.

My scalp tingling like it was covered in fire ants couldn't be a good sign, but instead of hopping in my car to rush back to the salon, I ran inside to the bathroom, cracked the door, and gave it a whiff.

Nothing.

I stepped closer to Simon and sniffed harder. *There.*

Maybe. I wasn't sure.

I tugged at the collar of my blouse. Had it always been this warm in here? I hadn't noticed yesterday.

Stop it. It's fine. Mr. Goodreaux's words were getting to me. That's all. It wasn't hot. My air conditioner wasn't going out. Simon didn't stink.

Yet.

Rather safe than sorry. I snatched my diffuser from the living room and loaded it with lemongrass oil, then moved it to the bathroom and plugged it in. I sprayed Simon with Lysol. It wasn't a permanent solution—in fact, it wasn't even a good temporary solution—but it would have to do for the moment.

I hollered upstairs to Mango that I'd be back soon, then locked the front door and hurried down my driveway.

Mr. Percival stood in front of the driver's-side door of my car, his arms crossed, his frown pulling at the loose skin of his face, turning the lines between his eyebrows into canyons.

"Can I help you?" I asked.

He shook his head. "Something ain't right over here."

"I don't know what you're talking about," I said.

"Oh, I think you do."

My head burned. My eye wanted to twitch. But I forced a smile onto my face. "Water your own grass, Mr. Percival. I have to go."

I reached around him and opened my car door, forcing him to step out of the way. If the groomer didn't have a cancellation so I could get that damned dog washed and back to her home, I'd shave Mango myself because I wasn't sure how much more of this angry little man I could take.

What if Mr. Percival followed through on his threat? What if he did call the police and they heard those horrible goatlike chortles? Would that give them reason to enter my house?

No way. That wouldn't happen. He was bluffing.

I hoped.

At the stop sign, my phone chirped, and the voicemail icon showed on the console screen. I pressed it.

"Hey, Cordelia. This is Dr. Ezelle's office again. Call me back when you get a chance. This needs to be handled, and the sooner the better." There was a pause on the line, and then the caller spoke in a quieter tone, all pretense of professionalism gone. "This ain't going away without you getting in touch with me. You don't want to ignore me, hear? Maybe we can help each other out."

The message ended.

I slumped forward in my seat.

Normally this would make me angry—because how dare she speak to me that way—like I was powerless. I was not a woman to be messed with.

But at that moment, I felt exactly like the woman people messed with.

Another foil landed in my lap.

Things were unraveling, one thread at a time.

Drewy was pissed. She waved her assistant away, and led me straight to a shampoo chair herself, wincing as she unfolded foils.

"How bad is it?" I was afraid of the answer.

"Oh, it's... You should be happy it isn't *all* completely overprocessed."

The relief I felt over my hair was silly compared to everything else in my life. "That's good news, right?"

Drewy frowned. "I have to cut it."

"That's not so bad." I loved my long hair, but a new style wasn't the end of the world. Maybe something short and fun...

She shook her head. "Let me finish. I'll have to cut it after we do a demi color in a darker color. I'm thinking like a level six point three. Think a warm toffee shade."

"Warm toffee?" No way.

"It'll look great with your complexion."

"No. I'm blond. It's who I am."

"Not anymore. That's what happens when you ignore a professional and do what you want. Unless you'd rather keep this streaky, messy, splotchy hair. In that case, I won't be able to rebook you.

My name cannot be associated with this train wreck." She flicked her hand in the direction of my hair.

Tension knotted my shoulder blades. I was not a brunette. Cordelia Black was sunshiny, damn it. Occasionally, I was icy. Sometimes I was cornsilk or honeycomb. I was never, ever *warm toffee*. I inhaled a steady breath.

Drewy was the best of the best. If she was saying I had no choice. Well. "Fine," I said. "Warm toffee it is."

The process took over two hours. Drewy turned off her hair dryer and spun me around to face the mirror. "What do you think?"

My voice stuck in my throat, but my horror must've been written across my face because she quickly added, "Keep in mind this was a corrective process and will fade a little."

It wasn't that the hair color was ugly. It was that it was reminiscent.

This shade of brown did not resemble warm toffee. No, it was too close to the dark mousy color I'd inherited from my mama. This shoulder-grazing bob—though sleeker and more stylish—was too close to the severe cut I'd worn growing up, one given in our trailer by a pair of old kitchen scissors. The woman staring back at me from Drewy's mirror wasn't Cordelia Black.

All around me ladies sipped sangria while their stylists foiled and painted and snipped. Drewy searched my face in the mirror for clues as to how I felt, while in the next station, another stylist stole glances away from his own client.

I clenched my hands in my lap, my nails making half-moon

indentions in my palms. I searched for the correct words. Bright words. Chipper words. Maybe a witty, sarcastic remark. Or even something snarky and self-deprecating. Something biting—words with teeth.

I opened my mouth.

Nothing came out.

I tried again.

Any words—anything at all—besides the soggy, pathetic one that ran through my mind. A single name. *Joanie.*

Joanie. Joanie. Joanie...

I'd worked so hard—killing my past—burying it deep where no one would find it.

Yet here she was.

Joanie was staring back at me from beyond her grave. *My* grave.

I hated her. I'd killed my past self methodically, one carefully curated decision, one meticulously planned course of action at a time, until there was space to become who I was meant to be. Until I died as Joanie and resurrected as Cordelia.

I snapped my mouth closed.

With my lips pressed into a hard line, I slapped cash onto Drewy's station and waltzed from the salon with my head held high. My eyes remained focused, not daring to break from their course. I had to get out of there.

Even in the safety of my car, I held it together.

I made it all the way to the highway before the tears spilled, tracing dark tracks of mascara down my cheeks.

Cordelia Black was a fraud. She wasn't real.

21

MY ANXIETY BELONGED TO JOANIE—THE ONE THING OF hers I'd kept. Not that I'd had a choice. I highlighted my hair and straightened my teeth. I changed my clothes, corrected my elocution, and unlearned all the toxic internalized misogyny that had victimized my youth. I'd cut ties with every part of myself that even hinted at vulnerability—even parts I'd liked. I pushed every piece of Joanie down deep and visualized her lying in a grave with me tossing dirt over her. She was gone. Dead. Buried. I'd killed her. It hurt—*God how it had hurt*—but I'd done it.

The anxiety? It remained—a steadfast reminder of who I'd been. Joanie Brown. Spineless, trembling, twitchy-eyed nobody.

I wiped my eyes, and my fingers came away with soupy black smudges, but I didn't dare flip down the visor mirror and risk stealing a look. She'd still be there, in my reflection, mocking me.

I sniffed hard. What was I going to do? Not look in the mirror ever again? Because of a bad dye job?

That was weak.

That was Joanie.

So what if I had dark hair? So what if I had the corpse of my best friend's boyfriend in my bathtub? So what if I lost my biggest money-making account and a good portion of my regular clients resented me? So what if a horrible redneck receptionist was going to try and hold me hostage?

So fucking what?

The traffic light changed, and behind me someone beeped their horn. I forced myself to look into my rearview mirror before accelerating.

My cheeks were red and splotchy. My hair, which once hung down my back in honey-and-wheat sun-kissed waves, now grazed my shoulders and washed out my complexion.

But the reflection staring at me? She wasn't a scared girl. Not anymore. This reflection wasn't someone begging for love, so desperate for it, she didn't care if it was delivered with teeth and claws. I was simply me—overwrought and emotional. Cordelia Black.

I'd worked so hard to leave Joanie behind—to kill her—but it was Joanie who led me to Cordelia. She'd been weepy and needy, but she'd also been a survivor. She'd done what it took to get out of Sunnyside, and that hadn't been easy. Making it to college despite zero stability? The odds had been against her from day one.

Maybe there was no Cordelia without Joanie. I had her anxiety. But also, I could thank her for my grit. The kind of grit you don't get from having things handed to you. The kind of grit you can only obtain through overcoming.

And damn. Joanie had been a pro at overcoming.

Something inside me cracked open at this realization and more tears leaked from my eyes.

I'd never go back to being scared. To running. To not demanding respect from the world. But I could use a dose of that old tenaciousness that had cocooned Joanie like the exoskeletons of the beetles that had flown into the dim porch light of Mama's trailer. Like...like armor.

In my mind I heard Mama's slow drawl telling me to quit my crying. That the world was tough, and if I cried it would swallow me up.

Mama had given Joanie over to the very worst of the world, but she'd had a point about tears. Crying was a luxury I'd never had, so there was no point in starting now. I *knew* better.

Sugar was safe.

Diane was safe.

And I was fine.

As long as I kept it together. As long as I got a handle on things and made no more mistakes, it would stay that way. Was I really going to sit here and weep because, what? Life was hard? Give me a break. When had life not been hard?

I sniffed back the final sob and wiped my eyes with the backs of my hands.

My cell rang again, and this time, my stomach didn't flutter with nerves when I checked to see who was calling. If Practical Family Medicine wanted to do battle, then I'd make them rue it.

But the picture that flashed on the screen of my smartphone was of Diane and Sugar.

By the time I pressed the answer icon on my steering wheel, the tears and shame were gone from my voice.

"Hey you." I ran my fingers through my sleek tresses as I spoke.

"Hey yourself," Diane replied, sounding cheery.

"What're you and Sugar up to?"

"Samantha's visiting my parents this weekend. I thought I told you that?"

"You probably did. I've been a little distracted," I admitted.

"The whole Bosephan thing... It really sucks."

"You can say that again," I said.

"It'll all go away soon, right?" Diane couldn't imagine a problem that didn't have a happy ending. "Surely they'll settle."

"Maybe," I said. "I need to not think about it. Want to get pedicures or see a movie? Can you believe I actually have some free time? Oh. And I have brown hair now."

"Can't," she said. "I made plans with Simon."

Simon wouldn't be meeting anyone.

"That's why I'm calling." She paused.

"Oh?"

"We're going for a hike. I thought maybe you'd come with us? I want you two to spend more time together. Y'all hit it off so well at the barbecue, and I don't want you to be mad about the whole travel-nursing thing. I promise I'm still only thinking about it. Besides. This hike is supposed to be amazing. Simon knows this place way out near the Mississippi line, he promised there's actually waterfalls and... Wait—you what?"

"What?" I asked.

"You have brown hair? Why do you have brown hair?"

"Oh. I wanted to try something new." Complete lie. Lately, I'd had enough "new" to last a lifetime. I'd take my old boring blond monster-killing life back, thank you very much.

"But your hair? You loved being blond. It was your whole thing. Like, if God was typecasting for a blond bombshell, you'd have been the lead choice."

"Diane, you know blond wasn't my natural hair color, right?" I'd been a drugstore bottle-blond when we'd met, before I could afford professional highlights. We'd lived together, she'd helped with my roots, but turning the whole thing into a joke was easier because the truth was depressing.

"I can't believe you went *brown*. That's so, well, boring." Her comment stung. "You could've at least joined team ginger with me."

"You know how to make a girl feel good about her decisions, you know that?"

Diane sighed. "I'm sorry. I'm sure it looks great. I'm just... shook."

Sugar's eyes would roll right out of her head if she heard Diane say *shook*, and I resisted the urge to snicker. "It's fine. Call me if your plans change, okay?"

"Wait. You won't come with us? It'll be fun. Please?"

"Well," I considered. As much as I truly hated hiking, it was my fault Simon wouldn't be showing up. Diane would be devastated when he "ghosted." She'd need me, and didn't I owe it to her? "I guess since you said please," I snarked. "Okay. Sure."

"You mean it?" Diane's voice pitched an octave higher, and

in my mind I saw the glow of her smile. "You—Ms. I-hate-the-outdoors—are willing to come hiking?"

"Do you want me to go or not?" I flashed my turn signal and entered my neighborhood. Mr. Percival was nowhere to be seen. Great.

"You know I do. I'm just—"

"*Shook*?" I said.

"Cordelia Renee? Are you making fun of me?"

"Still not my name," I said. "Give me a few minutes to change clothes, and I'll come over and ride with y'all."

"Okay," Diane said. "We can take my Jeep. I'll take the top off. Yay! My bestie and my boyfriend are going to be best friends!"

A pang of guilt rattled my chest. "Uh huh. Talk to you later. Love you." I ended the call quickly.

If Diane could see herself as I saw her, a guy like Simon wouldn't have a chance, even if I hadn't killed him. Even if he wasn't a monster.

Simon was handsome enough but—at least the nonmonster Nice-Guy version he'd presented Diane—was the human equivalent of a yawn. If he were a food, he'd have been cold unsweetened oatmeal. Except it would be like if someone poisoned that oatmeal, and then the best person ever thought it was gourmet and took it home to serve to her daughter for breakfast.

I had no regrets about what happened—I only hated to think of Diane hurting.

But that pain wouldn't last long. She had me.

22

I CHANGED INTO MY FAVORITE BLACK YOGA SHORTS AND hot pink tank, then touched up my face. The dark hair color meant I'd have to buy all new, bolder makeup.

Other than that, my hair wasn't *so* bad, was it?

I frowned. No. It definitely was.

I grabbed a cap and shoved my hair beneath it. Better.

Mango barked to go out. "Fine," I said, because apparently we had conversations now. She followed me downstairs.

Passing through the living room, I thought I caught a whiff of something...something not good.

No way. The handyman and his self-proclaimed super-sniffer were making me paranoid—that was all. I hadn't smelled anything when I'd come home, but I'd also run straight upstairs.

Mango did her business outside, and we hurried back to the fridge for her slice of cheese.

I sniffed.

There.

There was something...different...in the air.

It couldn't hurt to check.

The thought of going into the guest bathroom turned my stomach. My monsters, drained of blood and cold on my worktable, were things of beauty. Art in its rawest form. Simon, with his waxy skin and sunken cheeks, was a creature stitched of nightmares. The last thing I wanted was to look at him, much less sniff him.

Did I have a choice?

Mango took her slice of American to the living room, while I headed toward the hallway. I opened the bathroom door and stepped inside.

Nothing.

Simon watched with his dull gray orbs, blank and bleak and accusatory. I leaned close to his face and inhaled.

No...there *was* something. Something earthy and funkish, buried beneath the scent coming from my oil diffuser. It wasn't putrid—not yet. I backed up to the door and sniffed again. Now that I knew it was there, it couldn't be missed. The scent wasn't strong enough to be called an odor, but something told me that wouldn't be the case for much longer.

I should've known. The kitty litter worked by wicking away moisture, but it was no match for our oppressive humidity—the air so wet, old folks joked it took gills to breathe. Louisiana was, at its core, one big swamp. Things rot faster in the swamp. My first kills had taught me as much.

I fanned myself with my palms. My freshly applied makeup was in danger of sliding off my face. It *was* warm in here. *Shit.*

In his current state, Simon wouldn't keep until Friday, when I'd planned on meeting Clarence. Why hadn't I trusted myself and gone with the ice? What possessed me to listen to shitty-kitty Betty? It hadn't been twenty-four hours and I was already regretting the decision.

There was no way around it; I had to make the switch from litter to ice. And sooner rather than later.

There were other options. I considered packing Simon into an ice chest and storing him at my workshop, but that would be a mistake. One, where could I find an ice chest big enough? Rigor mortis had set in, so bending Simon wasn't going to happen. And two, I needed him where I could keep an eye on him. The urge to move him out of my house was strong, but it wasn't worth the risk of someone finding his body. If everything worked out—and everything *had* to work out—then Simon would only be staying a few more days. I could manage.

I stepped into the hallway and closed the bathroom door.

I pulled out my phone to call Diane and cancel the hike; there was too much to do. But she'd already texted me.

DIANE: How long before you get here? I need you.

She needed me. I sighed and scooped up Mango from her perch on the back of the sofa. The ice could wait a few hours because I'd never put Simon's needs before Diane's. I would always be there for her.

CORDELIA: On my way!

The late afternoon sun reflected off Diane's copper hair in a fiery halo. Even frowning she was gorgeous. She sat on her front stoop, clad in teal tights and matching crop top, lost in her own world with her chin cradled in her palms and her elbows propped against her knees. A small line deepened between her brows, and her lips puckered as if she'd bitten into something sour.

When she saw me, she ran her index fingers beneath her eyes and smiled. It was fake—stretched too wide and too tight—and it hurt my heart knowing I was at least partially responsible for her misery.

As I got closer, Diane's mouth dropped open, her brows shooting toward her hairline. She bounced to her feet. "Okay. Let's see it."

"Huh?" I was confused.

She bounded down the walkway, meeting me in the middle, and pulled the cap from my head. My brown hair spilled around my collarbone.

"It's so bouncy! I love it." She ran her fingertips through the ends of my hair.

"You do? I worried I'd made a big mistake." As if I'd *chosen* to chop my hair off and color it Joanie brown.

"No, it's perfect," Diane said. "I thought about cutting mine, but Simon likes it long."

"You should do what you like, Diane. Not what *he* likes." It was an old argument that spanned years. Diane's appearance changed with each relationship.

"I know, I know," she said.

"Where is Simon, anyway?" I looked up and down the street, pretending to notice for the first time that his truck was nowhere to be seen. "Is he inside? Did you pick him up or something?"

Diane hugged her arms across her chest, the way she did when she was upset but trying not to be. "No. He was supposed to be here over an hour ago, but he hasn't shown up, and he isn't answering his phone." She bit her bottom lip. "I don't know what's going on."

And she never would.

My brow furrowed. My lips pressed into a line. It was a carefully orchestrated expression of concern; I'd practiced it on the ride over.

How often had I manipulated my actions, my expressions, my entire fucking personality to trap monsters? Still, it felt dirty to almost lie to Diane.

My voice ticked higher as I asked, "You mean you haven't heard from him at all? Since yesterday?"

Her curls bounced against her collarbone as she shook her head. "Not a word since last night. You think something's wrong? Should I—I don't know—call the police?"

Only if you want me to go to prison.

My eyes widened. "Why?"

"Because it's not like him to disappear like this, you know? What if you called McSmiley? Maybe he could—"

I held up my hand. "Sweetie, no. I'm sure it's fine. If you report him missing or have me check in with Christopher after only a few hours, it could look a little, I don't know, stalkery."

And that's the story of how I gaslit my best friend. I hated Simon for lots of reasons, and now, for what he was making me do to Diane. I'd never want her to doubt her instincts, but it wasn't like I could let her call the cops. What if there were red light cameras that caught Simon on his drive to my house? Easy enough to explain away—if he wasn't rotting in my bathtub.

Until his body was gone, I wasn't safe.

I pushed forward with my lie. "Is it possible he was called in to work? He is an ER nurse, after all."

"I guess so." Her brow furrowed. "But he could've texted."

I cocked my head to the side and shrugged as if to say, *Men*.

Diane kept talking. "It's not like him to go dark like this."

"Diane. *Go dark*?" More gaslighting. "That's a little dramatic, don't you think? Besides, how long have you known him? A month? Maybe two?"

She nodded.

"Don't take this the wrong way, but maybe this is *exactly* like him. Maybe the honeymoon phase is over, you know? I wouldn't worry—not yet. I'm sure he's fine. He probably got busy, that's all."

Busy decomposing.

"What if he's ghosting me?" Her arms wrapped across her chest, and she swayed from side to side.

This was her real fear all along. The words were heavy, landing like stones sinking into a puddle. She'd hoped there was another explanation—any other explanation. Well. Almost.

I touched her arm lightly. "Don't think that. Seriously, I'd bet anything he got called in to work. That's all. Now, we still doing this or what?"

Diane threw her arms around my neck. "You're the best, Cor. You always know exactly what to say. You're right, I'm being dramatic. We've only been together a little over a month, right? This is no big deal."

My insides felt as if they would pull apart—guilt and shame mixed with the pride of doing the hard things to keep my family safe.

Diane stepped back, her hands sliding down my arms until she got to my wrist. "Hey. You took it off." She ran a thumb over the place where Sugar's friendship bracelet normally lived. "Did something happen to it?"

"No," I lied. The bracelet had been pushed further to the back of my mind with each fire that sprung up. Diane's question was a glass of cold water thrown in my face.

"I was working on a project. I guess I forgot to put it back on."

"You said you never took it off," she teased. "I've kept this piece of ratty yarn on my wrist for years because you're a closeted sentimental softie."

"Yeah. Well. This was a real Jackson Pollock situation; I couldn't risk ruining it." The lie was flimsy, but also not. My kitchen could have passed for the famous abstract expressionist's studio. Which reminded me… "Hey, since Simon didn't show, do you mind a change in plans? There's a new trail I want to try out."

Diane's face scrunched. "Wait. You? Want to try out a specific hiking trail? Where did you hear about it? Who do you even talk to—besides me—that spends time outdoors?" She paused, rocking back on her heels. "Cordelia Renee, are you talking about the outdoor mall?"

"First—still not my name. And no. McSmiley told me about this trail," I said without thinking. "We're supposed to go together, but I want to check it out first. If it sucks, I don't want to get stuck there on a date."

This was the perfect chance to see if there were more game cameras, and who knows; maybe I'd find the bracelet too.

Diane nodded, smirking. "Okay. I get it."

"Get what?"

"You really like this guy."

"What?" I asked.

"When have you ever worried about how you'd come across on a date?"

"You misunderstood. I don't want to risk being stuck on a long difficult trail with a guy I'm still getting to know, that's all."

"Boo." Diane rolled her eyes. "McSmiley's such a sweetie. He brought you dinner."

"Excuse me, but you told him to. That's basically like you got me dinner. He just delivered it," I said. "And besides, you know I hate surprises."

"No one hates surprises that end with free food," Diane countered.

She had a point.

It had turned out to be kind of perfect. Cleaning up a crime scene really worked up an appetite.

WE WERE IN DIANE'S JEEP WITH THE TOP OFF, TWO MILES from our exit, singing along with Taylor at the top of our lungs, when a blue pickup truck merged into the lane next to us, speeding until we were behind it. My heart stopped.

No. Impossible. When I'd abandoned Simon's pickup late at night with the keys still in it, I'd assumed it would get chopped for parts. Or that whoever stole it would at least paint it before joyriding in it.

Calm down, Cordelia. Old Toyota trucks were a dime a dozen in Louisiana.

We inched closer. There was no reason to think the truck was Simon's.

Except. *Oh no.* Simon's truck had a large sticker on the tailgate. I couldn't remember what it said exactly, something about nurses and saving lives and blah blah blah. The thieves who'd taken the truck peeled the sticker away, but the paint underneath was darker, giving a perfect shadowy imprint of its shape. What were the odds that this truck—same color and body style—happened to have had the exact same sticker in the exact same spot? Zero. The odds were zero.

I cut my gaze to Diane, forcing myself to continue to sing along, but stumbling over the familiar lyrics. Keeping time was impossible while my heart was a metronome doing double beats. Diane was still bobbing her head to the music, swaying in her seat. She hadn't noticed the truck. Maybe she wouldn't.

Simon's truck gave its signal. It was merging directly in front of us.

Fuck.

At least the car thieves had changed the tags. Still. A blue truck, the same make and model, with the perfect outline of a specific sticker...

"What the hell?" Diane punched the gas, crawling onto the truck's bumper. So much for her not noticing.

"What are you doing?" I yelled over the wind and music, morphing the anxiety in my voice into something like surprise. "Diane, slow down."

"That's Simon!" Her eyes narrowed in fury. Her temper didn't make an appearance often, but when it did, well, there's a reason there's a stereotype about redheads. "That asshole couldn't text me, but there he is. Right freaking in front of us!"

"Diane, that truck has Arkansas plates."

"I don't remember what plates were on Simon's truck. He's lived all over the place. It's one of the reasons he's excited about travel nursing. They could've been from Arkansas. And look—that's his head. And there's a woman in there with him."

Shit. Maybe the thieves hadn't changed his plates. And as bad luck would have it, the driver's short blond hair was visible through the back glass. The person next to him had dark hair pulled into a high ponytail.

"Still, Diane. Slow down. You're going to get a ticket! Or get us killed."

She ignored me.

"What's your plan here?" I yelled.

"Cordelia Renee—"

"Not my name!"

"Cordelia Renee." Her voice grew in volume and pitch. "You've known me for how long now? And better than anyone. What makes you think there's ever a plan?" She was right.

One thing was certain—it was not Simon driving the truck. How would I handle this situation if he wasn't a corpse? If we'd really caught him with another woman? I'd be pissed—exactly as I had at the restaurant. Before I'd killed him.

I slid into protective best friend mode. "Okay then. I guess we're giving the asshole a piece of our minds."

The driver of the truck tapped their brakes, and Diane backed off their tail; then without flicking her blinker, she careened one lane over. Diane punched the gas and sped up next to the truck.

The driver had Simon's fair complexion and blond hair. Unlike Simon, he sported a scorpion tattoo on his protruding jaw. He scowled at us. The person in the passenger seat, a man with deep brown skin and, honestly, really great eyebrows, leaned forward and flipped us the bird. Diane deflated but kept pace.

"Diane, slow down." We didn't need trouble with these guys. And scorpion dude looked like someone who wouldn't mind a little trouble.

Diane didn't seem to hear me.

The driver looked our way a second time. He blared his horn, then angrily mouthed a string of profanity.

"That's not Simon," Diane said softly. I could barely hear her over the wind and Taylor.

"No. It's not. Now slow the hell down."

"And that isn't a woman."

"No. I don't think it is," I said.

"And did...did he call us cunts?"

I don't know why it was so funny to hear Diane say *cunts*. Maybe it was the wispy, disbelieving tone of her voice. Maybe it was because she was walking, talking sunshine and rainbows, a person who couldn't believe someone would ever call someone else a vile name.

"Yeah. He did." I giggled. "Now slow down. God."

She eased off the gas, and the truck sped away. I was relieved the driver wasn't the kind of asshole who'd slow down and follow us.

"I...I must seem crazy." Diane shook her head. "I thought that was him. That truck—"

"It's fine. You're stressed. It's understandable. And that did look like his truck."

Because it was his truck.

Diane exited to the highway that ran outside of town. The

silence between us felt heavy, almost uncomfortable. Weird. Our silences were never strained.

"Admit it. You think I'm pathetic," Diane said after a while.

"What? Why would you say that?"

Now that we weren't zooming on the interstate at seventy-five miles an hour, it was easier to understand each other. I flicked off the music.

"You don't have to lie." There was a hardness in her words as she turned onto the lonely stretch of road that would take us to another, lonelier stretch that turned to gravel before dead-ending in the forest. It was a familiar route. "You would never have done that. Christ. I chased down a truck. What was I thinking?"

"I don't think you're pathetic—I could never..." I paused, pointing out the upcoming sign so she wouldn't miss our turn.

We weren't far now.

"For what it's worth," I said. "I have no idea what I'd have done." I let out a deep breath. "I can't imagine feeling that strongly about a man—about *anyone* romantically—that I'd lose my mind. I'm not bragging; it's not a strength. Like how love makes you crazy sometimes isn't a weakness. Maybe that's why we work so well together."

Diane smiled. "I hadn't thought about it like that. Maybe so. Still, I can't believe I thought that was his truck. What am I going to do? Go insane every time he doesn't text back? Chase every ugly blue truck in Baton Rouge?"

I shrugged. "That would keep things interesting."

"Shut up." She laughed.

I pointed again and she turned.

A few miles slipped by silently before Diane asked, "You sure we're in the right spot?"

The road was riddled with potholes and bumpy enough to chatter your teeth. I could dodge them with my eyes closed, but Diane hit every single one—almost like she was trying to.

It had been ages since I'd been here in daylight. With its dense, scrubby landscape, the stretch of back road wasn't exactly scenic. Everything was a shade of gray or brown or dark green. "Yeah." I forced brightness into my tone. "Christopher said once we get to the trail, it's gorgeous."

"Okay." She sounded pensive. "If McSmiley says so—because it looks like a bunch of swampland to me. Creepy."

She turned the Jeep onto the final road. In another mile it would give way to gravel. The closer we got to the dump site, the small knot in my stomach tightened. Silly. There was nothing to be nervous about. Hopefully, I'd find the bracelet right away, and *not* find any other cameras at all. And who knows—maybe we would have a nice hike. Yeah, right. There was no such thing.

The faint echo of tires screeching against pavement, along with a high-pitched whining sounded from somewhere far behind us.

"What's that?" Diane asked. The whining grew louder. "Sounds like a siren."

Before the words were out of her mouth, a cop zoomed behind us, siren blaring. A second later, there was another one.

My throat constricted, and my vision went fuzzy and bright around the edges. This was it. They'd somehow found Simon and tracked me down.

How?

I'd gotten my key back from Mr. Goodreaux.

It had to be Mr. Percival. He'd made good on his threat and convinced a cop that I'd stolen his dog. They'd entered my home and found the body. That had to be it.

I grabbed the Jeep's oh-shit bar in front of me. My fingers wrapped around it, squeezing until my knuckles burned. Cold, clammy sweat bathed every inch of my skin. I wasn't afraid—not exactly. What I did was right and good. I had no regrets.

But to go down like this? With the body of a monster in my bathtub packed with kitty litter; it would be a media frenzy.

Oh god. The true crime podcasts would have a field day.

Diane would never forgive me. Sugar would hate me because for the rest of her life she'd be the goddaughter of that deranged lunatic Cordelia Black. Even McSmiley's life would be ruined. *Hey are you that cop that was dating that serial killer and never even knew?*

I was an albatross strangling the ones I cared about.

"Cordelia?" Diane slowed the Jeep to a crawl. "Are you okay? You're white as a sheet."

My eye twitched. Joanie was here with me—I could feel her—wanting to break down. To confess while there was still time.

The cops were closer now, directly on our bumper. With the top off the Jeep, the sirens blared so violently my molars ached. Maybe I could make Diane understand. Maybe she'd stand by me. We were Cordelia and Diane, weren't we? Vintage?

So why did I feel like Joanie?

"Cor!" Diane yelled, but I barely heard her.

She pulled the Jeep to the roadside. She had no idea she was carrying what the police were after, and if she pulled over, they'd follow. Why else would three police cruisers show up with blaring sirens in the middle of nowhere?

The cops must've discovered my car at Diane's, and assumed we were together. It would be easy enough to find two women in a bright yellow Jeep. It was hardly a needle in a haystack. Baton Rouge wasn't huge like Atlanta or Houston.

"You don't look so good," Diane yelled.

This time I turned to face her. I blinked. My mouth opened, but I snapped it closed, realizing my fatal mistake in all of this.

We were together. The cops were going to think she was in on it. Simon was her boyfriend, after all.

"I'm so sorry." The words came out in a whisper. Or maybe they didn't come out at all.

Time meant nothing. The moment lasted forever. Joanie scratched beneath the surface, but I didn't give in to her tears. *If you cry, the world'll swallow you up!* Mama's words echoed.

Sugar. What would happen to her? Would she end up in foster care? Or be shipped to Florida to live with Diane's snobby, estranged older sister?

My hands shook, the sensation moving up my arms and taking over my body. I didn't fight it, nor the twitchy eye. It didn't matter. None of it did.

Diane's gaze burned a hole through me as she slowed to a complete stop and shifted to park.

"I'm sorry," I whispered again.

"What? What are you saying?" Diane yelled over the noise. "You look like you're going to pass out."

The police cars didn't stop.

They flew around us, barreling down the road. Soon, even their sirens disappeared.

I was…*safe*?

Diane eyed me, her expression dripping with concern. I was Cordelia—the strong one. The one who had it together, always. She'd never seen me almost lose it before.

"Cor…what were you saying?" she asked again.

A deep breath filled my lungs, and I released it with a loud, steady whoosh, throwing my head back. It was like, in a moment, all at once, everything released in me. My stomach felt as if it were full of Jell-O, and every nerve and muscle and tendon went slack.

We sat on the roadside for at least five minutes, not speaking, while Diane rubbed away the gooseflesh that had sprouted across my arms.

"You want to tell me what that was about?" she asked.

"I—" I bit my lip. "I don't think I know. The sirens… Probably childhood trauma shit."

She nodded gravely. Diane didn't know everything about my past—she didn't know Joanie—but she knew enough to understand why anything to do with sirens could be triggering. Using my shitty upbringing as an excuse may have been an easy out, but damn. I'd survived it, so it might as well serve me as an adult. And if keeping my best friend from thinking I'd gone off the deep end wasn't serving me, then nothing was.

"Don't take this the wrong way," Diane said. "But I don't feel like hiking anymore. Raincheck?"

I nodded my agreement.

I couldn't have hiked if I'd still wanted to. Everything that was supposed to hold me together and give me form had gone wobbly. I felt boneless and wrong. I collapsed back in my seat and didn't talk. I'd only wanted to protect her; instead I'd put Diane in a different kind of danger.

We rode back to the interstate in silence, not bothering with the radio.

I felt better by the time we reached Diane's, but she decided she needed a nap, so we said goodbye.

On the drive back to my house, something bothered me. It was right there in the recesses of my mind, its nagging buzz like a mosquito you could hear but not kill.

Then. It hit me.

The cops zoomed around us and disappeared. But there was nothing on that road—it turned to gravel and dead-ended at the forest where I exchanged bodies with Clarence.

They hadn't been after me, but they would be soon. Because where else could they have possibly been going?

There must've been another camera. Somewhere some poacher saw something that made him call the police.

I wasn't safe after all.

THE URGE TO RUN WAS INTENSE, BUT I WASN'T SOMEONE who could simply disappear, abandoning Diane and Sugar without a trace, only to be named a suspect on the news. I'd never do that to them.

And then there was Simon. Once he was found—and he *would* be found without me around to hold things together—everything would be over.

There was a chance I wasn't recognizable on whatever footage the police now had.

If they even had any.

In a way, getting caught would feel better than this uncertainty. Jumping out of my skin each time headlights bounced across the window blinds. Horrible scenarios playing on loop in my mind.

I paced the floor. *Living room. Kitchen. Living room. Kitchen.* Sitting here doing nothing would drive me insane. I needed a task—something I could control.

I sniffed the air.

Simon's odor was stronger. *Garlicky. Earthy.* Not overwhelming, nor, I suspected, identifiable, but noticeable in a way it hadn't been that morning. Well. That was a task. Time to put Simon on ice.

Kitty litter, it turned out, was the glitter of the pet supply world. It got everywhere and stuck to everything.

The clay kernels scattered across my bathroom tile when I pulled Simon, and then his tarp, from the tub. Pellets dug into the monster's every crevice and crease, but I had my nifty shop vacuum. I'd bought it to keep my car tidy. Who knew it would be so good at cleaning kitty litter out of a dead man's armpits? It deserved a rave review online: *Five stars! Works perfectly to clean up life's little messes.*

I double-bagged the tarp and litter, and vacuumed up the stray pellets. Mango growled from the corner of the room as I worked. "I know exactly how you feel," I assured her. Simon still raised my heckles as well.

Once finished, I heaved the monster's corpse back into the tub, and made a grocery run, where I purchased fifteen large bags of ice. When I returned, my driveway wasn't filled with police cars. Always a good sign.

I packed the ice around Simon, leaving only his head visible. It reminded me of a nature documentary I'd watched once, about alligators during a North Carolina winter. The beasts would sleep beneath icy water, nothing showing but their snouts. They were slow from their lowered body temperatures, but they were dangerous all the same. Just like Simon, dead and frozen, was still a danger to me.

By that evening, cops had not burst down my front door waving a warrant.

I was too keyed up for bed, even though it was—*no way*! How was it only seven o'clock? That couldn't be right; it felt so much later.

I checked my phone: 7:08 p.m.

And a missed text from Christopher.

CHRISTOPHER: How are you feeling this afternoon?

How was I feeling?

Oh. Right. He thought I wasn't well.

CORDELIA: Better, thanks.

Complete lie.

Mango twined through my legs as I surveyed my kitchen. When Christopher didn't immediately text back, I set my phone on the counter.

I pulled my caddy of cleaning supplies from beneath the kitchen sink and got to work scrubbing the previously missed splotches. As I mindlessly washed the monster's blood from my grout, I relived the thrill of my screwdriver pushing through his skin, through his fascia, and through his muscle with a satisfying *pop*.

Killing Simon had been extraordinary, but by doing it without a plan, I'd given him control, which he still held on to. He sat in my home, bloating and smug. If I was caught, if everything in this life I'd worked so hard for came apart at the seams, it was because of him. He'd laugh if he could. A man like Simon? He'd enjoy holding that power.

I squirted more cleaner across the tile—the same tile where less than a day before, he'd been splayed out, bleeding for his crime—and scrubbed harder than necessary. A low whine came from Mango as she watched from her perch on the back of my sofa. "It's fine," I lied. "Everything is going to be okay. You'll see."

She cocked her head to the side as if she didn't believe me. Why should she? I didn't believe me.

Every push of the sponge, every spray of cleaner grew more intense.

Still no cops.

What was I missing?

I tossed my sponge into the trash bin, then stared at it for a moment, doing nothing except feeling my heartbeat and listening to my racing thoughts.

Since becoming Cordelia, I'd only felt like this—spiraling out of control—one other time.

In the beginning hunting was messy and scary, but I'd been in charge of each and every scenario. There'd been no reason to harbor such erratic fear because I'd left nothing to chance. My wits—planning and executing—were impeccable, and I'd never had a reason to doubt myself. Every monster was researched. Even before Clarence, even on the darkest days, I'd known exactly how things would go, from start to finish.

The one time I'd lost control hadn't been from a hunt. It was from before I knew my calling. Before I'd understood *why* I was so compelled to become Cordelia in the first place.

That kill—like Simon's—had also been for Diane.

It was an accident. I hadn't stalked him. He'd let me into his home, his wife was out of town. The powder I'd slipped into his drink was supposed to only knock him out; that was what the internet had promised. He wasn't supposed to die—he was only meant to sleep. I would take compromising photos of him. Photos that would make him stop. Make him leave Diane alone. But he'd had a reaction, and when he'd sipped his poisoned whiskey, his hazy eyes rolled back into his head, and foam leaked from the corners of his mouth. He'd made a clicking sound as he'd dropped to his knees, as if pleading for help.

I'd watched, unable to move at first.

And then, I ran.

The news of his death splashed across the television in our dorm a few days later. Diane cried, mistaking my silence for shock. I'd hated him—what he'd coerced Diane into. How he'd made her agree to things she didn't want. Things she'd whispered to me about after we turned off the lights each night, she in her bed and me in mine. She'd hated herself for what he made her do. Diane—*my Diane*—had said that; he made her hate herself.

And he wasn't going to stop. Diane was hardly the first. He was Peter Pan, and our school was Neverland.

But still, when we'd watched the news of his death, she'd cried real tears, so I couldn't tell her what happened. How he wasn't supposed to die. How I'd been there.

For days I'd waited for the police to show up. To haul me from our dorm and off campus. To arrest me. I'd finally cried—but not because I'd been responsible for his death. No, Joanie's tears had leaked from my eyes at the idea losing Diane. But it never happened, and not too long after that, Diane discovered she was pregnant, so I'd done the thing I was so good at—the skill I'd honed since my birth; I'd pushed the trauma down and buried it alongside my former self, and instead focused on helping my friend. She'd needed me, and I'd always be there for her.

What I felt now—the helpless, hopeless weight of emotion—it was akin to what I'd felt that bleak night when I'd accidentally poisoned our history professor.

I'd learned a lot when Sugar's sperm donor had died, and it wasn't long after when I discovered, and heeded, my life's calling. Because the lesson that I'd been taught was I could get away with killing bad men.

I inhaled a shaky breath.

Maybe I hadn't lied to Mango. Maybe everything was going to be fine. Simon was a bad man. No—he was a monster. *There'd been smoke. This was my calling.*

So what if it happened a little differently than usual?

Time for a break. I picked up my phone and walked to the living room and collapsed onto the sofa. Mango jumped down from her perch and snuggled into my lap.

Christopher had texted back.

CHRISTOPHER: Good. I'm glad you're better. I wanted to check on you sooner but today has been insane.

Insane. The police cruisers were so prevalent in my memory that when I shut my eyes, I could hear the echo of their sirens. See the red and blue flash of lights behind my eyelids. Taste the bile that had bubbled up my throat. *Insane...how?* Did Christopher know what happened on that lonely stretch of back road? Had they found the dump site? My mouth went dry but I channeled Sweet Cordelia.

CORDELIA: Aw. I'm sorry. Anything I can do to help?

CHRISTOPHER: I'd love to hang out if you're feeling up for it...

Perfect.

CORDELIA: Give me an hour to shower and change.

CHRISTOPHER: Great! 😃

He dropped a pin, and I ran upstairs to get ready, with Mango right behind me.

25

MCSMILEY'S HOME WAS THE END UNIT OF A TIDY ROW OF cheerful yellow townhouses, about twenty minutes from my own place. When I arrived, the sky was darkening, and everyone's porch lights glowed softly with waxy light, reminding me of miniature full moons.

Purple flowers bloomed in oversized pots flanking Christopher's front door. *Interesting.* It was the kind of thing Diane would love—that despite his hectic career, McSmiley managed to keep plants alive. Again I thought of how much easier life would be right now if she'd met McSmiley instead of Simon.

I raised my knuckles to knock, but the front door opened before I had a chance. Christopher's damp hair fell artfully away from his face, and he smelled clean, like Irish Spring. "You made it," he said. "Come on in." He stepped back and, with a dorky swooping gesture, ushered me into his home.

The living room screamed *bachelor pad*, filled with a worn leather sofa and a monstrous flat-screen balanced on an ugly glass and metal television stand. Two gaming consoles were tucked beneath. There wasn't a book or throw pillow or scented candle in the place, but several pages of a kid's artwork—*Olive's, perhaps?*—were tacked to the far walls. Yep. Diane and her exploding ovaries would've fallen for Christopher, hook, line, and sinker.

"I hope you're hungry." McSmiley smiled—because of course—and nodded toward the coffee table, which was littered with take-out containers, opened to reveal steaming dishes of roasted chicken doused in sweet sauces, shrimp fried rice, crispy green beans, potstickers, and more.

"Always." My stomach rumbled. "Mmm. Smells amazing." The spicy aroma was an upgrade from the odor at my house, but anything was better than pine-scented dead guy.

"Good. My last attempt at feeding you the best Chinese food in the city didn't go over so great. I hope to redeem myself." As he spoke, Christopher watched my face intently.

"What?" I asked, throwing in a Sweet Cordelia dip of the chin for good measure.

"Your hair. I love it. Dark hair and dressed in all black, you look like a cat burglar."

"Cat burglar, huh?" My lips pursed into a smirk. I'd carefully chosen tonight's outfit. Casual. Sexy, but not obvious. I'd nailed it with high-waisted black leggings and a cropped black tank. No jewelry. Simple makeup. Easy. The fitted outfit not only showed off my curves, but Christopher wasn't wrong—it paired perfectly with my new hair color. I tucked a sleek strand behind my ear. "That's what does it for you, huh?"

Christopher shrugged. "You can't hold what I say against me when you show up looking like this." The corners of his eyes crinkled. "Can you do a French accent?"

I swatted his arm and peeked at him from beneath my lashes—full-on Sweet Cordelia. "You do *not* want to hear me attempt *any* accent, I promise."

It was the truth. The process of correcting Joanie's backwoods elocution had been more painful than fixing my teeth.

Christopher scooped food onto paper plates, and we ate. The meal was even better than I remembered. Of course, last time, I'd inhaled lukewarm noodles straight from the container while eyeballing Simon's fresh corpse. Christopher's living room could use a style upgrade—pretty sure his wobbly coffee table was rescued from the side of the road—but there were no dead bodies.

"I'm glad you came over." Christopher pushed fried rice around his plate. "Perfect ending to a crazy day."

"Me too." I made room on the coffee table and set my plate down. I thought of the police cruisers barreling behind Diane and me. How I'd frozen in place, sure I was caught, my entire life as I knew it over. This was my opening to find out what I needed to know. "I wonder if your crazy day had anything to do with what Diane and I saw."

"I don't know." Christopher's head tipped to the side. "What did you see?"

Silence lingered between us as I considered my best move. *Innocent. Oblivious. Sweet.* I clasped my hands in my lap. "After my hair appointment, Diane talked me into going on a hike. I hate hiking, but Simon was supposed to go but couldn't, and Diane been looking forward to it for days. The trail he'd told her about was way out near the parish line—you have to go down this dead-end back road to find it. Simon called it a hidden gem." Wasn't like Simon could correct my lie. "Anyway. These cop cars appeared out of nowhere and flew around us like bats out of hell. It was so strange because there was no one else around."

"Wait. Were you out near Old Hound Road?" Christopher's dark brows furrowed, and he leaned forward slightly. There was a seriousness in his tone that wasn't there before. "Why the hell would y'all go out there? It's nothing but overgrown swamp."

"Um." I pretended to think. "Maybe. I don't remember the road names. Simon said the trail was a great find." I shrugged. "But I don't know, we didn't go on the hike. The cop cars freaked us out so we turned around and left."

"Simon is an idiot." Christopher's tea-and-honey eyes flicked over me as he sat up straight, his jaw suddenly tight. It was a look I recognized, both from the monsters I hunted and the doctors I dealt with day in and day out at my job. It was an appraisal. I didn't like it.

"Y'all should stay away from that area. Cordelia, you need to be careful." He shook his head, and when he spoke again, it was more to himself than me. "I can't believe Simon would suggest y'all hike out there. What was he even doing out there to find a hiking trail?"

"Be careful of what? We're adult women and there were the two of us." I rubbed my palms over the length of my thighs. "And

I agree—Simon is an idiot. But that aside, if something is going on—Christopher..." My voice trailed off. I hope I sounded worried. Afraid. Which, okay, I kind of was, but not because of what was down Old Hound Road. I was anxious for obvious reasons.

McSmiley was silent, the muscles in his jaw twitching as he clenched it tight, his thoughts warring over his handsome face. He wanted to tell me—I could see it—but he wasn't sure if it was the right thing to do. "I...I know I'm being weird." He sighed. "This case...well, it's a lot. I didn't mean to scare you."

I rested my hand on top of his and leaned close. *Trust Sweet Cordelia.* The thought ran on repeat, as if I could beam it from my mind directly into his. *Protect Sweet Cordelia.* "Is there something I should know about? To stay safe, I mean? Did we almost stumble into something...something bad?"

"Okay." He nodded after a moment. I'd done it; he was going to tell me what he knew. "We got word of something illegal out there. I can't answer specifics." Sure he could. "But I've seen some things." He raked a large palm over his face. "That sounded stupid. What I mean is I don't scare easy, and this whole case gives me the heebie-jeebies." He looked deeply into my eyes, no smile on McSmiley's face. "Promise you'll stay away from that whole area—you're not missing anything; it's a dump on the best day. Trust me."

"But why? What has you so freaked out?"

Something was happening. Something big.

Stay away. Heebie-jeebies.

At least I could safely rule out another camera. No way I'd be sitting here having dinner with a cop if they'd found one. That was good news.

What else was there? What could I have possibly missed? Because that had to be it. Why else would the cops haul ass to such an unremarkable piece of swamp? We sat, with Christopher staring at me, and neither of us speaking. My chest tingled with a feeling like spiderwebs brushing against my insides. I closed my eyes and inhaled. It was fine.

Everything was fine.

"I'm not freaked out," Christopher said carefully. "Just concerned." His eyes narrowed. "Are *you* okay? You look a little... flustered."

I gathered Sweet Cordelia around me like a shawl, pushing the spurt of anxiety *down, down, down.* The police cars hadn't been for me; that was all that mattered at the moment. Whatever they found out there—why they were there in the first place—it was fine. Cordelia was always fine.

Sweet Cordelia sighed, oh so softly. "I'm okay. It's strange though, to think we were randomly so close to a crime scene. Scary."

"It is." Christopher nodded. "Random, I mean. I should have a chat with Simon."

Good luck with that. Then, *Does he suspect Simon of something?*

I tucked the little nugget of information away—it could be useful. Or dangerous if he decided he needed to find Simon sooner rather than later. *Great.*

"Cordelia?" Christopher took my hand in his.

"Huh?" I blinked, smiling wanly, glancing down to where his fingers clasped mine.

"You're okay. Diane's okay. Nothing happened."

"What are you talking about?"

"You have this strange look on your face. It's the crime scene, isn't it? I freaked you out. I shouldn't have said anything. The last thing I wanted to do tonight was upset you." McSmiley squeezed my hand and I stared into his face. There was nothing there but concern. True concern. "Guess when it comes to good dates, I'm oh for three."

It was kind of cute, the way he worried about me.

Unnecessary, but cute.

"You didn't do anything wrong. I asked, remember?"

"Yeah. But I know better." He tucked a piece of hair behind my ear, and my eyes darted to his. "When you see crazy things on a regular basis, it's easy to lose perspective on what would freak out most people. Accidentally walking into a crime scene is a lot. Being told not to go somewhere because it could be dangerous? Not exactly date night conversation. I warned you on our first date I wasn't that good at this."

"You're fine," Sweet Cordelia said without hesitation. *Keep talking; tell me your secrets.* "For what it's worth, I'm having a great time."

Christopher's expression shifted to his *I want to kiss you* face. Of course a damsel in distress would get him all hot and bothered. I'd predicted as much on the first date. It was the whole reason I'd trotted out Sweet Cordelia to begin with.

I had to admit: McSmiley was cute. And—okay, yes the fact that he wanted to be a knight in shining armor was super annoying—but he was sweet. Someone who wanted to be a real good guy, not a phony Nice-Guy like Simon. Maybe kissing him could be fun.

My eyes lingered on his full lips, the kind of mouth *made* for kissing. For the second time since I'd met him, I considered it. Not because I was attracted to him—I wasn't, not really—but because I wondered what kissing McSmiley was like. He was probably good at it. It would probably lead to other fun things, and I needed to blow off some steam. God. How long had it been since I'd gotten laid?

It would be so easy to let it happen.

But no. It was the wrong move. Not part of my plan. Christopher would get super attached, I could tell. It wasn't a complication I needed. Not right now.

I dropped my gaze and he took the hint. Sweet Cordelia—the little minx—required things to move very slowly, apparently.

He cleared his throat and asked, "You want to watch a movie?"

Anything was better than hanging out at home with a smelly, decomposing monster.

"Sure," I said. "What do you have in mind?"

"How do you feel about rom-coms?"

"Love them." Not a total lie. I could appreciate nineties Tom Hanks as much as the next girl.

"Great. This is one of my favorites." Christopher selected a movie older than me, starring Meg Ryan and Billy Crystal. No Tom Hanks, but it was fine. We lounged on the couch, our limbs gradually tangling together.

My ovaries remained in no danger of exploding, thank you very much.

My eyes popped open and for a moment I panicked. Where was I? Whose arms were around me? What was that noise? I stiffened, afraid to move but also wanting to run. To bite and kick and scratch and get away.

Slowly, my thoughts untangled themselves from nightmares and I relaxed.

I was lying next to Christopher on the sofa, his arms draped over me as he softly snored. The television screen was dark. What time was it?

I blinked the sleep away, my eyes adjusting. The faintest hint of dusky pink sunrise showed around the blinds.

I'd spent the night. *Not part of the plan.*

After the first movie, we'd tidied up. Christopher had brought out ice cream; then we'd started a second movie. I should've known better; I could never stay awake through two movies. But Simon was at my house and not thinking about him had felt so nice. I'd fully meant to get up, to leave. Eventually.

I needed to go. I had work. And Mango needed breakfast and to pee. And I needed to check on Simon...ugh.

Fucking Simon.

Christopher's arms and legs were looped around me, and I considered the best way to free myself without disturbing him.

I rolled onto my side, and something on the coffee table caught my eye.

Christopher's phone. He'd set it on the table after picking up our mess from dinner.

Would there be another, more perfect opportunity to find out *exactly* why the police had barreled down the desolate stretch of back road? What had given Christopher—as he put it—the heebie-jeebies? It had to be something big. He'd wanted to chat with Simon for simply telling us we should hike the area.

Christopher snored loudly.

Okay.

With a deep breath, I scooched softly to the edge of the couch without sitting up, stretching my arm toward the table. *Almost there.*

Christopher snuggled closer to me. I froze. What was my plan if he woke up?

I could say I was...looking for the remote. That would work.

I strained forward, my fingertips on the dark plastic of his phone case, and slid it to the edge of the table. Very carefully, I lifted it up.

It was locked. Of course it was locked. Who didn't lock their phone?

What number or word was important enough for Christopher to use as a passcode? Maybe something to do with his niece, Olive? Had he mentioned her birthday? No. Not to me.

I didn't even know *his* birthday.

His gentle snores grew into a steady buzzing, and his arm

tightened over my waist. The phone slipped from my fingers and bounced from my chest to the floor with a thump.

I waited, and when Christopher didn't wake up, I eased his arm away, so slowly and so surely, and again rolled to the edge of the oversized sofa. My fingers walked over the floor until I had the phone in my hand.

This time I took a moment to inspect the device.

Diane had this same model, and she used face ID to unlock it.

I rolled over until my breasts smushed against Christopher's chest. He stirred and smiled in his sleep, but his eyes remained shut. I held the phone over his face, gripping it tightly so I wouldn't drop it.

Come on. Work.

Christopher wiggled.

Don't wake up. Don't wake up.

My "looking for the remote" excuse wouldn't work now.

Christopher mumbled something and blinked, his eyes opening into slits, my heart leaping into my throat. *Shit.* There was no explaining this away.

But as quickly as they fluttered open, his lids closed.

The brief eye contact was all it took. The phone clicked and I was inside.

I rolled onto my side and held the phone over the side of the sofa, close to the ground, just in case. I opened his messages. Lots of names I didn't recognize. There was my text thread under CORDELIA FUMBLE. I rolled my eyes, but kept scrolling until I found one that looked promising. It said BOSS.

It was a group text. I clicked on it.

BOSS: Good job today. Things didn't pan out how we hoped, but progress was made. Don't worry. He'll talk eventually. Keep things by the book. We are so close. Remember, this one stays quiet.

He?

Nothing about bodies or a pirogue.

What could possibly have given Christopher the heebie-jeebies? He did seem a little dramatic, didn't he? There was the cupcake of deception and the way he'd showed up late at night with food.

Yeah. He probably liked the attention. Liked warning Sweet Cordelia to be safe. Total superhero complex.

The whole thing, it was probably nothing but another drug bust. Maybe a meth lab in the woods. Wouldn't be the first time. Or even the second or third. They'd never happened near my body-exchange site—one of the reasons I'd chosen the isolated location—but if that was changing, it would explain the camera. And last week Tanisha Harris had reported on—

"You awake?"

The phone fell from my fingers.

"Sorry didn't mean to startle you." Christopher's morning voice was deep and gravelly. His breath was warm against my neck. It wasn't terrible.

I rolled to face him, breast pushed strategically against his body. *Don't look at the ground, McSmiley. Nothing to see there.* "I guess we fell asleep."

"I guess we did." Christopher gave me a squeeze. "You want to get some breakfast? How do you feel about Egg McMuffins?"

Okay. He didn't know I'd had his phone. Not if he was talking about breakfast sandwiches. Also—way to spring for the good stuff, big spender. *McDonald's* after I spent the night? *Really, McSmiley?* I smiled. *McSmiley. McMuffin.*

McStupid.

"What're you grinning about?" he teased.

"Nothing," I said. "And I can't. I have to get home and—" I almost said *Let Mango out* but caught myself. "Get ready for work. Busy day."

"At least stay for coffee."

"I really can't." Sweet Cordelia gave him what I hoped was an apologetic look. I needed to get out of here, to gather my bearings. I wouldn't be out of the woods until Simon was out of my house, but everything I'd found out was good news, and I'd take it.

His fingers traced my arm, stopping at my wrist. "Hey. You took off the bracelet."

"You noticed." What I meant was, *shit shit shit.* Things were going too well.

"Yeah." Christopher ran his fingertips over my wrist. "I thought it was sweet."

The moment on the back road had rattled me worse than I'd realized. Why else would I make such an idiotic mistake? Of course McSmiley noticed; he'd noticed the bracelet at the zoo. I should've worn long sleeves. No, I should've bought some pink yarn and made a decoy bracelet. Something. Anything.

I'd foolishly thought that with Simon dead, the bracelet posed no threat. The swamp was dark and deep, and the bracelet was several inches of ratty pink yarn, and it might not even be there.

But it could be.

And Christopher could find it.

He would recognize it. I know he would.

He'd remember my story of me and Diane going hiking in the area, and he'd know something wasn't adding up. Maybe it wasn't a smoking gun. Maybe it was a long shot—but a long shot was still a shot.

I'd not planned for this. For any of it. And now I was going to pay, because that was how life worked.

Calm down. This is nothing.

But it wasn't nothing.

What did I know about this man, anyway? What if my gut reaction the night after Diane's barbecue had been the right one, and Christopher could see right through me? What if this was all an act? Why would he bring up the bracelet without good reason? He didn't know I never took it off. I hadn't told him that, had I?

Had I?

Had I?

I couldn't remember.

God. I was spiraling. *Get a grip, Cordelia.* My eye twitched.

"I'm glad you stayed over," Christopher said, oblivious to my silent meltdown. "Spending time with you was exactly what I needed to get my head right."

Jesus, how did he not feel my heart pounding?

He smiled, and it wasn't his McSmiley grin.

This smile felt intentional—deep and something like smoldering? Was he watching me, analyzing how I'd react? It was a tactic I used often: ruffle feathers and people slip up.

But not me. Not Cordelia Black.

I mirrored Christopher's sexy morning smile with my own—minus crinkly eyes because thank you, Botox—and before he could ask another question, I leaned forward and pressed my lips to his. Was it planned? No.

But it would work. He'd wanted to kiss me for weeks.

His thumbs pressed into my hip bones, and he deepened the kiss.

Good.

You didn't kiss people you suspected of murder.

THE KISS WORKED. SORT OF. I MADE IT OUT OF Christopher's house without any more talk of the bracelet. Maybe he'd forget about it.

Yeah. Sure.

As for the kiss? It was...fine.

Okay. It wasn't fine. It had felt like kissing my brother. He hadn't said so, but I was pretty sure McSmiley felt it as well. His dopey kiss-me expression was wiped away after a single lip-lock, and he hadn't begged me to stay for more.

It was kind of disappointing—not because I *wanted* to kiss McSmiley. But because I'm a good kisser, damn it. And a sore loser. This felt like losing.

Besides, I'd worked too hard on McSmiley to lose my in with the police now, when I needed it most.

Maybe we could be friends. *Yeah.* That could work—you confide in your friends, right? My experience in the matter was limited, but I told Diane everything. Well. Almost everything.

Okay, actually, that was a bad example because there was a whole hell of a lot I didn't confide to Diane. But *she* confided in *me*. So would Christopher.

My thoughts were still spiraling between the kiss, and the bracelet, and, well, everything, when my phone rang.

Not my smartphone. No, the ringing was from the phone that was kept for a single purpose. The one I trashed and replaced each month without fail.

My simple disposable, untraceable phone. It had no internet, no Bluetooth. It didn't even have caller ID.

The cheap contraption was only important because it was my singular line to the body snatcher.

Since Clarence was never to call me—a fact I'd made sure he understood the very first time we'd done business—there was no reason for this phone to ring. *Ever.* I'd never even had so much as a robocall on one of my burners.

The muffled sound came from the glove box.

Without stopping my car, I reached over and dug the phone out, clutching it so tightly my fingers ached. What was the move? What was the right plan? Before I could decide, the ringing stopped.

I punched my brakes and slid onto the shoulder of River Road. The urge to chuck the phone out the window and drive away was strong, but that wouldn't solve a thing, would it? I was in no position to let things such as random phone calls to untraceable burner phones go. The last thing I could afford to do right now was make yet another mistake.

Think, Cordelia.

Should I call him back? *Of course not.* Could I even be sure it was Clarence? It had to be; he was the only one with this number. I never bothered blocking the number when calling because I changed burners so often. He'd have it from the last body drop.

My head buzzed with terrible possibilities. I should've answered. Knowing what was happening was always better. No matter what.

When the phone rang a second time, I didn't hesitate. I clicked the answer button, but said nothing, refusing to show my hand. I breathed heavily into the receiver, signaling that, yes, I was here.

"Hello?" My body snatcher sounded nothing like the slick businessman from the medical device conventions. His usual smooth tenor was nasal, pitched an octave higher. His panicked breath crackling through the receiver of the cheap phone tricked my ear into feeling damp. I switched sides and wiped away the imagined wetness.

Why was he doing this? There was too much at stake for him to break the rules. A man like Clarence only cared about money—he would never risk losing such a lucrative business deal. Unless he didn't have a choice.

Unless he was desperate.

Heebie-jeebies. He'll talk eventually...

Fuck. Clarence was a he. And if heebie-jeebies were a person, they'd be Clarence. The slender trout-mouthed man with the greasy comb-over and grandpa cardigans was creepy, no doubt about it. And he was the only other person who knew what went down on the deserted swatch of land at the end of Old Hound Road.

I pressed the phone harder to my ear, letting out another round of heavy breaths.

"Hello? Is that you? Are you there? Listen, I need a body. Tonight. Hello? It's important. I, uh." Clarence stammered. "I, I know it isn't our meeting day and I'm not supposed to call you—but this... I'll pay you double—you hear me? A thousand dollars! Two thousand! Hello?"

This wasn't right. Nothing about this was right.

First the camera.

Then the police.

And now Clarence.

There was no way this was all a coincidence.

Without saying a word, I ended the call. I pulled the battery loose then lay my forehead against the leather-wrapped steering wheel and shut my eyes. Droplets of sweat tickled my cheeks as they traveled from my temples, sliding down my face, landing in my lap, making wet circles on the thin material of my leggings. My eye twitched.

I could no longer hold the scream inside. It tore from my throat, giving voice to the rage and fear and anxiety that had all but consumed me since the very first moment Simon had given me that prickly feeling in Diane's kitchen.

Fucking Simon.

I sprang from my car and jogged up the steep hill to the levee, which ran alongside the road, then reared back and slung both pieces of the cell into the Mississippi River, panting as they disappeared below the rippling surface. As they sank, something cracked open inside of me and relief flooded out, diluting the panic and anger.

I screamed again, but this time, the primal sound came out as laughter. My shoulders shook with the absurdity of everything. My knees buckled, and I sank to the isolated sidewalk. There was no sound but the lapping water and my gasping breath.

I sat and laughed, shoulder-shaking belly laughs, until I was empty, and only then could I see the situation for what it was. And that nagging tickle in my hindbrain? Those almost thoughts that kicked up anxiety and dredged up Joanie with her useless panic from the ether of my subconscious and made my eyelid do the cha-cha? In a single moment, it all quieted.

I squinted into the sunshine, my lips spreading into a grin as the river breeze kissed my face. The sky was blue, the air was clear, and it was beautiful out. I pushed to my feet and dusted off my pants.

Whatever was happening to Clarence, didn't mean it was bad for me. I'd been smart from the beginning; Cordelia had planned for everything.

If Clarence had somehow managed to get himself caught—if the police were questioning him or if he was working with them—then this phone call did nothing but prove I was going to be okay. Because if he had any inkling of who he was dealing with—of who was leaving him bodies—then I wouldn't have gotten a call on the burner. It was a last-ditch effort on his part. It had to be.

I'd planned for this, hadn't I? Clarence was smarmy and

off-putting—an easy scapegoat. Neither was he innocent. He tricked the dying and pilfered them for profit. There was no need for me to feel guilty. And I didn't.

My steps were lighter as I turned to walk down the hill. I was halfway to my car when the sense of smug well-being evaporated.

I'd delivered Frank to Clarence on Friday, then harvested Simon later that night. I'd put off calling Clarence so as not to raise my body snatcher's suspicions. I'd originally had every intention of meeting him this weekend.

Depending on when Clarence got himself in trouble, I'd likely avoided a close call by waiting. What if I'd gotten spooked by Handy Heroes or Mr. Percival and called Clarence and insisted on meeting him earlier? What if he was already talking to the police? He could've set up a sting.

What if I hadn't found that camera when I did?

Then it would be me at the police station desperately making calls to save my ass.

I opened the car door and slid behind the wheel. Everything worked out for Cordelia Black. I followed my code. I made plans. And okay, so lately I'd had a few slipups, but I was back on track.

I pressed the button to start, shifted to drive, when everything ground to a halt.

The call meant I wasn't a suspect.

But it meant something else as well.

Something bad.

Because Simon was at home in my bathtub.

And without Clarence, I had no way to dispose of the body.

I was distracted when I got out of my car at home, so lost in my own thoughts that I stood on my stoop, key in hand, before I realized something was off.

At first it was a only feeling.

Until I noticed the gate to my backyard.

It was open.

The police. My heart thumped. *Were they inside waiting on me?*

Clarence had known it was me all along, and he'd delivered his misfortune to my doorstep. My gaze darted left, then right. Was my street quieter than usual, an eerie silence before a storm?

No. I'd spent the night with Christopher. The BRPD didn't suspect Cordelia Black of anything.

Still, the hairs on my arm remained on end. No one had reason to be in my yard.

Had someone broken in to rob me? That would be horrible under regular circumstances, but right now my life was *not*, by any stretch of the imagination, regular circumstances.

Holding my breath, I stepped through my fence into my backyard.

"Mr. Percival?"

The man was pulling on the doorknob to my back door.

"What the hell do you think you're doing?" I asked.

His shoulders hunched near his ears, his face whipping toward me. He blinked.

"Well?" I asked.

"I know." He wagged his index finger at me. "You're hiding something. I know what I heard. That handyman said you have a dog, but you don't!"

"You need to leave," I ordered. "Right now. Or I'll call the cops."

He crossed his arms over his barrel chest. "Good. Call them. Then maybe they can check your house for me."

"You're insane," I said. Did I have his dog? Yes, okay? Yes, I did. But he had no reason to know that. Besides, who in their right mind acted this way? "Leave. Now."

He marched toward me. "I'm watching you, Ms. Black."

My eyes narrowed, but I held my tongue as he walked out my gate. I followed and locked it behind him.

BY THURSDAY, SIMON STANK—NO SUPER-SNIFFER required—and I still had no plan for how to get rid of him.

Even after the painstaking process of cleaning out the kitty litter (which I still found in random corners and crevices in my bathroom) and covering him with ice, he was beginning to bloat.

I refilled the diffusers with more lemongrass and sprayed so much lavender mist that it coated the tile floor and turned it slick, but air freshener and essential oils did little to help the odor, which in turn did little to help my mood.

On top of everything else, the groomer hadn't called back. I'd bathed Mango two more times, until finally, annoyed and desperate, on Wednesday I'd bought a pair of clippers from the big box store because I figured, how hard could it be to shave a dog? Turns out—very.

The blades kept getting clogged and Mango yelped as if I were hurting her. By the time I gave up, she looked worse, as if she'd lost a fight with a lawnmower.

Every single time I left my house, I could feel Mr. Percival's eyes crawling over me, staring from behind his curtains.

Things weren't good.

Simon's mouth had fallen open then frozen rigidly in place, and his eyes were caught in an eternal hollow-eyed scream.

"Oh, shut up." I blasted him with a squirt of Lysol. "Why are *you* screaming? You aren't the one with anything to lose."

The gunmetal gray of his irises had faded to the frosted-over color of muddy ground after the first winter cold snap. Purple pooled in the hollow spaces of his face. The gash in his neck was a black hole. No way Diane would find him handsome now. "It's all your fault, anyway," I snapped. "If you'd have left my family alone, neither of us would be in this mess."

I closed the bathroom door, feeling a little like Joanie for ignoring the problem.

Mango weaved through my ankles, chortling until I pulled a dog treat from the pocket of my robe and tossed it to her. She nabbed it midair, and my frown softened. "Good devil dog." We'd been working on the trick for a few days.

I sank into my sofa and picked up my phone.

ME: Hey you!

DIANE: Hey yourself. ☹

ME: Where've you been, stranger? Long time no see.

For most people, going a few days without contact wouldn't be considered long, but I'd talked to Diane at least once each day since we were dormmates.

Three full days without as much as a text was unheard of. I was a bad friend for not checking in on her, but between feeling guilty over her heartbreak and not having a plan to fix things, I worried I'd make everything worse.

DIANE: 😢🤬😠 Physically I've been here. Emotionally? All over the place.

ME: What happened?

As if I didn't know.

DIANE: 🤬 Simon.

...

...

DIANE: He still hasn't shown up or returned my texts. Don't say a damn thing. I can't handle I told you so.

ME: I'd never say that. Are you going to work today?

DIANE: No. 😢💔 I've been taking sick days this week. What if I run into him? I'm pathetic.

No, she wasn't.

ME: I'm coming over.

DIANE: You're the best.

ME: 😎 I know. You're lucky to have me.

DIANE: Bitch. 😍

I knocked twice, then let myself into Diane's.

With Sugar at school, her house felt too quiet. Sweaters hung from the backs of chairs, and the floor was littered with abandoned shoes. Tattered paperbacks sat in a tumbling stack across a small table near the front door, next to a lipstick-stained mug that seemed to be at least a few days old. Diane's sloppiness had driven me crazy when we were roommates. Now it was simply a part of who she was.

"Honey? You downstairs?" I called out as I crossed the living room.

I'd brought with me a box containing my French press and some breakfast goodies. I shifted it in my arms, then slid it onto her dining table. "Diane?"

"In here." Her voice came from underneath a mountain of blankets in the living room. I'd walked right past her and hadn't noticed.

"Oh, babe." I sat down near her feet. "Tell me all about it."

She sat up, pulling her covers tightly around her shoulders. "I thought he loved me—or at least liked me a lot. I'm such an idiot." She groaned. "He didn't even care enough to call and break up. I tried to give him the benefit of the doubt when he missed the hiking trip, but he *never* called." She fell back into her nest. "Samantha was at my parents' house spending the night. I didn't tell you because I was embarrassed, but I'd planned for that night to be the first time he slept over. Hell, it was going to be our first time...you know..."

"Fucking?" I offered.

"God, Cordelia. No." She frowned. "With Simon, it was supposed to be more than that. It was supposed to be special. Or at least *I* thought it was." She grabbed a chartreuse throw pillow and pressed it over her face as her body shook with sobs.

I squeezed her foot and let her cry. This was the part I'd dreaded: Diane's epic heartbreak.

After a few minutes, she screamed into the pillow and then threw it across the room. "Tell me the truth. Is there something wrong with me? Am I so gross that a person would choose to disappear rather than sleep with me?"

Simon hadn't chosen to disappear, but I couldn't tell Diane that. "There's only one explanation." I patted her foot. "He's an idiot."

Diane, with her tear-streaked cheeks, puffy eyes, and runny nose, was miserable, and seeing her this way, knowing I'd had a hand in it—it made me miserable too.

"Aren't you glad you found out now instead of later? The guy's a loser and totally not worthy of you."

She shrugged. "I thought he was different."

"You *always* think they're different," I said. "You *love* love. It's sweet."

"I'm not sweet." Diane scowled. "Don't call me that."

"Sure, honey. I didn't mean anything by it. Now lie there while I fix you some coffee and a bagel. You want cream cheese and raspberry jam? I got it at the farmer's market downtown and it's amazing."

"I'm not hungry." Diane moaned.

"I'm going to make you one. You don't have to eat it." For a moment I felt as if we were college kids instead of thirty-three year old women. Some things never changed. I'd always take care of Diane when she needed me, no matter what that entailed. If it meant putting my own freedom at risk—well, it was a burden I'd carry time and again. No question.

Diane sobbed silently into the pillow, and my head spun with contradicting thoughts. *I was a horrible friend for killing Diane's boyfriend. I was a great friend for taking out a predator who meant her and Sugar harm. She'd hate me if she knew. She'd love me if she knew*. Unable to handle it, I grabbed the remote and clicked on the television to drown out my thoughts. Diane still had cable, and the commercial playing caused me to do a double take. It was the singing kitties—the one shitty-kitty Betty had blathered about. I shook my head as I went into the kitchen to put the kettle on and toast the bagels.

"Aren't you going in to work today?" Diane called from inside her cocoon.

"Ha. That's...complicated at the moment." I scooped the proper amount of coffee into the press.

My three scheduled clients had cancelled their appointments because of Bosephan. They had to blame somebody, and as the evil drug rep who'd touted its safety, I was their most obvious scapegoat. It was great time to finally use some of the sick days I'd banked.

Then there was Practical Family Medicine. That awful office manager had left two more messages. I couldn't put them off much longer.

But Diane didn't need to know any of this. She was dealing with her own stuff.

"I hope everything's okay? I heard things have heated up with the lawsuit..." Her words trailed off.

"Don't worry about me." I popped the bagels into Diane's dollar-store toaster. If they didn't burn it'd be a miracle. "I'm always fine."

"If that isn't the absolute truth. You were a cat in another life. You always land on your feet."

I hoped she was right.

When the coffee had steeped long enough, I brought the French press to the table in front of the sofa, along with two mugs and the food, which I'd attempted to arrange artfully on Diane's favorite yellow trays.

I settled in next to her, and she asked, "Where do you think he is? Do you think he met someone else?"

"Who?"

"Simon. Jeez."

The coffee steamed as I filled her mug. She sat up, and I passed it to her. "I don't know." The lie was effortless. "Anyway, who cares? I know I'm a broken record here, but he wasn't good enough for you."

She took a deep drink, then set her mug on the table and sniffed. "Obviously."

I passed her one of the saucers with a bagel on it, and she took a bite. With the curtains closed tight, Diane's face glowed in the television's light. On the screen, a woman appeared way too excited about dryer sheets.

Diane spoke around her mouthful of carbs. "What if he's with someone at work? I'll be so humiliated. He was always insistent that we didn't let anyone at the hospital know we were together.

He blamed human resources. But what if it was because he was seeing someone else?"

My mind flashed back to the woman from the restaurant. Was she missing Simon, same as Diane? Was she out there looking for him? Reporting his absence to the police?

I studied Diane's face. She needed reassurance. Compassion. "Doubtful. Who'd want him?"

"Cordelia, really?" Diane set the rest of the bagel on the coffee table, then licked her fingers clean. "That's cruel."

"I meant he won the lottery with you. And lightning doesn't strike twice; he couldn't do any better."

"Thanks. I think?"

On the television, two officers escorted a familiar face into the police complex. I froze.

The man stared at his feet, and his comb-over was mussed, with the sides of his dark hair obscuring his face, with only his hawklike nose peeking through, but I'd know him anywhere.

"Help me find the remote." I grabbed throw pillows and tossed them to the floor. "Come on—*quick*."

Diane pulled it from between the couch cushions. "What is it? What's wrong?"

"Shh. Turn it up!" My hands flailed. "I know that guy!" I pulled the remote from her fingers and cranked up the volume. Her brows pushed together in confusion.

The voice of a male reporter spoke as scenes flashed over the television screen.

"*Clarence Elgin of Slaughter, Louisiana, was arrested in a bust of his Baton Rouge business, located on Industriplex Boulevard. The fifty-six-year-old is being charged with fraud, though our source says that further charges are likely, possibly including murder. Elgin is listed as the owner of Spirited Gifts. The company's website describes the business as a compassionate resource dedicated to helping people donate their bodies to science, contributing to the greater good. But behind Spirited Gift's benevolent exterior was what our source claims could only be described as a house of horrors. Police were granted a warrant to search his facility after neighbors complained about blood in the parking lot, and a stench like rotting meat."*

The camera flashed to a woman. The words scrolling across the screen identified her as a worker from the tax office next door to Spirited Gifts. "*The smell was... You wouldn't believe it,*" she said, shaking her head.

Tanisha Harris came on the screen. "*This report contains disturbing content and viewer discretion is advised.*"

"Jesus, Clarence," I mumbled. "What kind of operation were you running?"

"Wait, you mean you *really* knew that guy? For real?" Diane's eyes rounded.

"Yeah. From a pharmaceutical convention. Now, shhh."

"*Bodies of at least two missing Baton Rouge men were discovered among the recovered remains, which included a freezer drawer filled with hands and at least four heads in a meat locker.*"

Fucking shit. I thought of the phone call on the levee, and of Clarence's panicked voice. I'd wondered if he was working with the police or if he'd been arrested. Now I had my answer. A chill laced my spine. I'd been close to getting caught.

The reporter continued.

"*After multiple complaints were filed, police traced the stench to the yard behind the facility, which is enclosed in an industrial twelve-foot privacy fence. A torso, believed to be male and Caucasian, appeared to have been lying in the open for days.*"

The camera cut to another business owner, and on the other end of the couch, Diane's mouth hung open. "I can't believe you knew someone so evil."

Tanisha sat behind the news desk. "*Our source tells us the investigation took an even darker turn when two of the bodies were discovered to have died under suspicious circumstances. Police are awaiting autopsy.*"

The couch squeaked as Diane wiggled from her nest to perch on the edge of the cushions. "What the hell is wrong with people? Who could do that? Maybe I need to get a dog. A German shepherd or Doberman or something..."

The reporter continued. "*Stay safe, Baton Rouge. It seems we might finally have the name of the Red Stick's serial killer.*" Tanisha looked solemnly into the camera until the screen went to commercial.

I bristled at the word.

No mention of Old Hound Road. At least there was that. The police must be keeping it under wraps.

Diane sniffed back tears.

"Oh honey, what's wrong?" I scooted closer and put my arm

over her shoulders. "Look, no one said anything about missing women. We have nothing to worry about. But if a puppy would make you feel safer, then get one. I'll even help you pick it out."

Not only had I caused Diane's heartbreak with Simon, but thanks to Clarence getting himself busted, I'd inadvertently scared the shit out of her as well. Those suspicious circumstances the reporter mentioned—that was me. I was a terrible friend.

"It's not that. What if…?" Her voice trailed into sobs. "I'm sitting here thinking the worst about Simon, but what if he isn't ghosting me. What if he's dead? What if he's in that awful place all cut up, and I'm over here cursing his name?"

"Sweetie, listen to yourself." My voice was stilted, but Diane didn't seem to notice.

"I know. I sound crazy, right?" The look in her watery eyes begged me to tell her she was wrong.

Simon was dead, but I could truthfully vouch that he wasn't in Clarence's house of horrors.

"A little bit," I said. "Those guys on television? As horrible as it was, they were probably mixed up in something terrible. Simon is probably—"

"Probably off dicking around with some other woman." Her shoulders slumped forward, but at least she was no longer sobbing. "It's weird, because if he's cheating, then I could kill him. But when I think of him as…that"—she gestured toward the television—"I…" Her voice cracked.

I shook my head. Frazzled brown hairs escaped from my stubby ponytail and swished around my face. "This isn't healthy. Get dressed. We're going for brunch. My treat." I glanced around the messy room. "You've got to get out of this house."

"I don't feel—"

"No excuses." I stood and clapped my hands. "Chop, chop."

"But we just ate," she whined, making no move to stand.

"Do you have something against a second brunch?" I pulled her to her feet. The mountain of covers and pillows fell to the floor. "Go put on those ugly overalls you love and let's go."

My friend needed to get her mind off Simon.

So did I.

28

WE HAD BRUNCH AT RONALDO'S CAFÉ. IT WAS A QUAINT eatery inside a converted historic warehouse, once owned by a company that sold gas lamps. The restaurant only took up a small portion of the ground level, and with its concrete floors, exposed brick walls, and large windows, it felt more like New Orleans, Baton Rouge's popular older sister. The two of us split the special—Eggs in Purgatory. The food wasn't great, but it didn't matter. We were together and Diane was no longer crying.

Probably because I'd made it my mission to ensure her mimosa was truly bottomless. I signaled the waitress, and she set a fresh drink in front of Diane, who couldn't stop giggling. In that moment, it was easy to pretend the monster my bestie had been crying for wasn't dead by my hand, and that my biggest problem was my credit card bill. .

"To Simon." Diane raised her glass, orange juice and champagne sloshing over the rim. Her eyes were glassy, and her words poured lazily from her mouth. When I didn't move, she insisted, "Go ahead, raise your glass."

I held up my glass of water.

"May that asshole rot." Diane drained her mimosa, then set the goblet on the table with a forceful *thump*.

"You want his asshole to rot?" I teased.

Diane leaned forward. "No. He's an asshole. I want *him* to rot. Duh." She paused, lips pursed. "But if his asshole rots, that's okay too."

She was in luck, I guess. Most of Simon would be rotting, asshole included.

"I think it's time to get you home," I said, watching as she wiped her mouth on the back of her hand, then smacked her lips.

"No," she insisted, hands waving in front of her face. "I never get to have fun. Just...jus' one more." Her words slurred.

"Okay." Again, I signaled the waitress. "But only one." While Diane was distracted with something in her purse, I quietly told the server to make this next mimosa only orange juice.

A moment later, the waitress set Diane's drink in front of her, and she clapped her hands. "You're the best."

"I try," I said.

Diane slurped her drink and rattled on about Simon, as I absent-mindedly swished my fork through the the marinara on my plate, spilling some of the red sauce on the white tablecloth. It reminded me of Frank, and I felt guilty.

Even though his kill seemed like a million years ago, it had been the same night Simon had shown up uninvited, interrupting my ritual and taking over my thoughts. Frank's blood was supposed to become art; it was the promise I made to all my monsters. Their final transformation from hatred into beauty, a form of postmortem atonement. Yet, his blood remained in a can in my fridge. Another day or two, and I'd have to move it to the freezer. The second Simon was out of my life for good, I'd use it to create something mesmerizing. I owed it to myself. In a way, I owed it to Frank.

"What's wrong?" Diane leaned across the small table and clutched my wrist.

I smiled. "Nothing. Why do you ask?"

She swayed in her seat. Ordering her OJ instead of another mimosa was the right call. "You looked so...beautiful but so sad...so *very* sad. Cordelia? What's that word? You're beautiful but sad?"

"I don't know? Melancholy?" I offered.

"Yes. That's the one. You looked so melancholy. Like you should be wandering the moors searching for your lover's ghost."

"I'm not melancholy," I promised. "And the moors? Searching for my lover's ghost? That's what I remind you of? I should invest in a better under-eye concealer."

"What—that's not what I—" She blinked rapidly, as if suddenly fighting tears. "I want you to be happy. That's all. So, so happy. I tried to get McSmiley to—"

"Oh sweetie," I said. "I *am* happy. I tell you all the time. I'm *so* happy. I don't want McSmiley or anyone else. I have you and Sugar."

"I know you *say* that, but I want you to have something good. Something like me and Simon—" She cut herself off, and I knew she'd remembered through her drunken fog there was no more "me and Simon." Her face fell.

I'd wanted to help her feel better—to forget her problems for a little while—but I'd made it worse. I'd been doing that a lot lately.

It was time to call it. "You ready?"

She nodded somberly, and I paid our bill.

For most of the ride back to her house, Diane leaned her head against the passenger window, silent, while Sugar's playlist spilled through the speakers. We were a block from her house when her gaze settled on me.

I tried to sound bright, nervous I'd set off another round of tears. "What is it, sleepyhead?"

"I was thinking..."

"Oh, yeah. About what?" I glanced at her. Her eyes were narrowed into a scowl.

"It's your fault."

"What is?"

"Simon. You never liked him. I told myself I was being silly, but I know you didn't." She wagged her index finger at me. "He could tell too. That's why he disappeared—because of you."

She didn't know what she was saying. It was ridiculous to let her words sting me, but they did. They did because they were true. I was the reason she was heartbroken. If I'd have followed a plan, I could've dealt with Simon without trampling Diane's heart in the process.

I said nothing. She wouldn't remember this conversation. Or if she did, she would be embarrassed. Apologetic.

She was drunk. She was sad. Drunk, sad people say hurtful things. Mama taught me this at a young age.

Diane laid her head back, and a soft sob escaped her lips. She cried silently the rest of the ride to her house.

I helped her inside, then tucked her into her cocoon on the sofa. I put a glass of water and some Advil on her coffee table, and her phone on the pillow next to her head, with the alarm set for half an hour before Sugar was due to get off the school bus. Diane would rally and put on a happy face for her daughter.

Diane's forehead was warm as I smoothed back her hair. She dozed, her mouth slightly open with spit collecting in the corners, and every so often, her nose whistled.

She hadn't meant what she'd said in the car; she didn't blame me.

Did she?

The images from Simon's phone flashed through my mind and I shivered. If after all of this, Simon ruined our friendship...it would hurt. But at least she and Sugar were safe.

My phone rang, cutting through the quiet. I pulled it from my bag and answered before it could wake Diane.

"Hello?" I whispered, as I walked toward the front door, exiting, then locking it behind me. "Oh. Okay. Sure."

Finally. Some good news.

The phone call was the groomer. There was a last-minute opening, if I could get Mango there immediately. Hell yes I could.

After a mad dash to pick up the devil-dog from my house, we made it across town to the quaint shop in record time. A bell chimed as I pushed through the door and set crusty Mango on the table to check her in. The groomer's brown eyes widened. "What in the—"

"It's blood," I said.

"Is she okay?" The groomer, whose name tag read, *Mitch they/them*, ran a hand lightly over Mango's back.

"Oh," I said, realizing how my words sounded. I'd figured out the story on the ride over, but obviously my delivery needed work. "It's not *her* blood. She went out to potty and found something dead to roll around in." I shrugged as if to say, *Dogs, what can ya do?* "When y'all didn't have an opening, I tried to handle it myself and, well..." I gestured to Mango.

Mitch chuckled. "Yeah. It's that poodle hair. If it gets wet or dirty, and you don't have the right products, it turns into a tangled, knotted mess. Regular clippers won't cut it. No pun intended." Mitch petted Mango softly, and she licked their arm. "These little dogs are still dogs; they don't know they're supposed to be fancy. People are always surprised when they get into something dead or dig in the trash. Don't worry." Mitch shook their head, amused. "Give me an hour and I'll have her good as new."

I left Mango in Mitch's capable hands and got back into my car. I didn't want to go home and hang out with Simon.

Diane was sleeping off her bottomless mimosas.

For the first time in for as long as I could remember, my mind was blank, and not in a relaxing way. No plans for hunting or shopping or things me and Di and Sugar could do. Just...blank.

So I drove. No destination. Going nowhere in particular, simply killing time.

How had things gotten so off course?

Mango was going home soon; that was good.

But Diane was mad at me. Okay, maybe she wouldn't remember what she said, but those feelings of blame and anger, they had to be in there, right? They weren't manufactured by alcohol. All the mimosas did was loosen her lips.

I had no plan for getting rid of Simon. It was not supposed to end like this. He was ruining my life.

I'd worked so hard to become Cordelia Black. I thought out and followed meticulous plans. Paid attention to minute details. And for what? To keep from finding myself in the exact kind of predicament I was currently in.

On top of everything else, I was probably going to lose my job. Dr. Ezelle's office manager had left me another hostile message, and Margery was not happy about me using my sick days while the company was in crisis mode, though we both knew she couldn't legally stop me.

I was stuck. Hollow. Nothing but a husk. Nothing but Joanie in mascara and better shoes.

By the time the groomer called to let me know Mango was ready, I was no better.

Again, the bell chimed as I entered, and Mango was back on the front table, but now she was naked.

Like, *really*, naked.

Mitch, who'd been jovial when I'd dropped the dog off, frowned. "I need to show you something."

Their warm eyes hardened as they pointed to Mango's hindquarters.

"What's that?" I traced my fingers along the raised whelps criss-crossing her pink skin. "Did...did I do that when I was trying to clip her?" The idea that I'd accidentally hurt Mango made me ill.

"No," Mitch said. "There was a little razor burn, but I haven't seen anything like this—not from clippers. These are healed lacerations. Any idea how they could've happened?" They crossed their arms over their broad chest.

Mitch thinks I did this.

"No." I'd never hurt an animal. Ever. Not after the doe Tim had made me dress down. It haunted my memories. "I...I haven't had Mango very long. About a week."

Mitch nodded. "Okay. That makes sense. Some of these rescue dogs have a very traumatic history. I hope you'll take good care of her. Someone who survives what Mango has likely survived deserves a safe home and family who loves her." They looked down at Mango. "And you, little lady, stay away from dead things." Mango yipped.

The entire drive home, I thought of what Mitch said—how someone who survived the abuse Mango had, deserved a safe home and a family who loved her. By that logic, didn't I deserve the same? Those two things, safety and family, were all Joanie had dreamed about, and I'd let both slip away.

I sat in my driveway with Mango in my lap, patting her head and running my fingers gently over the web of bumpy scars. *What if I kept her a little longer? To make sure she's safe.* I couldn't wrap my head around it. Surely there was a reason for the scars. Maybe she'd been hit by a car or any number of other things—the world is a dangerous place for everyone. Especially when you're eight pounds soaking wet.

No. I couldn't keep her. Mango's face was everywhere, signs pleading for her return with the offer of a reward. It was too dangerous, considering what I was hiding in my home. Besides, I had no reason to believe that Mr. Percival had done anything to harm his dog. I didn't like the grouchy little Boomer, but an animal abuser? Didn't seem likely.

I patted Mango one final time; she was a different animal without her matted hair. "You know," I told her. "Don't listen to anyone. It's a look." She snuggled close to me, and I kissed her head. "You can come get cheese any time you want. Just, you know, it would be nice if you pooped in your own yard."

She chortled and licked my face. *Devil dog.*

Before I could change my mind, I cradled her in my arms and marched her across the street, shoulders stiff and jaw set.

Mr. Percival stepped onto the stoop before I could knock, his shoulders slumped forward, and there were bags under his roomy eyes. He looked sad. Exhausted.

The man's permanent scowl softened when he realized the wiggly dog I held was naked Mango.

I thrust her into his arms.

He looked from her then to me, then back to the vibrating pup.

“She’s…she’s bald,” he said.

“I found her.”

“But—”

I held up my hand, and he hushed. “She was funky. I got her groomed before bringing her back. You’re welcome.” Without waiting for a response, I turned and marched home, ignoring the ache in my chest, the one that tempted me to snatch Mango away. Was this how Tim felt when Mama’s addiction finally pushed him to leave? When he’d disappeared down our driveway without so much as a backward glance for Joanie? Even though he’d had no legal rights in the matter, had part of him ached at leaving such a broken thing behind?

Mango didn’t belong to me. Giving her back was the right thing to do.

So why did it feel so wrong?

I WENT TO BED EARLY BUT COULDN'T SLEEP WITHOUT Mango snuggled next to me. After hours of tossing and turning, I took my pillow and a blanket, and moved to the couch. Despite being logged in to every streaming service known to man, there wasn't a bingeable show in sight.

I threw myself back into the cushions and stared at the ceiling until the first rays of sunshine slid through my window blinds. Great. It was going to be a long day. I got up and put on a pot of coffee. Margery had left a message yesterday evening. It suggested I return to work today if at all possible. I wasn't sure if I would.

I sniffed the air and frowned. I'd grown used to Simon's odor—which wasn't necessarily a good thing—but he needed more ice.

Without bothering to change out of my pajamas, I took my small wheeled cooler to a local ice kiosk I'd discovered the day before, and got my roommate a refill.

The trip took less than half an hour, there and back.

In the kitchen, the cooler's wheels wobbled, and before I could steady it, it tumbled to its side, scattering ice across the floor.

I wasn't even mad.

Maybe it was dumb—because Simon certainly didn't care—but the fact that his ice was now grimy with floor dirt and random hair, it gave me a petty thrill, like when I'd waited tables in college and secretly spit in flirty men's drinks before serving them. Sometimes it's the little things.

I pushed open the bathroom door, and it was like walking into a wall of funk. I'd lied—there was no getting used to this. Simon was getting worse daily.

Maybe hourly.

The smell made me cough as I dumped the dirty ice over Simon's frigid torso, refilled the diffuser in the bathroom, and pushed towels under the crack at the door's bottom, but the odor stuck in my throat, tickling my tastebuds in the worst way.

Something had to be done, and soon.

Without my body snatcher, I didn't want to contemplate what this meant.

When I passed the fridge, I stopped and grabbed a slice of American cheese, but Mango was gone, so I tossed it in the trash.

My phone rang. It was Diane.

I let it ring.

I'd never ignored Diane in my life. So what if she'd been a little mean when she was drunk? This was silly.

I took steadying breath, then tapped the answer icon. "Hey."

"Hey yourself," Diane said. "I'm so embarrassed. I can't believe I got college drunk on a weekday at brunch."

"You needed a break." It was true, though brunch hadn't really offered her one. I glanced at the time on the oven clock. "You taking today off?"

"God, with this headache, I don't have a choice. Samantha sounded like a herd of elephants on the rampage this morning. It was all I could do to hold it together until she got on the bus. Besides, I've been taking sick days all week; what's one more? What about you? Don't you ever go to work anymore?"

"I have some later appointments," I lied, waltzing into my living room.

"Honestly," Diane said. "I could rally and go in, but I need another day without worrying about running into Simon. Can you believe that coward still hasn't called me?"

Oh, I could believe it. "I don't blame you. Although you aren't the one who should be embarrassed. He's the loser."

A silence settled between us a beat too long. "Listen, Cor. About what I said. On the car ride home?"

"You remember that?"

"Well, yeah. I wasn't *that* wasted." She sounded miserable. "I'm really sorry."

"It's fine," I said.

"No, it's not. You were trying to help me feel better, and I was being a brat."

I didn't correct her, because it was true. But that didn't mean she was completely wrong. That she didn't have a right to her feelings. "Do you...? Is that how you truly feel? You think I'm the reason Simon disappeared?" I moved my phone from my right ear to my left.

"No." She didn't sound certain. "Of course not. If he ghosted because he doesn't like my best friend? Good riddance." Her words gathered confidence as she spoke, as if saying them made her realize they were true. "If I had to choose between you and someone I was dating, I choose you every time. Simon can go to hell."

"Yeah." I smiled into the phone. "I choose you too."

"Listen, you want to hang out today? I know we got brunch yesterday, but we could finally get that pedicure, maybe have lunch or window-shop or something? Girl time with absolutely no guy talk. What do you say?"

There was nothing I wanted more. But...

I sniffed, frowning at the lingering funk.

"Can't today." It physically pained me to say it. "Later, though?"

Diane's voice deflated. "Okay. Sure. Talk soon?"

"Yeah. Soon," I said, but Diane ended the call before I got the words out.

She was still upset after all. I tried to push the gloomy feeling away. I hated when things were off between us.

It was ten thirty when my phone rang again, and I rushed to answer because for a moment I thought Diane was calling me back.

But the screen read Practical Family Medicine.

I was running on zero sleep and my emotional tank was on empty, but I was done with stalling. Waiting for the right moment was getting me nowhere. Besides, Cordelia Black didn't hide from problems. Even Joanie had cut her teeth on hard situations. I pressed answer. "This is Cordelia."

"Hi, Cordelia. This is the office manager at Practical Family Medicine—"

"Yes. I know." I didn't bother to mask my irritation. Clearing my throat, I continued in a less hostile tone. "I got your messages."

There was a pause.

"I see. I thought maybe I had an old number since you didn't call us back. Especially considering how important of a matter this could be for you." Her words hinted at a threat.

"I'm sorry." I pulled my legs into the crisscrossed position. "I guess I don't understand what you mean?"

"It'd be better for us to speak in person."

My mind was foggy from stress and lack of sleep, but clear enough to realize I couldn't let her know she had the upper hand. "Why's that?"

"There's an issue with several of the signatures not matching. I *hate* to imply anything, but this could be difficult for you if someone wanted to cause a scene."

"And who'd want to do that?" Keeping my demeanor positive took every ounce of self-control. "It's common knowledge that Dr. Ezelle had a stroke, *bless her heart.* It makes sense to me that if some of the signatures don't match up, which I personally find hard to believe, it's because of her diagnosis. If someone wants to accuse me of something, I hope they think long and hard about it." I smiled into the phone. It felt good to use my claws.

It would feel even better to bare my teeth and turn loose all the anger I harbored—anger mostly toward Simon, and maybe to a lesser degree, myself. I could unleash it all on this woman. But this problem needed to go away with as little fanfare as possible. “Using the good doctor’s misfortune to get ahead isn’t a good look, and this is a small community.”

The office manager didn’t miss a beat.

“Okay. You want it plain; here it is.” What little pleasantness she’d held disappeared and her accent thickened from sweet country lady to shotgun toting hard-ass. “I think someone forged these forms. I don’t know why, and I don’t care. Come see me, today, and we can work somethin’ out. If you don’t, then I’m gonna make a stink about it. Maybe I’m wrong—I don’t think I am—but do you want that stain on your reputation? Like you said, *this is a small community*. We close at four.” The line clicked.

THE DOOR TO PRACTICAL FAMILY MEDICINE WAS STUCK AS usual. I pushed it hard with my hip and stumbled into the waiting room. My tan and white Louis Vuitton Neverfull was slung over my shoulder, while I managed a splashy bouquet with tropical flowers so tall I had to peek through their stalks instead of over them. In my other arm I held the largest box of macarons available. As it stood, I was over two hundred dollars into foliage and sugar.

"Good morning." I regained my balance and sashayed through the shabby reception area with its beige floors and brown paneling. Scratched end tables were covered with ancient *Woman's World* and *Redbook* magazines, the cover models' clothing so dated they were back in style.

"Good morning," the receptionist countered, her husky voice flat. In puke-colored scrubs that soured her fair complexion and faded sandy hair with gray roots, she fit her surroundings like an animal in its native habitat.

I heaved the vase filled with lilies, ferns, and birds of paradise onto the counter, followed by the box of sweets. The heavy Louis was pulling on my shoulder, so I set it on the desk in front of the woman. I rubbed the side of my neck. "Sorry, this bag is so heavy."

Her eyes slid over my purse.

I nodded to the flowers and sweets. "I brought y'all a treat. For being so kind to me throughout my career."

The receptionist smirked then narrowed her gaze. "How nice of you, Ms. Black."

She went back to filing a stack of papers into assorted folders. Whoever had taken over the practice obviously hadn't sprung for updated systems.

A minute ticked by—literally. The analogue clock on the wall was loud in the empty time capsule of a room. *This is ridiculous.* I tapped the toe of my shoe against the tile, louder and faster, until finally the woman looked up, her lips pursed.

"Yes?" she asked.

"Is the office manager here? We need to have a little chat."

Her pencil-thin brows rose as she stared at me a moment, before calling to another lady, hidden behind a wall-sized shelving unit filled with folders and charts. "Carlene, Ms. Black is *finally* here for you."

Carlene grunted and walked through the reception room to the front door without sparing a glance in my direction. "Come on," she said. "Let's go outside where we can talk."

I grabbed my Louis and followed her out.

There was a bench near the front door of the office, and she sat. She pulled a soft pack of menthols from the pocket of her scrubs and thwacked them against her palm before lighting one up. I glanced to the sign on the door that said the office was a smoke-free facility, but let it go.

"So." I fanned the cigarette smoke away from my face. "You wanted to see me?"

The office manager wore her wiry auburn bangs feathered away from her face, which reminded me of a creased paper bag—Caucasian skin tanned to an unnatural shade of orangey-brown, lined and rough and in desperate need of retinol. She blew out a stream of smoke as she spoke. "I bet you don't even know my name."

"Sure, I do—it's Carlene."

Her lips curled into a mean grin. "You heard Patty say it in there, didn't you?"

She inhaled another puff.

"That's silly, Carlene." My voice tightened, as if I'd been caught. As if I were nervous. "You said there was a problem with the forms. I wish the good doctor was here to clear it up. But to show you how sorry I am for this inconvenience, I brought you the treats in there." I angled toward the door. "Does this square us? Are we good now?" I clutched my purse over my stomach.

"No."

"*No?*" I asked. "What do you mean *no*?"

"The way I see it, you and I both know that ain't Doc's signature."

My eyes widened and I regurgitated the familiar excuse. "She had a stroke, Carlene. If the forms don't match, it's probably because she was having some preliminary symptoms. That's all."

"Maybe." Carlene shrugged. "Maybe not."

"Look, I'm telling the truth. But my boss made it clear; there can be no drama with this case. *None.* I'm doing my best to make everyone happy. It's what I do."

Carlene nodded. "You need me to shut up and be sweet. Is that it?"

"Yes." My words came out rushed and worried. "I brought you that beautiful bouquet and that box of macarons. Neither were cheap, by the way. That should show you how much I want to make this right. Y'all have been clients of mine for years."

The woman shrugged again. "Robin was your client; I was her employee. Flowers die, and I'm diabetic. I'm not trying to draw this out or ruin your career, just so we're clear. I'm no criminal." Her words left her mouth in a cloud of menthol. "However, the way I see it, I'm doing you a favor, so I should get something for it. Something I'd actually want, that is."

"What is it you want?"

"A thousand ought to cover it." Carlene's puckered frown deepened the lines that webbed her mouth.

I gulped. "A thousand dollars? I don't know... You've heard that Bosephan went under? That's my only good product." My gaze dropped. "If you give me a few days, I could get some of it. Maybe borrow it from someone."

I shifted my weight, nudging my bag forward, drawing her gaze, before she again met my eye.

"No," Carlene snapped. "This needs to be handled today. Right now. How is it you have all these fancy belongings but no money?"

I peeped up from beneath my lashes, clasping and unclasping my hands. "I'm in a lot of debt. If you can give me some time. Please."

"Not my problem." Carlene's gaze settled on the Neverfull bag. "How about that?" She tilted her head toward the purse. "I like that bag. Ain't it one of those Louise Vee-tawns?"

"This?" I asked. "Yes, this is a Louis Vuitton. It's a two-thousand-dollar bag. *This* is what you want?" I sounded appalled. "You said you only wanted a thousand."

She nodded. "Yeah. Well, like I said, that ain't my problem. I always wanted a nice purse and now I reckon I'll have one. Or maybe I can sell it on the Marketplace. That is, unless you want me to cause a stink?"

I couldn't wait to be done with this woman. "If I give you this, we're square? No drama. You promise?"

"Promise," she said.

"Okay. Deal." I sighed. "You're really holding my feet to the fire."

Carlene thumped away her cigarette butt, and I followed her back into the office. Her grin could only be described as shit-eating as she gave me a plastic bag, and I dumped the contents of my purse into it, then handed over the Louis.

"Let me get those forms for you right now," she said, sitting down at the reception area's lone, outdated computer. She tapped away, and a moment later, an ancient printer loudly cranked out the desired papers. Carlene adjusted the strap of my Louis on her shoulder, then scrawled her signature in the appropriate places before sliding my copies back across the counter. "Pleasure doing business with you."

I snatched the documents and smiled. "Likewise."

The gaudy bouquet remained on the counter, but I grabbed the box of macarons on my way out. No point in letting them go to waste.

That last smile I'd given Carlene was genuine, and it stayed on my face the entire trek back to my car, even as I swung the plastic bag on my arm. It stayed on my face as I cranked my vehicle and pulled out of the parking lot. It stayed on my face as I drove home. The box of macarons sat on the passenger seat. I popped a pistachio-flavored one into my mouth.

The thing is, I understood people.

Sizing them up was my job, from doctors to monsters. I watched and assessed and judged. When Joanie didn't get in the way, I was good at it.

Making deals was my language. I recognized bad ones, but more importantly, I knew what it took to negotiate a good one.

I molded myself and my behavior into whatever version would get the job done. Sometimes that meant wigs and sunglasses and socks with ballet flats. Other times it meant a Stella McCartney dress and an $800 pair of heels.

To say Dr. Ezelle's office was run-down was being nice. And I may not have known Carlene's name, but I'd recalled her face. I remembered her demeanor from each time I visited Practical Family Medicine. The way she'd scoffed each time I signed in at the desk. The way her eyes had narrowed and her lips pursed whenever I'd said good morning.

The day's outfit had been chosen with care. My shoes were some no-name brand Diane had left at my house. The dress was off the rack from a low-end department store. And the oversized Louis on my arm? The one I'd claimed retailed for two thousand dollars? The one I'd given away without so much as a debate?

It was a fake.

My one and only. A two-hundred-dollar fake, purchased for when I traveled. Maybe it was my poverty-stricken childhood that made me paranoid, but I'd never risk ruining one of my good bags by shoving it under an airline seat.

Some people are intimidated by nice things and respond accordingly. My gut told me that Carlene was not one of those people. She'd both wanted something *from* me and had something *on* me. Intuition whispered that the more I appeared to have, the more she'd try to take. I'd known better than to go into the meeting shining like a Cartier. The fake bag was the single extravagant item. You didn't have to appreciate the finer things to recognize certain brands. Yes, even backwoods Carlene had known a "Louis Vee-tawn" when she saw it.

In my book, the deal counted as a win, especially since I kept the macarons. I popped another into my mouth. *Yum, raspberry.*

I texted Margery that I could meet her at the office. Less than twenty minutes later, I was on the elevator, and as I exited its sliding doors onto my floor, more than a few people's gazes followed me. My smile was enormous, all lips and poison. My hips swayed as I walked, and the papers were clenched in my fist, swinging next to me.

The bitch was back. I was one step closer to reclaiming my tight-clawed hold on my life.

Margery's door was closed, and I didn't knock before barging inside. She stood beside her desk, wearing a shapeless gray wool pantsuit despite the heat, and listening intently while scowling into her phone. Whoever was on the other end of the call was giving her an earful.

What? she mouthed.

I held up the forms and shook them.

Margery's eyes narrowed. "I'll call you back." She hung up. "What are those?"

"What do you think?" My voice was cool. Bored.

My boss's squat heels snapped against the tile as she crossed the room to stand in front of me. She snatched the forms from my hand and looked over them. "How did you get that redneck office manager at Dr. Ezelle's to sign? I was certain she'd be a problem."

"Doesn't matter." Buying off Carlene with my purse wasn't the most badass way to handle business. Margery's imagination could do better.

"You're a piece of work." She sighed. "I don't care how you got her to sign, only that she did. Good job."

"Thank you," I said. "Now that we're squared, let's talk about my career. Bosephan was my big account and it's gone."

"And you want to make sure you are getting seniority on something new? Don't worry, that won't be a problem."

Actually, I wanted to make sure I still had a job once everything was said and done, but sure, seniority would be great. "Fabulous," I said, and left without another word.

THE ELATION OF KNOCKING SOMETHING OFF MY LIST OF problems was short-lived when I walked into my home and gagged.

Louisiana was always muggy, but the past week had been unseasonably warm. At the moment, my air-conditioning hummed along, but maybe the handyman was right. Maybe it was struggling to keep up. Because inside my house was almost balmy. I fanned my face—not sweating. Not yet. *Great.* The absolute last thing I needed right now was for my AC to go out. Keeping Simon cool was hard enough as it was. And it wasn't like I could risk having a repairman come over.

This wasn't sustainable. I needed a plan. ASAP.

I pulled my hair into a quick ponytail and untucked my shirt to cool off. I focused on only breathing out of my mouth but—*oh god*—I could taste him.

It had only been a few hours, but in that short amount of time, something about the body had changed—something vital. Ashes to ashes, dust to dust, but apparently there was a vile middle stage that the folksy old saying chose to omit.

As much as I didn't want to—and I *did not* want to—I opened the bathroom door.

Since the last ice-dump, the drain of the tub had clogged. Probably remnants of that god-awful kitty litter. *Thanks Betty.* The melted ice mingled with body fluids turning into a stagnant brown pool in my once nice Jacuzzi guest tub.

There wasn't enough bleach in the world to sanitize those jets.

Simon's face was changing, and with his deepening vacant star and unhinged jaw, he reminded me of an Edvard Munch painting. It would've been interesting if it weren't so horrifying.

"Shut up," I hissed, then made the mistake of taking a deep breath. The odor of human decomp wormed through my lungs, burrowed into my stomach, and twisted. I stumbled to the toilet and retched. No, this could not continue.

It was time to serve Simon his eviction notice.

I had a plan. I hated it—but it was the best option.

The only option at the moment.

After chugging two glasses of wine, I grabbed a binder clip from my studio and pinched it over my nostrils. Taking only shallow breaths, I did my best to ignore the bitter taste in the air. In a paper bag, I placed my good sharp kitchen knives, two Costco rolls of aluminum foil, and some masking tape.

On a whim, I threw in the remainder of my kitchen trash bags, because they might be useful. Once I started, I didn't want to stop until I was done, because if for some reason I stopped, I knew I wouldn't finish.

And I had to finish. It was time to put this—*all of this*—behind me and get my life back.

The only other time I'd separated a corpse had been my first intentional kill.

It was terrible, everything about it. The kind of terrible that stays with you. This was before Bosephan. Before my workshop. Before I understood the importance of what I was doing, but somehow knew it must be done.

The first man who'd hurt Joanie hid his irises behind heavy drugged lids. When he'd released me, I'd fallen to the ground, a simpering, scared mouse of a girl, and he'd laughed a deep, croupy laugh that still haunted me. It was then that I'd first witnessed the smoke.

By fifteen, I knew what smoke meant. I saw it often and hid from it whenever I could.

At twenty, I'd accidentally killed a man—our professor who'd hurt Diane. This taught me I was capable of getting away with execution.

I was twenty-two before I understood I was put here to do more than bear witness to the evil of monsters, and twenty-three before I'd intentionally heeded the call.

As things often did, it began with a familiar face.

It was the evening of my first real adult job interview. Things had gone better than I'd ever dreamed, and it felt as if my life was finally on track. At the red light nearest our apartment, I happened to glance at the car next to me. I recognized the driver. It was a shock at first. His reddish-blond hair was thinner. His sharp cheekbones softened, as was his once-handsome cleft chin. His SUV gave him away; it was the same one his wife had driven, back when he was a coach at my high school. The back window had a decal of an orchid and something about coexisting.

When he glanced over, his eyes were hazy and glazed. Something snapped when I saw the car seats in the back of his vehicle, and it was like fingers reached deep into my center and squeezed.

Him. The word was as clear as if I'd heard it aloud.

This man continued to hurt innocent people. He hadn't stopped when he'd been fired from teaching. Hadn't stopped when he'd been charged and the girls he'd coached came forward. He hadn't stopped when he had kids, and if I didn't kill him, he'd never stop. I *knew* this. I don't know how, but I knew it the same way I knew to breathe or eat or sleep.

A month later, after research had proven me correct, I'd done it.

And I'd spread his body through the swamp.

Call it God.

The universe.

An eye for an eye.

Karma.

A Greater Power had sanctioned me to deliver vengeance to monsters and justice to victims.

Even believing it all the way to my marrow, that first disposal had still nearly undone me. I wasn't sad I'd ended a bad man, but I'm human, and chopping someone up isn't easy.

Afterward, I'd made myself the promise—the one I was about to break. The promise of *never again*. Still covered in that old coach's blood, my face wet with snot and tears, I'd decided if I was going to do this, then I'd find a way to kill that would not unravel me.

Now, here I was, brought full circle back to the darkness. To the rank disgust.

Heaving a deep breath and steeling my nerves, I shoved open the bathroom door and set my bag of supplies next to the tub. Slumping onto the toilet lid, I leaned forward to hold my face in my hands. *I can do this. I can do this. I can do this...*

This was the plan. There was no other way.

A whole and complete body dumped into the wilderness was easy to discover. And once there was a body, there was a case.

I straightened my shoulders. I'd suck it up and do the hard thing. I'd take Simon apart. Then I'd wrap him up and store him in my fridge until I could dispose of him piece by piece. One drive to the marsh, to the river, to the dump. One body part thrown away at a time, until he was gone from my life forever. It wasn't perfect, but it was all I had, and it had to work.

Simon White would not be my downfall. I'd left Mama's trailer behind, and though Joanie had found me in my new life, things were different. I'd never again suffer because of a bad man. Especially not a dead one.

Steadying my hands, I set to work.

THE WATER IN MY EN SUITE SHOWER WAS CRANKED TO scalding, as if that could wash away the images seared into my brain. As if the hissing spray from the shower could drown out the sound of knife against flesh and meat and bone that echoed through my memory. As if the steam could somehow cleanse Simon's decaying stink from the back of my throat.

When I was a girl, Mama's boyfriend Tim had taught me to butcher a doe. The way we'd sliced the innocent deer to pieces for processing—slow and methodical—it had broken my heart.

Simon was only another animal, one less innocent than that doe, and more deserving of his fate. My breaths had come shallower with each slice, but my actions were sanctioned, so I forced a smile with each cut, my lips pulled tight like a plastic snarl.

There are moments—good and bad—that change us forever. Butchering the doe had been such a moment and taking apart Simon White was another. His face would forever remain right there, behind my eyelids, hollow-eyed and leering.

I'd finished the job, then pushed aside the meager contents of my fridge and freezer and stacked Simon in front like a side of beef bought and packaged by the butcher. His unwrapped head was shoved into the empty vegetable crisper like a melon being chilled for the fourth of July.

When this was all over—once I had my life back—I was buying a new refrigerator.

And a new guest bathtub.

Actually, I'd need a new house.

I slid down the tiled shower wall to sit in the bottom, pushing thoughts away until I wrangled my mind into serene, delicious blankness. It was a skill honed by Joanie—disassociate for a moment of peace. Water ran over me for minutes, maybe hours. Time didn't matter.

The shower spray was freezing when I came back to myself, and I shivered as I pushed awkwardly to my feet and shut off the faucet. Stepping from the shower, I felt like a caterpillar who emerged from her cocoon still a caterpillar. Vulnerable and small and ugly.

The first time I'd sliced apart a monster, moroseness had plagued me for weeks. The dark feelings were always there, lurking like the boogeyman waiting for its moment to snatch Joanie into its tangled claws and take over my life.

It wouldn't happen, because *I* wasn't Joanie. I wasn't. I was Cordelia, and Cordelia wasn't controlled. She took control. I'd fought my entire life. I wouldn't stop now.

Simon was out of my bathtub, but still in my house. I needed him gone. Really gone.

Forever.

Why put it off? I'd already done the hard part. I could get rid of him now.

No.

No. This required a plan. Impulse decisions led to trouble. That's what had gotten me here in the first place. Simon would not further manipulate my actions. Would not turn me reckless. He would leave, but it would be on my own calculated terms.

I toweled off and frowned. Purple half-moons colored my under-eyes making my washed-out pallor even more sallow. The mousy tangles around my face amplified every shadow and line, and my fingernails, normally manicured professionally every two weeks, were jagged and chipped.

Who was this woman, aged ten years in a matter of weeks? This wasn't the reflection of Cordelia Black. It wasn't Joanie, either. This woman looked defeated. Bone weary and tired.

This haggard person staring back at me was Simon's doing. She looked like someone who could have a body in her fridge, and that wouldn't do.

Simon couldn't win; I wouldn't let him. I'd get myself together—a little skincare, a coat of nail polish—get some dinner, and work out an eviction plan. A good one.

The swamp at the end of Old Hound Road was off-limits, but there were many places to disappear in south Louisiana.

Everything was going to be okay. I—*Cordelia Fucking Black*—was going to make it okay. I spritzed volumizer onto my roots and worked it through my hair with trembling fingers.

Thirty minutes and a quick blow-dry, some tinted moisturizer, and a coat of Dior show mascara, and I wasn't back to a hundred percent—my manicure was still garbage and I was still a brunette—but I was damn sure closer. More importantly, I felt better.

By the time I'd pulled on my favorite Fendi midi skirt and cropped tank, things appeared marginally less hopeless. Women in Fendi didn't chop up bad men and wrap them up in their fridge. *Never.* A smile spread over my face as I turned off my bedroom light and headed downstairs to leave for some dinner. Planning was done best on a full stomach.

I was locking my door when Mango yodeled.

She was in her front yard all alone. I'd thought Mr. Percival would do a better job keeping up with her, considering.

"Hey, you devil," I called out. Okay. Maybe I missed the little shit.

She bolted toward me, making it to the edge of her yard before yelping a loud, painful sound. She scurried back, her tail tucked and her head low.

"What's wrong?" I jogged across the street and crouched to pet her. "Is this a new collar?" I ran my fingers over the tough nylon. A large plastic box was fastened to Mango's scrawny throat, with two metal teeth jetting into her delicate skin like fangs.

"A *shock* collar?" Mango was only eight pounds. The chunky plastic strapped to her chicken neck was obviously intended for a much bigger animal.

Why would Mr. Percival do this? Shock devices weren't illegal, but Mango was so tiny, and it seemed so cruel. She'd do anything for cheese—she didn't need to be zapped. All he had to do was stand outside while she did her business.

I tugged furiously at the collar. The nail of my index finger caught on the nylon and tore into the quick. "Sonofabitch."

I'd let Diane down. Maybe I'd protected her, but I'd also broken her heart.

I'd let myself down. I'd allowed a monster to figure out what I was, then goad me to action instead of following a plan.

Now, it seemed I'd let Mango down too.

I worked my thumbs beneath the collar, and the snug torture device loosened, but before I could remove it, Mr. Percival appeared outside his front door, eyes narrowed. My skin crawled under his beady glare. "Mango! Here!" he belted.

Mango darted to him obediently, and the two disappeared inside.

I'd been sure that Mr. Percival would never hurt her. Sure, he was a cranky old man, but he'd seemed so worried when she'd disappeared.

Didn't I know better than anyone that what people chose to show the world wasn't usually the whole story? People worked hard to keep their dark bits hidden. Just ask the coaches and pastors and scout leaders who'd lain upon my table.

I stared at the peeling hunter-green paint of Mr. Percival's closed door. I was so tired of bad men hurting those I loved. I had to do better. To be better.

Thunder cracked in the far distance.

No more failing.

No more excuses. No more waiting. It was time to take back control of my life.

And that started with Simon.

You need a better plan. The words whispered through my mind. Did I, though?

It had taken months to lay the groundwork and iron out the details with Clarence. I didn't have months. Not this time. In the end, my last "perfect" plan had fallen apart, anyway.

All of my plans had fallen apart.

Maybe it didn't matter. Maybe there was no meticulous plan. Maybe there was only not getting caught.

Getting rid of *all* of Simon this evening wasn't possible. He hadn't spent enough time in the fridge to temper his stink, and no way did I want his odor to stain my vehicle. But I could get started, at least.

My stomach growled, but dinner could wait. I had something more important to take care of.

I ran inside to grab a little something from the fridge.

THE GRIT OF THE SIDEWALK CRUNCHED BENEATH MY HEELS as I walked along the levee, acutely aware of the appendage in my purse.

Simon's hand was wrapped in aluminum foil. It didn't smell great.

The idea of coming to the levee hadn't been a conscious one. I'd imagined going to one of the many swamps, possibly hopping on the interstate and heading for the Atchafalaya Basin and letting the alligators help me out.

Once behind the wheel, I'd gotten lost in my thoughts—*Mango, Diane, Mr. Percival, Sugar, Christopher, Clarence, Simon, Mango, Diane*—and ended up here. The river. The familiar spot where Diane and I often came when stressed or excited or to share big news. The spot from the photograph of sophomore year—Diane pregnant and me determined to be there for her. The photo we each kept framed in our homes. *Our spot.* It made sense to come here, at least for a moment.

Usually people milled around, riding bikes or snapping

pictures, but with the sun dipping below the horizon as bloated clouds grumbled overhead, I was alone. The churning brown water of the river, which comforted Diane, was ominous, making me feel small and deflated.

Making me feel like Joanie.

The sky muddied from pink to gray, as the rumble of thunder grew louder. Minutes later, a steady drizzle began to fall, dampening my cheeks and collecting on my lashes. Thankfully I'd grabbed my trench coat before I'd left the house and now pulled it tighter around me, against the weather. I couldn't turn back—not anymore. I sank onto Diane's favorite levee bench. My Louis, the real one, slouched open next to me, its contents exposed.

There was no one around, but even if there had been, the small package I pulled from my purse could easily be explained away as a po' boy. People see what they want to see. A woman dressed in a Marc Jacobs trench would never have a hand in her bag.

Handbag. I snorted. Diane would love that.

Through the foil, I squeezed Simon's fingers in mine as I looked out over the river.

What was my plan, exactly? Oh. Right. There wasn't one.

This felt dangerous, like the night Simon had appeared in my home, and I knew—*on some level I knew*—I was going to kill him. Sitting here, holding hands with a monster, anything could happen. A thrill climbed my spine. I wasn't acting meticulous like Cordelia. But neither was I afraid like Joanie. *Look at me, living on the wild side.* Damn it felt good.

What if I unwrapped this appendage and chunked it into the

water? What if I did this piece by terrible piece until all that was left was that melon of a head, staring from my fridge drawer with those cold, hollow eyes?

No.

No no no. I couldn't do that. There was being free, living on the wild side, and then there was being stupid. Cordelia Black was never stupid. Neither was Joanie.

This piece of Simon could be found. Netted by unsuspecting fishermen or dropped to land by a bird who'd thought it was diving for a fish. What if it rained for a night, and the river swelled its banks again and stranded this hand on the sidewalk? Flash floods weren't that uncommon in Baton Rouge and always left debris. I could see it, some helpful citizen cleaning up litter and discovering Simon's pale palm.

Eventually he'd be identified, and the police would investigate, which would lead them to discussions with Diane. What if they listed her as a suspect?

The gaping flaws in my not-a-plan were obvious. How had I not even considered fingerprints?

I turned the package over in my hands and slid my nails beneath the tape that held it closed. The ridges along Simon's bony fingers felt rough as I rubbed lightly over his knuckles. This man—*this monster*—had caused so much trouble.

On the other side of the river, thunder cracked louder, and as if on a timer, the drizzle thickened to a soupy downpour.

I didn't move.

Marc Jacobs was no match for the rainstorm, and in a matter of minutes, water soaked through the coat, but I sat and stared across the water, stroking the back of Simon's hand like it was a deranged pet. The sun sank over the horizon, bathing everything in a dusky grayish lavender as the lampposts that lined the sidewalk blinked on. I shoved the hand back into my bag and stood.

There had to be a solution—one that made sense. However, tossing Simon's hand into the river? That wasn't it.

That first instinct—*my Cordelia instinct*—had been correct. Rushing to get rid of Simon was a bad idea. This was the home stretch. Now wasn't the time to screw up.

My stomach growled, reminding me that I hadn't eaten. I sighed. Time to grab some food and head home to regroup.

Water squished between my toes and dripped from my hair. Mascara smudged into my eyes, and when I ran the back of my hand along my cheek, it came away streaked in black.

Clearly I was losing it; wearing anything but waterproof mascara when there was a chance of rain was psychotic. Could this be Cordelia's epic descent into madness? Standing in a rainstorm near Diane's special place, clutching Simon's hand? Running makeup adding insult to injury?

I clearly—*clearly*—needed to get a grip. I walked faster.

My car was only yards away when something in my purse moved, and I nearly dropped the designer bag in a puddle. I stood frozen, then burst into laughter. My phone was buzzing. What had I thought? Simon's hand had come to life?

I answered.

"Hey, you!" Diane's voice sounded far away.

"Hey yourself," I said.

"Where are you? I've tried to text you like five times!"

"Sorry." I pushed wet hair away from my face. The rain was picking up. "I didn't see it. Been a little preoccupied."

"What?" The phone crackled. "Cor? You there?"

"Hello?" I said louder, as if that would help with a crappy connection.

"I can hear you now," Diane said. "A little anyway. Listen, I'm sorry if I was weird this morning."

"It's okay," I said. "You weren't."

"What?" Diane's voice was muffled. The connection buzzed.

"I said it's okay. Don't worry about it." Lightning popped overhead, illuminating the sky. I ran the last few feet to my car and hit unlock on my key fob.

"I can barely hear you," Diane said.

"It's this storm," I yelled. "I'm near the river—near our spot. The reception is always crappy over here."

"Aw. You went to our spot? Cordelia Renee."

I slid into my car and slammed the door against the downpour. My hair and clothes dripped onto the tan leather interior.

"Is not my name." I smiled into the receiver. "Hey, I'm free now if you want to get some dinner? How about at that little diner over on your side of town? The one with the burgers that Sugar likes?" I looked at the foil-wrapped hand in my bag. "Give me about thirty minutes to drop something off at home first."

The line clicked with static. "Hello?" The buzzing grew louder. "Hello?"

"Hello?" Diane said finally.

"Hello?" I said.

Diane laughed. "This is ridiculous. I'm hanging up. I'll see you in a minute."

"Wait!" I yelped. "What do you mean you'll see me in a minute? Do you and Sugar want to meet at that burger place near your house?"

"Oh. I'd love to get something to eat, just me and you. But I'm not near my house. Listen, you've been the best ever." The phone buzzed louder, muffling Diane, but I strained to hear. "Seriously, the best friend I could ever ask for."

I wasn't so sure about that. "Diane—"

Another bolt of lightning illuminated the sky.

"No, let me say it. I haven't been a good friend to you. I'm so sorry for what I said the other day, and I mean what I told you earlier today. I'd pick you every time."

More buzzing. Then: *Click. Click. Click.* Had the call dropped?

Diane's voice came back onto the line midsentence. "—you something, and I'm almost to...to drop it...I can't wait...your face—"

"Sorry?" I moved the phone from one ear to the other. "Di, I didn't catch that last part—"

"I said I'm almost to your house! I made you something! I still have the...you gave me...remember?"

My heart raced, and my throat grew thick.

The line hummed with Diane's voice, but her words were unclear. "Key... Christmas... See you..."

"Diane? Diane! Where are you?" I screamed into my phone. "What do you mean you're almost to my house?"

This was bad. Really bad.

Diane had a key to my home. In the unraveling of my life I'd forgotten about it, just as I'd forgotten about the handyman and so many other things. So many things Cordelia Black would never forget.

I'd given it to her last holiday season so she could drop off Sugar's Christmas gifts. My goddaughter was a world-class snoop, and Diane needed a good place to hide them. This entire time she could've popped over at any given moment…like right now.

"Diane!" My voice came out in a rasp.

"I'll see you in a minute. Love you!"

"No! Don't go in my house! Diane! Wait in the driveway, I'll be there soon!"

But as I said the words, the line clicked and she was gone.

I screamed and threw the phone into the passenger seat.

Why had I ever given her a key? How could Cordelia Black ever forget such an important detail?

Cordelia wouldn't forget—never. It was Joanie—right there under the surface—wearing my skin like a costume. Maybe all of this was her. I bent forward and took a deep breath, willing my eye not to twitch, my fingers to remain still.

Joanie's neurosis would not be my downfall. When I'd tried to kill her, it was for good reason.

I'd hardened my heart because the world is a hard place. I'd changed my appearance because the world listens to beautiful people. I'd even rewired my brain, because no one cared about a mousy, soft-spoken pest, no matter how intelligent she may be. Cordelia was confident, and driven, and stunning. Cordelia could handle anything. Including this.

But was I Cordelia right now?

Had I ever *fully* been the shiny, starched, perfect Cordelia Black at all?

My tires squealed against the wet pavement as I hauled ass from my parking spot, soon reaching eighty miles an hour, zooming down side streets and ignoring neighborhood stop signs.

I punched the brakes in my driveway, and the car jerked to a stop, parking next to Diane's Jeep. I leapt from the driver's door, abandoning my keys, my purse, as well as any rational thought other than getting to Diane before she opened my refrigerator.

WATER PUDDLED AT MY FEET, SLICKENING THE FLOOR AS I stepped carefully into my house. "Diane?" I called softly. My curtains were pulled closed against the gray evening, and the only light was from the small fixture over my kitchen island. I blinked as my eyes adjusted to the dimness.

My heels clicked against the floor as I stepped carefully into the room, shrugging off my rain-soaked trench, leaving it in a heap on the floor.

Diane's favorite hand-painted platter sat on the island, glowing beneath the pendulum light. It was chipped on one side, as if it had been dropped. Misshapen, overly large macarons spilled onto the counter. She knew how much I loved macarons and must've made these for me. I was touched.

A mewling whimper came from the other side of the island.

"Diane?" I eased toward the sound.

A slice of light shone from the cracked open door of the fridge.

If it had been open for any amount of time, it would have shut off automatically.

Diane hadn't been here long.

A few seconds had changed everything.

She sat huddled on the floor, her knees pulled in close to her tear-streaked face. In one hand, she held one of my steak knives. In the other, a cell phone.

The phone was more threatening than the knife. "Diane?"

"Stay away from me." She jabbed the knife in my direction.

Rookie mistake. Her hands trembled, and I could've easily taken her wrist and twisted the knife to the ground.

But then what? If I fought Diane and won—and I would win—what was the endgame? If I held the knife and made her drop the phone, what would I do next? If I explained, and she didn't believe me, then I'd always worry she'd call the police. And eventually, she would.

Diane could never understand. Violence was the language of bad men and one I'd learned early, forced into fluency.

But Diane? Sweet, kind, and thoughtful? She would have to tell, or it would break her.

The only way to stop her would be to *ultimately* and *completely* stop her—the way I'd stopped predators my entire adult life. I couldn't do that. I couldn't take my friend's life to avoid a jail cell. The image of Diane with a knife plunged into her abdomen, her leaking blood mingling with the remaining flecks of Simon's...no. I pressed my eyes closed and shook my head. *Never.*

Another high-pitched cry floated up from my best friend's throat.

I did this to her. She won't forget this. I ruined us. And now she would tell and I'd go to prison and no one would be left to protect the innocent. No one would protect Diane or Sugar.

But that was my fault, not hers.

I let Diane keep her knife.

She again swung it in my direction. Would I let her kill me? If sending me to jail wasn't her goal, would I let her drive that knife into my chest? Or pull its blade across the tender flesh of my throat? Where was the boundary of what I'd do for Diane—the only person who'd ever cared about me? Wrong question. Was there a boundary at all?

"Diane." I held my hands in front of me, a show of surrender. "We need to talk. Have you called the police?"

She looked blankly at the phone in her hand, as if she'd forgotten it was there. That look, along with the lack of sirens in the driveway, gave me hope.

I took a small step back.

Diane struggled to her feet.

If I'd wanted, I could've kicked her over. I could've taken the knife. I could've taken the phone. I could've ended everything within a minute. Instead, I allowed her to get awkwardly upright.

"It's not what you think," I offered quietly, my voice as strained as the look in her eyes.

"How do you know what I think?" A fresh stream of tears wet her cheeks. "What've you done? Cordelia, you killed him. You murdered him and you let me think he disappeared. Fuck—you comforted me." She neither came toward me with the knife, nor made a move to use the phone. My best friend sobbed as she spoke, the delicate bones of her shoulders shaking violently. "Why? Was it because I was happy? Because it was someone besides you? Tell me!"

I remained neutral, hands up, face blank.

"What's wrong with you?" Her scream gutted me. "You stand there like that, when I've found Simon's head—" Her voice trailed off, and she gestured to the fridge.

"Let me explain. Please, Di."

"No. Don't. What was your plan, anyway? Kill me too?"

I ached to throw my arms around my friend. To console her, but I didn't dare. "I'd never hurt you. Never," I said. "You have to believe that."

"How do I know? You're a killer! A monster, Cordelia." Diane coughed, then lunged for the sink and retched. She wiped her mouth on the back of her arm, still awkwardly clutching both knife and phone.

That word—*monster*—it was barbed, piercing my skin. It tore at my flesh and broke my heart. She could've chosen any word. Any other word at all. "Simon was the monster. I didn't do this to hurt you. I did it to save you."

"Save me?" Diane coughed again and spat bile into the sink. "Save me from what?"

I took a small step toward her, testing the water. She didn't flinch. "Diane." I reached outward oh so slowly. "I'll make us some tea, okay? I'll explain everything. You'll see. I know you will."

"Back up!" She screamed as she brought the serrated knife down and pulled it across my reaching forearm.

Her wobbly slice was weak, and the cut was shallow, but the knife was sharp, and a thin line of blood bubbled to the surface.

I yanked my hand back.

The small trickle of blood slid down my arm, collecting in the crease of my elbow.

Diane paled at the sight. "Oh shit." She sucked in a deep breath. "Oh no, oh shit." The knife clattered to the ground as she brought her palm to her forehead, keeping a firm grasp on the cell in her other hand.

Her weight shifted. She was going down.

35

DIANE SWAYED, TOO WOOZY TO PULL AWAY AS I SLID MY arm beneath her armpits, catching her weight. The trickle of blood smeared against the white fabric of her tank top as I guided her to a chair.

"Sit here. I'll get you something to drink," I told her.

She slumped forward and rested her head between her knees. Her shoulders trembled from the release of deep, choking sobs.

I'd forgotten Diane had such a strong aversion to blood.

Of course. Seeing a head in a lettuce drawer would bring most people to their knees.

"Diane, honey, I know this seems crazy, I do. But I promise, it's going to all make sense. You'll see. I did this for you."

Diane said nothing, but at least the guttural sobbing had stopped. "Why don't I make you some tea, hmm? Some chamomile? Then we can chat, and you'll see. I know you will." I didn't believe my own words. Diane could never understand, but I had to try.

Running my fingers over the neatly arranged row of mugs gave me a second of peace, because if I was doing such a menial task—making Diane a mug of tea—then maybe things would work out. Friendships didn't end while partaking of something so comfy and warm. You didn't have tea and then go to prison. That wasn't a thing that happened.

It would be fine.

It *had* to be fine.

Finally, Diane spoke, her whispered voice raw and beaten.

"Is this the first time?"

I said nothing, only continued rummaging through the canister where I kept my best teas. Everything *was* fine, see?

"This isn't the first time someone close to me has died. What about...in college."

She didn't say his name; she wouldn't dare. It hadn't crossed her lips since we were huddled together under a blanket watching the news of his death on television in our dorm.

Tension bunched in my shoulders. The question stretched between us. Miles and miles long. An eternity.

"Answer me," she whispered.

I couldn't. Even with tea, there was no coming back from that. No way to make her realize the truth after such a long time. Such a long silent deception.

I sucked in a breath, preparing the lie on my tongue. The shame I felt wasn't shame for the death of a monster. The shame was only for this moment.

I'd lied to Diane before, but this felt different—somehow more personal. It had been an accident; I should've told her then. But she'd cried for him. There'd been so many tears. I couldn't.

I couldn't now. "No. Of course not." I dug around for the kettle, unable to look back at my friend. "I...could never."

It was all I could manage.

Behind me, Diane said nothing.

Then.

My front door banged closed.

The kettle clattered to the ground as I spun around. Headlights flashed through the window, followed by the sound of tires peeling against the wet pavement.

"Diane!" I screamed. "Diane, please wait!"

I ran after her, toward the door, pausing in front of the buffet table.

Proof. I had proof!

I grabbed Simon's phone and SD card from the drawer, and hurried outside.

My best friend's Jeep wasn't in the driveway.

Diane was gone.

MY TIRES SCREAMED AS I SLAMMED INTO REVERSE AND peeled out of Diane's driveway.

She wasn't at home. I'd stood outside her front door, no umbrella or jacket and soaked from the storm, with my blood-crusted arm on full display. Sugar answered my knock with rounded eyes, her babysitter standing behind her. *"She's not here, CiCi. I thought she was going to your house?"* Sugar's voice had wavered. She was afraid.

My fault. It's all my fault. This could be the last image my god-daughter ever had of me. Sorrow ballooned in my chest. Coming here had been a mistake. This was the memory I'd given her: her godmother the serial killer standing in the rain like a deranged lunatic.

No. I had to keep going. If Diane hadn't come home, where would she be? The police station?

If she were that afraid there was no way she wouldn't get Sugar first. Diane was a good mother. No, a great mother.

I racked my brain for an answer.

Suddenly, I knew.

The place where Diane always went—the same place I'd gone earlier without thinking.

Slamming on my brakes, I cut a U-turn in the middle of the residential street and sped toward downtown.

I didn't slow down until I reached the riverbank. Diane's favorite benches were ahead, and if I squinted through the drizzle, in the glow of the streetlights, I could make out someone slouched and staring out at the Mississippi. Gold lamplight glinted off of copper curls. It had to be her.

I parked on the roadside and marched up the levee steps.

During the drive here, the rain had eased to a mist. I slid onto the bench next to my best friend. Water glistened on her shoulders and arms. She must've come directly from my house and sat here during the storm.

Diane glanced at me and then back at the river.

"I guess you didn't turn me in," I said.

"Thinking about it." She shrugged. "Maybe I will."

A ship's horn echoed across the water. The urge to reach out and touch the top of Diane's hand was so strong, but I clutched my fingers in my lap. Our silence had morphed into another living thing existing in the space between us. I couldn't take it anymore.

"I went by your house first, and—"

Diane whipped her face toward mine. "Why? What did you do? Is Samantha—"

"What did *I do*? You mean...you think... God Diane, I'd never hurt you or Sugar. I'm the same person I've always been. The same person who's been there for you since college."

"No." She shook her head, her sopping curls swinging. "No. You aren't who I thought. The woman I know would never—"

"If you truly believe I'm a danger to Sugar or you, then why haven't you gone to the cops? I won't stop you." It was a bold statement, but it was true. I'd decided there was nothing to do except explain myself and let the chips fall where they may.

Not all friendships could come back from finding your boyfriend's head in your best friend's lettuce crisper, but I clung to the hope that I could make Diane understand. We were *Cordelia and Diane*. We were *vintage*.

She searched my face, her eyes narrowed. "Back at your house, when I found..." Her words caught in her throat. She sniffed and began again. "At your house you said that you did this *for me*. I...What did I do to make you think I'd want that? Was it something I said? Because I never..."

"No." I shook my head. "You didn't do anything." I wanted to tell her the truth—my real, honest-to-god truth. But that could never happen—and not only to protect myself. Diane could never know about my calling for her own good. Once she told authorities about me killing Simon—once they started investigating—if Diane knew too much, they'd never believe she wasn't a part of it. And if they kept digging, there was also Sugar's dad, way back in college. Two men romantically connected to Diane, dead.

"What, then? Cordelia, why?"

My face pointed at my lap, where my hands clenched and

unclenched as I considered how to do this. "I didn't mean to hurt him. It just...it just happened."

"What are you talking about?" Diane's gaze bore into me, and she sat deathly still except for the rhythmic rise and fall of her chest. "How does something like that *just happen*? His head was in your fucking—"

I cut her off. "I caught him—Simon—out with another woman. I was minding my own business, and there he was."

"So you killed him? For being a cheater?"

"No. Of course not. Just...let me finish." I took a deep breath. This was easier before Diane found her voice. Before she asked questions. "It was weird, okay? *He* was weird, like he was a completely different person—the way he moved and dressed." I spoke carefully, evenly, as I recalled the memory for Diane. I had to get this exactly right. It was my only chance to make her understand, to blend the truth into something she could digest. "He pretended he didn't know me at first, but showed up later at my house, completely enraged. We argued, and I told him to leave y'all alone. He said some vile things. Disgusting things about you. About Sugar."

Diane chewed her bottom lip, but said nothing. Was it shock or disbelief? I pushed ahead, determined to get the story out.

"Hearing him, it made me wonder about the time we'd spent together—if there was something—an inappropriate gaze or touch—something we could've noticed. Something we explained away." I shivered. "I don't know what happened next. I think he attacked me; I'm almost sure of it." It was a small, necessary lie, braided in with mostly honesty and some murky gray half-truths.

"Next thing I knew, I'd stabbed him. There was so much blood. He—he was dead. Diane...I...I panicked."

"No. You're lying." Diane blinked rapidly. "Simon would never. These are all lies—gross lies."

"Diane, you *have* to believe me!"

"Cor, but I know him, and—"

"You know *him*? What about me? Diane, what about *me*?"

"What about you?" She shook her head. "He... His..." Diane's voice cracked. "Cordelia, what about what I saw in your fridge? I don't know you at all."

She didn't know me at all? I'd risked my freedom—*my sanity*—to keep her and Sugar safe. To rid our city of one more predator.

I closed my eyes and focused on my breaths. I could deal with prison. With becoming a headline. A punchline. I could deal with the world hating me. I could deal with it because I knew why I'd done it. I'd do it all again to protect my family. But those words—*I don't know you at all*—they were cutting. Razors scraping off my flesh.

Because I had no one but Diane—*and she knew me.* We'd been through everything together. Freshman year, when Diane found out my scholarship didn't include meals and I'd been living on packs of twenty-five-cent instant noodles. She'd snuck me food from the dining hall. I'd gone home with her on holidays when she'd found out I was staying on campus alone. I'd held her hand when she'd told her family she was pregnant and refused to name the father. I'd been in the room when Sugar was born.

Diane had never met Joanie, but she knew my childhood sucked and had been there when I was figuring out exactly who Cordelia was. She'd witnessed the remnants of the broken girl I'd been. Everything that made me who I was—*Diane knew.* The small part—the miniscule part—I kept from her? That was for her own good.

"You don't know me at all? Diane, how can you say that?" Joanie's vulnerability swelled, pressing, clawing, marching like ants beneath my skin. "You know me." Tears welled in my eyes. Heavy, full tears. Tears for everything I'd been through, everything I'd done. I sobbed because what was the point of any of it if I lost Diane? She could be angry at me. She could even hate me. But she knew me. How could she say she didn't?

Diane watched my breakdown in disbelief. When she spoke, her voice was soft. "Cordelia?"

"I'm...I'm sorry, Di. I'm so sorry. I didn't mean for any of this to happen, but I'm telling the truth. And you *know* me—don't say you don't. I'm Cordelia—*your Cordelia.*"

"It's...it's okay," she said, her tone suggesting maybe she didn't mean it.

No, it's not. Joanie whispered in my mind. *Nothing will ever be okay, again.* Mama's voice followed on her heels. *You go to crying and the world will swallow you up.*

I tried to sniff back the tears, but there was no stopping them, and on some level, maybe I didn't want to.

Why had I ever listened to Mama anyway? She'd never cared for me. Never taught me anything. But I'd glommed onto *don't cry* like it was the damn gospel. Maybe as a kid, on some level I'd understood that if I'd allowed myself to begin crying, I'd never have stopped. It wouldn't have been tolerated and Joanie would've died in that trailer—in that life. A true death. Instead, I'd become the person I'd always so desperately needed.

"Cor?" Diane pressed her hand to my cheek, her fingers cool against my burning face. I leaned into her touch, remembering how, as a girl, I'd seen mothers on television caress their daughter's cheeks, and I'd longed for it. Yearned for someone to care for me like that. Diane tilted her head and murmured, "I've never seen you cry before. Not once."

Shit. I wiped my eyes with my palms. Was I having a breakthrough? Was this what people meant when they said things like crying was cathartic? I always thought that was a stupid saying to make people feel better. I smiled and sniffed. "That's because I don't," I said. "Or, I guess, I usually don't. But the idea of you thinking I'm just some stranger capable of—"

Then, I remembered. I stood abruptly. "I have proof." I had Simon's phone. I pulled it from my pocket of my skirt, clicked the SIM back into place, and powered it on. I tapped the screen, but it was locked.

"Cordelia? What are you—is that...?" Diane hugged her arms around her torso and swallowed. "That's Simon's phone."

"Yeah. It is." She'd see soon enough. She'd see and she might not understand, but maybe she'd forgive me. She'd realize she still knew me. That Cordelia—*her Cordelia*—would never hurt her. That I had a reason, a damned good reason, to end Simon White.

"It's locked, but I know how to open it. Don't move. I'll be right back."

I turned and hurried toward the steps.

Simon's hand was in my bag.

I HATED LEAVING DIANE, EVEN FOR A MOMENT. I TOOK THE levee steps two at a time, grabbing the railing for support more than once.

At my car, I unwrapped the aluminum foil from Simon's hand, thinking of how if I'd filed off his fingerprints, this would've been the end of the line. I'd never have gotten back into the phone, and Diane would hate me forever. I guess the panic and anxiety that had clouded my judgment wasn't the worst thing that could've happened. In a way, Joanie had helped me.

I squished Simon's index finger against the screen and unlocked it, then dropped the hand back into my bag and left it in my vehicle. I wasn't easy to run on wet concrete in heels—even short ones—but I made it back to Diane in no time flat. I clicked to the not-so-secret album, then held out the phone. "Here."

There were no sounds except for the eerie lapping of the river and the faraway hum of traffic as Diane flicked through the photos. The horror in her eyes grew wilder with each swipe of her finger.

Diane's knuckles whitened around the phone.

"Do you see now?" The question hung in the air. "I had to do it."

And you know me. Say it.

She stared in silence, and I gently took the phone from her fingers, worried that in her horror, she'd chuck it into the river. The phone was my only proof as to who and what Simon was—proof that could be useful when Diane turned me in. I powered it off and again removed the SIM before sliding both into my pockets.

Diane inhaled a rattling breath. Her cheeks paled until her freckles stood out like flecks of mud. There was a limpness to her that reminded me of how I felt the day the police zoomed behind us, sirens blasting. She didn't speak for a long time. We sat. And watched. And listened.

Until.

"What's wrong with me? What's so broken in me that I brought *that* into my daughter's life?" She stared into my face, her pupils like black saucers. The tiniest spark of hope ignited in me. Was it possible?

A few photos, and Diane feelings had done a one-eighty.

"Nothing." I scooted cautiously toward her, speaking calmly as if mollifying a scared animal. "There's *nothing* wrong with you. Men like that, they know what they're doing. Listen to me, sweetie. This is *not* your fault." Oh so slowly, I laced her fingers into mine. "Simon sought you out *because* you're good. He was a predator."

"You think...you think he targeted me? Because I'm, what? Because I'm nice?" She contorted her face as if the thought pained her.

"That's exactly what I think. I killed him, and I have to live with that." I'd gladly live with that as long as Diane didn't hate me forever. "What I couldn't live with is going to prison without you understanding why I did it."

"Prison?" She jerked her gaze toward mine. "You saved us. You can't go to prison."

"Diane," I said. "If anyone finds out, then I'm one hundred percent going away. Probably for life. He isn't only dead; he's chopped to pieces and stacked in my refrigerator."

"But he's...he's... The women in those photos...they were... One was..." Her complexion tinged green, and her voice dropped to a whisper. "And he's a *pedophile*." Saying the word knocked the air out of her.

Diane leaned forward on the bench and sucked in a gulping breath. She untangled her fingers from mine and gripped the bench's metal slats as if she were afraid the seat would buck her off.

"Yeah, and I didn't call the cops when I found out. I didn't even call them after I killed him. If I had, then maybe...but I didn't."

"Look, I'm glad he's dead, okay? But why didn't you?" She tilted her face to the sky, bathing her features in the soft glow of the lamplight.

Why? She could never know why. I considered my words. "I guess I panicked. The news has been talking about a serial killer. I had this crazy idea that I might get blamed for that. I know it's nuts, but I wasn't thinking straight."

It wasn't a great excuse, tangled somewhere between truth and lie, but it was the best I could do for her.

Diane crossed her arms over her chest and nodded. "Too bad you can't make him disappear."

Hearing my sunshiny friend speak these words as plainly as if she were ordering brunch was bizarre. *Too bad they don't have bottomless mimosas. Too bad they don't have a seafood option. Too bad you can't get rid of the corpse in your fridge.*

But also, it was amazing, and I stopped a smile a millisecond before it spread over my face. "Yeah, too bad." As if it were a new consideration instead of the single thought that consumed my every waking moment for over a week.

"Wait a minute." Diane grabbed my hands and leaned close, her face inches from mine.

"What?" I asked.

"What if we could?"

My heart sped, and for once the tremble that threatened my hands wasn't from Joanie and her anxiety. No, it was from Diane. She'd said...

"We?" My expression fell completely blank. Diane didn't need to know that these words out of her mouth were better than any I could've hoped for.

Diane—*sweet Diane*—might not, under any other circumstances, be able to contribute to a plan to make a corpse disappear. However rage has a way of evolving us. Fury can take us to the next level. That old cliché about pressure changing coal into a diamond was true. Because once upon a time, I, Cordelia Black, had been timid Joanie Brown, beaten and broken. And while I'd always hold part of her inside me, fury had changed me into so much more. I was only Cordelia—a protector—because I'd been someone who needed protecting. Joanie had been ignored by women who could've helped, and in response, I'd become that kind of woman, only I didn't ignore bad men. I didn't ignore people who needed me. I was strong now because Joanie felt weak.

Now, Joanie whispered, *maybe you can be both.*

"What are you saying?" I asked.

I knew firsthand that all evolutions were possible. Even this one.

"I think I have an idea. It's crazy, but not crazier than, well." She shrugged, gesturing wildly with her arms and buzzing with the same energy that took her over whenever she began a new DIY project. "You've heard me talking about that new medical waste incinerator, right? How it cost a fortune?"

I nodded. Who hadn't heard her talk about it? Diane never missed an opportunity to point out how the purchase had thrown the hospital into financial crisis.

"You've done the dirty work. All we need to do is sneak Simon into medical waste. I'm not sure about..." She paused and swallowed. "About the head. The rest of him shouldn't be too hard. I can't do it all at once, but, little by little."

"You can't do it at all." The idea was appalling. There was no way she could be responsible for dumping body parts—she'd almost passed out from a tiny cut on my arm.

"Cordelia, you saved us from a predator. A predator that I brought home, for god's sakes! I want—no, *I need* to help you. Hell, you've always been the one looking out for me. In college after Samantha was born, you rearranged your classes—your entire life—so I wouldn't have to drop out and move home. You've helped with her tuition, her birthday parties, every breakup I've ever had. You've been my ride or die, *always*. And what have I done? I've put you in a position where you had to kill someone. *Fuck.*" Her voice hitched. I squeezed her hand tenderly. "Let me help," she begged. "Please."

I pressed my lips into a tight line and looked at Diane, my best friend, PTA mom, cookie maker, faux-finisher extraordinaire. Her uniform of tanks and paint-stained overalls and happy smiles that could keep you warm all winter. This change would've been unbelievable, except the love that poured from Diane to Sugar was as fierce as a river. And rivers bring life but are also capable of crushing cities.

"Please, Cor." Her eyes shined with her entire heart. She wanted to help me because she loved her daughter, and maybe, just maybe, she still loved me too. I should've said no, but I couldn't. I'd never been able to hold out with Diane.

"Okay," I relented. "But we do it my way. No questions."

Diane nodded and leaned back into the bench, gripping my hand in hers. She smirked.

"What?" I asked.

"This is the absolute last place I saw the night going when I got the idea to bake you those macarons."

I snorted. "I bet so."

"Can I ask you something?" She let go of my hand and turned her body to face mine, pulling her feet onto the bench and hugging her knees close to her chest all in a single fluid movement.

"Anything."

"How long have you been keeping this secret?"

Thinking of the stress, of Joanie threatening a coup and my life snowballing out of control, I shook my head. "Too long."

Diane dropped her feet the ground and slid closer to me. She slipped her arm around my waist and squeezed me into a side hug, laying her head on my shoulder. I returned the embrace. "I love you," she said. I knew she meant it. "Forever?"

"And ever," I agreed.

"We're vintage, right?" She held up her pinky, and I linked it with my own.

"Vintage. Definitely," I finished.

The fluorescent orange of Diane's friendship bracelet glowed under the lamplight, next to my naked wrist.

OUR PLAN WAS ONLY *MOSTLY* FOOLPROOF.

As I tucked my car into an overly snug space in the parking garage at Mercy Hospital, I mused over the fact that if the past month taught me anything, it was that *mostly foolproof* was the best you could hope for. *In life. In love. In body disposal.*

It was a tough lesson, one I'm not sure I'd have learned if Joanie hadn't come out to play, but I was better for learning it. That's me, Cordelia Black—growing as a person. Diane and I had chosen the garage instead of the employee parking lot, even though the employee lot was closer to the side entrance I'd been using. The garage was less risky. The employee lot required badging in and out, and while Diane had nabbed me credentials (whose photo I'd altered), using them to enter and exit the lot would leave a trail, which was never ideal.

I flipped down the visor mirror and pushed my wig's long bangs from my eyes. This was my favorite Mercy Hospital disguise yet. The ashy mouse-brown bob with wiry fringe and severe lines was so wrong for my sharp chin and short forehead that, with miniscule effort, I was unrecognizable. A little contour (okay—a lot of contour), some oversized thick glasses, and perfection was achieved.

Carefully, I opened my door and squeezed out. Today was going to be a good day, I could feel it. It was our last load. Adrenaline zinged so heavily through my system that my cheeks were rosy with it.

Beneath the scrubs (also nabbed by Diane—she was surprisingly good at this) I'd padded a pair of shapewear to round out my booty and stomach. In the snug space between my car and the giant pickup truck parked next to me, there was just enough room to admire my distorted reflection in my vehicle's door. A girl could get used to these curves.

I straightened my spine and looked around, clearing my throat as I smoothed the front of my clothes with my palms.

Besides the addition of my new ass, my C-cups were strapped down beneath two sports bras, and I have to say, I wasn't mad at the support.

I whistled as I walked around my car.

That old song, the one about getting by and help and friends, had been stuck in my head since the morning after the levee, when Diane and I had begun piecing together the plan. Now it was all I could do to keep from belting it out as I popped the trunk and hoisted an oversized, Simon-filled backpack onto my shoulders.

When Diane stopped by my house earlier this morning to run through the plan, something she'd insisted on doing before each and every disposal day, she'd been even paler than usual, and her eyes were puffy. She'd tried to hide it, her nerves as frazzled as her appearance, and I hadn't had the heart to tell her the extra concealer and bronzer weren't working.

"Breathe," I'd instructed her. "It's all going to be fine. Today is a good day. This is the last time. Easy, remember?"

"How are you always so calm?" She'd bit her lip pensively. That look—worry and dread—had only grown heavier with each and every Simon delivery. I'd hoped by now she would've relaxed a little, but it wasn't happening. "You act like it's no big deal."

"I guess I'm glad to be kicking Simon out," I'd said. "He doesn't pay rent or clean up after himself. He's a terrible roommate."

Diane hadn't smiled. Mental note: too soon for jokes. But god, I felt good. Like my old self. *No, that wasn't quite right.* I felt like my *true* self. Confident as Cordelia, vulnerable as Joanie, able to make jokes because whatever happened, I could handle it.

With Diane on my side, I could handle anything.

And Simon was finally going to be out of my life once and for all.

Well. Mostly.

"Remember." Diane had shifted nervously from one foot to the other. "Mercy Hospital—"

"Is divisive between doctors and nurses and support staff—*completely* toxic." I'd smiled, my hands resting on her shoulders. "Diane, relax. We've been over it a thousand times. Everything will go off without a hitch, just like it always does. I'll be wearing the right things, and moving in the right spaces. I'll be fine. Stop worrying."

I didn't mind her anxiety because Diane being a part of the experience was a new level in our friendship. She'd hugged me three times, squeezing me progressively harder with each embrace, before hopping into her car and zipping off to work in her section of the hospital campus.

This morning's exchange had left me feeling surreal. Before Simon, I'd always worked alone, yet here I was, sharing the experience with my bestie.

My joyful whistle grew louder as I slammed the door of my trunk and marched toward the hospital.

The deposits had taken place over the course of two weeks, with me sneaking in pieces of the predator at varying times during varying hospital shifts on varying floors. As I trudged toward the doorway, beads of sweat slid down my temples. From exertion, not nerves. Joanie and her anxiety were still here, tucked away like a note into a pocket. Once I'd made peace with her—*with us*—and made space for her in our life, her anxiety—*I mean our anxiety*—became manageable once again. Though, I suspected, it would never fully leave. But that was okay. I'd deal with each moment as it came.

The incinerator was housed in its own building on the edge of the Mercy Hospital campus, but it would appear suspicious to the security cameras if I went straight there. Instead, I marched through the side entrance of the main building.

When I pushed open the door, cool air blasted me. All around, buzzing fluorescent light bounced off the pale walls. Nothing about the place seemed conducive to healing, which didn't matter to me. My patient was already dead.

No one in scrubs gave me a second glance as I hit the up button and stepped onto the elevator.

The doors slid open to the fourth floor, and I fell into the busy stream of foot traffic.

Simon had been a nurse in the pediatric emergency room, a fact that, after seeing the photos on his phone, turned my stomach. He'd talked extensively to Diane about his work, and thanks to him, we'd known to look for each floor's clean room, where the fresh biohazard carts were stored, along with those red medical waste bags.

Today I was going to the fourth floor, where orthopedic surgeries took place. Between shifts, Diane had located their clean room on the other side of the floor, past the nurse's desk and another bank of elevators. Being sneaky was a good look on her.

Keeping my eyes trained straight ahead and my shoulders back, I walked down the hallway as if I belonged.

"Excuse me," a gruff male voice called. "You with the backpack!"

Oh shit.

Dueling ideas rushed through my head. Ignoring the man was tempting, but I couldn't shake the image of being chased down and having the wig snatched from my head like the unmasking of a Scooby villain. No. That wasn't the move.

Happy but dumb employee was the correct play here; it had already saved my ass once, on day two of dumping Simon.

"Yes," I said, with too much sugar in my tone.

The man was shorter than me and wore his resentment on his ruddy face like a Mardi Gras mask. His russet hair was thinning, and his scrubs were a different color than mine, his baby blue and mine hunter green. He peered at me from across the desk. "Lose the backpack. I don't know why I must keep saying these things to you orderlies. No personal effects on the hospital floor. Consider this a warning. Next time I'll report you and you'll be written up."

I flashed him what I hoped was an exasperated smile. "Sorry. I didn't realize I still had it on. I'll take care of it right now."

He glared. "See that you do."

The rubber of my athletic shoes squeaked as I hurried away with my chin tucked low.

I circled back in the other direction, taking the *very* long way around, but eventually I arrived at the clean room without drawing any more unwanted attention.

The "room" was barely more than a dimly lit closet, but like the clean rooms on the other floors, its shelves were crammed with rolls of red biohazard bags in different sizes, and two pristine red carts were pushed into the corner.

I stood in front of the closed door in case someone tried to open it from the outside, and slid my backpack from my shoulders. I got to work unwrapping pieces of semifrozen Simon and sealing him in the biohazard bags. I pulled the nearest cart closer, and after placing the backpack in its own red bag (I wouldn't be needing it after today), I stacked Simon in the cart, then tossed the pack on top.

Now for phase three: the escape.

With a quick look up and down the hallway, I counted to three, my heart gaining speed with each number, then dashed out with my cart.

After today, this would all be over. My life would be back to normal. *Maybe even better than normal—at least with Diane. Friends who slay together, stay togeth—*

"Please tell me you're going to OR five?" A tall woman stepped in front of me, blocking my path. Her black hair was pulled severely away from her pretty face and tucked beneath a colorful cloth hat. She wore the same shade of scrubs as the ruddy little man, but unlike him, the light blue color worked with her tan skin. Her name tag was nowhere to be found.

She frowned at the cart. "They've been waiting for a tech to bring a cart for over fifteen minutes. It's unacceptable."

"I was taking this one to waste disposal," I said.

The woman shook her head. "You came from the clean room. I hope you didn't take a contaminated bin in there. Why in the hell would you do that? Were you in there playing on your phone? Or vaping?" Her mouth twisted in horror at the idea.

The wig bounced around my chin as I shook my head, fully committed to the part of happy-dumb employee. "No...I don't know why I said that. Must be first day jitters."

She narrowed her eyes. "That doesn't make sense."

"I—"

"Are you lying now or were you lying before?" She stared me down, and I'd have died before dropping my eyes. I thrust the cart at her. "Why don't you check inside if you're so curious? I told you, I don't know why I said that. It's first day jitters."

She tilted her head, considering my challenge. My stomach fluttered with the anticipation of what could happen. If I was written up for contaminating the clean room, it would take five seconds for things to fall apart—mostly because I didn't work here.

"Hey, Kim," a chipper blond woman called to the snotty brunette, giving me a break from her scrutiny.

I let out a deep breath as silently as I could. That was close, but there'd been no eye twitch. No trembly hands. No panic attack. Only the familiar urge to pounce. To come out on top at all costs. Joanie was a part of me, but moments like this were for Cordelia alone.

The blond threw a glance my way, sizing me up. I grinned, happy-dumb. Her brows scrunched, and she turned her back to me to speak to the bratty brunette, Kim. "That foxy brother of yours is waiting on you at the desk."

Kim rolled her eyes, her mouth still twisted in disdain. "Thanks for letting me know. We have plans to grab some lunch later, but he's the worst about showing up whenever he wants."

I considered pulling my cart quietly away, but before I could, Kim caught my eye. "We aren't finished," she snapped, then turned back to the blond. "Can you tell him I'm dealing with something?" She gestured to me. "I'll be there as soon as I can."

"Yeah, sure." The blond nodded and trudged back down the hallway.

"It's your lucky day. My brother's here and that puts me in a better mood." Kim pursed her lips. "I'll walk you to the operating room."

When we got to OR 5, Kim nudged me inside, then beat a hasty retreat. Thank god.

A man and woman, both in green scrubs that matched mine, were cleaning the room. Near the door, there was a tray stacked with three or four of the red medical waste bags—much smaller than the ones I'd used for Simon—filled and securely closed.

"About time." The woman frowned and scratched her frizzy gray hair. "Wait, where's Caitlyn?"

I shrugged. "All I know is they pulled me from my regular floor and told me to come help." Cue happy-dumb grin. My cheeks were starting to ache.

"Might as well get to it." She didn't bother asking my name, and the man in the corner didn't stop mopping to look up.

The woman took the biohazard bags from the tray and moved to open my cart. My first instinct was to pull away, because I had a plan. And that plan said that no one else touched this cart but me. Until now, it had been me alone delivering my carts to waste disposal. But having Simon mixed with legit waste could only help things. I relaxed and nudged the cart toward her.

The woman gave me a funny look as she opened the lid, and without even glancing inside, dropped the bags into the bin and refastened the latch. "Now, why don't you let me take that to the dirty room? On second thought, I'm going to go ahead and walk it to the disposal building. I need to stretch these old legs."

Again, my hands squeezed the cart handle, and my ever-present grin grew tight around the edges. The plan was for me to take the cart, and the plan was important.

However...

"Sure." I let her pull it from my grasp.

Putting another degree of separation between me and Simon could only be a good thing. And it wasn't like she was going to dig through bags of medical trash looking for treasure. At least, I hoped she wouldn't.

Once she was gone, I mumbled an excuse about needing the bathroom and darted out the door.

The bank of elevators was around the corner. As soon as they were in view, I stopped short.

Snotty Kim was waiting for the elevator, but that wasn't why I put on the brakes. It was who she was with—the man who had to be her brother.

Oh no.

He was tall with dark hair and filled out every inch of his snug tee. The two siblings were deep in conversation, their heads tilted toward each other. When he smiled, his perfect teeth gleamed. *Hello there, McSmiley.* Of course. Because things were going too smoothly. I hadn't seen him in person since our less-than-stellar lip-lock, though we'd texted a few times.

I took a step backward, trying not to draw attention, but stumbled over a *wet floor* cone, barely catching myself before falling. Christopher's gaze landed on mine, and we both froze.

I should've worn more costume makeup. I should've—

Kim looked up. The smile she'd beamed at her brother never

dulled. Her tone was sugar and spice, but I knew better. "Finished already?"

I nodded, opening my mouth to speak, then snapped it closed.

It was easy to hide from monsters, but I'd never hidden from someone I knew before. There was a brief flashback of Simon recognizing me in the restaurant on the night everything fell apart. I pushed it away. Simon couldn't upset me now. Cordelia Black remained calm under pressure. If I kept my mouth closed and the encounter brief, everything would be fine.

I was certain of it.

Almost.

Christopher's eyes pulled me like a magnet. The urge to search his face for any sign of recognition was strong, but I resisted, carefully keeping my sight trained on Kim.

The elevator dinged and the doors opened. Kim stepped on, tugging her brother behind her. Christopher continued to stare at me. It was rude, really. He finally glanced away, raised a finger, and opened his mouth, then shook his head, closed his mouth, and gave me one more hard look.

Why hadn't I been more careful? Did he know? Could he tell?

"Are you getting on?" Kim asked me.

"Um..." I took a step back, this time managing not to stumble.

"I'm sorry," Christopher said. "Do we know each other?"

His gaze lingered on my face. It would've been funny, except it was terrible.

He smiled—because of course he did—and touched his chest with his palm. "I'm Christopher. You look so familiar."

And then—before I could respond at all—the doors shut.

I raked a hand across my forehead, no doubt smearing my heavy makeup or unsettling my wig.

That was too close. Thank goodness we were finished. Simon was gone forever.

Mostly.

The elevator dinged, and I was struck with the image of the doors bouncing open and Christopher pointing a single finger at me in a complete *aha* moment. No way was I waiting around for him to figure it out. I bounded down the hall, taking the stairs and bursting outside, not stopping until I was inside my car.

I blasted the air-conditioning full force as I dug around my tote for my phone, then texted Diane the thumbs-up emoji.

She immediately responded.

DIANE: Thank god. 🙏

ME: No. Thank you! All done. Your plan worked perfectly. After sending, I reconsidered and added, Or almost perfectly.

DIANE: It was our plan. What do you mean almost? Everything good?

We'd discussed what was okay and not okay to put into text, but if Diane got emotional, I didn't trust her to remember the rules. Nothing about the hospital. Nothing about a body (obviously). I answered before she snowballed.

ME: It's fine. Ran into McSmiley. He didn't recognize me.

Dots bounced across the screen, and I played around with my music playlists until I found the song I wanted.

DIANE: What do you mean he didn't recognize you?

She must have written and deleted several messages before settling on that one.

ME:

...

...

DIANE: Ugh. Men!

Only Diane would be pissed about this right now. She still held out hope that I would eventually wake up and realize I was head-over-heels for McSmiley. It wasn't going to happen, not even to make Diane happy. I could only pretend to be Sweet Cordelia for so long.

She was the hardest part to play.

On the way home, there was a wreck on the interstate, and I had to slam on my brakes to keep from rear-ending the car in front of me. My purse flew from the passenger seat and spilled its contents everywhere. When I finally made it back to my house and was picking up the mess, something caught my eye in the crack between the seat and the middle console. Something hot pink. I pushed my hand into the tight space and on the third try, pulled out Sugar's bracelet.

It had been in my car the entire time.

I'd searched high and low—even in this same spot—and it had never shown. This tiny piece of yarn had caused me so much anxiety; it had kept me up at night. And now...here it was.

As I fastened it onto my wrist, I decided that it must be a sign. Sugar's bracelet was a good omen that everything was going to work.

There was only one more loose end for me to tie up, and this would all be over. Diane and I would be home free.

And all because of Frank.

TWO WEEKS LATER, AFTER A LUCRATIVE MONSTER STALKING session, I tossed my wig onto the dining table, where it landed splayed out like a dead cat. I shook out my hair, giving my scalp a good scratch with the points of my stiletto nails; I'd finally gotten a much-needed manicure. Killing was off the table for now, until I figured out a way to get rid of bodies. But stalking was fun.

Mango's nails tapped against the floor as she ran into the room. Her hair was slowly growing back. "There's my murder-mutt." I'd become one of those people who baby-talked to their pets. Sue me. "Devil-baby want some cheesy?" I grabbed a piece from the fridge and unwrapped it. She snapped it up, then curled up in her spot on the back of the sofa.

I pulled my sweats from the dryer and tugged them on. Comfort and wine were the ticket.

My stomach growled.

Or maybe comfort and a snack.

There was a box of breakfast pastry in the bottom of my freezer.

Diane had gotten me addicted to the sugary strudels in college, and somewhere along the way they'd become comfort food.

My hand was on the freezer door when my phone rang.

"Hey," I answered brightly.

"Hey yourself," Diane said. "I haven't heard from you today. Is everything okay?"

Her voice was tight with barely restrained annoyance, and a full octave higher than her usual husky pitch. Diane hadn't quite bounced back from, well, everything.

She worried if an entire day passed without hearing from me. It was kind of nice, to be honest, but I missed her old carefree way.

Good thing I knew exactly how to help her get it back. It had taken over a week of meticulous Cordelia-level planning, but once she saw the evening news, everything would be better.

"Sorry." I pulled open the freezer to grab the box of pastry. Simon stared at me with an open mouth. Crystals formed across his eyelashes, and his skin had finally taken on a lovely hue, though not the blue I preferred in my monsters, it was much improved from the waxy yellow. "I've been stupid busy."

She let out a heavy breath. "It's fine. Sorry, I'm just—" There was a pause, then she asked, "Can I come over?"

"Of course." I eyed Simon. "But maybe leave Sugar at home. Just in case."

"Cordelia Renee...still?"

"Not my name, and I'll see ya in a bit." I hung up, annoyed at the judgment in that one word: *still.*

Yes, still.

It wasn't like I was going to keep Simon's head forever—I wasn't crazy.

I slid my phone into my pocket, then grabbed the yellow box from the bottom of the freezer, but instead of closing the door, I paused for another long look. Rigor mortis had caught him with his mouth open, and when he'd been spending his days soaking in an ice bath, I'd thought he was stuck in an eternal scream, but now I realized that wasn't the case. No, he wasn't screaming at all. He was singing. Singing to wish me an amazing day.

Serenading while refrigerating. Clever. I snorted and bumped the freezer door closed with my hip.

I was pulling the sheet of pastries from the oven when Diane shuffled in, breathless. She hadn't been sleeping well and her exhaustion was obvious in the dreamy, underwater way she moved as she slumped onto a barstool.

Mango chortled, hopping down from her post and scampering to Diane for pets, which my bestie obliged. "It's so weird how you ended up with your neighbor's dog," she said.

"Yeah. Tragic, really." I shrugged, remembering the way Mr. Percival had looked, his head twisted at an odd angle at the bottom of his staircase. Weird was one way to put it. "He should've been more careful using the stairs at his age, especially having a small dog underfoot."

Mango yipped in agreement.

Diane's gaze darted to my fridge, threading a chord of tension tightly between us. I ignored it, focusing instead on squeezing frosting across the strudel's flaky crusts.

I scooped one onto a plate and slid it in front of her.

"Gross, Cordelia." Diane paled. "Are these…? Were they in the freezer with…you know?"

"Don't be so dramatic. It's not like they were touching." I poured her a cup of coffee. "They're strawberry, your favorite."

The whites of her eyes doubled in size. "I don't get how you can even sleep with…with his…with that thing still in your house You have to get rid of it."

"I will." Eventually. I set Diane's plate on the floor. Mango had no problem with snacks that shared a space with Simon.

But to answer Diane's question: I slept great.

Simon was a monster, but he was also more than that. He was a token. A totem. Simon's head was a reminder of how our friendship had done what I'd never dreamt it could; it had survived my truth. Well, my *mostly* truth.

But my truth, nonetheless.

"I was about to watch the news," I said, masking my excitement.

"Yeah, keeping up with the news is a good idea." Diane took her coffee into the living room and clicked on the television.

I slid a pastry onto a plate and followed, then curled into one of the wingback chairs. Mango padded over and hopped into my lap.

On the screen, the male news anchor smoldered into the camera. His matte powder absorbed the glare of the studio lights, giving his skin the appearance of smooth marble.

Diane clutched her mug in two hands. The face she was going to make when she saw this report would be epic. *Thanks, Frank.*

The camera zoomed in. "*Shocking update on the story of local university arborist, Frank Turner. According to police, Turner's blood was found in the apartment of Mercy Hospital employee Simon White. Police say that White was not home when they received a distressed call about a possible murder in his home. Illegal pornography was uncovered at the scene."*

I stroked Mango's back, my pastry forgotten on the end table as I watched Diane watch the television. Her mouth dropped open, and her coffee mug tumbled from her hands. It hit the ground with a thump and splashed deep brown liquid across the rug. We both ignored it.

"What the hell?" She gasped and walked closer to the television.

The camera switched to a shot of Simon's apartment door covered in police tape. "*The body of Frank Turner was originally found in the Baton Rouge warehouse of accused murderer and businessman Clarence Elgin, along with the bodies of other missing Baton Rouge men, including the remains of social worker Gerald Montelero, one of the most recent men reported missing. Elgin has maintained his innocence in the murders and claims he had a source supplying the dead bodies, but that source had yet to be found.*

"Since the identities of both murdered men have been confirmed, two former clients of Gerald Montelero's have come forward with allegations of abuse. The victims' names are being withheld to protect their identities, but Montelero was their mental health counselor for the past two years. Montelero is now the third missing man to be accused of physical and/or sexual crimes. When asked why they were coming forward now, the victims said they never felt safe until Montelero was confirmed dead."

A surge of pride bloomed in my chest and gooseflesh erupted across my skin, despite the warm puppy in my lap. Victims hurt by monsters were coming forward. They felt safe.

Because the monsters were dead.

Because I'd killed them.

The report continued. "*Simon White is wanted by police for questioning regarding involvement in the murders of the long list of victims discovered in Clarence Elgin's warehouse. His whereabouts is unkown, but police consider him dangerous and say if you see Simon White, do not approach, and call nine-one-one.*"

Diane turned toward me with an eerie stillness. She was rarely still. When she was mad, she raged. When she was happy, she bounced or twirled. When she was sad or nervous, her hands twisted or flapped.

"Diane, honey, are you okay?"

"I'm fine." Her face was stone, but she slumped back to her chair and gave her full attention to the news report.

I'd been thinking of Diane when I'd disguised myself as a cleaning lady and broke into Simon's apartment, armed with the can of Frank's blood. Diane would need closure; she wouldn't feel protected until she had it, and Simon's death wouldn't be enough.

So, I'd done what any best friend worth their salt would do in this situation.

I'd given her that closure.

Frank's congealed blood was smeared around Simon's apartment, in his bathtub, on the walls, and in his bed. I'm no blood-splatter analyst, but I thought I'd done a pretty good job.

Simon's phone had been unlocked and all pics of Diane and Sugar deleted, though the other pictures had not. It was the smoking gun left at the crime scene. The call the cops received from a hysterical maid had come from an untraceable burner phone, one that would never be found. If they bothered looking into it, they'd discover it was the same number that alerted the media.

Yes, with Frank's help, I'd tied things up nicely. Clarence, who'd still serve some jail time, now had a small chance of not going down for murder—which I guess was a good thing, since the only crime he was guilty of was being creepy as hell and illicit business practices. And, okay, maybe accessory after the fact.

Once the police connected the dots, then Baton Rouge would have the name of its possible newest killer, and the answer to why men went missing. Simon would be pinned as the man who'd met Clarence with bodies in the swamp. Knowledge of the contents of his phone would leak, causing people to dig into each of the missing men, discovering their secrets. The press would have no problem filling in any blanks with whatever they felt would garner clicks and sales. Local conspiracy theorists were guaranteed to do their part on social media.

We would be free from scrutiny. Any lingering sadness plaguing Diane—any weird feelings toward me—would go away because I'd killed not only a predator, but a suspected serial killer. Diane could be proud.

And by the time police discovered Diane's relationship with Simon, she'd be prepared for the attention. I'd make sure of it.

SIMON'S GRAY EYES BORE INTO MINE. HIS HEART KNOCKED three loud, succinct beats against his chest—a sound I'd heard before but couldn't place.

How dare he be awake; how dare he look at me? He was dead. Didn't he know? Didn't he remember? I opened my mouth to protest. He had to go and never come back, but before a single sound could cross my lips, he kissed me. It was wet, and sloppy, and tasted like...cheese.

American Singles.

My eyes fluttered open. Mango's wet tongue was buried in my mouth.

I coughed and pushed her away, then wiped my tongue on the back of my hand. Gross. Still better than kissing Simon.

In all my nightmares, all the horrible dreams left over from childhood, I'd never dreamt of a dead monster before. I hoped this wasn't the start of something new and horrible. Maybe it was time to get rid of his head. Diane would be happy.

The sound of a car backing out of my driveway sent me hopping out of bed and hurrying to the window in time to see a UPS truck pull away.

Mango yodeled, telling me we had to move quickly. I scooped her up and hurried down the stairs and out the back door. When she was done taking care of business, we went inside, and I started the coffeepot.

I remembered the UPS truck and retrieved the package from my doorstep, then flicked on the television, selecting the platform that played local news. Settling into my sofa, I slid my fingernail beneath the packing tape of the small parcel, opening it easily enough.

Inside was the memory card converter—the one I'd ordered the night Simon had, well, had turned everything upside down. I hadn't forgotten about it exactly, but saying there'd been more pressing things to deal with was an understatement.

The memory card was still tucked away safely in a drawer. I retrieved it and my laptop, bringing them back to the sofa.

On television, the music played, signaling the local morning news, and Tanisha's cohost recapped the story of Simon's apartment. Good, the story was sticking. The more it was reported, the truer it was. That's how things worked. It was appropriate background noise for the job at hand.

I snapped the converter into place on my laptop, then clicked the memory card into its slot. It was time to finally get some answers about this damned camera.

The pictures loaded, newest to oldest. The camera must've

operated on a motion sensor. Intermixed with random photos of squirrels and one of a bobcat, there was me walking toward the camera. Before that, me driving up, collecting my money from beneath the pirogue. Clarence. His SUV. Me dropping the body off.

Then.

"No," I whispered. "That little shit."

Why hadn't I considered this? Of course, it was the only thing that made sense.

I'd been so certain it was some Bubba who'd planted the camera and it was just my bad luck, that I'd refused to see the obvious culprit.

I stared at the photo of the man's face. His pointy chin and nose. His thick coke-bottle glasses. His flushed white skin and trout lips.

Clarence. The greedy, money hungry, no-good business partner of mine.

It made perfect sense. I've said before that Clarence was driven by greed—it's what made him a good accomplice. When nothing else was reliable, greed held steady.

Even if he'd been successful and figured out who I was, it wasn't so he could do the "right thing" and turn me in to authorities. A man like Clarence doesn't suddenly grow a conscience; he wouldn't have ratted me out. This was about extortion. I'd bet, before he'd gotten caught, he'd planned on using the footage to bleed me dry. Metaphorically, of course.

I scrolled back and forth through the photos.

"Well, Clarence," I said aloud. Beside me, Mango cocked her

head. "That's what you get for trying to screw over Cordelia Black." I scratched Mango's ear. Karma was on my side—this was only more proof. If Clarence's attorney was even halfway decent, he wouldn't go down for murder. However, he'd likely spend enough time behind bars to think about what he'd done. I wondered how often he spouted off his crazy story about a camera in the woods that disappeared.

I ejected the memory card and snapped it in half, then erased the photos from my computer. On my way back from the coffeepot, something on the television caught my eye.

A story that made national headlines.

Brett Turner's mug shot flashed across the screen, followed by an action shot of him leaving a courthouse.

My eyes narrowed. Brett Jameson was what hunters like Tim referred to as big game.

The Tallahassee college junior was caught red-handed by two of his fraternity brothers with his pants at his knees, on top of a passed-out freshman girl behind their frat house during a Halloween kegger. They'd pinned him down and called the cops. His case had received national attention because it followed on the heels of another controversial high-profile case. (There was always a new high-profile case, wasn't there?)

Every news organization worth its salt had covered the story in some form or another.

The judge was expected to send a message by punishing Brett to the full extent of the law. His own fraternity brothers testified against him. The victim had given a heartbreaking account of the night's events, keeping her chin up even when Brett's lawyers—the best his daddy's money could buy—ripped her character to shreds. *Why was she drunk? Why was she passed out? Why had she worn such a slutty Halloween costume? Surely, she knew what she was broadcasting? Was it possible she'd agreed to the encounter? Didn't she have a lot to gain by making this accusation, possibly interviews and a book deal? It was about attention, wasn't it? Wasn't it?!*

She'd never faltered.

So why was Brett smiling as he walked to a waiting car?

I grabbed the remote and cranked up the volume, standing a foot away from the television screen.

"*In what can only be described as an astonishing turn of events, Brett Jameson was sentenced to two months community service, and will not be required to register as a sex offender. The judge presiding over the case commented, saying that he was reluctant to ruin such a promising young life for making one bad decision. Brett's supporters have heralded him as nice young man, raised in the church, and an athlete on the school's badminton team, who drank too much and made a mistake. Others have pointed out that the mistake he made was rape.*"

"No way." My fingers twitched as a familiar rage kindled in my bones.

The camera cut to a scene of a young woman wiping her eyes as she exited the courtroom. Brett had been all relieved smiles, but this girl's shoulders rolled forward with her chin tucked to her chest, and her long jet-black hair forming a curtain around her face. It was obvious she wanted to be anywhere else. What had they promised her? If she testified, he'd go to jail? If she were brave, she'd get justice?

My jaw ached, and I realized I was baring my teeth.

"*I'm sorry, but this is bullshit.*" Tanisha Harris's words came from off camera.

"*Tanisha, your mic is hot,*" the male anchor said in a singsong tone.

"*I stand by what I said,*" Tanisha told him. The scene on the television blinked back to the newsroom where Tanisha Harris, Baton Rouge's favorite newswoman, was standing rigidly behind the desk. "*This isn't—what did you say Jim?—'an astonishing turn of events.' No, this is complete and utter misogynistic and dangerous bullshit.*" She tore her mic from her shirt, then stormed off set.

Jim's eyes rounded as he stared blankly into the camera. "*That, uh, well, um...*"

Someone cut to commercial.

Tanisha Harris was correct. This was bullshit.

Brett had gotten off way too easy, but that didn't mean he wouldn't face justice.

It was too soon for me to kill in Baton Rouge, but workaholic that I am, I'd accumulated some vacation time. And I'd always wanted to visit sunny Florida.

People in the spotlight deserved karma as much as anyone else—maybe even more so since it could be argued that they were examples.

It would take planning. Patience. *Perfect* attention to detail. All the things I was good at.

There was a pharmaceutical convention near Tallahassee in six months—that would give me an excuse and more than enough time to plan.

My mind buzzed with excitement as I rolled the possibility around in my head. How I could do it. How it would feel. How I would establish an alibi.

What I'd do with the body. Alligators were literally everywhere in Florida.

There would be no room for error, but if everything worked out, and the stars aligned, Brett could be my masterpiece. My *Mona Lisa*. My *Starry Night*. My magnum fucking opus.

The beginnings of a plan took shape—a plan that required my cotton-candy-pink wig and thigh-high leather boots. I bounced on the balls of my feet and clapped my hands. Oh, this was going to be too much fun.

Filled with a new, optimistic energy, I jogged upstairs with Mango following behind.

Brett Jameson would not escape justice.

It was going to be a long six months.

THE END

READING GROUP GUIDE

1. Cordelia is so protective of her found family, Diane and Sugar. How does this contrast with the crimes she commits? Does her love for Diane and Sugar absolve her other actions?

2. How do you interact with your best friend? What would you do to protect them?

3. How does Cordelia use how people see her (and women) to her advantage?

4. What do you make of Cordelia creating art from her kills? Is this just a serial killer trait (like collecting a trophy), a way for her to express herself, or something else entirely?

5. Cordelia is clearly traumatized by her childhood experiences. Does this change how you see her actions now? Does it make anything she's doing better or more justified?

6. What do you think of the "smoke" Cordelia sees in her victims' eyes? Is it instinct or a figment of her imagination?

7. Do you have a "Sweet" version of yourself like Cordelia does? Do you have other versions of yourself that you use in particular situations?

8. Cordelia and Sugar make a big deal of Simon calling Sugar "Samantha" and not anything else. How do names give us power or other people power over us? Why is it important that we get to choose how we're called?

9. Is Cordelia murdering people for "good" reasons? Despite her altruistic intentions, how else is she personally benefiting from these interactions?

10. Do you think Cordelia actually sees the "smoke" in Simon's eyes, or is she simply seeing what she wants to see?

11. Everything begins to spiral out of control for Cordelia after she murders Simon. How much of what happens is due to bad luck, and how much is a direct result of her prior actions? Do you have days or weeks where every little thing feels like it's going wrong?

12. What does Cordelia's reliance on designer brands tell you

about her? How much can you tell about a person based on the clothing they choose to wear?

13. How well (and accurately) can you read people? Do you have an instinct for knowing whether a stranger is "good" or "bad"?

14. Were you rooting for Cordelia to escape her predicament? Why or why not? Why might being in someone's perspective make us more sympathetic to them?

15. Do you think Cordelia deserves to be free at the end?

A CONVERSATION WITH THE AUTHOR

What was it like to write from a serial killer's perspective?

Honestly, it was a bit cathartic for me. Many (too many) years ago, when I was eighteen, there was a serial killer in Baton Rouge preying on women and college girls. I, like all teen girls in the area, was gripped with a terror that I was forced to push down and ignore and keep going with my life as if everything were normal—as if a monster wasn't hunting and killing women. I specifically remember one time someone putting up a missing person flyer where I worked (at a bridal shop), then a few weeks later, when the body was discovered, coming to take it down. We—the shop girls—had to continue to smile, assist customers, and act as if everything was completely normal. Coming of age during this time left its mark on me. The lingering effects of that fear, of always feeling as if I could be a victim, still sneak up on me from time to time. I think all women know some version of this fear, though we all deal with it in different ways.

Maybe creating Cordelia Black was my writer-brain's response. Cordelia is fun. She's flawed. She does bad things (for good reasons). She is far from perfect. But she isn't afraid of anything. (Except losing her found family and, okay, maybe bad highlights.)

What do you think of Cordelia? Is she admirable, or is she the real monster?

Cordelia is complicated. If she is a monster, it is because she was turned into one. I can definitely see her coming from a well-adjusted family, from a loving environment, and using her cunning senses to make millions of dollars instead of killing predators. But...that didn't happen, and so here she is. Living her best life, as she'd put it.

Do I think she is admirable? I don't know. Besides being a killer, Cordelia can be shallow. Overbearing. Self-absorbed. Focused on the wrong things. She is also loving, loyal, funny, and smart. When I created Cordelia, I wanted her (outside of being a killer) to feel like someone you could know in your life. Not perfect. Not necessarily a badass. Just a woman getting things done. Only, the things she is getting done involve a kill room and painting with blood.

What was the most difficult part of this book to write? The easiest?

I spent a lot of time figuring out exactly who Cordelia was outside of her...special interest...before figuring out the killer part of her. Digging into her trauma and poking her wound was by far the hardest part of the story to write. (That and keeping up with fashion trends—which I'm not a hundred percent sure I did.)

The easiest, most fun part? Absolutely Mango. Hands down. Fun fact, Mango didn't come into the story until after draft two or three. I decided Cordelia needed a dog, and so the devil dog was born.

What kind of research went into this book?

One of my best friends is an artist and another is a therapist—so there were some interesting conversations with each of them. To their credit, they didn't blink at my weird questions about painting with blood or why Cordelia might behave in certain ways.

Another time, I fell down a research rabbit hole involving the flow and congealing of blood, and let me tell you...I took liberties in the kill room scenes because otherwise there would've been way too many intricate details involving the best way to position a corpse and how one might go about doing it. Better to give you the basics and let you use your imagination. Trust me. (Maybe I should apologize to my literary agent, who read those early, detailed scenes. Sorry, Ann!)

Probably the most interesting research is something I stumbled into when the idea for this book was barely a spark in my imagination—and that is body donation. The process of donating a body to science is highly unregulated and very profitable for the broker. Clarence might be the most realistic character in the entire book.

What do you want readers to take away from Cordelia's story?

Honestly? I hope readers take whatever they need. I know that sounds like a fake answer—but I truly mean it. If you read this as a funny thriller about a serial killer and her best friend, well I hope you had a great time. If you read a book that hits you in your feelings about a damaged woman hurting men who hurt women, I hope you are happy with the way things ended for my stabby girl. I believe that once a book is in a reader's hands, it is theirs. And often, even if we are opening the same book, we are actually reading different stories, depending on what we bring to it from our own experiences.

What are you reading right now?

I am such a chaotic mood reader and am currently reading quite a few books, including *The Hollywood Assistant* by May Cobb, *So Thirsty* by Rachel Harrison, *You Will Never Be Me* by Jesse Q. Sutanto, *My Darling Dreadful Thing* by Johanna van Veen, and (to lighten things up) *Worst in Show* by my good friend, Anna E. Collins.

I am listening to the audiobooks *Midnight Is the Darkest Hour* by Ashley Winstead, *The Locked Door* by Freida McFadden, and anxiously awaiting my library hold for *Blacktop Wasteland* by S. A. Cosby.

In nonfiction, I just got a memoir titled *Sociopath: A Memoir* by Patric Gagne Ph.D and am looking forward to reading it. Also, on a recent thrifting trip, I nabbed *Kitchen Confidential* by the late Anthony Bourdain and can't wait to dive in.

ACKNOWLEDGMENTS

My road from writer to published author has been long and winding. Along the way, I've met all kinds of people, and I owe so many for their encouraging words, their gentle nudges to keep going, their tough love, their uplifting spirits, their listening ears, and their eyes on early versions of my work. If we've crossed paths somewhere along the way and you were kind—from the bottom of my heart, thank you. (For the few who went out of their way to be unkind...well...I suppose spite can be a useful tool as well. Maybe I owe them a debt of gratitude? No. I don't think so.)

Justin. My person and the most steadfast, patient, human ever (who somehow fell in love with an ADHD gremlin who possesses no chill. Oops.). Thank you for being my cheerleader, biggest supporter, my sounding board, a shoulder for me to cry on, and for celebrating every single milestone, from first finished manuscript to book deal. But most importantly, thank you for always being an example to our kids (and anyone who knows you) of what a good man should be. Love you, soul-matey.

Ann Rose (affectionately known as Ann *Freaking* Rose) is my dream agent. Seriously—I don't know how most literary agents operate, but Ann goes above and beyond. Ann, I am so thankful for everything you've done for this book and my career. You recognized something in Cordelia when she landed in your slush pile, and I will always be grateful for the brainstorming sessions, the texts, and your unwavering belief in this story.

To my editor, MJ Johnston. From our first phone call, I knew you "got it." Every author hopes for an editor who will love their book and advise them on how to make the story the best it can be without changing its heart and soul. I absolutely hit the jackpot with you and am so thankful for all your hard work in shaping Cordelia's misadventure.

Mandy Chahal is the best publicist, and no, I will not be taking any questions on the matter, thanks. Mandy's excitement for TGAK is contagious, and (*gasp!*) she makes marketing so much fun. Thank you, Mandy, for not only answering my millions of questions but doing so thoughtfully and enthusiastically and for always helping me point the firehose in the right direction.

The team at Poisoned Pen Press has been nothing but amazing and proved to be the perfect home for Cordelia Black.

A huge thank-you to cover designer Tim Green/Faceout Studio for using your brilliant, beautiful talent on *This Girl's a Killer*. I am truly obsessed with this cover. (That blood splatter on the sunglasses? Perfection.)

To my first (and best) author friend, EJ Wenstrom. Girl. What. Can you even believe you are holding this book in your hands right now? I still remember telling you, "I think I want to write about a serial killer." From conception to querying to submission to deal announcement, you have kept me sane in this wild industry.

The biggest, hugest of Thank Yous (and that still feels woefully inadequate) to some of the best women I know: Lana, Lisa, Megan, Anna, and Julia. From making Simon just the right amount of slimy to finding the book's opening line (which I'd cleverly buried in the second paragraph) to gut-checking me on murder scenes—you've all been crucial in helping figure out Cordelia's story. Your publishing insight and writing advice are invaluable, but your friendship is everything. I am so lucky to know you.

Author Layne Fargo supports women's wrongs. *Always*. Years ago, she took time out of her busy schedule to read the (probably god-awful) *very first* version of Cordelia, and this year she read the (hopefully much improved) ARC. Thank you for your kindness and encouragement, Layne. I am forever a fan. If you write it, I'm reading it.

To Amy for beta-reading a super early draft. And for explaining how hospital clean rooms work. Surely Cordelia would've gotten caught without your insider knowledge.

To artist Courtney and therapist Anita for answering questions about art and trauma. And from time to time, dragging me away from my computer to ensure I got a little sunlight and touched some grass. Thank you.

To my family:

My sons. You two make me so proud every single day. I love you big.

Mom, you knew I was a writer before I did and have always been so supportive. When I was a kid, your belief in me taught me how to believe in myself. Dad, you taught me early in life to take up space and not back down. All of these lessons have served me well. Thank you.

I have the best in-laws ever. Papa-Day, I'm still not convinced you aren't secretly Superman. It's truly mind-boggling the number of times you've come to my rescue with a gas can or an extra car key because I was lost in my own head, figuring out "the plot." Doda, your enthusiasm is unwavering and unmatched. For that, I am so grateful. Thank you both for everything.

To Jill and Lou and Garrett and Caleb—because better sisters and brothers do not exist. You are who I'm calling if I ever happen upon a corpse in my bathtub.

To my officemates/writing partners, the good boy duo of Gryff and Winn—who would never ever roll in a bloody corpse (that would take too much energy). And who always come when called (especially if cheese is involved).

And finally—I've waited a *very* long time to write this.

To that one third-grade teacher. It never pays to be cruel—especially to a child who is struggling. I hope you see this and know you were wrong. Daydreaming *did* get me somewhere in life (*hello book deal*). I'm not lazy. I'm not stupid. I have ADHD. And I win.

ABOUT THE AUTHOR

Emma C. Wells is the author of *This Girl's a Killer*. She loves antiheroes, dark humor, witty banter, twisty plots, and ride-or-die friendships. Emma lives in Louisiana with her family, where her time is split between daydreaming of story ideas and searching for her car keys.